The Kindness of Strangers

The Kindness of Strangers

Emma Garman

Virago

VIRAGO

First published in Great Britain in 2026 by Virago Press

1 3 5 7 9 10 8 6 4 2

All characters and events in this publication, other than those clearly in the public domain, are fictitious and any resemblance to real persons, living or dead, is purely coincidental.

A CIP catalogue record for this book is available from the British Library.

Hardback ISBN 978-0-3490-2018-1
Trade paperback 978-0-3490-2019-8

Typeset in Garamond by M Rules
Printed and bound in Great Britain by
Clays Ltd, Elcograf S.p.A.

Papers used by Virago Press are from well-managed forests and other responsible sources.

MIX
Paper | Supporting responsible forestry
FSC® C104740

Virago Press
An imprint of
Little, Brown Book Group
Carmelite House
50 Victoria Embankment
London EC4Y 0DZ

The authorised representative
in the EEA is
Hachette Ireland
8 Castlecourt Centre
Dublin 15, D15 XTP3, Ireland
(email: info@hbgi.ie)

An Hachette UK Company
www.hachette.co.uk

www.littlebrown.co.uk

I must find myself a life, a new life,
even if all of life consists only of an
endless search for life.

ROBERT WALSER

Prologue

Friday 27 March 1953

Jimmy was cold, paralysingly cold, and sticky-wet above the waist. Blood soaked his jersey, churned in his throat, filled his lungs. He tried to move, to turn onto his back, but an iron bar of pain held him in place. Circling above like seagulls' squawks were voices discussing, with maddening dispassion, if he was alive or dead. None of them tried to help. Why would they? To be rid of him was their dearest wish. Honor was smoking – sucking on her eternal cigarette holder – and casually speculating whether his heart was still beating. Even little Mina seemed unperturbed that a man was dying right there on the carpet. She might have been watching a scene in a film.

A soft warm hand grabbed his wrist, and he wondered if it meant to pull him from the black hole that swayed beneath, engulfing him with nausea – until, in an instant, all physical sensation ceased and he saw himself lying face-down on the floor. Honor, Georgina, Mina, Saul and Robbie were cheerfully looking at one another, and at him. Except it was no longer him: it was only his body. He hovered somewhere near the ceiling. Slowly, he noticed a sphere of bright white light drawing him higher. It was surprising, how he longed to submit to the light. That would mean letting them, all of them, get away with it. With him gone, their problems would disappear. And who would mourn him, let alone avenge his death? No one. The injustice was unbearable.

Part 1

1

An Unconventional Situation

Five weeks earlier

How did Honor Wilson arrive at her place in the world? None of the explanations were quite satisfactory. Her late husband, a publisher she met during the war, had many useful friends and even more enemies, as befitted a prestigious man. Yet people said it was Honor, not Gerald, who had 'married down' (an expressive phrase, used freely back then). Others remarked on their age difference – thirty-five years, maybe more – with all the given connotations. Honor seemed an unlikely coquette, with her boyish figure and literary pretensions, her sexless aura. And such unusual colouring, that coal-black hair and bloodless complexion. There were whispers of ancestors in a bygone Middle-European crown land, Moravia or Carinthia.

Even of royal blood, a rumour Honor did nothing to dispel.

'Well, you know, my dear,' she liked to remark dreamily, 'I *have* come down in the world.' But this was the early 1950s. Who hadn't?

Her home, at least, was a kind of queendom, where she held official sway over a collection of lodgers. 'My dear house guests', as she called them. This happy menage lived at 42 Tregunter Road, just east of Brompton Cemetery, whose headstones, supposedly, had supplied Beatrix Potter with character names. Honor's house was medium-sized, a rectangular semi-detached Victorian with its mirror image next door. Dingy cement-coloured stucco rose halfway up the frontage, giving way to yellowish brick. There were five floors if you included the attic and basement, and overgrown gardens front and back.

On one especially bitter evening in February 1953, a moonless dusk obscured all but a silhouette of the front garden's unkemptness. Not that the stranger approaching the front door would have passed judgement. For many years he'd lived in a place devoid of greenery and foliage, of joy in all its forms.

From the back kitchen, George heard the doorbell's chime and went to answer it with a sigh. She wasn't in the best of spirits. Her period was two weeks late – just her rotten luck – and her back hurt from holding a position in Auden Quennel's draughty studio. George worked as an artist's model, the least worst of several demi-monde professions she'd dabbled in. During today's sitting, a mouse had run over her bare foot, making her jump up. 'Keep still!' shouted the rude bugger (Auden, not the mouse). She had burst into tears, then wondered what the hell was wrong with her. Usually she gave as good as she got. How else was a girl to survive in this blasted world?

In any event, her nice manners weren't on full display to the tall, overcoated figure who stood on the doorstep. 'Ye-es?' she said, holding the front door only slightly ajar. She peered at the man, who had an angular, clean-shaven face and dark shadows under his eyes.

'Good evening,' he said cordially. 'Is Mrs Honor Wilson at home?'

George opened the door a little wider. As the entrance hall's electric chandelier subsumed the weak glow of the porch lamp, she assessed the stranger. He was somewhere in his twenties, she decided, and not bad-looking. Not her type, though. George liked well-fed men with twinkly eyes and languid movements. Men who seemed durable, brimming with life. 'And you are?' she enquired. Some sort of charity collection, she suspected. Or one of those Jehovah's Witnesses.

'The name's Jimmy Sullivan. I hope Mrs Wilson won't mind me dropping in like this. We knew each other years ago, you see.'

George didn't see. In her conceptions of Honor's past lives, there weren't any young men who – she glanced down – wore spiv's shoes and spoke in unmistakable cockney tones. 'You'd better come in,' she said. 'I'll go and see if Mrs Wilson is at home.'

Mr Sullivan stepped inside, bringing the mingled smell of fog, tobacco and Old Spice. George saw him look at her chest. Admirable at the best of times, it was emphasised by an accidentally shrunken white pullover, the only clean thing she'd had to wear that morning. *Men*, she thought with infinite weariness.

They went into the drawing room and she invited Mr Sullivan to sit down. Glancing around, he removed his hat and half smiled, perhaps a little awed by the surface grandeur of the high-ceilinged room, with its maroon velvet sofas and antique-looking rug, the cherub-carved marble fireplace and chandelier made of glass fruit. As George left him alone, it crossed her mind that he might steal any number of things. Or was she being a dreadful snob? Thievery was unconfined by class, after all. One of her school friends had a brother in Wormwood Scrubs. Wartime profiteering. Nevertheless, she hastened her step on the stairs.

Honor was in the so-called office, from which she published her literary quarterly, *Vista*. From a glance, she appeared a handsome woman in her thirties. Her eyes were a deep china blue and her black hair was fashionably short, coaxed into waves around her white-powdered face. The effect was striking: she looked like a silent film star, or a French chanteuse in a faded professional photograph. She had spindly fingers, indeed a spindly physique altogether, and wore neat high-necked blouses, jewelled brooches, and mannish trousers. A pair of tortoiseshell spectacles hung around her neck on a gold chain. She was seated at a large squat desk with her back to the window, mustard-yellow curtains drawn against the dark evening. On the desk was a typewriter, a glass holding an inch of whisky, and a jumble of typescripts, books, and magazines. At her feet, almost hidden from view, lay her little white mongrel, Lulu.

'George, darling, whatever's the matter?' she said by way of greeting. 'You galloped up those stairs like you were running from an axe murderer. Is someone here?'

Robbie, cross-legged on the rug with some marked-up page proofs spread out in front of him, merely glared at George. Robbie was thirty-two, but he had the thwarted, perplexed air of a teenager. His hair didn't help: wiry and buff-coloured, it resisted all attempts to smooth it down. When he wasn't swatting hair from his forehead, he was pushing his spectacles up the bridge of his nose. Impatience emanated from him, as though he were unfairly held back from some glorious destiny. Perhaps he was. The son of a parson in Dorking, he had planned to go straight to Cambridge from his middling provincial grammar school. For years, he'd survived on the knowledge that at university, his evident genius (thus far underappreciated by the third-rate minds in his midst) would set in motion a virtually effortless ascent to renown. The war got in the way, of course. Eventually, his youthful immodesty relinquished somewhere in North African enemy territory, he spent three undistinguished years at Downing College. He then loitered, not entirely fruitlessly, on the fringes of the London literary world, until coming to Honor via a family connection. That was nearly five years ago. He had a wife somewhere or other, but no one had ever met her.

'Nothing's the matter,' began George, 'but—'

'You *do* look cross. Doesn't she look cross, Robbie?'

Robbie sighed as if making a huge effort and looked at George. As usual, she got the feeling he disliked her. But what she'd done to offend him, she couldn't imagine.

'You've a visitor,' she said. 'A young fellow. Drat, what was his name? Jimmy something. I put him in the drawing room.'

'A writer, I imagine,' said Honor. 'It's a bit much, calling at this hour.' She glanced at her wristwatch: gone six o'clock. 'Robbie, are you expecting someone?' Writers, invariably young men, occasionally came knocking with pages in hand, hopeful of an audience with Honor. She enjoyed making someone's day by praising their work. This happened rarely. She also enjoyed taking some overentitled twerp down a peg, opportunities for which were more frequent.

Robbie began to deny he was expecting anyone, and George said: 'He's not a writer. At least, I don't think so.'

Honor got to her feet, drank what was left in her glass and said: 'Ah well, no rest for the wicked!' She was incongruously prone to these washerwoman phrases. Another favourite was: 'This won't get the greens on!' As if she knew one end of a cabbage from the other, thought Robbie.

George and Honor went downstairs. As they entered the drawing room, the visitor stood up and came towards them.

George felt Honor stiffen and gave her a sideways glance. Her nonchalant expression hadn't altered.

Mr Sullivan spoke first. 'Good evening, Mrs Wilson? As I was saying to the young lady, I hope I'm not intruding. I was wondering if we could have a talk.' He glanced at George. 'Alone?'

'Gosh,' said Honor. 'This is all very mysterious. Very well, then.' To George's surprise, as she'd never known Honor to care about privacy, she added: 'Be an angel and shut the door behind you, would you?'

Up in her room George kicked off her shoes, got into bed fully clothed, and pulled the grimy pink counterpane up to her neck. Pondering on her absent period, she soon forgot about the visitor. She was never late, was the thing. Obviously, if she was up the duff, she couldn't have it. It was simply a question of getting hold of some money. Whose fault was it, she wondered, other than her own? She cast her mind back. Christopher Maidstone or Julian Fyfe, it was one or the other. Julian was richer, but he was also a Roman Catholic. Imagine if he proposed? George lit a cigarette and contemplated being Mrs Julian Fyfe. Mrs Fyfe would carry a shopping basket and wear headsquares tied under the chin. She'd make jam and give some to her neighbours, who'd think her a wonderful woman, a credit to her husband. When she put on weight – for Mrs Fyfe, bless her, could never resist a second slice of Victoria sponge – she wouldn't mourn her nineteen-inch waist. She'd have more important things to worry about, like organising the bring-and-buy sale for the WI and ironing Mr Fyfe's shirts.

Suddenly nauseous, George stubbed out her half-smoked cigarette.

She'd go cap in hand to Christopher, then. He already had

a wife, so no fear there. But even if she scrounged together the money, where did one find a safe abortionist? A girl she knew had gone to a Harley Street man, who declared her mentally unfit to be a mother and thus was the operation done: quick, clean, and perfectly legal. The trouble was, George doubted Chris's funds would stretch to Harley Street. And she didn't fancy being classified as crackers. It felt like tempting fate.

There were her sisters: a farmer's wife in Eastleigh who wore old tweeds and bred Alsatians, and a banker's wife who did heaven knew what in an overdecorated house near Regent's Park. George was the youngest by some years – she'd been an unwelcome surprise – and she doubted either sister would offer much sympathy for her predicament, each being a mother several times over. They took gleeful pleasure in talking about the revoltingness of the whole business, the bulging veins and stretch marks, the swollen breasts and leaky nethers. Why should George get to opt out? she could imagine them thinking. Wasn't it high time she stopped gadding about having her portrait painted, or however she spent her days?

She could confide in Honor, she supposed. Somehow Honor had managed to never have a baby, so she must know a thing or two. Then again, she could be oddly prudish. George recalled making some throwaway lewd remark to her about a friend's honeymoon, only for Honor to turn all red and stuttery. It put George guiltily in mind of her school's biology mistress, the most spinsterish of spinsters and terribly sweet with it, who almost wept when she had to describe frog reproduction to a bunch of nasty sniggering girls. Except Honor wasn't a spinster. Her marriage to her late husband had been very happy, supposedly. And she and Saul were once lovers, it was gossiped, although George could scarcely credit this. Oh well, she'd thought, Honor's bedpost notches are none of my affair. Still, her embarrassment at a mere allusion to sex had cast her in a new light. Not such a seasoned sophisticate after all.

George liked living at Tregunter Road. All she needed was to be thrown out on her ear. Before she'd moved in, nearly a year ago, she'd rented a shabby bed-sitting room off the Earls Court Road. The gas fire positively ate shillings and the window panes rattled at the lightest breeze. But even in warm weather, she dressed and undressed under the bedclothes: she suspected her landlord, who had a droopy brown moustache, of spying on her through a crack by the ceiling light fixture.

So when Auden's wife, Edwina, had told her about Honor's house, George had begged to be introduced. 'The situation's a bit unconventional,' said Edwina, who vaguely knew the girl moving out, a student at the Slade who was getting married. 'She rents out all her spare rooms, and yet one can't imagine she really needs the money. I suppose she's playing out a bohemian fantasy of communal living.' Her tone was disparaging. She regretted marrying a penniless artist and longed for suburban comforts, a brand-new little house with a fitted kitchen, wall-to-wall carpets, and a mint-green bathroom suite. 'To each their own,' she went on. 'She runs that magazine from home, too.' The word *magazine* was given verbal inverted commas. 'I'm not sure it would be your cup of tea.'

But George thought it sounded fine. If ten years at boarding school had taught her anything, it was that privacy and solitude were luxuries, not necessities. Edwina duly telephoned Honor, who invited George round for tea. An anxious George sat in the drawing room at Tregunter Road, wearing a striped dress with a full skirt and matching jacket, her best outfit, while Honor talked about herself, the writers she liked, and how everyone said she ought to write a novel. George hadn't the first idea what to say. She'd last read a whole book when she was twelve and an illicit unexpurgated copy of *Lady Chatterley's Lover* was passed round the dorms. It was sufficiently enlightening that any further literary education seemed pointless.

Honor barely seemed to notice her silence and chattered gaily on. Finally she said, as though they'd been discussing the room the whole time, 'It's one pound and three shillings a week. Can you manage that? I'm sure you'll be happy here.' George, whose bed-sitting room was two quid, could hardly believe her luck.

There was a loud knock at George's bedroom door. 'Hang on,' she shouted, getting out of bed and smoothing the covers. 'All right, come in.'

Robbie entered. He exuded even more discomfort than usual, as well he might: he'd never visited George in her room before. 'Sorry,' he muttered. 'I just wanted a word.'

'By all means.' Her tone was bright. She kicked a pair of drawers under the bed and pointed to her little horsehair settee. 'Won't you sit down? Can I offer you a drink? There's only gin, I'm afraid. No tonic. But Mina might have some.'

'It's all right. I don't want anything.'

'If you're sure.' George took a bottle from the tray on the sideboard and half filled a tooth glass with gin. Wasn't gin meant to be helpful in her circumstances? She took a gulp, scalding her throat and bringing sour saliva rushing onto her tongue.

Robbie sat down, a tad gingerly, she thought. He crossed his ankles, exposing the worn soles of his brogues, and said: 'I wanted to ask you about that person in the drawing room. Have you any idea who he is? They've been shut up in there for an age.' He caught George's look. 'I know. It's nothing to do with me. But I happened to catch a few snatches of their conversation. It sounds like he's going to be moving in.'

'Really?' She perched on the edge of her bed and thought about this. 'I must say, he doesn't seem Honor's type. Though I only exchanged a few words with him. He claimed they knew each other years ago, which struck me as queer. And there's no room, surely?'

'The only space is the other attic bedroom. You know there's a smaller one just across from mine? It's basically a box room now, full of old junk. But it could be cleared out.'

She saw what he was getting at. 'And you're accustomed to some degree of privacy, up in the roof by yourself.'

'Well, quite. The only time I've got to write are the evenings. You know how I'm run off my feet with *Vista*. Supposing he has noisy friends over, or listens to the radio at odd hours? I need my sleep. I'm useless if I don't get eight hours.'

George was touched he was confiding in her, even if only to fret and complain. She wasn't sure she'd ever heard him speak so many words in a row.

'Yes, I do see your concern.' She sipped her gin, more slowly this time. 'I suppose I could say something to Honor. It wouldn't seem quite right, having a strange man sleeping above our heads. Especially for Mina. She's only seventeen, you know. And sometimes she wanders about in her nightdress. What would her parents say?'

Robbie grinned. 'What about me – aren't I a strange man?'

'Oh, you know what I mean!' But George realised she'd made a faux pas. The notion of Robbie as someone to protect young girls from – as a viable romantic figure, come to that – had never even passed through the outskirts of her mind. She wasn't sure why. He was married, allegedly. And he was pleasant enough to look at, if a bit on the scruffy side. He was an intellectual, that was the problem. All his vitality was diverted to his brain. 'You're so evidently a decent chap,' she assured him. 'Didn't you come to Honor via a family connection? It's hardly the same.'

Robbie laughed. 'My dear George, please don't worry. I'm not offended. I grew up with four sisters. Haven't you noticed that girls invariably feel comfortable around a man with sisters? We've had some of the masculine corners rubbed off, or something.'

'What an interesting theory. I think you might be right.' Pish, she thought. She'd known plenty of utter scoundrels with sisters. 'In any case,' she went on, 'why don't we wait and see if this fellow actually is moving in? Perhaps you misheard.'

'Perhaps.' He frowned and fixed his gaze on the ashtray at George's bedside. 'Are you going to finish that cigarette?'

Taken aback, she passed him the ashtray. 'Be my guest.'

Robbie found some matches in his trouser pocket and lit the fag end. Then he asked, belatedly, after George's well-being.

'Why, do I look ill?' She felt it, though she was dimly aware it was too early for morning sickness and all that malarkey.

Robbie, exhaling a stream of smoke, looked alarmed. 'No . . . I mean, of course not. I was only—'

'I think I'm preggers, which is an awful, *awful* bore.' She hadn't planned on telling him, of all people. She was rather tight, she realised. Several ounces of gin swirled acidly in her empty stomach. If she finished the bottle while lying in a hot bath, would that do the trick? It wasn't her day for a bath, but Mina might swap with her. Especially if she explained why. Mina would enjoy being enlisted into a crisis, would think it a learning opportunity. She regarded George as something of a mentor, the older girl being a bona fide deb who'd received an expensive education. For all the good it did her. Mina, the daughter of a coach driver and a district nurse from Essex, had left school at fourteen. She'd worked as a packer in a chocolate factory until she'd saved enough to move to London. Courageous little Mina wanted a glamorous career or a rich husband. It hardly mattered which. When she wasn't attending classes at Mrs Morley's Charm

Academy for Young Ladies in Shaftesbury Avenue, she worked as an usherette at the local Classic Cinema.

'You'll keep this under your hat, won't you?' George said to Robbie. 'I especially shouldn't want Honor finding out. And it might be a false alarm. Fingers crossed.'

'By all means. I shan't breathe a word. What are you going to do?'

'Get rid of it, of course.'

Robbie couldn't help being shocked by the baldness of her statement. George saw his face and said: 'Oh, come on. It's not a baby yet. It's no bigger than your fingertip. If it exists at all.'

'If this isn't too gauche a question, have you . . .'

'Told the would-be father? No. Bit of a snag, there. I'm not entirely—'

'George, no!' The words burst out. 'But how many have . . . not that it's any of my—'

'Goodness, keep your hair on. Only two.' She pointed an accusing finger at Robbie, a representative (albeit barely) of the sex that had got her into this mess. 'Count yourself lucky you were born a man. Not that any man would do otherwise, unless he were a bloody fool.'

A look passed across his face – of scepticism, of disagreement? – and he opened his mouth to respond just as Honor's voice trilled up the stairs. 'Darlings! George! Anyone? Could you please gather in the drawing room? There's someone I'd like you to meet.'

2

Living Cheek by Jowl

On the stairs Robbie and George, hearing animated voices and laughter, exchanged a bemused glance. They entered the drawing room to see Honor and her guest sitting on a sofa, both in an alert, raised-chinned posture. Saul Reznikov, the poet-refugee who lived in the basement, sat on the facing sofa, a drink in his hand and Lulu the dog in his lap. As he stroked Lulu's head, he wore his habitual expression of abstracted benevolence. Catching George's eye, he conveyed with a lightning-fast smile-shrug that he too had no idea what was going on.

'Ah, here they are,' said Honor. 'Allow me to present Mr Robbie Trafford and the Honourable Miss Georgina Mountford-Owen – though of course you've already met. George is very much the linchpin of our little coterie, aren't you?'

George offered a wan smile and went to make herself a drink.

'This is Mr James Sullivan,' continued Honor. 'An old family friend.' On the last word her voice quavered almost imperceptibly. Between her long fingers she twisted the fraying fringe of a cushion.

If I didn't know better, thought Robbie, I'd say she was nervous. But the man standing up and extending his hand didn't seem at all frightening. He was tall and narrow-hipped, wearing a forest-green jersey, dun-coloured corduroy trousers, and black suede brothel-creepers. His dark hair was close-cropped, and freckles faintly dusted his hands and face. There was something callow about him, something innocent and unworldly, that made Robbie think of the young privates he'd fought beside. 'How do you do,' he said, grasping Mr Sullivan's hand extra firmly.

'Pleased to meet you,' returned Mr Sullivan, saying it as a single four-syllable word. 'And please, call me Jimmy.' He sat back down and looked at Honor, as if for guidance.

George, who was busying herself with whisky bottle and soda siphon, asked over her shoulder if Robbie wanted one. He didn't normally drink, being irrationally fearful of what he might say or do under alcohol's disinhibiting influence. But the strangeness of the occasion seemed to warrant a loosening of his rules. He was unnerved, too, by George's news. What did she mean by telling him? He hated keeping secrets. And her predicament was the ultimate irresponsibility. Extramarital sex was one thing – he took no moral position on either side – but innocent babies ought to have willing mothers. His estranged wife, Pamela, had used an apparatus whose intricacies he took care to know nothing about. Suffice it to say, she knew what she was doing. She always did; she was an extremely capable girl.

He accepted the drink George proffered, watching uneasily as she sat down next to Saul and took several unflinching gulps from her own glass. Robbie, rather than sit too close to anyone, pulled over a cane-backed chair with deflated upholstery. As he sat, broken springs jabbed him. He shifted, and tried to think of something to say.

George leant forward and addressed Jimmy. 'You're a family

friend, are you? How . . .' She paused to concentrate on accepting a cigarette from Saul's silver case. 'How nice. What's the connection? Honor's past is an enigma to us. Has she always been such a dark horse?'

Honor stared at her in frank astonishment.

Jimmy cleared his throat. 'Well,' he began, 'my mother—'

Honor interrupted. 'Jimmy's mother was in service at my grandmother's house, in Windsor. We were all devoted to Mrs Sullivan. Sully, we called her. The kindest of women. Jimmy used to visit on school holidays, didn't you, Jimmy dear, and when my cousins and I were staying we would all play together.'

Robbie considered dubiously if Honor and Jimmy were close enough in age to have played together as children. He placed Honor at around thirty-eight. As for Jimmy, it was difficult to tell. But there was surely a decade between them. At minimum. So it didn't quite add up. He tried to picture Honor as a child. It was impossible.

'Have you lived in London before?' Saul asked Jimmy.

Jimmy hesitated, then said: 'I haven't, no. As Mrs Wilson said, I grew up near Windsor. Always wanted to live in London, though.'

'What did you do in the war?' asked Robbie.

'Really, Robbie!' said Honor, laughing. 'As if anyone wants to talk about the war. The point is that Jimmy is going to live here, at least while he looks for a new job.'

Jimmy, glancing from Robbie to Honor, nodded. 'I'm ever so grateful. And I promise not to get under anyone's feet. You won't even know I'm here.'

'Nonsense,' said Honor, patting his knee. 'Saul, darling, how about some music?'

Saul, who kept his own collection of gramophone records in the drawing room, chose a Shostakovich symphony. Its strings blared out with, thought Robbie, profound foreboding. He shivered and looked at his empty glass. Probably a bad idea to have another.

In showy appreciation of the music, Honor placed her hand on her chest and closed her eyes. When she opened them, she looked around and frowned. 'Now, Jimmy, there is someone missing. Has anyone seen Wilhelmina? Is she at that job of hers?'

She spoke, thought Robbie, as if Mina's job were a needless frivolity. As if Honor wasn't the one charging the girl rent, due promptly each Friday.

'I believe the only evenings she works are Fridays and Sundays,' said Saul unexpectedly. 'On those days, she lets me in without a ticket after the programme has started. If the auditorium isn't full, naturally. Dear girl.'

Robbie felt slighted: Mina had never offered him this favour. Saul belonged to that magical club of men whom women adored, a club Robbie had no hope of joining. The trick, he suspected, was being handsome but purporting not to realise it. Saul was in his forties, the most attractive male age in Robbie's opinion, and knew how to look understatedly suave. His shirts were always crisply ironed, his ties spotless, even though he had no woman taking care of him. Noticing an ink stain on his own shirt cuff, Robbie pulled his threadbare jersey sleeve over it.

'Where's your accent from,' Jimmy was saying to Saul, 'if you don't mind me asking? It's not English, is it?'

Saul smiled. 'How clever of you to notice. The place I'm from no longer exists. I come from Bukovina. Which means I was born in the Austrian Empire. Then, when I was a child, the Bukovina became part of Romania. Today, it is gone from the map. Poof!' He made a fist and flung his fingers open, like a magician revealing a vanished coin.

To this startling answer, Jimmy could only blink and nod.

Robbie felt sorry for him, and said to Saul: 'But geographically, your birthplace is in the Ukraine now, is that right?'

'Indeed so,' said Saul. He turned back to Jimmy. 'I have lived in your country for nearly six years.'

'Will you stay for ever, do you think?' asked Jimmy, back on firmer ground.

'That depends. If I am allowed to, then yes. Why not?'

Why not indeed, everyone murmured, as the slam of the front door shook the house, signalling Mina's arrival. Honor sent George to fetch her, and the girls' voices drifted in from the entrance hall. Robbie, sitting nearest the ajar door, heard Mina say: 'But I look a fright. It's filthy out tonight. All right, let me hang my coat up.'

Mina followed George into the drawing room and saw, unusually, all the residents sitting together, along with a man she'd never seen before. He looked clean and tidy, but she knew, before he'd even opened his mouth, that he wasn't of means (*a kind girl will never encourage advances from a man in a subordinate position*). Cosh-boy shoes, for a start. She stopped caring about the droplets of sleet clinging to her drooping pin-curls and the ladder creeping up her stocking.

Honor made the introductions. He had good teeth, noticed Mina. She'd give him that. Saul offered to get her a drink. She saw they were all drinking whisky, which in her opinion tasted like petrol. 'A drink?' she said, as if equally tempted and scandalised. 'I'll have a very small sherry, if I may.' She looked at Honor, who was normally a right stingy cow with the booze. But apparently it was a very special occasion, as Honor just smiled.

Mina sat on the end of the sofa (*back straight, ankles crossed*) next to George. Saul handed her a large sherry with a smile. He was a good old sort. A Jew, of course, and a foreigner. But Mina took as she found. And Saul had always been kind to her. Said she reminded him of his daughter. They got separated in Hitler's war, Saul and his daughter, and he never saw her again. Nor his wife. Poor sod.

'Have you been out somewhere nice this evening, Mina darling?' asked Honor. Nosy parker, thought Mina. What business was it of hers?

'I had an extra dancing class with Mr Romano,' she said. 'He's not at all satisfied with our progress on the slow foxtrot. You know what a taskmaster he is!' Gabriele Romano from Florence – né Malcolm Sidebottom from Yorkshire – was a stalwart of Mrs Morley's Charm Academy for Young Ladies, much relied upon for his expertise in Deportment, Carriage and Sitting. Mina squirmed to remember how, as an uninitiate, she would sit with her hips too near the edge of a chair.

'Ever been to the Lyceum Ballroom in Covent Garden?' asked Jimmy. 'I can just imagine you there, on the dance floor.'

'I haven't had the pleasure,' said Mina. 'I've been invited a few times, though.'

George, cheeks flushed and eyes glazed, circled an arm around her. 'I'm confused,' she said, cocking her head at Jimmy. 'Didn't you say you had only just moved to London?'

'That's right,' he said quickly. 'A friend told me about the Lyceum Ballroom.' He saw he'd have to be careful around this one, the posh blonde. As for the brunette, she wasn't fooling him. He knew when someone was putting on airs and graces. She wasn't bad-looking either. Neat little pointy face, ringletty hair. But too slight in the figure. The way she'd tightly belted her costume, with its big skirt, couldn't hide that she had hips like a young boy. And bee stings for thrupenny bits. Then again, she was only a kid. Maybe she had some growing to do. Not the blonde. She was fully grown and then some.

George noticed Robbie peering into the bottom of his empty

glass, looking worried. 'Honor,' she said, 'I was just wondering: where will Mr Sullivan sleep? There's not a great deal of room, is there?'

Honor frowned again. 'I suppose there isn't. Jimmy, for the time being we'll have to put you in an attic bedroom, across from Robbie. It's not ideal – rather cramped. I'll ask Greta, our daily woman, to organise it in the morning. No doubt she'll bite my head off, but that can't be helped.'

This crucial question settled, Jimmy jumped to his feet and explained that he had to be getting back to the Fulham Road YMCA. Everyone dispersed in their respective directions, except for George, who lingered, and Honor, who was brushing invisible lint from her trousers and considering the full ashtrays and dirty glasses. 'Greta can deal with this tomorrow,' she said, more to herself than George. Then: 'What was that?'

George repeated: 'Can I have a quick word?'

'You can, but I'm famished, aren't you? You could do with something to eat, I'm sure. A cup of strong coffee, too. Come on, I'll make us some supper.'

They walked through the dining room, which was separated from the drawing room by double doors and never used except for parties. Instead, people ate in the kitchen, a squarish low-ceilinged room overlooking the garden. There was a cavernous larder but no fridge, an electric washing machine, an enamel gas stove, and an ancient mushroom-coloured dresser with an inexplicable funnel-type structure built in. (Only Honor knew this was a flour hopper, for sifting, but she feigned bafflement.) A more modern touch was the table, hyacinth-pink Formica and pale wood, around which the residents sometimes gathered for breakfast. Their rent didn't include board, only light and heat, but a system operated whereby ration coupons were pooled and, for unrationed staples, a kitty maintained. Greta, the daily woman, presided strictly over the kitchen economy, terrorising shopkeepers with her Slavic thrift and merciless haggling. The local butcher, a sixteen-stone former POW, had taken to retreating into the back room at the sight of her, leaving his assistant to be accused of rigging the bacon scales. Honor, for her part, seemed to require remarkably little nourishment and subsisted mainly on MacVita crackers and king-size Pall Malls.

This evening, however, she insisted on preparing for herself and George a concoction she called 'egg in a nest' – a slice of stale National Loaf topped with powdered egg and fried in lard. It wasn't bad, thought George, as she ate and considered what to say about Jimmy.

'Listen,' she ventured. 'I know it's not my place. But is it entirely appropriate for Mina to be living cheek by jowl with a strange chap? You know me, I'm a tough old boot. I'll be twenty-six soon, God help me. But she's just a child, however much she tries to pretend otherwise.'

'Oh dear,' said Honor. 'You don't think she'll want to move out, do you? I never promised to provide a female-only environment. After all, Robbie's here, isn't he? I must say, I don't really understand what you're getting at.' She of course knew exactly what George meant. And she was right to speak up. Robbie wouldn't touch a hair on a girl's head unless expressly invited to do so. Even then. Whereas she'd seen the way Jimmy had looked at Mina and George. He didn't realise he was doing it, of course. For men like that, it was a reflex. And Mina was just a child. Still a virgin, Honor imagined. But that clock was ticking. Must she be *in loco parentis*, though? She thought of herself at Mina's age. No one had protected her. She'd learnt the hard way what beasts men were. All the more reason, then, to look after Mina. As for George – well, it didn't bear thinking about. But George had standards. Of that Honor was quite certain.

'Oh, Robbie,' said George. 'He's like a brother. This Jimmy Sullivan character – well, are you positive he's the sort of person you want to have around? It's terribly nice of you to help him out and all that. But couldn't he stay on at the YMCA? I gather those places are quite comfortable.' In the summer of 1949, George had spent several nights at the YWCA in Bloomsbury, sharing a room with four other girls. In the mornings there was a deafening waking-up bell, like you were in prison. And in the evenings, a ten o'clock curfew. One night she'd rolled in at 2 a.m. with her fourteen-year-old roommate, who was three quarters cut and wearing a sequinned cocktail dress of George's. They'd been at the Café Royal, being stood round after round of drinks by some merchant seamen on shore leave. The YWCA's battleaxe in charge had thrown George out there and then. She'd spent the rest of the night in a twenty-four-hour milk bar off Leicester Square, repelling the attentions of pimps and one very persistent old girl who claimed to want to recruit her to MI6.

Honor speared a burnt crust with her fork and sighed. 'It seems he's had a little trouble at the YMCA. And I do feel an obligation, you know. To his poor mother. Sadly, she's not with us any more. But she was very kind to me as a girl. No one else was, you see. I hope you've never known what that's like, to feel so alone. You never forget it.'

George, who had wolfed down her food, was now sober. She was also numb with fatigue. She opened her mouth to speak, but no words came out. Probably for the best. She didn't trust herself not to blurt that she was pregnant, as she stupidly had to Robbie. Embarrassment clenched her stomach. He must have been horrified.

'Look,' said Honor, not unsympathetically, 'why don't we see how it goes with Jimmy? If you girls feel uncomfortable, or if he misbehaves in some way, then I'll ask him to leave. I'm afraid that's the best I can do.' My hands are tied, she thought miserably.

Saul had repaired to his basement quarters, where he had his own kitchen annexe with a bath (saving him from participation in all the coupon-pooling business, which he found tawdry). Close at his heels was Lulu the dog, who hoped for a treat. 'Oh, little one,' said Saul. 'That we could all be like you, content with a scritch on the neck and a bit of liver sausage.' Lulu accepted this morsel from his hand and pressed her pink and white snout against his leg in gratitude.

He made himself a simple meal of sliced apple and Jacob's Cream Crackers as he pondered the fact of Mr Sullivan. His arrival wasn't a happy event, that much was evident. But would Honor explain? You'd think she might trust him, given the past they shared, the confidences he'd kept. Of course, that was – what was the English saying? – all water under the bridge. Up until a year or so ago, they would still occasionally sleep together, always in his bed, after the house had gone quiet and the young people were either out gallivanting or fast asleep. By the end of their affair, he sensed her heart wasn't in it. She had begun making excuses to avoid spending time with him, and when they were together, he seemed to get on her nerves. Not daring to bring about any type of confrontation – for he couldn't bear to cause bad feeling and risk losing her as a friend – he mirrored her coolness, her withdrawal. And so it was that a fresh layer of sadness settled on the older layers petrifying in the pit of his stomach.

They'd first met in 1947, during the last days of that strange, sultry summer. Britain's hottest of the century, supposedly. For reasons lost to time, Saul had attended a publishing company's party in Bloomsbury. The large, square office-cum-reception-room, with its oil paintings and glass-fronted book cabinets, had impressed him as more like a comfortably appointed home than a workplace. He had hovered on the outer fringes of the sizeable gathering, by an open window. You could see directly into the building over the road, its rooms sliced open to reveal floors gnarled with desecrated belongings, wallpaper sun-bleached and caked in filth. Like a hellish doll's house. The man who'd invited him – they'd shared a publisher in Paris, he remembered now – noticed Saul standing alone and said: 'Oh, but you must meet Gerald and Honor Wilson.' He conducted him over to the couple. Saul politely shook Gerald's hand, brought Honor's lightly to his lips. Poor Gerald was already ravaged by lung cancer, his face withered to its skeletal constitution, eyes huge. And yet Honor held onto his arm, standing slightly behind him, as if she were the one in need of protection.

It didn't matter. Saul was irresistibly impressed. Not by Honor's appearance, immaculate though she was in a violet suit, expertly tailored to emphasise her hand-span waist. And he couldn't honestly claim that anything she said was remarkable or original. No, it was her stately demeanour that drew him, her air of lofty self-absorption. This belied a generous nature, he discovered. She became his champion, shepherding his work into publication, recommending him to editors and newspaper people. At times it was almost stifling, the role she took as his advocate. He was, in a sense, her creature. Yet how could he mind? Without her, God only knows what might have become of him. He had helped her too, he hoped. It was Gerald who had asked him to move into Tregunter Road, during the poor man's last days. He may have known about our affair, mused Saul. May have been glad of it.

An odd life I lead, he thought as he polished off his solitary meal and gave Lulu the plate to lick. When that young man had asked if he meant to stay in England for ever, he had thought: But I exist minute by minute, hour by hour. To contemplate beyond tomorrow was somehow impossible. He filled his days with work, and in so doing, he felt he managed commendably. Sleep, food, reading, writing. Sex – well, occasionally, but it wasn't a priority. The cinema was a more reliable balm, that escape for hours into a dark, smoky room, alone and yet safely alongside others. He liked comedies best. To try and make people laugh was to Saul the very essence of goodness.

He heard Honor's step on the stairs. Come to fetch Lulu, he thought, and indeed the little dog jumped down from a chair, ready to greet her mistress.

'Come in,' he called. Honor glided in with her usual light-footed grace, but her small shoulders were stooped and she looked tired. Pensive. As though the bright social performance of earlier this evening had taken a particular toll. 'I've just had a bite to eat,' he said. 'Can I offer you anything?'

She picked up Lulu, then turned to him, smiling and making more effort. 'Well, I wouldn't say no to a drink. So long as I'm not disturbing you.'

'You? Never.' He gestured to the leather sofa and poured two whiskies. As he sat down next to her, he murmured: 'Is everything all right, Honor dear?'

She smiled again, nodded. 'Of course. Just one of those days.'

'Because if there's anything you want to talk about . . .'

'I know. Thank you.' She said no more, but seemed content to sit and sip her whisky.

'Is this young man's arrival something of a burden? You know, you can't always be everyone's saviour. You must think of yourself. Who is he, anyway?'

'As I said, his mother—'

'His mother worked at your grandmother's house. I remember. But this is me.' He placed his hand lightly on her forearm. 'We don't need to have secrets, do we, you and I?'

She gave him a plaintive look and asked for a cigarette. He sensed she was about to offer some confession, that she had reached, precariously, some emotional brink. 'I do know him from a long time ago,' she said. 'That much is perfectly true. As for the rest – well, it doesn't matter. But I wonder if . . .' She stopped and watched the bluish smoke stream from the corner of her mouth.

'What? Tell me. Is there something I can do?'

She smiled again, but with sadness. 'You are sweet. You've always been sweet to me.'

He looked at her enquiringly, and her eyes filled with tears. She took an intake of breath and brushed both cheeks with the back of her hand. Thus composed, she said: 'I know you work awfully hard, and have precious little free time. But I wonder if you might come upstairs more often. Not for any reason other than I think the girls will feel better with your presence. As a paternal figure.'

He understood. 'In case that young man thinks he can get away with any hanky-panky.' Mina had taught him the phrase, but he'd not yet had the chance to use it. 'Say no more.'

Honor laughed, then sniffed. 'I couldn't have put it better myself.'

'Speaking of the girls,' said Saul, 'George wasn't herself this evening, was she? Is she unhappy about something?' He hated to see a woman not in control. It was so undignified. His own mother, of blessed memory, never took a drink except for a sip of wine on Shabbos.

'She was drunk! Disgracefully so. I don't know what on earth has got into her. It's setting a poor example for Mina.'

'Oh, I wouldn't worry about our little Mina. I sometimes

think she's cleverer than all of us put together. George . . . well, I just hope she's not in any trouble.'

Honor widened her eyes. 'You don't think . . . No, George would never be so foolish. She was presented to the King at Buckingham Palace!' She spoke as if this were a magic spell against future disgrace. And in a way, perhaps it was.

Friday 27 March 1953

'All right,' said Robbie. 'I'll take one end, and Saul, you take the other. Ready, so, on my count of three. One, two, three. That's it.' Christ, he thought, he's heavy. He'd always thought of Jimmy as weightless, graceful. Like a ballet dancer. *Me, a ballet dancer,* Robbie heard him say. *You're having a laugh.*

George, seeing Robbie and Saul struggling, came and supported the middle of the rolled-up rug as they inched towards the door. Robbie muttered thanks. The familiar smell of George – flowery scent, unwashed hair, alcohol-tinged breath – mingled with the coppery smell of the blood-soaked rug.

Robbie's stomach rose into his throat. He feared his knees might buckle.

'His foot!' cried Mina suddenly. 'Oh God, his foot is sticking out.'

'Calm down, for goodness' sake,' said Honor. 'Let's just get him into the Anderson shelter for now, so we can clean up in here. Then tomorrow we'll decide what to do.'

3

Unwelcome Details

George didn't feel magically shielded against catastrophe. Not by a long chalk. As a younger girl, it was true, she'd operated with a sort of reckless entitlement, an assumption that everything would work out all right in the end. And usually it did. She'd got into plenty of scrapes, but nothing that couldn't be fixed. This wasn't even her first time with a bun in the oven. When she was eighteen, she'd taken a nasty tumble from a horse and was knocked out cold. She came round in a little country hospital to be told, sadly, that there was no longer a detectable heartbeat. 'No heartbeat?' she said. 'But wouldn't that mean I'm dead? I'm not dead, am I?' The ruddy-faced old Irish doctor exchanged a look with the matron. There had been a babby, he gently explained. George understood: the babby was no more. 'Good heavens,' she said, sitting up. 'Do you know how far along I was?' Don't worry about that now, she was told. They were going to put her back to sleep and do a little operation. Politely rebuffing the matron's offer to ring up her husband, George sank back on the pillows and marvelled at her extraordinary good fortune.

But lightning wasn't going to strike twice, however tempted she was to go horse-riding, or take up circus acrobatics, or throw herself under the wheels of a vehicle. In diagnosing her condition, the National Health Service quack had supplied two small yellow pills: after she took them on consecutive days, he promised, menstruation would recommence, unless she was *enceinte*. Alas, as she told the good doctor, her menses remained stubbornly AWOL. Case closed, apparently, because he immediately enquired if she was getting married. No, she confessed, marriage wasn't on the cards. This brought forth a philosophical sigh and a speech, clearly well rehearsed, about how a great many couples, through no fault of their own, were unable to have children and would love nothing more than to adopt a little newborn. It was straightforward to arrange. George thanked him very much. She saw he meant well.

The next person she told was Chris, who had a fifty per cent chance of being the father. As far as she knew; she was no mathematician. A different sort of girl, she supposed, would work out the true culprit by cross-referencing diaries and cycles and so forth. George was nowhere near that organised. Even if she were, she didn't particularly care to know. She had decided this was Chris's cross to bear. She rang him up at his office (Chris worked in some government department or other; George was hazy on the details) and told him they needed to talk. Would he meet her at their pub? Affable as ever, he said certainly.

George had deliberately used the standard verbal formula for implying bad news. Better to prepare him, she thought. But when she joined him in the Six Bells, he happily kissed her hello and went back to drinking his pint, not a care in the world. 'I got you a gin and French,' he said. 'How've you been, anyway? I haven't seen you for a while. I thought you'd gone off me.'

Ah, thought George. He thinks that's the bad news. Maybe

he'll be relieved! She tucked her musquash coat over the back of her chair and girded herself to make the announcement. At least Chris wouldn't make any kind of scene. He wasn't the type. 'You did *not* think I'd gone off you,' she cajoled. 'What rubbish. Since when've you ever had a moment of self-doubt? Handsome brute like you. I bet you've never been chucked in your life.'

He grinned at her. She wasn't kidding. Chris's appearance was his main attribute, the secret of his many successes. He possessed an overall glimmering blondeness: hair, brows, lashes, silkily furred forearms. In winter, his skin was white, with rosy tinges on his cheekbones; after a few days of summer, he turned a freckle-less matt brown. His eyes were amber-ringed pale grey and might have been too femininely pretty if not for their shape: narrow and deep-set, shadowed by a prominent brow-bone. Chris was easy-going, affectionate. A Labrador in human form.

George drank half the contents of her glass and said: 'The thing is, Chris darling, that, unfortunately . . .' She glanced at her lap and back to his face. 'Unfortunately, I'm going to have a baby. Or rather, I shall if I don't do something about it. Sharpish. Which I fully intend to. As soon as I can, that is.' She heard herself babbling like a lunatic and stopped talking.

Chris stared at her with incomprehension. George looked back at him and the background hubbub seemed to recede. He drained his pint, replaced it carefully on a beer mat and said: 'Bloody hell, Georgie. Are you sure?'

'Quite sure, I'm afraid. I went to the doctor this morning.'

He nodded, digesting this. 'You're not saying . . . you're not saying it's mine?'

'What on earth do you mean?' Her voice was dull, unconvincing.

'Come on, old girl. I can't be the only . . .' He twitched his finely sculpted nostrils in consideration of the right word. 'I can't be the only candidate.'

The nerve, thought George. The bloody nerve. 'And supposing you are? What then?'

'Then I'd say you're not being fair. I mean, how many times was it? Twice? And on both occasions we were in our cups!'

'Believe it or not, Christopher, none of that is relevant to the outcome.'

He frowned mutinously. She wanted to walk out in a strop. Equally, she wanted to force him to help her. She had a grim operation in store. (How grim? Better not to think about it.) All he had to do was open his wallet. She wasn't willing to let him off the hook even more easily.

'Look, I'm told I'll need about fifty quid. That's the minimum it will cost, apparently. I rather think it's the least you can do.'

'Fifty pounds?' He looked aghast. 'Aren't there pills you can take or something? I've heard about women taking pills.'

She said nothing. Of all the ways she'd imagined the conversation going, this was worse.

Chris turned towards the bar, as though someone might come and rescue him. Then he sighed and looked at George. 'I didn't want to tell you this,' he said. 'But Eleanor is pregnant. Any other time, I'd have the money to give you. As things are . . .'

'You do realise an actual additional baby will cost more than fifty pounds?' She almost shouted the words, and the group of girls at the next table, secretaries or shop assistants, started giggling and whispering.

His cheeks had turned scarlet. 'I don't wish to be ungallant.' He said each word with slow precision. 'I really don't. But the financial responsibility shan't be mine.'

George stood up and grabbed her coat, blinking back furious tears.

Outside, the murky chilled air filled her nostrils and stung her eyes. Chin down and hands in pockets, she strode off in the direction of home, wondering if Chris would come after her. What a fool she'd been. Of course, his marriage was no secret, she'd known their affair didn't have a future – and yet she'd believed he cared about her, in some small, essential way. Seeing that ruthless withdrawal had felt like a physical blow. But she only had herself to blame. You're never safe as an unmarried woman. That was what you were always taught. And if you went your own merry way regardless – well, what on earth did you expect?

On the corner of Edith Grove, she heard a man come up behind her and say, 'Miss Mountford!' She swung round, confused and relieved. But it wasn't Chris. It was Jimmy Sullivan.

'Oh,' she said. 'Hello there. It's Mountford-Owen. But please, call me George.' Since Jimmy had moved into Tregunter Road a week ago, she'd hardly seen or heard him. Perhaps he'd meant it about not getting under their feet. Or perhaps Honor had warned him to stay out of the way. In any case, she hadn't given it much thought. She hoped Robbie wasn't too put out by him, habiting as they did across the landing from each other. But she had her own troubles.

'I saw you walking past,' he said. 'I was just having a drink.' He pointed to the King's Arms. 'Why don't you join me?'

The question of how he'd seen her through the pub's opaque windows skittered into her mind, then out again. 'Thank you,' she said, 'but I've just had a drink with a friend.'

'Let me buy you another.'

Oh, what the hell, thought George. Why not. In the pub, she sat down and Jimmy went to the bar. The girl serving laughed at something he said, leaning towards him and fluttering her thickly painted lashes. When he came back with their drinks, George gave him a knowing smile. 'I think you've got a fan there, Jimmy.'

'Who, the barmaid? Nah. It's her job, isn't it? Make all the blokes feel like she might take 'em home at the end of the night.'

'Is that what you'd like, then?' George was in a dangerous mood.

'Don't be daft. Course not.' He was blushing.

'I'm sorry,' she said. 'Ignore me. I'd have been better off not getting out of bed this morning.'

'That's a shame.' He didn't ask her to elaborate. 'Still, tomorrow's another day, eh?'

She smiled with jaded effort. 'What about you – how are you settling in at Honor's?'

'All right, I think. I try to be out most of the time. You know, so I'm not a nuisance. I've been looking for a job, so that takes up a lot of the day.' He had a quiet, deep voice, and spoke slowly, tentatively.

'What sort of work were you doing before?'

'Me? I've done all sorts.' He took a sip of beer. 'When I was a kid, I wanted to be a policeman. But I failed the medical examination.'

'Oh really? Why?'

Jimmy hesitated. 'It's silly. I had asthma. It wasn't even that bad.'

'So were you . . .' She stopped, cleared her throat.

'What were you going to say?'

'It's just . . . I was remembering that evening you first visited us, when Robbie asked what you did in the war and Honor shut him up. I thought perhaps you'd been medically exempted and Honor didn't think it was any of our business. Which it isn't. But then I realised you're probably too young to have fought. What are you, twenty-five?'

He shook his head, smiling. 'I've got one of those faces. Hasn't changed since I was twelve. I'm going to be twenty-nine next month.' Looking down, he tapped his cigarette ash. 'But you were right. I was exempted on medical grounds, when I was eighteen. I was gutted. The worst part was seeing the look in people's eyes. You know, they'd see me, a strapping great lad, and wonder why I wasn't away fighting. It's not like being blind or a cripple, something you can see. I looked like a coward, one of those . . .'

'Conscientious objectors,' said George.

'Yeah, one of those lot.' He wrinkled his nose. 'Anyway, enough about me. Tell me about you. How do you know Honor? Do your families know each other?'

George shook her head. 'Nothing like that. I just heard about a room that was going begging, from some mutual friends. But I didn't know Honor before.'

'Seems like you're good pals now, though.'

'I suppose we are, yes. She's been a saint, really, in putting up with me. I'm not the most domestic creature to have about the place!' George remembered the time, not long after she'd moved in, when she'd arrived home a little the worse for wear, decided to run a bath, and promptly fallen asleep. Honor, herself asleep in bed, had been woken by water pouring onto her face. To George's immense relief, she just laughed it off and didn't even let her chip in for the cost of repainting the ceiling. And yet when Mina took a teaspoon of Honor's black-market sugar without asking, the poor girl was rather forcefully upbraided. Honor then accepted a farthing in recompense, shocking George, who'd witnessed the whole brouhaha. People were inconsistent, she thought, impossibly so. It wasn't advisable to set too much store by their past behaviour.

'What about your parents?' asked Jimmy. 'Why don't you live with them?'

'I left home years ago,' she said simply. 'Daddy and I never really saw eye to eye.' She smiled. 'Do you know, Honor's is the nicest place I've lived, ever since coming to London when I was nineteen. My goodness, I've lived in some funny places. I once shared a room with a friend above a Maltese restaurant in Chalk Farm. At night, they would bring in girls, smuggled into the country for nefarious purposes. You'd hear them sobbing and banging on the walls. We told the police, but they didn't pay any attention. Thought we were silly women who'd overheard a domestic squabble and turned it into some elaborate fantasy. And eventually I started sleeping through it. Turns out you can get used to anything. That's what I've learnt, anyway.'

As George told this story, Jimmy grimaced. He wanted to tell her how well he understood. You *could* get used to anything. But that was how you stopped being truly human, wasn't it? By closing yourself off to feeling anything at all, by expecting nothing so you couldn't ever be disappointed. 'Maybe you can,' he said calmly. 'But you didn't ought to. Don't be a frog in a pot. That's the worst thing you can be.'

It made a horrible sort of sense to George. Perhaps she was a nearly boiling frog. 'How do you avoid it, though? We humans are nothing if not adaptable, aren't we? It's how we survive. You can't go leaping away at the first hint of discomfort.'

And sometimes, reflected Jimmy, you've got nowhere and no one to leap to. 'Why didn't you and your father get along, then? Did you disappoint him by not marrying some Lord Fauntleroy or other?'

'Something like that. I've got two older sisters who did everything right. I've always been treated like the runt of the litter. Obviously, he wished I'd been a boy. That might have made up for the fact that I came along when my parents were, shall we say, advanced in years.'

'Doesn't seem to have done you any harm, though, does it? Not from where I'm sitting, anyway. I mean, have you looked in the mirror lately?' He immediately regretted his words, which had sounded so much better in his head. He'd been doing all right till now. It was the longest conversation he'd ever had with a girl, let alone one who seemed so impossibly worldly.

How bored I am of being judged by my appearance, George was thinking. She was even more bored of having to feign gratification. Every man was under the impression that, while lesser beings may have complimented her beauty, only his opinion carried true weight. 'Ah, but for all you know I'm hideously ugly on the inside.'

Jimmy widened his eyes, nonplussed. Then he laughed, and so did George. 'My dad didn't like me much either,' he said. 'The old bastard's dead now, and I can't say I'm sorry.' He sighed. 'Listen to us, proper pair of miseries. Let's talk about something else. So you don't want a husband, or a big house. What *do* you want?'

'What a question! To be the right amount of free, I suppose. Free enough that I can run my own life, but not so free that no one cares if I'm happy or sad, or cares where I am at three o'clock in the morning.' As the words came out, they seemed to describe a considered philosophy, rather than an answer she'd pulled out of the air. What she'd said wasn't untrue, though.

'And you believe that's possible, do you? To have your cake and eat it too?' His tone was gently reproving, but for the most part, he wanted the same thing. Unless, he thought, if by 'run my own life' she meant having no one to look after her, no one to come home to at night. Sometimes Jimmy felt it was all he wanted, just to come first in another's thoughts.

'Of course,' she said, exhaling cigarette smoke and frowning. 'I must believe it. Otherwise I might as well just throw in the towel.'

Somewhere behind them a glass smashed on the floor, and

they both started at the noise. Then Jimmy said: 'So do you work on Mrs Wilson's magazine, what's it called . . .' He knew what it was called.

'*Vista*.' George gave a quick little chuckle. 'Gosh, no. That's not my bag at all. I can't even type. I began a secretarial course once, and after two days the teacher said, very kindly, that she would refund my fees as it was clear my talents lay elsewhere.'

'But the magazine is successful, isn't it? I mean, people read it?'

'It depends on what you mean by successful. Certainly people read it. But it's not hugely profitable. There are subscribers and advertisers, I gather, but most of that money goes to pay writers.'

'Oh.' He thought about this. 'So the writers are well paid, are they?' It didn't make sense – why would Honor, of all people, carry out work without a financial reward to herself?

'I don't know the details,' shrugged George. 'As I say, it's not my world at all.'

Jimmy let it drop and suggested they have another. George thought: Sitting here drinking isn't going to solve anything. Still, she said yes, and they talked for nearly another hour. Eventually it crossed her mind that she ought to call a halt to the proceedings, as Jimmy would happily stay there until chucking-out time. So she said: 'Well, I mustn't keep you out until the early hours. Honor will think I'm leading you astray.'

'Will she indeed,' he said with good-humoured scepticism, but he finished his drink and stood up.

At Tregunter Road, George let them in with her latchkey. Honor was coming down the stairs, looking her most whimsical self in an oversized apple-green jersey. A purple paisley silk scarf hung unknotted around her neck, along with her usual spectacles chain and several gold necklaces. Between her fingers was a cigarette holder but no cigarette, as though she'd rushed from the room on hearing the key in the door.

Awkwardness thickened the air.

'Hello, Honor,' said George. 'Gosh, that green is heavenly on you.'

Honor smiled vaguely, looked down at her empty cigarette holder, then stared at the two of them. 'Where have you young people been on such a cold night?'

George meant to say they happened to meet in the street – no need for Honor to hear anything else. But she was distracted by Jimmy helping her with her coat as she shrugged it off. It wasn't an outrageous gesture. Just slightly off. And Honor was regarding them, George registered, with something approaching alarm. Jimmy said: 'George was nice enough to have a drink with me. We had a good old chat, didn't we?' He hung her fur coat on the rack, smoothing down its damp lapel in the manner of an overly intimate butler.

'How very nice,' said Honor, her face saying the opposite.

They all stood there beneath the electric chandelier for what felt to George like an entire minute. Then Jimmy said: 'All right then, ladies, night-night,' and headed off upstairs. Honor took hold of George's wrist. 'Come and have a drink,' she said in an urgent whisper.

'I've actually had . . .' began George. But she let herself be shepherded into the drawing room. Honor closed the door behind them.

'I must say,' said Honor, 'I'm really surprised by your behaviour lately. Is there something you want to tell me?' Her voice was quivering, whether with nerves or anger George couldn't tell.

George sat down heavily. Her legs ached, as did her full bladder. 'I'm sorry, have I done something to upset you? Because if so, I'm—'

'First you say you don't think Jimmy is a suitable lodger. Then you start accompanying him to goodness knows where.'

'It was only a drink at the King's Arms. We bumped into each other in the street. I assumed you wanted us to befriend him.'

'I'd like you to be friendly, yes. Nothing more.' Honor paused. 'You wouldn't, George darling, would you?'

Since when do you care whom I sleep with, thought George. 'It hadn't crossed my mind. I can't imagine why you think it should. Unless you believe I set my cap at anything in trousers, in which case—'

'There's no need to take umbrage. You're just much too good for someone like Jimmy. That's all I'm saying. I wouldn't want you to—'

'He told me why he couldn't serve, if that's what you mean.'

Honor blanched. She went to pour them both a drink, then sat back down and looked at George. 'What did he tell you exactly?'

'About being exempted from conscription. Because of his asthma. He seemed ashamed, poor fellow.'

Honor sipped her whisky, and some colour returned to her cheeks. 'Yes. Quite. I agree, it's hardly his fault. But George, I don't mean to ... I just don't see him as ...' She trailed off uncertainly.

'An eligible suitor for a *gel* like me?' George lowered her chin and raised her shoulder winsomely. 'In all honesty, I think I've squandered my chances for anyone presentable. But that's by the by. Please rest assured, I've no unwholesome designs on our Mr Sullivan.'

'He may feel otherwise, though. The way he took your coat ...'

'That was a bit odd, wasn't it? Perhaps an attempt at good manners. He may've thought it was like standing when a lady enters the room or something. I'm not sure we ought to damn him for misapplied etiquette.'

Honor laughed. 'You're a kind girl, George. I'm glad we had this talk. You'll stay out of his way, then? I do think it's best. I mean, we wouldn't want him to get the wrong idea. Get his hopes up, as it were.'

George promised to give Jimmy a wide berth and said goodnight. She went to the lavatory, then to her room. There was a block of Cadbury's in her bedside drawer, she realised with a drunken flutter of joy. Ever since chocolate came off the ration a few weeks ago, it had been the main constituent of her diet. Bliss. Curled up in bed munching, she remembered leaving the Six Bells in an awful strop. So much for Christopher. Rotten bastard. Could it be true that his wife was pregnant too? George was sorry for her, if so.

But she was more sorry for herself. She'd have to find some money. That was all there was to it. What could she sell? She looked around the room without much hope. She had a gold bracelet, an heirloom from her grandmother. But she doubted a pawn shop would offer more than a few quid for it. None of her clothes were worth anything. The only expensive thing was her fur. And that was ratty, with a torn lining. Besides, she could hardly be without a winter coat.

She heard Mina on the landing before she stuck her head around the door and said: 'Knock, knock.' Without waiting for George to respond, she came in and flopped on the little settee with a sigh. The hem of her mauve wool skirt slid up, revealing tidily darned clocks on the sides of her stockings.

'Tiring shift at the cinema?' asked George, passing her the chocolate.

'My dear, I thought I'd fall asleep on my feet!' Yet she looked as alert and pretty as ever.

'Well, you'll never guess where I've been. At the King's Arms with our new friend Jimmy.'

'You weren't! George. Don't tell me you like him.'

'Not like *that*, no. Give me some credit.' Was this really what people thought of her? That she'd throw herself at any Tom, Dick or Harry? 'He seems harmless, though. He confessed to me that he couldn't be a soldier because of weak health.'

Mina removed her gloves to break off a piece of chocolate (*a lady never wears gloves whilst eating or drinking*). 'You mean he didn't serve? Was he old enough?'

'Evidently so. He's nearly twenty-nine. But he suffered from mild asthma, so was exempted.'

Mina frowned and rolled her gloves into a neat whorl. 'He said that, did he? Sounds like a pack of lies to me. My eldest brother's got terrible lungs from catching TB when he was only little. He said the army doctor barely listened to his chest before giving him the all-clear. He was sent to the front and all. His pal, who had a gammy leg from polio, was still sent to Kenya instead of combat duty. They weren't picky, you know. Couldn't afford to be.'

'Oh.' George felt foolish. 'Gosh. I suppose you're right. Why lie about such a thing, though?'

Mina shrugged. 'Maybe he went AWOL. Maybe he's still on the run now, and that's why he's here. He was too frit to be a soldier. You'd hardly want to admit that.'

Surely Mina was being overly imaginative, thought George. The girl saw too many films and was prone to fanciful notions. 'But I told Honor,' she said, 'who already knew. She wouldn't lie on his behalf, would she? Or harbour a fugitive from justice.'

'So says you. Me, I'd not put it past her. She's a dark horse, isn't she? You said so yourself, the other night. More than a few skeletons in that cupboard, I reckon.'

'Did I say that? I can't think why. Honor's never given me any reason—'

'I mean, where are her people?' Mina raised her eyebrows.

'Doesn't she have parents? Or sisters, brothers, cousins? I don't think she even has friends.'

'She's never mentioned any family,' conceded George. 'Only her late husband.'

'How old was he when he popped his clogs, then? I heard seventy-odd.' Mina made a face. 'Can you imagine, marrying someone twice your age.'

Rather than respond to this, George ate another piece of chocolate. Then she said: 'There *was* something a bit strange tonight.' She got up and closed the door.

Mina was examining her face in a compact. 'Go on!'

George sat back down on the bed. 'Honor saw us as we arrived home. Me and Jimmy. She seemed in a thorough flap about us fraternising. Once he'd made himself scarce, she all but gave me a ticking-off. Then made me promise to avoid him. As though I were her virgin daughter whose prospects might be wrecked by parish gossip.'

'Golly. Honor being motherly. Will wonders never cease!'

'I know. But it was almost as if . . . as if it was Jimmy she was trying to protect. Thinks I'll break his little heart, haha. I suppose you ought to bear in mind, though, that these rules presumably apply double to you.'

'You mean what with me being an actual innocent young virgin?'

'Well, you are, aren't you?' George was curious, never having established this basic fact. Suddenly, fervently, she wished a lifetime of peaceful chastity for Mina. Why she wished this, she could hardly have said. Perhaps she wished it retroactively for herself.

'Too right I am.' Mina shuddered, as though only too aware that the alternative was ruinous. In truth, she'd only recently grasped what the whole business actually involved (George had helped enlighten her, albeit inadvertently). Now Mina was feeling queasy about marriage, though her broader plans for the future hadn't wavered. She wanted glamour, and comfort, and money, and most of all she wanted everything money could buy. A French-grey cashmere coatee with chinchilla trim. A suede box handbag with an ivory handle. Turquoise evening pumps by Roger Vivier for Christian Dior. Every colour of silk stockings on tap. A flat in Belgrave Square decorated in gold and eau de Nil, with new furniture from Harrods. If these blessings must come via a man, well, so be it. As a rule, Mina tried not to dwell on unwelcome details.

'Mina,' said George thoughtfully, 'how much do you earn as an usherette?'

'It depends on how many shifts I work.' Mina snapped her compact shut and put it in her pocket. 'About four pounds a week, usually.'

That was a pitiful amount. A waste of time. George could get more from a few sessions of figure modelling at the art school. Though she loathed doing it. Not that she cared about disrobing in front of strangers. It was merely boring and uncomfortable, even more so than sitting in a painter's squalid studio. In any case, no matter how much paid work she undertook, it would take too long to save up. Much too long. Time was very much of the essence. But supposing she borrowed the money somehow – could she then work all the hours God sent to pay it back?

'Why?' said Mina. 'Are you short? If you need me to lend you something, I—'

'No, no. Kind of you, but I wouldn't dream of it. I am in a bit of a tight spot, but I'll sort it out.'

'I can put in a good word at the cinema, if you like.'

'Thank you, I'll think about it. You get off to bed, darling, if you're tired.'

Left alone, George got back into bed herself and contemplated the last resort: asking her parents to lend her the money. If only there were an acceptable reason for needing such a sum. But even if she came up with the perfect excuse, merely asking would further lower her status in their eyes. In her father's, at least, and he held the purse strings. Charles Mountford-Owen was baffled by his wayward youngest daughter, unable to understand why she refused to settle down. And if she insisted on this odd existence of a modern bachelor girl, why must she be an artist's model? Her fellow debs, if they worked, did flower-arranging or cooked business lunches.

Perhaps, mused George, she'd have made a better fist of her romantic life if her father had been nicer. He'd always disliked her, even when she was a small girl. He never made much effort to hide the fact. To be fair, he treated all girls – and women, come to think of it – with a scorn that bordered on sadistic. Yet George had seemed to particularly test his patience. When she was about five, she got a kitten from a neighbour's cat's litter. Maisie, she was called. A fuzzy tortoiseshell with a squashed nose and white socks, Maisie sat on George's shoulder indoors, and outside she liked to nestle behind the lapels of her coat. One day they ate some blackberries in the garden, and Maisie, unused to such rich fare, greeted George's father by quietly vomiting on his shoes. Without speaking or exclaiming, he picked up the tiny creature by the tail and dangled her head in the pond until she stopped flailing. The cold cruelty of that act, George realised now, had deformed her faith in human goodness. He'd killed Maisie, she knew, not from an impulse to punish his daughter, or even because he'd simply lost his rag, but because George loved her and was loved back. In some perverse way, he found this insufferable.

So no: assistance could not be sought from parental quarters. She thought about going to see Julian, the alternative paternal candidate, to use Chris's fastidious word. But she instinctively recoiled against another humiliating confrontation. I'll decide tomorrow, she resolved, before closing her eyes and sinking into a delicious void. Along with arranging her body in useful poses, sleeping was George's great talent.

4

The Company He Kept

The uncomfortable subject of money preoccupied Honor. Dutifully at her desk on Monday morning, she was trying to read a short story set in a Ramsgate insane asylum. The writer was a woman, and Honor saw the story had merit. But she kept rereading sentences, taking nothing in. The thought juddering around her brain, short-circuiting all others, was this: how much would it take to be rid of Jimmy? There was only a tiny mortgage on the house. Perhaps the bank would lend her more. Then again, as a widow with a spotty income, she likely wouldn't qualify for a loan. And the house was all she had. It was her security. How she hated having to contemplate this! She preferred, as much as possible, to float above matters financial. Or rather she preferred purporting to do so. Like many acquainted equally with wealth and poverty, Honor was privately obsessed with the fate of every penny, while trying to appear blithe, absent-minded. To do otherwise, she feared, would attract attention from the gods, who might see fit to upend her relatively comfortable circumstances. Not that her comfort was undeserved, or unearned. Not if one looked at it in terms of general fairness and justice. So she told herself.

'Robbie,' she said, 'you liked this story, didn't you, the one set in a loony bin?'

He looked up from his own smaller desk, diagonally opposite Honor's. He was writing rejection letters and parcelling up manuscripts to be returned, a never-ending task. 'I have to say, I thought it was rather good. Derivative of Huxley, of course. But that's no crime.'

'Tell her we'll take it, then. I can't seem to focus this morning, but I trust your judgement.'

'All right.' He licked and sealed an envelope, then said cautiously: 'Is anything the matter?'

She smiled. 'No, nothing's the matter. I must be tired, that's all. Oh, incidentally' – she frowned as if the idea had just occurred to her – 'you haven't noticed George and Jimmy becoming friends, have you?'

Robbie removed his spectacles and rubbed the bridge of his nose between thumb and forefinger. 'Friends? How do you mean?'

'Oh, you know. I thought I detected a frisson. She's a very nice girl, our George. But she is awfully *sociable*.'

He hadn't heard this euphemism before. You don't know the half of it, he thought. 'She's never been very sociable towards me.'

'You don't invite it, Robbie, dear boy. You're always glowering at her, aren't you?'

Do I glower? he wondered. He hadn't realised. 'I suppose I've always found girls like her a bit frightening. All that to-the-manner-born confidence. Makes me feel like a forelock-tugging member of the lower orders.'

She laughed. 'You're not exactly Jude the Obscure. Isn't your father an archdeacon or some such? And George hasn't a farthing to bless herself with, you know that.'

'Ah, but it's not about money, is it? It's about social class.'

'Nonsense. Surely in this post-war age we're past all that? Everything's been levelled out, or so they tell us.'

'Not according to the Labour Party. Not until the means of production are nationalised.'

Honor gave a loud, deliberate yawn. 'Okay, Mr Orwell. Whatever you say.'

'Anyway, if social class no longer exists, why can't George make a boyfriend of Jimmy? Why would it matter?'

'I didn't say she couldn't. I merely asked a question.' She moved the pages she'd been reading onto a messy pile. 'But what about you? Have *you* made a friend of him?'

'I have, actually. We've had some interesting talks.' He paused. 'And I don't think you should worry about him and George. He told me he was, and I quote, off women.'

'Hmm.' A likely story, she thought.

They were both silent for a few minutes, then Robbie said: 'It must be a year now, mustn't it, since George moved in. I don't think I ever asked how you knew her.'

'Oh, I can barely recall. She was introduced via friends, you know, in the usual way. I believe I was importuned upon to rescue her from a sordid bed-sitting room. It is shocking the way some young women live today. In my youth, the idea of living by oneself would never have been countenanced. The connotations would be' – she paused, wrinkled her nose – 'untoward. Things are different now, I suppose.'

In truth, Honor could summon with vivid clarity the events leading to the advent of George. One evening, around Christmas

1951, she was leafing through *The Sketch* (which periodical provided light relief from the highbrow literary business of the day), when she chanced upon a society-page photograph. Taken at a Bond Street gallery's private view, it was of three women in evening dress with the caption: *The Hon. Miss Georgina Mountford-Owen, Miss Emeline Spencer, and Mrs Clarissa Smythe toast Mr Douglas F. Manning's dazzling new exhibition.* Gazing at George's smiling face, Honor succumbed to a volcanic eruption of long-repressed memories. George looked like a lovely person, she thought. Someone whose considerable beauty was more than skin-deep. The implications of this – the heart-clenching, unignorable implications – seized her as though by the throat. As she continued to examine the photograph, she became convinced of only one possible future course: she should get to know George and discover her character first-hand. A part of her realised this was insane. At the same time, she felt she had no choice.

But how might an introduction be affected? Mrs Clarissa Smythe, Honor was vaguely aware, was herself an artist who taught painting at the Slade. And *The Sketch* described Mr Douglas Manning as a former student of Mrs Smythe's. Honor's tenant Sadie Havers was a Slade student – she could be her emissary! They must throw a party. Mr Manning and Mrs Smythe would attend, and via quite natural conversation, Honor would lay some groundwork.

A date was set and invitations sent (Sadie, in agreeing to co-host, had no notion she was arranging her own dispossession). As it turned out, Mrs Smythe had a prior engagement. It didn't matter, because Douglas Manning proved both dupable and well placed to assist Honor in her quest. Having plied the young man with drink and compliments, Honor placed a hand on his arm and said innocently: 'Super turnout at your preview. I saw the photographs in *The Sketch*. Were they mostly friends of yours? It all seemed very grand to me. That pretty girl Georgina, isn't she the daughter of Lord Mountford-Owen? I once heard a speech he gave on education reform. Clever man. Rather fierce, I'd imagine.'

'You'd imagine right,' said Mr Manning. 'But George is a ripping girl. She's an artist's model, you know. Sits to several friends of mine. Not to me, I should add. She has a very classic sort of beauty, not quite my line.' This meant he found George extremely attractive and was annoyed at the predictability of his response. Dougie Manning had a raging phobia of being ordinary, and nothing was more ordinary than lusting after the buxom fair form of George. So he painted dark spidery girls with flat chests and gaunt austere faces, whom he also forced himself to seduce. Thus did he congratulate himself on his sophistication. He was miffed that no critic – not a one! – had yet compared his work to Modigliani's. Bloody philistines.

'How very interesting,' said Honor. 'Surely Georgina's papa can't approve of these activities?'

'I daresay he doesn't. Though I don't believe she always takes her clothes off. And I think the old man had practically disowned her already. Hence her being obliged to earn her own bread. Brave of her. She lives in a cheap bed-sitting room. Not far from here, actually. It's pretty seedy, poor girl.'

'Well,' said Honor, her mind working away, 'we can't have that, can we?' George could have Sadie's room, she decided. Getting rid of Sadie might take a bit of manoeuvring, but it shouldn't be too difficult. She was engaged, Honor knew. She hadn't planned to rush into marriage, but she'd see sense after receiving some heartfelt advice. Honor wouldn't like being left in the lurch, of course – it was terribly difficult to find the right sort of tenant – but Sadie's future happiness was all that mattered.

When George came to talk to Honor about taking the room, Honor had found herself nervous. She rabbited on about goodness knows what, while George sat serenely in a lovely striped costume, sipping tea and nodding politely at Honor's remarks. Afterwards, Honor realised she'd failed to ask any of the questions one might in the circumstances. That could have aroused suspicion. But she offered such cheap rent that George was unlikely to be put off.

And so it proved. The very next week, George arrived in a whirl of Miss Dior, effusive greetings, and carpet bags overspilling clothes. She declared herself thrilled with the room and the whole set-up. Before long, she had charmed the household – even Greta, the ill-humoured daily woman, hitherto supposed impervious to charm. Never mind that George's room turned into a constant tip. She flicked cigarette ash on the floor (even though Honor banned smoking in bedrooms), slept in complexion cream that made greasy marks on her pillows, and left dirty underclothes strewn everywhere. Lesser domestic crimes resulted, typically, in Greta withdrawing her labour. She wouldn't even run a duster over surfaces if she came upon a room in too much disorder. But George was exempt from the normal rules. Greta scolded her, but she was quickly placated by George's extravagant self-flagellation. 'You must think I was raised by wolves! How can I ever atone for my horrendous sluttishness? I'm a disgrace to my sex, aren't I?' And so on and so forth, until Greta was embracing her and clucking her tongue and saying now, now.

The only person immune to George's legendary appeal was Robbie. Why she stirred in him such antipathy, he couldn't explain. She just made him feel ill at ease. The worst was when he accidentally encountered her in the company of her men

reduced to selling their company in a seamy Soho nightery. Thus were many summer afternoons happily squandered.

Robbie had slightly exaggerated about making a friend of Jimmy. They'd shared one proper encounter, when Robbie invited him into his room for a cup of tea. It was late in the afternoon, and they'd met on the stairs.

'That would be very nice,' responded Jimmy. 'Very nice indeed. So long as you're not busy, that is.'

Robbie asked him to sit down while he lit the gas ring and put the kettle on. But Jimmy walked around the room, looking at everything: Robbie's shelves of books, his pictures, the Chinese bowl where he kept cufflinks and sentimental scraps like cinema ticket stubs. 'I must say, this is homely,' said Jimmy sincerely. 'You've arranged things well, haven't you?' He peered inside a découpaged metal box on a high shelf and lifted out a brown leather holster. 'Is this a pistol? From the war?' He opened the strap, ignoring Robbie's request that he put it back. 'Cor,' he said, holding the gun in his hand. 'That's smart! Is it loaded?'

'No, of course not. Sit down and have some tea.'

Jimmy sat on the desk chair and accepted his teacup. 'Who's that?' he said. He looked towards a silver-framed photograph of a young woman gazing unsmilingly at the camera. Her pale hair was shorn into a shiny helmet, and she wore long earrings and a choker necklace. 'Is she your girl?' He sounded faintly incredulous. Robbie was used to this. Pamela, whilst no beauty, had a sort of arresting sexiness.

'Yes and no,' said Robbie. He sat down on the rug, his shoulders against the wooden bedstead. 'It's my wife. We're separated.' He tried to think of the last time he and Pamela had been in touch. It was six months ago, maybe even nine.

'Oh dear, what happened? If you'd rather not talk about it, of course, I—'

'No, I don't mind. She got fed up with me, that's all. I can't honestly say I blame her. She was always wanting me to get a proper job. You know, instead of scrabbling together a living as a literary person. She wanted babies, and a nice house, and the usual things girls want. In the end, I told her she'd be better off finding someone else.'

'How long were you, you know, together?' How brave, thought Jimmy, ditching your wife like that, not a care for what people might think.

'Not long. We met at university. She's living in Cambridge now, working as a secretary in a solicitor's office.'

Jimmy frowned. 'But she must be mad. Who'd want to do that instead of sharing this life you've got? Living in London, working in publishing. It's much more exciting, isn't it?'

'It depends on how you look at it, I suppose. Not everyone wants excitement, do they?'

'Too true. I certainly don't.'

'Oh, why's that?'

Jimmy looked rueful, almost maudlin. 'When I was a kid I was a right little tearaway. I don't know why, even. I never meant any harm. I had too much energy or something. I was always getting into bother of one sort or another. The way I was going, I could've ended up in prison, like a few of my mates.' The first part, at least, was true. It was proving more difficult than he'd expected, sticking to a consistent story. He just hadn't expected these people to be so nice. Astonishingly, they seemed to find him acceptable. Whilst he knew he'd be better off keeping to himself, it was so novel, so strangely vitalising, to not be treated like scum, to enjoy intelligent conversation.

Robbie was mildly shocked by the mention of prison, but he

didn't want to show it. 'I think locking people up is barbaric, don't you?'

Jimmy laughed. 'I bloomin' well do not. Society's got to punish criminals, doesn't it? Or there'd be anarchy.' Only the cosseted upper classes, he thought, could ever imagine otherwise.

'Would there really, though? It's not as if we've ever tried, as a society, to solve crime with rehabilitation rather than punishment.'

Jimmy raised his eyebrows in amused forbearance. 'One of those bleeding hearts, are you?' He took a sip of tea. 'At least when criminals are locked up, they can't be a bad influence on others. Fathers passing down evil ways to their sons, and that type of thing.' He shook his head. 'All I know is, if someone murders your mother, you won't be thinking about how to rehabilitate him into an upstanding member of society. You'll be hoping they throw away the key. Better still, hanging.' He made an unnecessary noose-tugging gesture.

Robbie thought about his tyrant of a mother, who reserved all her affection for the three Border collies that followed her everywhere. She dressed year-round in a battered sou'wester and a green hunting jacket dating from Victoria's reign; her favourite activities were smoking, barking instructions at her social inferiors, and threatening cheeky village children with her shotgun (also of dangerously ancient vintage). You knew when Harriet Trafford was nearby from her particular smell, a mixture of Senior Service cigarettes and the rose water she brewed and splashed on in lieu of bathing, which she considered unhealthy. An abiding memory: when Robbie was six, he proudly presented her with a poem he'd written. A bleak little reflection on eternity, it went something like: 'The stars which shone/In our lifetimes/Will shine still when we're gone/The church bells, their chimes/Keep ringing though death has come.' She declared the poem 'a feeble effort', which 'lacked scansion' and was 'just doggerel, really'. His first harsh professional rejection, the taste of many more to come. Robbie tried to imagine someone murdering Harriet. He didn't fancy their chances.

'I suppose,' he ventured, 'I can understand the eagerness for capital punishment when the case is cut and dried. But it so rarely is. What about poor Derek Bentley?' He referred to the simple-minded young man who, just weeks earlier, had hanged for the murder of a policeman. 'Dead at nineteen. He didn't even hold the gun.'

'You want to know what I think about Derek Bentley?' Jimmy was suddenly vehement. 'I think he ought to have been a far sight more careful about the company he kept.' For goodness' sake calm down, he told himself. Don't take it to heart so. He went on, but tried to sound more casual: 'Christopher Craig – the actual shooter of that copper – his older brother, older by ten years, had got him into armed robberies when he was just a kid. The brother's in prison now, but too late for Christopher, who's there too. And rightly so.' He finished his tea. 'So you're not with your wife any more. Got any girlfriends?'

Robbie smiled at the conversational swerve. 'Not really. No one special, at least.' No one at all, but he didn't feel like announcing that.

'What about the girls who live in the house? They're both nice-looking, aren't they? I thought maybe you and Miss Mountford . . .'

'George? Gosh, no. She wouldn't look twice at me.'

Jimmy thought about this. 'I don't see why not.' He frowned. 'What did Mrs Wilson mean when she said George was the linchpin of the household?'

Robbie snorted. 'She meant George can do no wrong in her eyes, that's what. She adores her. Don't ask me why.'

'Yeah. I thought she seemed a bit stuck-up myself. But I'm off women, just for the moment. Got too much else to think about. Who needs the aggravation?'

'The aggravation,' echoed Robbie, testing the phrase on his tongue. 'Exactly.'

Later, in his own room, Jimmy went over their conversation in his mind. Had that declaration of being 'off women, just for the moment' sounded the right note? Robbie had seemed to take it at face value. A lot of people should find it suspicious: a man his age, still without a wife. No parents, either, though that was hardly his fault. They'd both died young, especially his mother, who was only fifty-three. But she was old for her age, worn out and sick of everything. She'd been like that for as far back as he could remember. His earliest memory: he was no more than a year old, in the drawer that doubled as his cot, breathing in the smell of beeswax polish, looking up at the white ceiling, and blubbing. Not wailing, just sobbing quietly. Nothing much was the matter probably, except for wanting to be picked up. His mother, father and sister kept coming in and out of the room, talking to each other whilst ignoring him. He knew – knew in some cosmic, prophetic way – that he was doomed to stay separate from them. They were a unit and he was unwanted, a nuisance, to be fed and clothed and kept alive, but only out of obligation.

As he grew older, he saw that other small children were liked by adults, even doted upon. But his essential wrongness somehow repelled affection. If a better explanation existed for why no one liked him, he couldn't imagine what it might be. He never asked his mother why she rarely touched him, or his sister why her expression always held such – this was the only word for it – such distaste. In the mirror, he saw a normal, nice-looking boy, so the problem had to lie deeper. When he was around ten, he resolved to not only learn what was wrong with him, but to fix it and live happily in the world, just like everyone else. Now he was nearing thirty, and though he hadn't managed to achieve his goal, he hadn't given up.

5

The Next World

On the evening of Jimmy's arrival, Saul was surprised when Honor, having wept intermittently and drunk too much, asked to spend the night. He'd thought that was all in the past, had come to terms with her unspoken rejection, even if he never quite understood it. Still, his heart was bruised, and he felt wary of repeating the cycle. And yet what could he say? He hated hurting a woman's feelings. Once, when Marya was tiny, Gila needed to stay in hospital for three days, and her sister, Malka, came to look after the baby. Every night his sister-in-law crept into his bed, as though helping Gila naturally meant performing her wifely duties. Were Malka young and beautiful, Saul might have demurred at her silent advances, out of connubial loyalty but also because nothing was more robust than the ego of a lovely girl. But poor Malka was nearly thirty, with a heavy figure and unplucked upper-lip hair. So he closed his eyes and did the kind thing. Malka's pleasure was excessive, as was her gratitude. Both were touching in a pathetic sort of way. For ever more she gave him satisfied complicit glances that went, thank God, unnoticed by Gila. Well, not for ever more. Malka and Gila had both been dead for over ten years. He hoped they were together in the *yene velt* – the next world – laughing at their silly husband and lover.

The next morning, Honor was back to her usual self: brisk, detached, haughty. As she went off to do whatever she did during the day, he reiterated his promise to show his face in the communal areas of the house, for the sake of George and Mina. 'Especially George,' Honor had emphasised. Saul wasn't sure why. Perhaps she thought George needed protecting from herself more than anyone else. That he could see. He liked the girl, but he didn't share Honor's elevated opinion of her. By no means was George too sensible to get herself into trouble, as Honor had said. In fact, she struck Saul as precisely the type to get into trouble. Girls with her wildness of spirit ought to be married off young. It was a dereliction of duty on the part of her parents. But the English, he reflected, were extremely stupid when it came to these things.

Saul had never got a woman into trouble, albeit more out of luck than design. Occasionally, when the barber suggested something for the weekend, he accepted out of a fleeting desire to make his life seem exciting. But he considered those devices degrading and wouldn't dream of using one. Instead, he was considerate (and unabashed) enough to make some relevant enquiries beforehand. The time of the month mattered, he was vaguely aware – something to do with the cycles of the moon. At the beginning of their affair, Honor had explained she was unable to have children, on account of a childhood illness. He was too tactful to ask for details. She hadn't seemed sorrowful about being robbed of motherhood. Matter-of-fact, you might even say. Still, he supposed she'd had her whole life to come to terms with it.

On first meeting Honor at that publisher's party, with her

dying husband, Saul hadn't contemplated a seduction. Not specifically. It crossed his mind that the connection might be professionally advantageous, but he hadn't pursued it. Then the strangest twist of fate occurred. He'd made his regular pilgrimage to Whitechapel, to eat a sandwich at Bloom's and visit his cousin Naomi Cohen. The woman who looked after Naomi answered the door and said, repressively, 'She's got a friend here.'

Sitting in the front parlour, drinking mint tea, was Honor. He might have assumed it was her doppelgänger, were it not for the expression on her face: guilty, frightened, *caught out*.

'Hullo, darling,' said Naomi from her wheelchair. 'This is Elizabeth, my old friend. She brought the most marvellous cakes, would you look at that.' On the table were two cream-filled sponges, one covered with glossy peaks of chocolate and the other with pink icing and strawberry slices. How many sugar coupons had been needed, Saul couldn't begin to calculate.

'How very kind of you,' he said. 'I don't believe I've had the pleasure.' As he took Honor's outstretched hand lightly in his, he gave her a smile that said: don't worry, whatever is happening here, I shall play along.

'Saul Reznikov is my cousin,' Naomi explained to Honor, who put down her teacup and said, 'Oh, is this your cousin who . . . the one from . . .' In her face Saul saw fear turn to panic. But he was used to this. People didn't know how to act. They worried about what to say. Was it rude not to offer commiseration? And yet what form of commiseration could ever be adequate?

Naomi rescued her. 'That's right. He's come to London from France, haven't you, darling? We hope he'll stay.'

Saul inclined his chin in affirmation, his mind ablaze with the possible meanings of Honor Wilson's manifestation, under another name, in Naomi's humble home. Faithful to his tacit assurance, he betrayed nothing. The threesome chatted about this and that while he, under urging from Naomi, ate two large slices of cake. After an hour, he glanced at the mantel clock and said he must be on his way. Immediately, Honor said that she too had to be going.

It was a clammy late-September day, a pinkish twilight shimmer in the air. 'May I walk with you?' asked Saul. If Honor hadn't wished to talk privately, he reasoned, she'd have stayed at Naomi's.

'Of course,' she said, and they set off down Whitechapel High Street. Despite her expensive pale-beige dress and matching coat, her crocodile handbag, Honor didn't seem ill at ease in the insalubrious district.

As if reading his mind, she said: 'My father used to take me to that café when I was a girl.'

She pointed to a small glass-fronted establishment with a red and white striped awning. Outside, a gang of young lads with pompadour-ish hairdos were smoking and lobbing saucy remarks at passing girls. Next door (except there was no door), several children played in the exposed cellar of a bombed-out building. They were inadequately dressed against the encroaching evening, the small girl in wrinkled ankle socks and a smocked dress faded from countless washings, the boys in obvious hand-me-downs. One child, a dirty-faced urchin in a sleeveless pullover – he couldn't have been more than four – saw Saul staring and winked at him like an old sailor.

'Going there was a special treat,' Honor went on. 'They served the most delicious lemon cheese tart. And iced coffee with ice cream! Yum.'

Saul asked, as he supposed he was meant to: 'So you grew up around here? How interesting.'

She nodded. 'I rarely talk about my childhood. Or the time before the war at all. It makes it easier, you see. Easier to forget the times I was unhappy. I just pretend, to myself and everyone else, that it all happened to a different person.'

'To Elizabeth.'

He said this as a statement, not a question, and she looked at him with gratitude. 'To Elizabeth.'

'Does your husband know about Elizabeth?'

'No. By the time I met Gerald, I'd already done away with her. He thinks I grew up abroad. That I have no family. That part is true, more or less.'

Saul thought this over as they stood aside to let two young mothers with prams pass by.

'But you've stayed in touch with Naomi?'

'Naomi doesn't know I'm Honor now. Naturally, or she wouldn't have introduced me as Elizabeth. I take it she hadn't told you about me?'

'Not that I recall, unless . . .'

'I'm a Gentile, in case you were wondering. Well, mostly. On my mother's side, there was . . . but that's not important. We were neighbours with Naomi and her family.'

'I see.' He sensed she was leading somewhere momentous, that this wasn't simply small talk. It didn't take exceptional powers of perception: she fairly glowed with intention. 'If you don't have any appointment to keep,' he said, 'perhaps you'll allow me to buy you a drink? If we can find anywhere suitable, of course.'

Honor smiled. 'That would be lovely.' She looked at her wrist-watch. 'It's opening time. I know just the place.'

She led them a couple of hundred yards to Aldgate High Street and an old pub, the Hoop and Grapes. Surprised, Saul followed her inside. The place was half full already, and a fug of smoke hovered beneath the low ceiling.

'Another of your old haunts?' he enquired.

'Heavens, no. Women didn't go to pubs in those days. Not

nice women, anyway. That's one good thing about the war, don't you think? A lot of the silly old rules fell away.'

Be that as it may, Saul couldn't see many women drinkers. One strikingly ravaged old lady, her face scored with criss-cross grooves, sat alone with a glass of beer. She wore a curious mix of rags and finery: a coat with a brown fur collar and a glittery brooch, and a dress that was patched and fraying. The once-elegant shoes on her deformed, swollen feet were reinforced with knotted twine. She gazed at some fixed downwards point, only occasionally reaching for her drink. There was a solemnity about her, a stillness, like she wasn't quite of this world.

The only other woman in evidence might have been cast as the ancient lady's foil, so pristine and contemporary did she appear. She was maybe eighteen, with black hair piled atop her head in Swiss-roll shapes (how, Saul wondered, was such a style achieved?) and fake pearls the size of marbles in her ears. Through her V-necked light pink jersey you could see the outline of her brassiere. This fact was certainly not lost on her companion, a swarthy youth with a tidemark on his neck. He was treating her to a half of stout and an explanation of why Britain must withdraw from Mandate Palestine. His voice was loud and authoritative, but his grasp of geopolitics was so tenuous that Saul had half a mind to set him straight. Except he could see from the girl's blank expression, the way she suppressed a yawn and concealed it with an encouraging nod, that she wasn't listening to a single word.

He was right. Blimey O'Riley, she was thinking. Some people do love the sound of their own voice. If I wanted a bloody lecture I could have stayed at home, listened to Ma jaw on about driving a Red Cross ambulance in France as a girl. If I never hear anything about wars and foreigners again it will be too soon.

Saul and Honor found a corner banquette and sat down with their Scotches (he'd thought neat whisky was a man's drink, but one learnt something new every day). He waited for her to explain further about her decisive reinvention. Instead, she told him of her plans to set up a literary quarterly.

'Perhaps,' she said, 'you might do me the honour of letting me publish your work. I know everyone must be clamouring to do so. And I certainly don't want any special favours. But I'm such an admirer. And if we were to have you in our inaugural issue – well, what a coup it should be! And not that this matters to you, I'm sure, but I intend to pay my writers above the going rate. After all, the venture will be nothing without them.'

These words fell delightfully on Saul's ears. As susceptible to flattery as the next man, he was also living hand to mouth, his main income coming from dribs and drabs of translation work. In common with many writers and artists, his once promising career had been derailed by Hitler. When he was thirty, an esteemed Romanian press had accepted his first poetry collection. The next day, Germany invaded Poland. Seven years later, the book was finally published in London, Paris, and Palestine. It received many nice notices. But as far as Saul was concerned, those poems were from another life, written by a different person. For the past two years, he had written poetry only in English, his mother tongues of Ukrainian, German, and Yiddish quite consigned to history. Four of his recent efforts had been published in *New Writing*, John Lehmann's anti-fascist periodical. Some journalism, too. But he needed more exposure, better connections. So with little hesitation, he promised to contribute original work to every issue of Honor's journal, as well as take on a to-be-defined role as European poetry editor. Only later, much later, did Saul wonder if Honor had invented this publishing venture on the spot, to make some sort of secret atonement.

'I'm hoping it will give me a purpose in the coming months and years,' she said. 'Gerald hasn't got long, you see.'

Saul dropped his hand over hers. 'How terrible,' he said. 'Is this what the doctors say?'

'We're looking at four weeks at the most, they think. I shouldn't be away from him now, not really. His nurse is there. She's very good. But I worry if I'm out. I've hardly left the house lately, so I was overdue a visit to Naomi. I do like to see her when I can.'

'I'm sure she treasures your visits. She lights up in your company, anyone can see that.'

'She really hadn't mentioned me to you before?'

'Is there a particular reason she might have?'

Honor withdrew her hand from his and ran a fingertip around the rim of her glass. 'No, no reason. How conceited of me to imagine I'd be the subject of your conversations!' She grinned abstractedly. 'Now, she said you were her cousin – are you actually cousins?'

'As opposed to what?' he said, laughing. 'Do you mean because she is so English and I am so foreign? Yes, we are cousins. Our mothers were sisters. Naomi's mother, my aunt Sylvia, she married an Englishman and came to London in the early part of the century. A lot of people were leaving the old country, you know, at that time. So we didn't grow up together, Naomi and I. But we did meet occasionally, at weddings and so forth. And now we are both here, and both widowed rather young.'

Honor opened her mouth to sympathise, but Saul raised a hand. 'A story for another day, perhaps.' He took a sip of whisky. 'I'm just glad to know she has a friend like you. By the way, how on earth did you wangle the coupons for those wonderful cakes? Or shouldn't I ask?'

'You probably shouldn't ask. But Naomi deserves a treat.' She smiled and affected a cockney accent. 'And what the eye don't see, the 'eart won't grieve over!' They both laughed, and she said: 'Speaking of which, paper is still rationed, of course. Our journal may have to be slenderer than I'd like. But I won't let it stop me.'

'I've got a feeling,' said Saul, 'that very little can stop you once you've set your mind on something. Now, how about another drink?'

She looked at her wristwatch. 'I really ought to be getting back to Gerald. But can I give you a lift somewhere? I'm going to find a taxi.'

Outside, a light drizzle was falling. As they walked in the direction of a taxi rank on the Commercial Road, the unlovely setting took on a strange enchantment. His destiny, Saul fancied, was switching lanes via the conduit of this puzzling woman, whose cryptic accounts of herself attracted him in ways he couldn't explain.

He didn't remember what they talked about during the taxi ride to west London. It was eclipsed by the memory that, as they parted, Honor said: 'Will you ask Naomi to tell you about me, about the history between my family and hers – yours? There are things you ought to know. But they're better coming from her. After you've done that, will you telephone me? We're in the book. Do phone, even if it's to say you never want to see me again.' She clasped his hand through the window. 'People used to call me Elsie,' she added as the driver sped her off into the night.

Saul rarely visited the East End these days. Naomi was dead: in the winter of 1950, she caught the flu, which turned into pneumonia. She was forty-three – no age at all. But she wasn't a strong woman, and the infection took her quickly. Now she lay next to her husband in the Willesden Jewish Cemetery. This was thanks to Honor, who paid for everything, including the plot and the marble headstone. By then, Saul understood why Honor felt a duty to Naomi, and to himself. He'd learnt, as Honor had put it, all about the history between their families. Still, he was grateful for her generosity. Naomi deserved a nice resting place, after all she'd endured in life.

But who will organise my funeral? he pondered as he stood outside the Classic Cinema on the King's Road, smoking and waiting for Mina to change out of her uniform so he could walk her home. He'd been to see *Angel Face* with Robert Mitchum: a bleak film, he'd thought, unwholesome in its preoccupation with sex and death. Perhaps Honor would see to the arrangements, if they remained friends until then. She was bound to outlive him. Whilst she'd always been coy about her age, he assumed she was five, even ten years his junior. Well, maybe not ten. She had lines around her eyes, he'd noticed lately. But her body hadn't changed one jot, not by one wrinkle or freckle or bulge. It was as taut and perfect as a girl's, with that sharp vertical crevice bisecting her midriff, and breasts that disappeared when she lay on her back, but for the large dark nipples, like ripe blackberries. Of course, it was having children that ruined women's bodies. From gestating one small baby girl, Gila had acquired lurid purple tiger-stripes on her belly, which hung down over her pubis like an apron. One of the sharpest disappointments of his life occurred when Marya was two and Gila stopped nursing. The high, firm globes of her breasts shrank and withered until what remained resembled Marya's little socks. No one warned you about these things before you were married.

'Oh, you waited,' said Mina, tucking her scarf more firmly into her coat. 'You are a dear. I hate going home by myself on these dark evenings. What did you think of the flick?'

'Not bad. Stylish and rather chilling.' He offered her his arm. 'Home, young lady?'

As they strolled, Mina told Saul about the new class she was taking, to learn how to be a mannequin. 'You probably think there's nothing to learn, that you simply wear clothes and walk up and down. But you couldn't be more wrong. For instance, there's a particular way to take off a jacket and still appear elegant. I'm naturally talented at walking, though. Signore Romano always says so. You ought to see some of the clumsy heffalumps who struggle with the basics. It's not complicated: chin up, stomach in, pelvis forward.'

Saul was only paying partial attention, whilst finding Mina's inconsequential chatter, as usual, extremely relaxing. When he noticed she'd paused, he asked: 'And so this will qualify you to work in a ladies' dress shop, will it? Parading the garments at their best advantage for customers?'

'Precisely. Or I could be photographed for magazines. Though I expect that's more competitive.'

'And if it was, what difference? Any competition, you would win. I only feel sorry for the other girls, the heffalumps.'

'You're too funny. The thing is, I'm not sure my parents would like me to do photographic work. It sounds a bit dodgy, doesn't it?'

'That depends,' said Saul reasonably. 'Presumably your parents wouldn't object to you being on the cover of *Vogue* magazine?'

'Now you are being a comic.' A wistful look crossed her face. 'You know what I'd love, though? My own fashion boutique. Can you imagine, choosing all the beautiful things to sell?' She pictured herself in a white-carpeted Mayfair shop, dispensing style advice to rapt women in fox stoles and pillbox hats, the air scented by a huge bowl of gardenias. 'Oh well,' she said, snapping back to dreary reality. 'Let's hurry, it's freezing.'

When they got home, Mina said: 'Will you have some cocoa?' They went into the kitchen and she put a saucepan of milk on the stove. When she gasped, Saul thought she'd burnt herself on the gas. But she said: 'Oh, I forgot to tell you.'

Saul smiled and lit a cigarette, expecting to hear that she'd received top marks in getting out of a motor car with her knees together. But she sat down, placed a hand on the table and said in a low voice: 'It's about Mr Sullivan. He told George some cobblers about getting medical exemption from serving in the war. Obviously a lie. I despise dishonest people, don't you?'

After a moment or two, Saul said: 'What makes you so sure he's not telling the truth?'

'He said he had a touch of asthma, and so was excused from duty. I mean, come on. Even if he couldn't do proper fighting and killing, he'd still have to do something. I had a feeling about him. Something's not right there, I said to myself.'

Saul opened his mouth to speak. Nothing came out. Mina stared at him in mild bewilderment. Luckily, the milk started bubbling over and she leapt up. By the time she put the mugs on the table, he'd gathered himself somewhat.

'Do you know how old he is?' he asked. 'I'd imagined he was around George's age, which would make him – what – only eleven or so when the war began.'

'He's twenty-nine! I was surprised too.'

Saul did some frantic calculations in his head. A shiver went through him, leaving an ache around his ribs. No, he thought. No. It can't be.

Mina clasped her hands around her warm mug. 'George went to the pub with him.' She raised her eyebrows. 'Honor didn't like that. Obviously she doesn't think Princess Double-Barrelled should be mixing with a commoner, seeing as the sun shines out of her behind.'

Saul laughed. It was rather sweet, he thought, the way Mina slipped into cockneyish speech when she was especially tired. 'What happened – did Honor warn him off?'

'It was George who got a ticking-off. If I were her, I'd have told Honor to get stuffed. What right's she got telling anyone what to do? She's not our mother. A funny sort of mother she'd be anyway. Can you imagine?' She frowned. 'Sorry. I wasn't . . .'

Sensitive girl, thought Saul. But he couldn't spend his life avoiding the subject of mothers and children. Not unless he moved to a desert island. 'It's quite all right. Now you, you'll be a splendid mother one day, won't you? How many children will you have, do you suppose?'

Mina wrinkled her nose. 'I'm not all that keen on the idea, truth be told. Two, I think. Two would suffice.' It wasn't babies themselves she didn't like. Some of them were nice enough. (Although, secretly, she much preferred puppies.) She just couldn't abide the mess they made. The last time she'd visited her nephew, who was about nine months, his mother plonked him onto her lap without warning. The little blighter's nappy leaked onto her apricot wool-jersey skirt, brand new from the Fenwick's sale, and his sticky paws left marks on her collar. (*A lady is never seen in public without a spotless collar and gloves.*) In any case, Mina remained decidedly on the fence about ever doing the thing to start a baby.

'Incidentally,' said Saul, 'is George quite well at the moment? We thought she seemed a bit out of sorts.'

'She does, doesn't she? The only thing I know is that she needs money. She mentioned maybe getting a job as an usherette. I felt like saying, my dear, you wouldn't last five minutes. It's real work, not like lounging on a settee in the altogether whilst someone does your portrait.'

'The altogether?'

She rolled her eyes jokingly. 'My word, how long have you lived in this country? And I'm still teaching you the King's English. Wearing her birthday suit. In the buff. Starkers.'

Saul looked even more baffled.

'Not wearing any clothes,' she stage-whispered.

'Ah! I see. Of course. But it's the Queen's English now, is it not?' He was glad to regain some authority.

'Blimey, so it is. You forget, don't you? She's too young to be in charge of us all, poor cow.'

'Mina, you'll tell me, won't you, whatever else you learn about Mr Sullivan? I'm rather curious.'

'Don't you worry. If there's anything else to ferret out, you can rely on me. To be honest, it's Robbie I feel sorry for. He's obliged to share close quarters with him, isn't he? He can't like that.'

'Oh, I don't know – I suspect sharing quarters with another young fellow should suit Robbie just fine.'

'Do you?' said Mina. 'I hope you're right.'

Saturday 28 March 1953

The sky was purplish black, the moon all but hidden by smoggy clouds, the only sounds spades crunching into the ground and the heavy breathing of physical labour.

'Boys, let me and Honor have a go,' said George. 'You've earned a break.'

She looked at Honor, who nodded her assent. George did look charming, she thought, in her headscarf and fisherman's jersey. Like a land girl.

The women continued digging by torchlight, and a serviceable grave began to take shape. 'How emasculating,' said Robbie, still slightly out of breath. 'You're making considerably faster progress than Saul and I were.'

Saul patted his shoulder consolingly. Honor, wiping her brow with the back of her hand, said: 'You had the hard work of the frozen topsoil. Now we're down to the softer silty layer.'

'I do wish you'd let me help,' said Mina. 'I feel so useless just standing here!'

'Nonsense,' said Saul. 'You're holding the torch, which is the most important job of all.'

Then it was time to do the process in reverse, and

replace the soil. Thank goodness for George's idea to roll the body in the rug. It was almost possible to forget that, contained in the disappearing coil of Persian wool, was the man they'd called Jimmy.

6

An Unanswerable Predicament

Grey raindrops pattered listlessly on the kitchen window, obscuring the thin morning light. Honor shivered and wished it wasn't too early for a drink. She scraped a dot of margarine across some toast, then dropped the knife on the floor as Saul, coming up behind her, said good morning with a certain insistence, as if not for the first time.

'Sorry, darling.' She picked up the knife. 'You made me jump. I was miles away. There's tea in the pot.' She sat down at the table. 'We don't usually see you for breakfast.'

He sat down across from her. As ever, he had dressed carefully, in a dark-blue Viyella shirt and wool waistcoat in a blue and brown check. His face was clean-shaven, and he exuded a pleasing melange of scents: peppery aftershave, musky hair oil, toothpaste.

'Well,' said Saul, 'you wished for my presence to be . . .' he raised his eyebrows, 'noticed more, didn't you? Because of—'

'Because of Mr Sullivan. I certainly did. You *are* thoughtful.'

Yet why, she wondered, was this the first morning he'd shown his face? The conversation in question had occurred some ten days ago, that night she went to bed with him. She'd been drunk, uncharacteristically impulsive. Stupid of her. This was the first time they'd been alone since then, she realised. There was an atmosphere between them. Did he imagine they were to resume their affair? More to the point, did he want to? Oh stop it, she told herself. As if everything wasn't complicated enough. She chewed a mouthful of toast – it tasted like dust – and tried to think of something to say.

Thank goodness for Lulu the dog: she padded over to the table and gazed up at Saul, tail down and eyes full of reproach. 'Don't fall for it,' said Honor. 'She knows you're a soft touch. She's had her breakfast. Naughty girl.'

But Saul didn't chuckle or pick up Lulu in sympathy. Instead he frowned, sipped some tea and said: 'How are you, Honor dear? I was wondering if perhaps—' He broke off at the sound of footsteps down the passage.

'Oh,' said Robbie. 'Good morning, Saul. Hello, Honor.' He seemed surprised to find them both there. 'Is there tea in the pot?'

'Why don't you make some fresh,' said Honor. 'Saul, what were you going to say?'

'I beg your pardon? What was I . . . No, nothing important.' Saul turned his attention to Robbie, who was examining some marmalade remnants at the bottom of the jar. 'Now then, how are you getting on with our new guest?'

'Our new . . . You mean Jimmy.'

Saul smiled. '*Jimmy*, yes. Are you two finding—'

'Mr Sullivan, I mean.' Robbie, feeling his cheeks redden, turned away and tipped the used tea leaves into the sink. 'As I was telling Honor yesterday, we've had a couple of chats. He and I. He seems like a—'

'Golly, I'm starving!' Mina, her slippered tread soundless, appeared as if from nowhere. Wrapped in a peach satin robe, face meticulously painted, ten or eleven metal cylinders arranged on her head, she looked like a cartoon android. Or, thought Robbie, an adolescent male's idea of one. 'Any marmalade left?' she asked him hopefully.

'Mina,' said Honor, in a tone of weary outrage, 'you didn't sleep like that, did you? How can you bear it?' And if I've told her once, she thought, I've told her a thousand times: dress properly before coming downstairs. For someone so preoccupied with ladylike etiquette, Mina had a slatternly side. Too heavy-handed with the maquillage, too. Honor remembered how, as a girl a year or two younger than Mina, she'd dared come down to breakfast wearing a smudge of black around her eyes, in timid imitation of Clara Bow. *You wipe that muck off your face this instant*, her mother had said, *or you'll feel the back of my hand*.

'One must suffer to be beautiful,' replied Mina. 'Who said that? Was it a foreigner? Whoever it was, she wasn't wrong.' She tucked a few renegade strands behind her ear. 'The thing is, mornings when I've got an early class, it's either sleep in my rollers or wake up at four o'clock to put them in.' This, her shrug indicated, was an unanswerable predicament.

Robbie brandished the marmalade jar. 'There's a bit left. You can have it.' Abandoning the prospect of toast for himself, he placed the refilled teapot on its coir mat at the centre of the table, then sat down next to Honor.

Mina opened the bread bin and continued: 'Perhaps I ought to get a permanent wave. I've got the right sort of hair for it. Takes a curl well.'

Honor stared at her, in no mood for a discussion of hair maintenance. 'Have you seen George this morning?' she queried.

Mina gestured to the ceiling with a breadknife. 'Still in bed. I won't repeat what she said when I put my head round the door, if you don't mind.' She scooped a dollop of marmalade onto a doorstop of bread and circled the spoon to spread it. 'When she got home last night, she asked me to wake her this morning. And that's the thanks I get. If she's late to an engagement, it shan't be on my account.'

'Oh, where did she go last night?' Honor half yawned with apparent disinterest. 'Anywhere special?'

'Lord only knows,' said Mina. She sat down and began cutting her bread into triangles. 'All I can tell you is that—'

Saul placed a hand on Mina's wrist. 'But Robbie was telling us his impressions of Mr Sullivan.' He smiled across the table at Robbie. 'Please, do go on.'

'Was I?' Robbie used his fingertips to sweep some crumbs into a small pile. 'Not much to say, really. He's a nice enough fellow.'

'Though not a soldier, I gather,' said Saul. He and Mina exchanged a glance.

'Is it true, Honor?' asked Mina. 'Was Mr Sullivan exempted for asthma? Because my brother, he—'

'If that is what Mr Sullivan says,' said Honor, more sharply than she'd intended, 'then that is what happened. It's none of your concern either way.'

Mina, her face the picture of wounded innocence, applied herself to her breakfast. Robbie tried to remember if he'd smoked his last cigarette yesterday. Saul felt in his pocket for his own cigarette case and Honor said: 'Darling, we're still eating.'

'Look, I do believe it's stopped raining,' said Saul. 'I'll go outside. Robbie, would you care to join me for a smoke in the garden?'

During the war Honor's late husband, Gerald, had planted fruits and vegetables in the garden, dutifully obeying the government's

'Dig for Victory' slogan. Under the supervision of his first wife, Barbara, he'd grown patches of onions, potatoes, cabbages, strawberries, and figs. The usurpation of the household by Honor (Barbara, elbowed into unmerry divorcee-hood, would put it less politely), someone who'd never touched soil in her life and didn't wish to start, reduced the bounty of these harvests. After Gerald died, grass and weeds spread until the only signs of his industry were wooden demarcation strips, mossy and swollen with rain.

Six months into Honor's widowhood, on a bright summer's day, she and Robbie went outside and he wondered aloud about reviving the kitchen garden. Spuds, after all, were still in short supply. Honor had clapped her hands. 'How I should love that! As you see, we've been lacking a capable man about the place.' Why Saul didn't figure in this calculation was unclear – perhaps, as a Jew, he was too effete for manual labour. (Robbie, who hardly knew any Jewish people, guiltily revised this opinion when told of Saul's years in a slave labour camp.) Anyway, Robbie hadn't actually meant to offer himself as the resident horticulturalist. As he'd soon learn, one had to be careful what one said to Honor. She had the enviable skill of interpreting everything in a manner most convenient to herself.

Robbie was twenty-seven when he moved into his room at Honor's. After coming down from Cambridge and getting married, he'd lived with his wife, Pamela, on the ground floor of a decaying terraced house in some nameless purlieu of Acton and Chiswick. Pamela's father, the proprietor of a factory in Surbiton that made metal tubes (for what purpose? Robbie didn't like to ask), subsidised the rent, 'just whilst you get on your feet'. As it turned out, to Pamela this meant 'until I badger my disappointment of a husband into respectable employment'. Since she'd successfully badgered him into marriage, you couldn't blame her friends. She would smoothly and warmly make introductions, only for Robbie to revert to a bumbling clueless undergraduate. He always imagined them discussing him afterwards. 'I know, darling,' George would say. 'Isn't he an odd little chap? I do my best to be kind, but really, what can you do with someone like that? He gives me the creeps, if I'm honest. That's Honor for you, unfortunately. She will adopt these pathetic little lame ducks.' And the man, who in Robbie's perception was always infeasibly handsome and athletic, the type to head a rowing or rugby team, would laugh briefly before forgetting about him entirely.

Robbie was intrigued to hear that Honor had rescued George from her previous situation. He'd assumed George floated from one congenial atmosphere to the next, invulnerable to distress or misfortune. Hence his surprise when she'd confided in him the other night. For the first time, he saw her as a vulnerable young woman, not the dauntless figure whose poise he so envied. Now he was the keeper of her shameful secret. Whoever would have thought it? And not one, but two of her exemplary specimens of manhood were in the frame! It wasn't surprising, he reflected. They all fairly oozed virility. Robbie wondered if he himself would ever have a child. The notion was somehow preposterous. It was disturbing to consider that at his age, his father the reverend had sired five children. Maybe that was Robbie's problem. Maybe growing up as the only and youngest brother to four sisters had warped him in some irrevocable fashion.

What was that game they used to play? Flapper, that was it. They'd dress up and pretend to be nightclub girls who danced with men for money. His eldest sister always took the part of the man, and the rules required her to start by offering a lavish compliment, in response to which they each told a wallet-loosening sob story, of escalating rococo-ness, to explain why they were for continuing with this approach. Her own occupation, attending a secretarial college in South Kensington to learn typing and shorthand, was deadly dull. None of her friends with husbands were expected to *do* anything. Robbie's comparative leisure, therefore, was all but intolerable.

Yet just as intolerable to Robbie was the denigration of his writing – that painstaking, near-constant effort – as leisure. He wasn't sitting around twiddling his thumbs, for crying out loud. Sometimes he even helped with the housework. If he needed a break from his typewriter, he tidied up a bit or took some dirty washing to the bagwash. Once, feeling especially energetic, he mopped the linoleum in both the sitting room and the kitchen. Meanwhile, the novel was coming along nicely. He'd recently published his first poem, in *The New Statesman and Nation*, no less. And a chap at *The Daily Telegraph and Morning Post* had promised him some reviewing work.

The final showdown occurred when Pamela proposed, in all seriousness, that Robbie take a job at 'Daddy's firm'. Daddy was keen to show him the ropes, she said. He'd have to start at the bottom, of course – maybe take some night classes in engineering – but within a few years he might be in management. He could still write his novel in the lunch break, if he really wanted to. The ensuing row crescendoed with Robbie storming off into the sunset. He really wasn't a storming-off sort of fellow. On reaching the Metropolitan Line station at Goldhawk Road, he realised he had nowhere to go, no friend whose sofa he might sleep on. None of his sisters lived in London. Even if they had, they were all married to ghastly men.

Not wanting to lose his nerve, he got on a train and rode all the way to Liverpool Street, where he alighted and went into the platform bar. A drink supplied the courage he needed to telephone his aunt Demelza, who lived above a pub in Bloomsbury.

As a self-described 'free spirit', Demelza might be sympathetic to his plight, he thought. ('Free spirit, my eye,' said Robbie's father. 'Try as nutty as a fruitcake.')

'Turfed you out, has she?' He heard the rasp of a match and the inhalation of a cigarette. 'That's some backbone, isn't it? Didn't know she had it in her. Well, I can put you up for a night or two. You don't want to go home, I take it?' She meant to his parents, and before he replied, she went on: 'No, I can't say I blame you. You'll have to stay out of my landlord's way, of course. He's fussy about non-paying guests.'

Demelza, who was into Eastern religions and miscellaneous spiritual mumbo-jumbo, answered the door in a loose straw-coloured garment not unlike a medieval monk's robe. With her fairish hair bound in two long plaits and an aureole of frizz around her face, she seemed even battier than Robbie remembered. He supposed that a woman deprived of both children and sex was unlikely to reach middle age without turning a bit strange. Of course, Demelza wasn't yet old. Only a few years his senior, he believed. But it was different for women. Especially those who insisted upon such flagrant eccentricity.

'You'd better come in,' she sighed, as though he'd dropped by unannounced. 'I'll put the kettle on. Have you got a shilling for the meter?'

Demelza got by on a war widow's pension, albeit one subsidised by some agreeable friendships. She was strict about assigned days for her chaps' visits, in this way keeping them innocent of their cooperative status in her life. Rarely did her husband, four years dead, even feature in her thoughts. She'd married him at nineteen, primarily because he said no one else would ever ask. On receiving the telegram from the Air Ministry, she'd struggled to understand her emotion until she realised it was joy: exalted, triumphant joy at her sudden liberation.

His aunt's digs weren't very cheerful, thought Robbie. The two low-ceilinged rooms were separated by an arch, across which she had strung up a beaded fly curtain, like at the butcher's. The larger room had a basin and shower, a single gas ring, and a round table covered with a pink crocheted shawl. In the smaller, windowless room was a single divan, untidily strewn with a red candlewick bedspread, and an imitation-walnut chest of drawers. Instead of electric lighting, there were gas jets on the wall. Outside on the landing was the telephone, with a jam jar for tuppences and a notebook to record calls, and a lavatory, shared by whoever had taken the downstairs bedroom for the night. 'We get all sorts,' said Demelza. 'Not Yanks, mind you. Geoffrey draws the line at Yanks.' She handed a cup of tea to Robbie, who looked at her quizzically. 'Too slow to join the Great War,' she said, with a forgiving little head shake.

Later that night Robbie lay on a blanket on the floor, in another man's pyjamas, underneath a quilt that smelled strongly of incense and, faintly, dog (but there was no sign of a dog), listening to Demelza snoring on the other side of the curtain. Was his life, he wondered, going to become as small, as impoverished and mean, as his aunt's? He contemplated going back to Pamela, even agreeing to work at the metal-tube factory. Trollope had worked for the Post Office, hadn't he? And a writer called Philip Larkin, an Oxford graduate, had somehow managed to publish a lauded poetry collection and two novels whilst working as a librarian, and still in his early twenties to boot. Robbie hadn't read these so-called novels; he was too jealous. They probably weren't very good. And supposing he did go and work for his father-in-law? Then there'd be no excuse not to have a baby. He couldn't explain why, but a child was not something he could countenance. Not yet.

He spent the next two days wandering around, leaving Demelza's rooms first thing and staying out until evening. It was mid June and the weather was dry, albeit rarely sunny. For long, stretched-out hours he sat on park benches, puzzling over the interplay of freely made choices and blind fate that had placed him in this quagmire. When the mental impasse of deciding how to live oppressed him too heavily, he retreated under a tree and napped. On waking, he bought sandwiches at a cheap student café. He thought about telephoning Pamela, but failed to do so. He couldn't imagine what he might say.

After a second day had passed in this desultory fashion, he was walking down Torrington Place at about seven o'clock and saw Demelza, who had a friend with her. 'Talk of the devil,' she said happily, 'and he will appear. This is my chum Sadie Havers. We've just been to a Theosophical Society meeting.' Demelza appeared to have dressed for the occasion, in a purple caftan and matching turban. 'Sadie, this is the out-of-luck nephew I was telling you about.'

Sadie was a tall, healthy-looking girl with a chestnut Eton crop, hatless, in a casual costume of wide-legged trousers and a filmy shirt with polka dots. She cocked her head and considered Robbie. 'Yes,' she said, thoughtfully. 'Yes, I think you just might be Honor's sort of thing.'

Demelza explained: 'Sadie's landlady needs help with a new literary venture. Apparently the pay will be rather modest, but you might negotiate some sort of live-in situation.'

They stood on the pavement outside the newsagent's at the corner of Malet Street. The sky was bleached white and the air smelled of warm tar and apple blossoms. Robbie digested Demelza's words – it sounded like a miraculous stroke of luck, which probably meant it was anything but – and Sadie said: 'No promises, of course. The lady in question is a bit . . . well, she's a bit rum. But I'll let you make up your own mind. If you like, you can come back with me now.'

'By "rum", Sadie only means unusual,' put in Demelza quickly. 'Artistic. It sounds like just the ticket to me. Sadie, you're a lifesaver. I'll telephone you tomorrow. Ta-ta.'

Robbie and Sadie watched her skip off, and he said: 'This is most awfully kind of you. Are you sure it's all right if I come with you this evening? Because I can easily—'

She laughed and shook her head. 'You'll be doing me a favour. Introducing you to Honor will raise my prestige. And to be honest, I could do with someone else nearer my own age in the house. Someone else full stop, actually. There's this fellow who lives in the basement – oh, he's nice enough, but he and Honor are carrying on an affair. I'm supposed to pretend I don't notice. It's awkward. Sorry, I'm not really selling it, am I? It's a lovely house. And I'm sure Honor's new venture will be very interesting to you. She worked for the publishers Wilson-Murray, you know – it was her husband's company, before he passed over to the other side.'

As Robbie later learnt, Sadie had been a Queen Alexandra's nurse in Normandy and Belgium, where she'd acquired a firm belief in this 'other side'. After the war, she became a private nurse to the terminally ill, living in at Tregunter Road for Gerald's final six months. Then she decided she'd had enough of broken and decaying bodies. I'm only twenty-four, she thought: I need some beauty, some *life*. So she applied to art school, but at Honor's insistence stayed on in the house. Her presence, she suspected, was a fig leaf of propriety, a diversion from Honor and her foreign chap shacking up before Gerald was cold in the ground (before he was anywhere near the ground, truth be told). But what did Sadie care, living in that big house for free?

*

'I've rather fallen down on the job here,' said Robbie now to Saul, accepting a cigarette and gesturing towards some sorry-looking broad-bean seedlings. 'I planted those two weeks ago, but I probably ought to have covered them. It's been so cold.' He cupped his hand over the flame of Saul's lighter. 'Thanks.' He blew out smoke. 'I'll try and do some tomatoes, I suppose.'

Saul, uninterested, said: 'It seems like a lot of effort. Honor's got you doing this every year, hasn't she? You know, you mustn't let her take advantage of your good nature.'

They were standing on the putty-coloured paving stones that extended around eight feet from the house. This patio area gave way to a rectangle of lawn, flanked by neglected flower beds and partly sacrificed to the vegetable patches that afflicted Robbie's conscience. An old Anderson shelter abutted the stone wall to their left. Lately used as a shed, it was almost hidden by dense ivy.

'So,' said Saul, in a brisk tone of changing the subject, 'as a war veteran yourself, what do you make of Mr Sullivan's claim to have failed his army medical exam? Mina seems to think it very unlikely. She's convinced Mr Sullivan is lying to conceal some sort of disgrace.'

Robbie was perplexed by Saul's interest. Why on earth did he care? 'Maybe he is. But aren't we all entitled to our secrets? In any case, Mr Sullivan is only here temporarily, isn't he? It's not very polite of us to poke around in his affairs.'

Saul smiled, and his smile said: oh, you English and your politeness. 'Did he tell you the same story, then, about being unfit for active duty?'

'As a matter of fact, it didn't come up. We talked about other things.'

'Such as?'

After a fretful pause, Robbie said: 'Um, he said he hasn't got a girlfriend. I told him I was separated from Pamela. We talked a bit about law and order, prisons, that sort of thing. I don't know how we got on to the subject. Oh yes, I said I thought Derek Bentley – you know, that feeble-minded young fellow, found guilty of the murder of a policeman – I said he ought not to have been hanged. Mr Sullivan had a different view.' He drew hungrily on his cigarette. 'Does Mina have any insight into the nature of his supposed disgrace?'

Saul looked at him with seeming hostility – perhaps, thought Robbie, because his question sounded sarcastic towards Mina. 'Mr Sullivan is of the opinion, then, that all murderers ought to be hanged?'

'I suppose that was the logical extension of his ... but look here, I'm only—'

Saul interrupted: 'Whereas you, you are against capital punishment in all cases? Or only in some cases?'

'Have I said something to offend you? I mean to say, the Nuremberg executions were certainly—'

Saul patted his shoulder. 'My dear fellow, you've said nothing to offend me, nothing at all. All it is ... well, I suppose I feel that you and I, as the men of the house, ought to know if there's anything untoward about Mr Sullivan. Honor can be a little too ... a little too willing to only see the best in people.'

Doesn't sound like the Honor I know, thought Robbie. 'Yes, I see what you mean,' he said, stamping out his cigarette under his shoe.

'Sit down, darling,' said Honor to George, who had at last appeared. 'Have some breakfast.'

'I'll have a cup of tea, then I must dash. I'm already fearfully late. Mina was supposed to wake me. I'm due in the West End at ten.'

'What on earth for?' Honor stirred an extra spoonful of sugar from her secret supply into George's tea.

'Oh,' said George evasively. 'You won't approve, I don't suppose.'

'Well, try me.'

'I answered an advertisement for some evening work at the Camera Club in Manchester Square. They pay models a guinea an hour. I'm going for an interview.'

Honor tried to keep the disapproval out of her voice. 'And what, pray, might you be expected to do for this princely sum?'

'You know. Pose in a swimsuit, or what have you.' The advert had stated 'nude but artistic poses'.

'In front of grubby blokes who fancy themselves photographers?'

George laughed. 'That's the idea, yes. I don't see that it's any different from posing for grubby blokes who consider themselves artists, do you?'

Honor frowned sceptically.

'Honestly, it's all perfectly decent and above board!' George drank some tea. A wave of nausea stirred her stomach. Oh hell, she thought, already? 'Anyway, it's only an interview. They might not accept me.'

'Don't be ridiculous. Good heavens, they'll bite your arm off. I'm only worried they'll move the goalposts. First it's posing in a swimsuit, then in underwear, then nude, then it's—'

'Being sold into white slavery?'

'You shouldn't joke about such things. Surely you won't want all those dirty Herberts owning photographs of you? They might sell them, publish them. Think of your future.'

But that's precisely what I'm doing, thought George.

'Well,' sighed Honor, 'I'm not your mother. I can't tell you what to do. I do worry, though. I can't help it.'

George remembered Mina's words. *Golly. Honor being motherly. Will wonders never cease!* It was true: there was something fundamentally unmaternal about Honor. It was connected to her strange androgyny. Her fleshlessness. George contemplated, as she occasionally did, the household lore that Honor and Saul were once lovers. Her predecessor at Tregunter Road, Sadie, had told Mina, who had told George. Honor could certainly do a lot worse. Saul was rather desirable, with his jet-black hair and foreign accent. Quite the epitome of the distinguished older man. But the notion of those two at it – no, it was simply unimaginable.

7

See the Pyramids Along the Nile

'Is bad soil for growing,' Greta told Robbie, the authority of this pronouncement undiminished by the clothes peg in her mouth. Not that Robbie would dream of arguing. Honor had tried going head to head with Greta, and it never ended well. *That bloody woman*, she would storm. *For two pins I'd sack her, if only I thought she'd find another job.*

Greta handed Robbie a peg so he could secure one end of the bedsheet to the line. He'd only come outside to look at his poor broad-bean plants. Now he'd been drafted into pegging out washing. Saul was right: people took advantage of his good nature. He glanced at the teetering basketful of freshly mangled bedlinen and wondered how to make a graceful retreat.

'You need,' she continued, making a flapping movement with her hand, 'I don't know English word. But I can get for you. Not expensive.'

'Manure?' he said. Was the flapping motion a horse's tail? 'That's very kind. I'll think about it. But I'm afraid I ought to get on. We're going to press today, and—'

'I saw new boy,' she said non-sequitously. 'He told me not to clean in his room. He is …' She squinted into the middle distance, considering the right word. 'He is not nice-mannered.'

'Why doesn't he want you to clean his room?'

'I cannot think of good reason. Can you?'

She stared at him until he realised it wasn't a rhetorical question. 'Oh,' he said. 'Well, I suppose if one isn't used to having servants or anything like that …' He stopped on seeing the expression on Greta's face. 'Not that you're a servant, of course! I only mean that—'

'No, is true,' she said philosophically. 'He is not like you, or George, a young person from good family. I am surprised that Honor lets such a person live here. She is always so, so …'

Snobbish, he thought. '*Particular* about people. Yes, isn't she just.'

'Blast,' muttered Robbie some hours later, getting to his feet and wiping his fingers on a handkerchief. He stood on the kerb, one hand on his bicycle seat and the other pushing his spectacles up his nose. To his added dismay, for he felt at a disadvantage, he saw Jimmy emerging from the house in his overcoat and a smart brown hat, new by the looks of it.

'Afternoon,' said Jimmy, walking over to him. 'Everything all right?'

'Hello. I've got a puncture, that's all.'

'Haven't you got a repair kit? I'll give you a hand if you want.'

'I'm already terribly late, that's the problem. I must get the new issue to the printer's by four, or there'll be trouble.'

'Why don't I drive you?' Jimmy brandished a key with a triumphant tinkle.

'Have you got a motor car?' In Robbie's mind, only rich people owned motor cars.

Jimmy laughed. 'That got your attention, didn't it?' He pointed to a rust-rimmed blue and cream Ford Anglia parked over the road. 'I've borrowed it from a friend. I do mean borrowed, by the way.'

'I wouldn't have imagined otherwise,' said Robbie primly. 'Gosh, you'd be doing me an enormous favour. The printer's some way away, I'm afraid – Clerkenwell. But if you're sure you don't mind.' He wondered if Jimmy had a driving licence but didn't dare enquire.

'Put your bike away and let's get going. I felt like a drive today anyway.'

A smattering of snow had fallen overnight but now the sun was out, touching the air with the faint scent of spring. Sitting in the passenger seat, Robbie was disturbed by the enclosed proximity. As Jimmy handled the gearstick, his elbow all but brushed against Robbie, who could smell the musty damp wool of his coat sleeve, as well as the man himself: Palmolive soap, Brylcreem, and some indefinable human essence. They set off at speed, and Robbie, biting a thumbnail and staring at his shoes on the worn rubber mat, ran through conversational gambits in his head.

Yet Jimmy wasn't in the least uncomfortable with the silence or their nearness. Unless, thought Robbie, he misread the fellow's apparent serenity.

Robbie remembered he had some cigarettes and got them out of his pocket. 'Would you like one? Can I light it for you?'

Jimmy smiled. 'S'all right.' With one hand loosely on the

wheel, he extracted a cigarette from the packet and deftly lit it. Then he blew three perfect smoke rings while doing a sharp left turn onto the Fulham Road.

Why did I ask that? thought Robbie. 'I heard you went for a drink with George the other night,' he blurted, desperate to redeem the situation.

'Did you now? She tell you that, did she?'

'Actually, it was Honor. I don't think she approves.'

'I bet she doesn't,' said Jimmy, under his breath. Then, in a more normal tone, 'Why, what's her problem with it?'

'Oh, I don't know. I'd better not speak out of turn. In any case, I thought you found George stand-offish or something?'

'She's all right. Just a bit full of herself. Thinks because Daddy's got a title, she can look down on the rest of us.'

Robbie was by no means George's greatest admirer, but this wasn't his impression. If anything, he thought, she slummed it far too readily. True, she made him feel provincial and plebeian, but she didn't actually mean to. At least, he didn't think she did.

'The only reason I bought her a drink,' Jimmy went on, 'is because I found her wandering the streets like an orphan. She wants to be more careful. Some funny people about, especially after dark.' He tapped his cigarette in the ashtray and shot a glance at Robbie. 'But as I told you, I'm off women. Even if I weren't, I wouldn't be interested in her.'

They hit a red light at Brompton Road, and Jimmy turned to face him. 'You came up, actually. She said you were a "decent soul", and that it was a shame your wife scarpered, and a shame that you didn't seem to have much luck with women in general. She thought, perhaps – and I'm only telling you this because you've a right to know; I'd want to know if people were saying it behind my back – she thought you might be queer.'

Robbie gave a brief alarmed chuckle and took a deep drag on

his cigarette. 'Did she really say that?' He was less offended at the aspersion than hurt by George talking about him in this manner. 'I mean, why would I get married in the first place if I were queer?'

'George said to conceal the fact, but then your wife probably found out and gave you your marching orders. I told her, I said that doesn't sound very likely. Robbie seems like an excellent bloke to me. She said, ah, but you see, you don't know him like we do.'

His cheeks burning, Robbie said: 'She's made all this up from whole cloth. She knows nothing about me or my life. We've never even had a proper conversation, she and I. Except for once. It was the day you first visited the house, in fact. Given what she told me that day, she's got a nerve gossiping about my personal affairs. A real nerve.'

'That's women for you, isn't it? Can't trust them as far as you can throw them. So what did she tell you, then?'

'She's going to have a baby.' The words escaped like mercury slipping between his fingers. 'And she doesn't even know who the father is.'

Jimmy made a whistling exhalation. 'My, my. What's Mrs Wilson going to say? Going out with the likes of me will seem pretty tame by comparison, won't it? Is she going to get married? Or give it up for adoption?'

'Neither, I don't think. She wants to – you know – end the pregnancy.' It's the size of a fingertip, she'd said. But that was nearly two weeks ago. How big would it be now? Maybe no size at all; maybe she'd already done the deed.

Jimmy ground out his cigarette and sped up to overtake a stuttering MG. 'But that's against the law. Not to mention immoral. Trying to kill a little baby, like it's an insect you step on. And what's she telling you for? She's made you an accessory to a serious crime. You could both be arrested.'

Robbie wondered whether that was true. 'I ought to have tried to talk her out of it. I suppose I didn't think it was my place. You won't say anything to anyone, will you? She told me in confidence. She definitely wouldn't want Honor finding out.'

Jimmy shook his head and tapped his nose. 'Mum's the word.' Frowning thoughtfully, he went on: 'You know what, let's agree to keep all of this conversation between ourselves. I shouldn't want George thinking I'm trying to be a troublemaker by repeating her remarks about you.' After he'd ascribed these opinions to George – which he'd done impulsively, curiously – Jimmy had pictured Robbie confronting her, accusing her of slander. Although perhaps it was no more slander than George being a baby murderess.

He imagined what he'd do if that was his baby. The mere hypothetical made him hot with anger. Then again, he'd never let the situation arise in the first place. The only woman he ever planned to impregnate was his virginal wife, on their wedding night. In his romantic imaginings, the act of congress with his lovely bride – whoever she was – would be incomparable to the handful of demoralising liaisons that were the sum total of his amorous experience. On his fourteenth birthday, his father had sent him to a local woman with a half-crown in his hand. Lily, she called herself. Her ground-floor rooms, in one of the streets behind St George's Brewery on the Commercial Road, smelled of cats and bodies, overlaid by a good deal of cheap scent. He didn't understand how anyone found eroticism in such a setting, or with such a person. Lily, raw-boned and coarse-skinned, seemed so old. Looking back now, she was probably no more than forty. As soon as he handed her the coin, she hitched up her skirts and spread her skinny thighs. She didn't even put her cigarette down. Not feeling he had any choice, Jimmy climbed on and attempted one blind thrust before falling out limply, at which point Lily pushed him off and told him to go home. When he asked for some change – he'd been there less than five minutes – she laughed like she'd never heard anything so funny.

More recently, he'd visited another professional, albeit a younger, cleaner girl who worked out of a white-painted Soho flat and made him have a wash first. Still, he was consumed by regret after. He felt impossibly sullied. He wished he could forget the feel of her insides, like being gripped by hot jelly. Why did his body respond, whilst his soul recoiled? He'd hated the metallic tackiness of her freckled skin, the penny-coloured stubble in her armpits, her breathily fake moans. It was absurd of her to feign enjoyment. It stood to reason that if a girl liked it, she'd be doing it for free. Like George. He remembered his aunt Marlene talking to Mum about the girls back in Cork who were sent away to the laundries when they couldn't behave themselves, when they'd disgraced their families. His mother had expressed sympathy with the fallen women, saying it was cruel, that babies should always stay with their mother. No, said Marlene, what was cruel was subjecting a child to illegitimacy and hellfire, rather than keeping your legs closed. His mother was too kind, thought Jimmy. At least, she was to other people. Not so much to him.

After dropping off the corrected page proofs, they got back in the car and headed for home. It was getting dark and Robbie was glad. The night felt like a shield. He couldn't stop thinking about George's words. At Cambridge, he'd known some unashamed pansies, men who seemed to enjoy playing up their femininity, as though they were daring the world to object. There was something heroic in their defiance. But Robbie had nothing in common with them, so he couldn't understand what George had perceived. He uneasily recalled that one of his hut-mates at

Aldershot, an unassuming dark-haired fellow from Eton, had made a pass at him. At least, it had seemed very much like a pass. But because Robbie wasn't certain, he'd decided not to report it and ruin the boy's life. It had never occurred to him that he hadn't been chosen at random, or merely from the convenience of nearness. Now he wondered. Had he revealed himself, however unwittingly, as somehow aberrant or corruptible? He almost wished he could ask the fellow, but there was no possibility of that. He'd been blown to pieces at El Alamein.

'Here,' said Jimmy, 'have some.' He handed Robbie a silver hip flask.

Cautiously, Robbie unscrewed the lid and sniffed the contents. It made his eyes water.

'Go on,' said Jimmy, 'it'll put hairs on your chest.'

Robbie took a swig and fire whirled over the back of his tongue and down his throat. He coughed, then swallowed down a jet of bile. 'What is that? Paint-stripper?'

Jimmy laughed. 'Russian vodka. A hundred per cent proof.'

'I'm not much of a drinker,' said Robbie, handing back the flask.

'All right, if you say so.' Jimmy took a sip himself. 'Have one more. Then you'll start to enjoy it. It's like smoking. Remember your first fag? I nearly threw up. Didn't have another one again for years.'

I'm not a child, thought Robbie. I'm nearly thirty-three, with an estranged wife and near-sole responsibility for an esteemed literary journal. Nevertheless, he drank some more and cheer began mounting irresistibly in his chest. They were driving through Piccadilly and the illuminated advertising signs danced across his vision, magically picturesque. Why hadn't he ever noticed them before? He frequently walked through the West End. But his eyes, he realised, were habitually on the pavement.

When he went to take another sip, Jimmy said: 'Easy now, you don't want to make yourself ill.' But Robbie had never felt better in his life. If this was drunkenness, he wished he hadn't denied himself all these years.

'D'you want to go to a pub once we get nearer home?' said Jimmy. 'I'll buy you some supper.'

'I,' said Robbie indignantly, 'will buy *you* some supper. You saved my life today, giving me a lift like that.'

'Let's not go overboard. Mrs Wilson wouldn't actually have murdered you for missing the deadline.'

Robbie sighed contentedly. 'She might have. You don't know what she can be like.'

Ah, thought Jimmy, but I do.

Throughout the next day, the evening came back to Robbie in fragments, like a chopped-up film reel. Sitting in the pub eating pork pies and crisps. Ordering more drinks. Telling Jimmy about his hairiest close shaves as a soldier, how he relived them in his nightmares yet still missed the war sometimes. A drunk woman singing that sad, sad song about her lover seeing the pyramids along the Nile. Stumbling as he walked home, so that Jimmy laughed and said to hold on to his arm. Jimmy's bare torso, dappled with fine dark hairs, palely beautiful in the dim gaslight. Holding his own arms up obediently so that Jimmy could lift off his jersey. Letting himself be kissed, kissing back, becoming no longer himself, but a new, unfamiliar person, one released from any form of reticence or fright.

When he opened his eyes in the morning, Robbie's mind was momentarily blank, amnesiac, even though he was abruptly alert, in contrast to his usual slow, groggy rise to consciousness. He was naked, he realised; that was why the sheets enveloped him with such softness. He stretched, noticing a tenderness in his stomach muscles, his thighs. It occurred to him to wonder why he didn't have a hangover – but, not having had one before, he wasn't sure how it was meant to feel. There was a knock at the door and he startled guiltily. 'Who is it?' he called out, and the reply came: 'It's me.' It was Jimmy.

He entered. He was dressed and had neatly combed wet hair. 'I wanted to see if you were okay,' he said. 'After all you had to drink last night.' He sat down at the foot of the bed and smiled.

Robbie sat up, keeping the sheet wrapped around his chest. 'I'm surprised I don't feel worse, actually. It was quite a night, wasn't it?'

'I'll say so. We had a grand time. Or I did, at least. I just wanted to make sure you knew that. I'm not sorry, not about any of it.'

'You mean . . .' Robbie hesitated. He wanted to explain that his memory was hazy, that he needed Jimmy to confirm what had taken place. But he feared it would be somehow rude, or might come across as though he wished nothing had happened. To his astonishment, that was the very last thing he wished. Was he still drunk? Maybe he was still drunk.

'We didn't do anything wrong,' said Jimmy. 'Nothing illegal. Not that it would matter if we had, because the only people who could ever know are us. And we'd never tell, would we?' He gazed at Robbie, who gazed back, his skin tingling with the collusion, the peculiar illicit romance of it.

'You believe me, though, that George was wrong, don't you? I've never been queer for anyone else.'

Jimmy smiled, almost shyly, Robbie thought. 'Me neither.'

The sound of female voices floated up from below. George

and Mina were up, engaged in their usual routine of borrowing make-up and hair ornaments from one another.

Jimmy got up and wedged the chair underneath the door handle. Then he came and took Robbie in his arms.

Later that day, Greta was in the kitchen, sighing and tutting in time to the hissing and puffing of her electric iron. Back and forth she slid it over a pillowslip, though no creases could be seen by the naked eye. Greta was a born perfectionist. *If you're going to do a job, then do it properly* was the maxim she lived by. Washing and ironing all the bedlinen was a monthly task to which several afternoons were devoted, in keeping with a complicated work schedule she had devised for herself. Greta was, to all appearances, indefatigable. Though she complained about her varicose veins and something she called carpal tunnel syndrome (a made-up condition, assumed Honor), it was clear these complaints were not to be taken seriously. Rather, they were offered as further evidence of her strength and virtue. *Though I suffer,* her ongoing publicity campaign reminded everyone, *my conscientiousness never wavers.*

Mrs Greta Kovačević, formerly of Yugoslavia, was somewhere in her fifties. She had dyed red hair (the packet promised Alluring Auburn, but she suspected, without regret, that her alluring days were over), wolfish amber eyes and the most restless of demeanours. No one in the house had ever seen her sit down, not even to drink a cup of tea. When beseeched to take the weight off her feet, to have some sherry, or a bit of cake, or a cigarette, she acted as if the beseecher were trying to hoodwink her, to seduce her into relaxing her steely discipline, thus impugning her claim that the housework left her not a moment for herself.

'You think I have time to sit?' she would demand. 'And when

washing-up is not finished and dog is not fed and floors are not cleaned, what then?'

Among the residents, Greta's omnipotence was accepted as part of the natural order. A Tregunter Road fixture since before Honor's reign, she was originally employed by Barbara, Gerald's first wife. The job had been quite different then: it was a family house, though the two sons were away fighting. In Greta's opinion, Barbara could easily have managed the housework herself, were she not such a lazy, vain woman. She saw no shame in lolling around with her feet up, examining her face in a hand-mirror, whilst someone else slaved. Greta kept these judgements to herself. As a refugee from Hitler's war, over forty and with poor English, she considered herself lucky to have found work that wasn't too arduous.

One morning in January 1942, as German bombs dropped on Liverpool, Greta arrived to find Barbara still in bed, sobbing and blubbering into a handkerchief. 'He's got another woman,' she wailed. 'Can you believe it?'

Is that all? Greta thought. Barbara hadn't seemed this upset when her sons were killed in action. 'Never mind. He says sorry? Men do silly things. He says sorry, you forgive him. Everything is all right.' Greta, who had a blanket contempt for the opposite sex, thought it beneath any woman's dignity to cry about a man's sexual incontinence. Her own husband, Vladko, had been a member of the Ustaše – the Croatian fascist party – and was publicly executed for committing unauthorised violence against Serbs and Gypsies. As a Catholic, Greta didn't believe in karma. But she did believe in the general principle of play stupid games, win stupid prizes.

'You don't understand!' Barbara's blubbering increased. 'He's leaving me for her. Some bloody little awful trollop from his office. Twenty-two! Says they're getting married. Not if I've got anything to do with it you're not, I told him. What kind of twenty-two-year-old wants to marry an old codger like you? Oh, he said, you see she's very sophisticated. An "old soul".' Barbara spat these words out. 'That's one word for it, isn't it?'

It's two words, thought Greta. She was itching to turn Barbara out of bed so she could strip it. Bloody little awful trollop or not, it was laundry day.

Greta had just folded one pillowslip and begun ironing another when Honor came in.

'Oh, Greta,' she said, 'I know we've been over this, but is it really necessary to iron the sheets and pillowslips? Nobody would care if they were a bit crumpled. I'm only thinking of you, standing there for hours operating that thing.'

Greta pressed a button to release extra steam and pushed the iron tip into a corner with vigour. 'You want people to talk about unkempt bedrooms, like you're running cheap bed and breakfast? I have my own reputation to worry about. Maybe you don't care how your house looks, but I care. Is reflection of me.'

Why do I bother, thought Honor, going to put the kettle on. 'Of course it is. And that is why I treasure you. Tea?'

Grudgingly, Greta nodded. She never refused a cup of tea, even if she didn't interrupt her work to drink it. Apropos of nothing, she said: 'What's his name, that new boy?'

'Do you mean Jimmy? Mr Sullivan?' Honor spooned tea leaves into the pot.

'Yes, him.'

After a pause, Honor said: 'Well, what about him? Has he done something wrong?'

'Depends.'

She could have reached across the kitchen table and wrung Greta's neck. 'Would you care to enlighten me on your meaning?'

Greta smiled with gentle malice. 'His bed was not slept in last night.' She shrugged, and her shrug said: there could be an innocent reason, but I highly doubt it.

Honor replaced the kettle on the stove. 'How on earth do you know that?' She'd seen Jimmy first thing that morning, making himself a cup of coffee. His hair was wet, as if he'd just had a bath. Greta must be mistaken, she told herself. Although now that she thought about it, he had been whistling and looking rather pleased with himself.

'I know because yesterday I strip and remake beds. Today I do quick hoover on stairs, top to bottom. Jimmy's door was open, so I could see bed still made.'

Honor opened her mouth to interrupt, but Greta pointed a triumphant finger upwards.

'I make beds yesterday.'

Honor understood. Greta put fresh linen on the beds once a month, but everyone was responsible for making their own beds in between times. Even if Jimmy had made the bed, his efforts could never match Greta's drum-tight tucking and military corners.

'Oh well,' said Honor lightly. 'He's a grown man. He probably stayed out late and slept on a friend's sofa.' She lifted the lid from the teapot and peered in. All this worry would make her ill, she thought. Running away and adopting a new identity for the second time suddenly felt very appealing.

'Robbie always makes his bed nicely,' said Greta. 'But Robbie is nice boy.' Jimmy, she thought, was not nice boy. And yet she was the only one who seemed to have noticed.

Honor passed her a cup of tea. 'Have you seen George today? I wanted to ask her something.'

'She got home little while ago. She was at one of her painters, but they *lost the light.*' Greta smiled, pleased at her reproduction of this artistic lingo.

'Did she? I might take a cup of tea up to her, then.'

Greta shook out her pillowslip and gave a shrug-nod as if to say: suit yourself.

'Knock, knock,' said Honor chirpily, standing at the threshold of George's ajar door. George was sitting at her dressing table, frowning at herself in the spotty mirror. She turned her head at the sound of Honor's voice.

'I thought you might like a cup of tea.'

'How nice,' said George sincerely. 'Thank you. Do come in and sit down if you like.'

'You look shattered, poor thing. Did you go out last night?' George's bed, under the window on the other side of the room, was in a state of some dishevelment. But that wouldn't stand up in a court of law, Honor reminded herself, not with George's domestic habits. Her pink eiderdown really has seen better days, she thought idly.

'Do I? Thanks a bunch!'

'I didn't mean . . .'

'I'm only teasing. I am a bit tired. How are you?'

'Oh, you know,' said Honor, 'soldiering on under immense strain.' But her tone was flippant, and she quickly went on: 'So what were you up to last night? A party?'

'No, I went to the pictures. Was in bed by ten. I think it's just the winter, dragging on, taking it out of us all. Or maybe I've got a cold coming on.' Or she was tired because she'd been chucking up all morning. Somehow, the vomiting made the pregnancy more real than the doctor's confirmation. 'Honor, I'm glad to see you, actually. I wanted to ask you something. I'm embarrassed to ask, but . . .'

Oh God, thought Honor. She wants to know if I mind, after all, her going out with Jimmy.

'Could I possibly touch you for ten quid? I'm a bit short at the moment. Owed money here and there. You know what it's like. I'll pay you back as soon as I can, naturally.' She'd found a man in Battersea who would do the operation for twenty-five pounds, so long as you weren't too far along. Two shifts at the Camera Club had already netted her six guineas, so if Honor gave her ten quid, she was sure she could cobble together the rest.

Honor hesitated. Her bank account was depleted, thanks to the money she'd given Jimmy.

'Don't worry if it's a problem,' said George. 'I can ask someone else.'

'If I give you the money, does that mean you won't need to do that evening job? Because in that case—'

'Exactly. You were right. I thought better of it as soon as I arrived for the interview.'

'I'm so glad. I'll pop to the bank in the morning.'

'Thank you ever so much. I do hate asking. It won't happen again.'

Honor gave a say-no-more head shake. 'So. Nothing else new with you? How are your current beaux?'

'Pretty much a dead loss, unfortunately. Never mind. Plenty more fish in the sea!' Just listen to yourself, she thought. The hollowness of that phrase. Yet Honor seemed to brighten at this evidence of the usual George: the flighty girl with delightfully loose morals who cocked a snook at convention and got away with it, who breezed through life exempt from comeuppance by the indulgent whims of fate.

8

An Impermeable Line

'As promised,' said Saul, 'the poetry slush pile, judged without mercy.' He placed the sheaf of pages on Honor's desk and sat down in her visitor's chair. It was early evening, but Honor hadn't drawn the curtains. In the dark window, Saul saw his reflection. I look old, he thought. No longer handsome, deserted by youth's last vestiges. When did that happen?

'All dreadful, were they?' Honor made a tutting sound. 'What a bore for you.' Saul's role as *Vista*'s European poetry editor, always rather nominal, had reduced over the years to be almost non-existent. Yet he remained on the masthead, and Honor kept up the polite charade that his opinion, his expertise, was indispensable. How funny now to think *Vista* wouldn't even exist if not for Saul. Her shock, her stupefaction at seeing him in Naomi's sitting room on an otherwise drab autumn afternoon had proved the unstoppable catalyst. During their first encounter, weeks earlier at a tedious publisher's party, Honor hadn't known *whom* she was meeting. An émigré poet, a Jew. Nothing earth-shattering about that. Even if she had found him vaguely attractive, with his sad eyes and deracinated air. He and Naomi were maternal cousins, it turned out; they had never shared a surname. Not that Honor remembered Naomi's maiden name. And 'my cousin Saul' was his only label.

The extraordinary tact he had shown – she would never forget it. Pretending they were perfect strangers, that he wasn't uncovering a fraud. A masquerader. Then they had walked up Whitechapel High Street and she'd felt an elated relief in confessing who she used to be. It was like taking off a tight garment you'd worn for so long, the discomfort had become part of you. For eight years not a soul had known of her prior identity. And Elizabeth – Elsie – existed only on occasional visits to Naomi, who'd never heard of Honor. Naomi's death, in 1950, severed the last link between Elsie and Honor. Or so she had hoped.

Would she have avoided going to Naomi's that day had she known Saul was to drop by? Without a doubt. He might have blown her cover, but more than that: she never wanted to think about the tragedy of his life, never wanted to see his face. Hence her gesture, the on-the-spot invention of a literary magazine. A pathetic form of reparation, obviously; no reparation at all. Yet he'd looked so pleased, so gratified, that she saw no alternative but to go through with it. And now she couldn't pack it in, because Saul believed it was her calling, her labour of love.

There was another, equally trifling act of reparation she had hoped to perform: buying back a painting of Saul's murdered wife, the valuable artwork he'd sent to England in the hope of making enough money to bring his family over. The painting's present owner, a Mrs Rebecca Levene of St John's Wood, had so far refused to sell. Honor wrote to her periodically, in case she changed her mind. Lately, though, a troubling thought had presented itself: supposing Saul didn't want to see the painting? Perhaps he coped by forgetting, by drawing an impermeable line between the past and the present, as Honor had always tried to do for herself. Now Jimmy had come along and made that impossible, and she didn't like it one bit.

'Incidentally,' said Saul, 'George was telling Mina that she needs money. Have you found out what the trouble is?'

Honor sighed. 'Between you and me, she was planning to do some very low-class modelling work. Almost pornographic, I think it's fair to say. In a photographic studio, not for painters.'

'Oh, Honor, surely not? A nice girl like that? You must put a stop to it.'

'I think she's seen sense. I lent her some money myself. Though what she needs it for, Lord only knows. It's not as if I'm a stickler about the rent. She's four weeks behind, and I haven't even mentioned it.'

'But you did scold her about going on a date with Mr Sullivan, I hear?'

'Who told you it was a date? Is that what George told Mina?' She looked so alarmed that Saul regretted his inquisitiveness in bringing it up.

'I thought they went to the pub last week, but I—'

'They happened to bump into each other in the street, that's all. And he offered to buy her a drink. She shouldn't have accepted. He probably caught her off her guard. I've told her there's no duty to be chummy with Mr Sullivan, just because he's an old family friend of mine. Naturally, any red-blooded young man will want to chance his arm with George. But she mustn't give encouragement. For the young man's sake as well as her own.'

Saul lit a cigarette, bemused. Policing George's social life was not normally a priority for Honor, so far as he'd noticed. 'What *is* your connection to Mr Sullivan?' he asked. 'I know, I know, you didn't want to tell me before. But I really wish you would. I—'

At the sound of footsteps on the stairs, Honor called out: 'Mina, is that you? Come in here for a moment, could you?'

Mina came into the office, her nose pink from the cold. She carried her gloves in one hand and a green mock-lizard handbag in the other. 'Still working?' she said. 'You two work too much. You deserve to take it a bit easier at your time of life.'

Sometimes Honor suspected the girl of deliberately trying to needle her. Let it pass, she told herself. 'We were just talking, actually. Come and sit down, Mina darling. Take Robbie's chair, he's knocked off for the evening. The thing is, we're concerned about George. Has she confided in you about anything that's worrying her?'

Mina cleared her throat delicately, covering her mouth with her hand. 'I can't say she has, no. I do know she'll be twenty-six this year, so maybe that's it. It's getting on a bit, isn't it, to still be on the shelf.'

'That's true enough,' said Saul. 'Perhaps she needs money to smarten herself up and find a decent marriage prospect before it's too late.'

'Mina,' said Honor, 'I don't mean to pry. But did George tell you she'd had a date with Mr Sullivan?'

'Yes, they went for a drink, didn't they?'

Honor's look of alarm was back, and Saul said: 'I'll have a word with him, shall I? Explain there are house rules about this sort of thing.'

'Oh goodness, no, that's not necessary,' said Honor. 'I shouldn't dream of putting you to the trouble, it's—'

'Nonsense!' He stood up. 'It's about time I got to know the fellow.'

'Truly, Saul, I'd rather—'

But he had left the room, Mina following behind and saying to Honor: 'I'll leave you in peace. You ought to put your feet up. You look tired.'

Honor almost went after Saul, and might have but for Mina, whose footsteps accompanied his down the stairs. Thick as thieves as usual, thought Honor with some bitterness. Then she remembered it was all her own doing. No point regretting it now. The obscure workings of fate had coaxed her into action, she reflected. Mina's own destiny, though she little knew it, was diverted by the death of a stranger: poor Naomi, who fell victim to that winter's terrible flu. At first, Saul had taken the sad news with his usual stoicism. But in the weeks after the funeral, a fog of melancholy settled upon him. He wasn't entirely morose or uncommunicative. Just absent, as though only the thinnest layer of his consciousness could stand to engage with the world.

One morning, in the hope of cheering him up a bit, Honor insisted he accompany her to a saleroom preview to look at some desks. He'd been using an old folding trestle table, and she wanted to find him something more attractive and functional. After all, wasn't work a writer's most useful resource in dark times? At Rogers, Chapman & Thomas on Gloucester Road, she had paused in front of a tortoiseshell-inlaid cabinet, which she thought might be nice for the drawing room. Saul, who had dawdled behind her, was talking to a child, a girl of about thirteen with dark hair in pigtails splayed out like scissors. She wore a navy gabardine mackintosh and carried a brown leather satchel, and her small pale face was serious as she listened to him.

'The guide price is in the catalogue,' he was explaining. 'Then you must bid for the items you want on the day of the auction.' The girl appeared downcast by this information, and Saul gently enquired who had sent her to the saleroom. Her mother, she said. They were opening a tea and dance room above their neighbour's fan shop, and they needed twenty elbow chairs immediately. As Saul and the girl discussed this enterprise, Honor stopped listening to their words and watched Saul's face. Who was this twinkling, animated man? He certainly wasn't the gloompot she'd woken up with that morning.

When his lightened mood persisted through the rest of the day, it occurred to Honor – and she wondered why it never had before – that he ought to marry again and have a child. A woman with her own money, she decided. A young war widow, and if she'd already got children, all the better. In bed that night, she broached the subject, quite carefully, she thought. But Saul took offence. He seemed to think she was giving him the elbow. 'You know,' he said, 'I can always find somewhere else to live.' He drew the blanket up to his chin and scowled at her, prideful and petulant, like a cat turning up its nose at an inferior meal. 'If that's what you want, just say so.'

Did their slow estrangement begin, wondered Honor now, at that moment? She had apologised, implored him to forget she'd ever said anything. She'd meant nothing by it, she insisted, nothing at all. The next day, she had another bright idea: she could foster a young girl, someone of around Marya's age, had she lived. A refugee, or an orphan. But then she realised certain checks might be involved in any official arrangement, which obviously wouldn't do. It wasn't until some weeks later that she found, in *The Lady*, under Houses and Flats, Etc., Wanted, this simple appeal: *GIRL (15), seeks small furnished room in London. Family home, convenient to West End preferred.* Letters were exchanged, and Mina duly presented herself for inspection at Tregunter Road. Honor asked Sadie to join them for tea, wanting to create the atmosphere of a feminine sanctuary. Although naturally Honor would be doing the judging, not the other way round. Her initial impressions were less than favourable. In Mina, so raw and avid, her clothes woefully misjudged – and that grinding lathe of an accent! – she saw something of her own younger self. For that younger self – for Elsie – she felt an unexpected pang of sentiment. All traces of her were banished so ruthlessly, albeit when she was older than this girl. Honor hadn't possessed the wherewithal to start her life, her real life, at such a tender age. Such pluck, she decided, ought to be rewarded.

It was ludicrous, really, how her scheme succeeded. With barely any interference, Saul and Mina became such fond friends that Honor felt spurned. Jealous, even, though she hated to admit it. ('Jealousy,' she heard her mother say, 'is a dark mischief.' Honor always thought this sounded like an expensive scent. *Dark Mischief eau de parfum by Guerlain, to heighten a woman's elusive charm.*) She was aware, had always been aware, of her inadequacy as substitute for Saul's dead wife. Yet this brash girl from the provinces could evidently serve quite well as a daughterly surrogate. After Mina found a job at the cinema, Saul began going every week, even though he'd never mentioned liking films. Honor was never invited along.

Clearly superfluous to requirements – in her own house! – she stayed out of Saul's way. Pleading tiredness, she slept more often in her own bedroom. With considerable effort she repressed her longing for their closeness, falling back on her own inner reserves of strength. Occasionally she thought she saw a puzzled look in his eyes. She wrote this off as her imagination.

Mina perched on the arm of Saul's worn leather sofa. She liked his rooms, despite their disorder and eccentric decor. None of the junk-shop furniture matched, and there were too many books everywhere. He also had a fondness for pointless bric-a-brac – coloured glass, weird foreign sculptures, fabric oddments – and ugly paintings. The largest picture, hanging between the windows, depicted an unhappy young man with jug ears and a great deal of dark hair. (Kafka, his name was, and Saul said he was a genius. Like most geniuses, he was dead.) Yet the place felt so safe and cosy, infused with an ineffable Saul-ness. On the door frame was a little plaque, brass and blue and white: a religious thing, he'd once explained. 'But you don't believe in God,' she'd said, confused. 'Certainly I don't,' he replied. 'Not in the conventional sense. But there is beauty and solace in tradition, in the threads that connect us across eras, is there not?' Mina found this a very attractive statement, aesthetically as well as philosophically. Beauty and solace, she'd murmur to herself in moments of low spirits.

'Did you see that?' said Saul now. 'My having a word with Mr Sullivan is the last thing Honor wants. But why, if she's so protective of George?'

'Search me. Are you really going to talk to him, then? What will you say?'

'I suppose I shall play it by ear. Unless you've got any suggestions?'

'I reckon you want to act pally. You know, talking man to man about the silly womenfolk. And whilst you're at it, ask him about his army record. See if he can keep his story straight. Here, I tell you what: try and catch him at the pub he goes to. You can pretend you're surprised to see him. The King's Arms – that's where he took George.'

Monday 11 May 1953

'Unfortunately, the man now going by James Sullivan, he . . . well, he appears to have absconded from his probation.' Detective Inspector Hilary Comyns spoke in a tone of casual contrition, as if Mr Sullivan were a dog he'd allowed off the lead. 'I shall visit his last-known address, of course. And question those with a vested interest in—'

'You think they've got to him, I suppose?' Roderick Smythe QC gave a rueful grimace. 'Damned nuisance if so. I thought all reasonable measures had been taken?'

'Indeed they had, and at this stage I can find no evidence that our measures were breached, or that Mr Sullivan was exposed as an informant. Of course, we—'

Smythe stood up. 'Sorry, old chap, duty calls.' Sighing like a theatrical old-timer about to tread the boards for the umpteenth time, he tapped his gleaming pate: he had to don his wig. 'I shall leave the matter in your capable hands. It goes without saying, of course, that without the fellow's testimony, things are looking very shaky indeed.'

9

Like Air Bubbles Rising

'Mr Sullivan, it is you. I wasn't sure. May I join you? What are you drinking?'

It was Saul's third time dropping into the King's Arms in the hopes of seeing Jimmy, and now here he was, sitting at the bar.

'Call me Jimmy,' he said cheerily, nodding at the barman to come and take Saul's order. 'And I won't say no, thank you. I'll have a pint of mild and bitter.'

Saul asked for a Scotch and sat on a bar stool. He looked around him and was about to remark on the congeniality of English public houses. But then he remembered to pose as a jaded habitué. 'Do you come here often?' he said. 'I don't believe I've seen you here before.'

'Oh, you know, now and again,' said Jimmy, accepting a cigarette. 'This your regular local, is it?'

'Mm, yes.' The barman placed Saul's drink in front of him. To his surprise, Jimmy said: 'I've read your poetry. I can't claim to be any sort of expert, but I enjoyed it very much. Do you like

Sassoon? Your style reminds me of his. Especially your sonnet "Last Day", which I—'

'You're very kind,' interrupted Saul. The boy couldn't possibly know (or could he?), but 'Last Day' was about his daughter, Marya. 'Fancy you reading my work. I'm touched.'

Jimmy nodded self-consciously. Perhaps he didn't ought to have said anything. The day after meeting Mr Reznikov in Honor's drawing room (was it really only three weeks ago?), he'd gone to Chelsea Library and, under a sort of helpless compulsion, read the poetry collection cover to cover.

In tracking down Honor, Jimmy's intentions had been perfectly reasonable. He needed a place to stay, and money to get back on his feet. Introducing some long-overdue discord to her unjustly cushy life was the icing on the cake. To find Mr Reznikov living there, after all this time, was the last thing he had expected. But by then his plans had gathered an unstoppable momentum. And it didn't matter, he told himself, especially given the size of the house. He'd simply stay out of the man's way. Of course, he'd meant to stay out of everyone's way, and look how that had worked out.

'Is that how you know Mrs Wilson, then?' he asked. 'From being a poet?'

'In a manner of speaking, yes,' said Saul. 'Though we're old friends now.' He paused. 'And you? I think I recall you and Honor knew each other as children?'

'Something like that, yeah.'

'But she's some years your senior, surely?'

Jimmy laughed. 'Don't let her hear you say that.' He quickly resumed a straight face. 'I only mean – women don't like to be asked their age, do they? I've never seen why it matters, myself.'

'Talking of Honor, I gather she was displeased about your consorting with George.'

He rolled his eyes. 'She tell you that, did she? Seems like it's all anyone can talk about. It was only a drink. Beats me why she gives two hoots.'

'I suppose she feels a certain . . . a certain responsibility for the young people living under her roof.'

'Well. If she wants to be George's moral guardian, she's got her work cut out for her.'

'What on earth do you mean?' said Saul, chivalrous to a fault.

Jimmy drank, then carefully placed his glass on a beer mat. 'I don't mean anything. The girl seems quite spirited, that's all. Her parents couldn't keep her in line, so why should anyone else?'

'All the same. It should be better, shouldn't it, if you remained on cordial but, but . . .' but what? he wondered, 'formal terms with the girls in the house.'

To this Jimmy gave a salute – a sarcastic gesture, suspected Saul, but it reminded him to ask about the army. As far as he could tell, the account Jimmy offered was consistent with the one he'd given George. He'd had asthma, though it had quite disappeared now, and he was deemed not medically fit to serve.

'Not even a desk job?'

'Nah.' Jimmy tapped the ash from his cigarette, then lowered his voice: 'What happened to you, then, when Hitler went on his march?'

Saul smiled. A clever if unsubtle way to redirect the conversation. 'You don't want to hear about all that.' He looked at the boy: did he resemble Honor? It was difficult to say. 'So you knew Honor when she was a child – I can't picture it! What was she like then?'

'You imagine, don't you, that she appeared on this earth fully formed. Smoking and refreshing her lip paint. Criticising people's dress sense and table manners. But yeah, she's always been the same. Except she used to have long fair hair. Not blonde. Sort of mouse colour.'

'No!'

'Yeah! She was much fatter too, as a girl.'

'Goodness me.' Saul shook his head in wonder. 'And you must know her parents – does she resemble them?'

'I think her parents are both dead, now, aren't they?'

'But you knew them? What was her father's job?'

After a pause, Jimmy said: 'I'm not sure, you know. You'd have to ask her.'

'Honor doesn't like to talk about herself. Perhaps you've noticed.'

He nod-shrugged non-committally. Saul, not wishing to belabour the point and make his motive plain, glanced at his wristwatch, then finished his drink. 'And I really mustn't talk your ear off all evening.'

They wished each other goodnight and Jimmy watched Saul leave the pub. 'Here, Graham,' he said to the barman, 'that fella I was just talking to. You ever seen him here before?'

Graham looked up from polishing a glass. 'Can't say I have, mate, no.'

Jimmy wasn't sure of Mr Reznikov's game. Did Honor send him to have a word, make it clear that George was off limits? Except Honor, surely, should hate the idea of Mr Reznikov and himself in a cosy tête-à-tête. And all the questions he was asking – he was obviously suspicious about *something*, even though he couldn't have been nicer and friendlier. There was no chance, then, that he'd caught even a whiff – a molecule of a whiff – of who Jimmy really was. The whole thing was puzzling. But it was Honor's problem, he reminded himself, not his. And once she stumped up enough money, he'd be on his way without a backwards glance. Disappearing on Robbie should be his only regret.

He felt an odd ripple in his solar plexus.

A mad idea flashed across his mind. Immediately, he quashed it. But the thought kept returning, like air bubbles rising to the surface of a dark pool. It was this: he might ask Robbie to come away with him. They could go to a place where no one knew them and live together in a little house with window boxes. And cats, boy and girl Golden Persians. Jimmy would get a job and Robbie would stay at home and write his books. The more he thought about it, the less mad it seemed. Couples, he'd always assumed, tolerated each other's perpetual company because they had no choice, because pairing off was just what you did. Now he understood that another person's presence in your life could suddenly feel essential, like water or sunshine. The trick, he supposed, was finding that person among the whole rotten morass of humanity. And yet, he thought, surveying the pub's denizens critically, surely it was less a matter of haphazard searching than of fate. If meeting Robbie was random, it followed that their rapturous affinity was commonplace. And at some bone-deep level, Jimmy knew that it wasn't. Robbie knew it too. He hadn't said so, but he didn't need to.

Finishing his pint, Jimmy remembered the words of Miss Lapham, the probation officer whom he saw fortnightly. On Friday, he had arrived at his appointment fizzing over with irrepressible joy, prompting her to remark on his good spirits. His reply had tumbled out: 'Well, you see, I've met someone special.' When she pressed him for details, he hastily described George. A half-truth, after all, was more convincing than a whole lie. Indeed, Miss Lapham seemed unsuspecting, even approving. 'For many a young man who's passed through my supervision,' she declared, 'marriage has been the making of him.'

*

Back at Tregunter Road, Saul poured himself another drink and sat down at his typewriter to compose a letter to Her Majesty's Prison Service. Had anyone glanced in from the street, they'd have seen a picture of brow-knitted concentration, the task at hand seemingly a matter of life and death.

It was a Sunday evening, customarily the time for languor and lethargy. Yet Saul's alertness matched the mood all around the house. Three floors up, George was counting and re-counting every penny she owned: it came to nearly twenty pounds. Not bad. Perhaps, she thought, she'd continue with the Camera Club even after the deed was done. It was better money than sitting for painters, and the men were far more appreciative. Some of them, she suspected, didn't even bother putting film in their cameras. But that was their business.

Across the hall, Robbie was in the bathroom, having spent longer than usual in his weekly bath. Critically, he examined himself in the mirror. Ought he start doing press-ups, or lifting weights? His body had never occupied his thoughts – it was just there, and it worked well enough – until this metamorphosis had occurred: this abrupt coming into being. The writer in him squirmed at the hackneyed phrase, but none other was as apt: he finally understood what all the fuss was about.

Downstairs, Mina arrived home from work and went to make herself a cup of tea. It had come to her, quite suddenly, what was the matter with George: she was up the spout. The other morning she was chucking up something terrible. And wasn't she bound to get caught eventually, the way she carried on? Mina couldn't fathom such recklessness. Honor would have a *fit*.

Honor, sitting in bed reading *The People*, remained in ignorance of George's unfortunate condition. For now, she was absorbed in an article about a seance during which Douglas Fairbanks, communicating from 'the other side' in an 'abyss of repentance', had apologised to one of his wives for his infidelity. He took his time, thought Honor: He's been brown bread more than ten years. Gerald, she reflected, had been notably silent since his passing in 1947. She looked up at the ceiling and said softly: 'Is there money hidden anywhere, darling? If not, you might let me know the next Grand National winner. That'd be super.' She paused and lit a cigarette. 'Even better: could you please arrange for Jimmy Sullivan, currently of this address, to join you in the spiritual realm?'

10

Goodbye, Tiny Sea Creature

George heard footsteps on the stairs. She tried to stand up from the spot on the landing where, five minutes earlier, her legs had given way. If only she could get into bed, she thought, she'd be able to manage. Her bedroom was no more than a few yards away. It may as well have been miles. Lying on her side, her knees to her chest, she shifted her weight onto her left hand and moved into a sitting position. As her head rose, spots floated across her vision. The pain in her abdomen kept coming in waves, as though something was squeezing and tugging at her insides. In her mind's eye she saw this thing as made of shining, sharp metal, like the device the doctor had used, but bigger and more complicatedly mechanical. The backs of her stockings were soaked, with sweat or blood. Perhaps both.

The footsteps drew closer and male legs came into view. Jimmy.

'George, what in God's name . . .'

‘My bed,’ she croaked. ‘If you could help me to my bed, I’d be awfully . . .’

He crouched down and considered her curiously. ‘Have you fainted? Are you hurt? Don’t try to move. I’ll get help.’

‘No!’ The word came out as a half-yelp, half-sob.

He gazed at her, perplexed. ‘But—’

‘Please don’t leave me. I mean, no need to trouble anyone else. I’m fine – it’s just . . .’ As she trailed off, she thought she saw his brow twitch with sudden understanding.

‘All right,’ he said. ‘Put your arm around my neck, that’s it.’ He picked her up like a baby, revealing a slick ruby crescent on the pale wood floor. The second she was less dizzy, she thought, she would clean it up.

Jimmy carried her into her room and lowered her onto the bed. As her head sank into the pillow and she inhaled the familiar musty perfume of her bedclothes, she began to feel less frightened. The pains didn’t abate. But she’d been told to expect some pain. She’d just stay in bed until the thing was completed.

How relieved she’d felt on leaving the doctor’s flat. She hadn’t for a moment imagined worse was still to come.

When she’d arrived there and Dr Jenkins opened the front door himself, she was surprised. For some reason she’d expected the presence of a wife, or a nurse, or some sort of female assistant. But no, there was only Dr Jenkins. Her first impression was of a short, anxious-looking man with a corrugated forehead, grey-bronze hair in a thin comb-over, and a map-shaped purple mark on his left cheek. ‘Come in, come in,’ he’d said, glancing left and right into the dim hallway of the mansion block. He took her coat and offered her a cup of tea. But he asked in a way that made it clear he wanted her to refuse, and so she did.

‘Well,’ he said, smiling and running his eyes up and down her body. He was trying to ascertain, perhaps, if she’d told the truth about being nine weeks along. Did women often lie? George looked the same as usual – if anything, she'd lost weight from being sick – but how would he know the difference?

They stood in his entryway, which smelled of furniture polish and coats drying after being in the rain. Eventually she realised that, before she was to be allowed further into the flat, he wanted his money. Flustered, she searched through her bag for the envelope, plump with crisp fivers. She handed it over and he fanned through the notes. 'Very good, very good. Follow me.'

This was the next surprise: it was to take place in the kitchen, as was evident from the narrow table covered with a frayed piece of oilcloth. At one end a floral towel had been laid, presumably for her head. On the counter, three feet away, were the remains of Dr Jenkins's lunch: a plate with some bread crusts, a stubbed-out cigarette, an apple core, a Wagon Wheel wrapper. Next to this was a tray – not a hospital tray, but a Bakelite tray decorated with a hunting scene – holding several metal instruments, including a large syringe, stainless steel with fingerprints on the handle.

George's stomach roiled. She almost lost her nerve. For God's sake pull yourself together, she thought. You're here now. Get it over with.

Dr Jenkins had removed his suit jacket and rolled up his shirtsleeves. He leant over the sink, washing his hands with Fairy Liquid and drying them on a limp tea towel. To reassure herself, George thought back to what Fiona had said. Fiona hadn't been to him, but she knew several girls who had. 'Poor old Monica was almost four months gone. Ghastly business. But I must say, she's none the worse for wear. Could get into her wedding dress, which was the main thing. It was a Norman Hartnell, you know. Of course you do, you were there. Nice do, wasn't it? I did think her bodice looked a bit snug, but that couldn't be helped. No one was any the wiser. So anyway, yes, this Dr Jenkins is a bit of an oddball, by all accounts. But perfectly businesslike. Or doctorly, rather. Discreet, naturally. It's one of those blocks on the wrong side of Chelsea Bridge. He works at the Westminster Hospital, so he knows his stuff. It's almost as good as going to a clinic. I'll talk to Mon and write to you with his phone number.'

When George rang him, she recited the script she'd been given. 'I'm a schoolfriend of your cousin Genevieve. She said you might be able to help me with a problem.'

'How long have you had this problem? Approximately.'

When she told him, he tutted stagily. 'Dearie me. In that case, it'll be thirty pounds. Upfront, in small notes. Wednesday afternoon at two o'clock. Does that suit you? Don't tell anyone where you're going. But you wouldn't do that, would you?' But I was told it would be twenty-five, she felt like saying. She had the distinct impression he'd detected affluence in her voice and bumped the price up. So far she'd only scraped together twenty pounds, and where the hell would she find another ten in two days?

In desperation, she decided to ask her sister Venetia. George slightly preferred Venetia to Arabella, the eldest, who was rather dotty and lived miles away in the country anyhow.

The following mid-morning, she caught the Tube to Regent's Park and, pretending to be passing through the neighbourhood, called at Venetia's house in Chester Terrace. Unflappable on principle, Venetia showed no surprise at the unannounced visit, even though the sisters hadn't seen each other in months. 'You look well, darling,' she said, leaning in to kiss George. 'Have you lost weight? You'll have some tea, won't you?'

Venetia's appearance was unchanged. She had the type of thin face and high cheekbones that didn't particularly age, although George calculated she must be forty-two now. Certainly, all her children were grown-up, or just about. George knew she was considered a contaminating influence on them, especially the youngest: sullen little weak-chinned Diana, who, her mother reported, was working as a chalet girl in St Moritz. 'Well,' said Venetia philosophically, taking a cigarette from the box on the table and tapping the end, 'it fills in the time, doesn't it? Until the season. And we're hoping she loses a bit of puppy fat whilst she's there. If not, I shall have to get her a prescription for Drinamyl. Oh, don't look at me like that, it's for her own good. She doesn't carry it as well as you. It's all in her hips and face, poor soul.'

Any superfluous fat cells on Venetia's skinny body, reflected George, would melt away from the sheer force of her contempt. 'Diana's doing all that, then, is she? Coming out.'

Venetia lit her cigarette and sucked on it deeply. 'I know you think it all very silly. And I can't say I disagree with you. But Dom is in favour. And I simply don't have the fortitude to go against the tide. That's where I admire you, Georgie. You don't worry about upsetting people. You go your own way, the court of public opinion be damned.'

It was hot and stuffy in the chintzy, over-furnished drawing room. Venetia was wearing buckets of scent – she always did – and George began to feel ill. She sipped some tea. 'How is Dominic? Still at the bank?'

'Of course. He works far too hard. Some days he's in the office until six o'clock! He's terribly conscientious. Can't bear the thought of letting anyone down.'

'Mm.' George used to go out with a chap who worked at Dominic's firm. Most days, he said, Dominic would go to the pub at twelve, followed by lunch, followed by an afternooner with his mistress *du jour*. George had once bumped into him walking down Queen Victoria Street with a girl on his arm. Bold as brass, as Mina would say. At most eighteen, Dominic's companion wore a mink wrap, large paste earrings, and a leopard-skin beret. She looked like a child who'd raided the dressing-up box.

Dominic, who couldn't have been less embarrassed if the girl was his dowager aunt he'd accompanied to church, introduced them as 'my colleague Svetlana' and 'my sister-in-law, the Honourable Miss Mountford-Owen'. Equally unfazed by encountering her sugar daddy's wife's sister, Svetlana offered a squeaky greeting more redolent of Liverpool than Leningrad. Get him to buy you some real diamonds, George felt like saying, and it still won't be worth it. Dominic was portly, florid in the face, at least fifty, the type of man whose waggish air didn't quite conceal a nasty edge. She'd contemplated telling Venetia about Svetlana. But she didn't want to make trouble for the girl. For all George knew, Dominic was the best of some even worse options. Also, she suspected the news would be received by Venetia as a hostile act on George's part. If George were honest with herself, that wouldn't be entirely untrue.

But of course, she thought. Why didn't I think of it before? She could get the money from Dominic. It wouldn't seem like blackmail, not really. The Svetlana incident was yonks ago. 'Anyway, dearest,' she said to Venetia. 'Afraid I must dash. Awfully nice to see you. Love to Diana and the boys.' If she hurried, she thought, she'd catch Dominic in his usual pub.

Disgusting man that he was, he read the situation in an instant. 'In the club, are we? Come on, you can tell your uncle Dom. Gosh, it seems only five minutes ago that you were a bridesmaid at our wedding. How old were you? Ten, eleven? You were such a sweet child. Like butter wouldn't melt. And now look at you, you naughty girl. Don't worry, I won't tell V.' He patted her knee. 'It'll be our little secret.'

'You just lie down on the table and make yourself comfortable, miss,' Dr Jenkins was saying. She could have sworn he put a sardonic emphasis on the 'miss'. How did he know she wasn't married? You could have a husband and still not want a baby. 'Nothing to be frightened of,' he went on in his faux-soothing way. 'I've done this hundreds of times. Nothing to it. Underclothes off, you can leave them on the chair there. You can roll your girdle up. Stockings on or off, it doesn't matter.'

George did as instructed, letting her stockings droop down her thighs. The table was hard against her back. She stared at the frosted-glass light fixture, its curved lip rimmed with dust and dead flies. The towel behind her head smelled strongly of bleach and washing powder. Then again, everything smelled strongly these days. The other day an Italian (she could tell by his shoes) sat near her on the bus, and his aftershave was so pungent she had to get off three stops early. But no one else seemed to notice. This must be what being a dog was like, she reflected.

Dr Jenkins loomed over her. She saw the spidery veins inside his nose, the metal fillings in his upper molars, the faint yellow stains under his arms. 'Now, young lady, I need you to relax. That's your only job. Relax, keep still and know that you're in excellent hands. If it starts to hurt, you can tell me and I'll stop. All right? All right. Now, I want you to bring your heels towards you and let your knees flop down. That's it, that's it. Good girl!'

She screwed her eyes tight shut. From one of the flats below came a baby's wail. How ludicrous, she thought. His hands were near her groin; she could feel the wiry hairs on the back of his fingers, the glass face of his wristwatch. A freezing cold, smooth object was pushed inside her, and she gasped in shock. He seemed to winch it open, and she squirmed involuntarily.

'If you wriggle, it will only take longer.'

She kept still and started to cry silently as he finished his winching.

‘There’s a good girl.’ Then, to himself, ‘Very healthy-looking cervix. No sign of disease.’ Humming under his breath, he unscrewed a bottle and fiddled with the syringe. He placed a dry hand on her lower stomach. Between her legs, metal clinking against metal preceded a sudden piercing agony. ‘It hurts,’ she yelped. ‘It really hurts.’ But he didn’t stop, and she heard herself scream. ‘Shush, shush,’ he said. ‘Come along now. Deep breaths. That’s right. Nearly done now.’ There was a crescendo of pain and she began to black out. She was brought round by the oddest sensation of a stinging chill spreading inside her womb. This is how I’ll die, she thought.

‘There,’ said Dr Jenkins, replacing his instruments on the tray and patting George’s shoulder. ‘All done. Now it’s simply a matter of time. Just go home and wait for it to start. It will hurt, but nothing too awful. Best to stay in bed. By tomorrow you ought to have passed the foetus. Look out for it. Then you’ll know it’s over. You’ll bleed for another week, but don’t go worrying about that.’

George fastened her stockings, pulled her dress down, and got up to put her drawers on. ‘The foetus – it won’t look like a baby, will it?’ No one had told her about this. She’d assumed it would disintegrate before she expelled it.

Dr Jenkins regarded her with weary condescension. These girls. Too squeamish to face the facts of what they were doing. But not too squeamish to sleep around all over the place, goodness no. He had more sympathy for the poor ones, the grey-skinned hussies from LCC housing who couldn’t be expected to know any better, whose only hope of any excitement was a knee-trembler in the alley after closing time. Or their mothers, exhausted from successive births barely a year apart, whose husbands still wouldn’t leave them alone. He saw those types rarely, of course. They couldn’t afford him. Their only resource was some wicked crone who charged five pounds to blindly inject a dirty cylinder of soapy water. But he saw plenty of this type: spoilt, frivolous, too sexy for their own good, never been told no and didn't know how to say it. They all assumed someone would always step in and fix their mistakes. In this they were usually correct.

'It will look like a very small baby,' he said patiently, as though explaining it to a slow-witted child. 'Like a jelly baby, in fact.'

She nodded, but she must have looked upset, because he said: 'Next time, come to me straight away. None of this hanging about. Then there'll be hardly anything there. The whole thing will be a good deal easier. You've got my phone number.'

'Thanks, but there won't be a next time.' Wild fucking horses, she thought, wouldn't drag me back here.

He gave her a 'that's what they all say, duckie' look and practically pushed her out of the door.

Lying on her bed, a tide of pain surging from her ribcage to her knees, George thought she'd be thrilled to see a little jelly baby foetus if it signalled the end of this. Even if it was kicking its legs and smiling, she'd be pleased to see it before she flushed it away. 'Thank you,' she said to Jimmy. 'I'll be fine now.'

'Got a towel? I'll . . .' He pointed to the landing.

'Oh, but . . .' She thought better of protesting. 'In the bathroom. There's a blue towel hanging over the bath.'

He nodded and left the room. She heard him going in and out of the bathroom. Then he went upstairs. Good, she thought. That was that. It was very embarrassing. Completely mortifying, in fact. Not that he'd cotton on to anything. He'd assume it was a nasty bout of the curse. No reason for him to think otherwise. Men knew nothing about such matters.

A minute or so later he was back, carrying two clean white towels. 'Look,' he said, 'why don't I put one of these underneath you?'

'I couldn't possibly . . .' George began. But she was too weak to argue. She let Jimmy undress her to her vest and girdle, wrap her in one towel, and lay her on top of the other. Then he covered her with a sheet and blanket. He did this all so tenderly, she felt like crying. 'Now, what can I get you?' he said. 'Cup of tea?'

'No, I don't want anything. You can leave me now, honestly. I'm feeling better.'

'But you can't be left alone. I know we can't call a doctor, but the least I can do is sit with you.'

'It's not what you think—'

'Shh,' he said, sounding like Dr Jenkins. 'Try to rest. Close your eyes.'

She did close her eyes, but the pain didn't abate, not for hours, or what felt like hours. A kind of delirium took hold of her: she kept hallucinating that she was floating up to the ceiling and looking down at herself. The blood kept spreading over the bed like flames. She feared she was bleeding to death, but Jimmy was right: they couldn't call a doctor. Eventually she must have fallen asleep, because when she opened her eyes, the room was in darkness and she was alone. She still felt a dull, low ache, and the mattress was probably ruined. But she was alive.

A few minutes passed, then Jimmy came in. 'You're awake!' he said. 'How are you feeling?' He switched the bedside lamp on. 'Blimey, you're as white as a ghost.'

'How long was I asleep for?'

'I dunno, about four hours? I sat and kept an eye on you. I only went to the lav just now. You gave me an awful fright. I thought you were a goner.'

She smiled wanly. 'Me too.' She remembered him undressing

her. 'I'll buy you some new towels. I wonder if you wouldn't mind not—'

'What do you take me for? Course I won't tell anyone else. Who did you go to, though, to get it done?'

She assumed he was asking out of concern, and couldn't see any point in dissembling. After all he'd witnessed, the game was up. 'It was a doctor. But not, you know . . .'

'No one who's on the up and up.'

'Quite.' She sat up, and he arranged her pillows so she could recline comfortably. 'Thank you,' she said. 'Thank you for everything. You're so lovely to have looked after me like this. I don't know what to say.'

'Don't be daft. I couldn't exactly leave you in that state, could I?'

As soon as he went upstairs, George pulled back the sheet and searched. She thought she remembered a particularly painful contraction, followed by the feeling she had passed something. But she wasn't sure. And she needed to be sure. She had to know if it was really gone from her body. Eventually, scanning the stiffening, burgundy-stained bottom sheet, she picked up a flesh-coloured lump. No bigger than a grape, it had discernible fingers, little slits for eyes, and a pin-dot for a mouth. The head was half the size of the body, which had a sort of tail. It looked like a tiny sea creature. Goodbye, tiny sea creature, she thought. I hope that didn't hurt you as much as it did me.

Robbie had spent the evening at his desk, working on his novel. He'd never be so grandiose as to say 'my first novel', as this presupposed publication, and also that a second and third would smoothly follow. He embarked on a new first novel every six months or so. The first few chapters always went so well that he looked forward to the glorious reception of his debut and – the true triumph – the chagrin of his enemies. Until, that is, around the thirty-thousand-word mark. Overnight, doubts and fears and general self-loathing illuminated the futility of his enterprise, his delusion in thinking he had it in him to produce a real work of literature, the shame of ever having harboured such ludicrous notions. Before long the cycle would begin again, usually when he read a splashy new novel he judged mediocre or worse. I can do better than *that*, he'd think indignantly. The younger the author and the more tediously 'modern' the style, the greater was his motivating pique. If it was a girl in her twenties writing autobiographically, the affront might sustain him for forty thousand words.

He'd long wondered if being in love would prove conducive to working, to inspiration, or whether the muse would desert him altogether. The latter seemed more likely, for Robbie imagined he wrote best when he was unhappy, which was most of the time. Yet current circumstances belied this. His and Jimmy's initial trysts had progressed to a full-blown affair, conducted on both sides with astonishing fervour. They had an established routine of tapping on each other's doors around midnight, after the house had fallen silent save for its own clanks and creaks. Before 6 a.m., they slipped back into their own beds. Robbie then floated through the day in a sort of haze, the previous night replaying like a mind-film as he worked. Even his mundane editorial tasks seemed to take on a new charm. And every evening, when he retired to his room to work on his novel, his fingers fairly flew across the typewriter keys. His brain swam with ideas; he could actually feel the sentences taking perfect shape and travelling from his head to his tingling fingertips. Despite hardly sleeping, he was never tired.

He kept looking back, with a kind of morbid curiosity, to the first time he and Jimmy properly talked, that afternoon in his room. He'd have sworn he had no inkling of what was to come. His blindness alarmed him. And yet nothing in his life had prepared him to recognise a lover. His marriage to Pamela – poor old Pamela, he thought with a fleeting stab of remorse – had left him unchanged. Untouched. He wasn't sure if they'd ever had a real conversation, not counting dreary spates of bickering. Whereas he and Jimmy talked voraciously, about everything and anything. No one, Robbie marvelled, had ever paid him such attention, listened to his opinions so eagerly. Except neither of them, it occurred to him now, were very forthcoming about themselves. Invasive questions were avoided, as though their communion was too exclusive, too precious to be sullied by the failures and cruelties life had doled out.

Glancing at the clock, he saw it was 11.30 p.m. Jimmy had been out this evening. At least, no noise had emanated from his room. He often went out. Robbie neither asked nor cared where he'd been – why should he, when their happiness in each other's company was unmistakable?

Getting up to brush his teeth, he heard voices from downstairs. He sometimes did: George's room was directly below, and there was a brass vent on the chimney breast. It sounded like a man's voice, though, which was odd. George wouldn't have gentleman callers at this hour. Honor didn't allow it, and quite right too. Intrigued, Robbie lay down on the floor and put his ear to the vent. He couldn't make out the words being spoken, but after a few moments he realised he was listening to George and Jimmy talking in low tones. His lungs tightened as he strained his ears, all his senses, to hear their conversation. Still he could only make out a few snatches. But it was enough. George: 'You're so lovely . . .' Jimmy: '. . . couldn't ever leave you . . . there's no one else but you . . .'

Robbie went over to the washbasin and quietly vomited. He cleaned up the mess, brushed his teeth, then lit a cigarette and lay on his bed. A sense of inevitability gripped him. Of course this would happen. How could he have foreseen otherwise? It was almost as though he'd hated George proactively, somehow knowing that one day he'd have a good reason. He'd never felt such humiliation. It was too awful to be borne. He wanted to crawl under his bed and hide away for ever. How long had it been going on? Were they laughing at him behind his back? Was George exultant that she'd been right to call him queer?

He'd have to move out of the house, obviously. He couldn't look either of them in the eye ever again. It dawned on him that Jimmy's purported dislike of George had been a ruse, a sleight of hand to conceal that he, like most men on earth, found her irresistible.

But why, Robbie puzzled, why did he bother with me? It couldn't have all been pretend, and even if it were, to what end? He had nothing to offer Jimmy, no money or useful favours.

The nicest weeks of his life had been obliterated in seconds. He struggled to think of a silver lining. No more subterfuge and secrecy counted as one, conceivably, except that didn't work, as the clandestinity, the whispering under bedclothes, the muffling of mouths in the heights of passion, the leaving of filthy little notes under each other's pillows had but added to the vertiginous thrill of it all.

When he heard Jimmy's tap on the door, the usual somersault of joy pulsed through him, chased within a split second by self-castigation. He wasn't sure if he could deal with a confrontation. But neither could he feign ignorance. His new knowledge would be written on his face. He got up and opened the door, then went and sat on his bed without saying anything.

Jimmy shut the door. 'Got you a present,' he said, handing him a packet of Spangles. 'You said they were your favourite.' He sat down on the edge of the bed and kicked his shoes off.

'I know,' Robbie said quietly. 'I know about you and George.'

Jimmy put his hand on the back of Robbie's neck and ran his fingertips in shivery circles around the soft hollow at the base of his skull. 'What about me and George?'

'I know you're having an affair.'

Jimmy laughed and didn't stop circling his fingertips. 'Are we? First I've heard of it.'

Robbie tried to pull away from him. 'I heard you, just now. In her room.'

Jimmy laughed again, but he was nervous. Obviously Robbie had it all wrong. Yet he seemed so angry, as though he might not be talked out of it. 'I don't know what you reckon you heard. But if you'd have seen the state of George this evening, you'd realise nookie was the last thing on her mind. With me or any other bugger. She's been to some butcher, hasn't she? Killed her baby, like you said she would. I found her collapsed on the landing. I've been watching over her, making sure she didn't bleed to death.'

'Oh my God! Oughtn't she to go to hospital?'

'She can't, can she? Not after what she's done. Don't worry, she'll live. Maybe this will be a lesson to her, eh?'

'Poor girl. Pretty tough lesson, isn't it?' He remembered George telling him, accusingly, that he was lucky to be a man. How keenly he agreed with her now.

Jimmy shrugged, rather unfeelingly, thought Robbie. 'No one had a gun to her head. She had a choice. Unlike the baby.' He sighed, then grinned. 'You were properly jealous, weren't you?' He took Robbie's hand, brought it to his lips and started kissing each of his fingers. 'Did you think I'd thrown you over for her? Now why would I want to do a thing like that?'

Robbie closed his eyes as Jimmy drew his fingertips between his teeth.

'Were you furious?' said Jimmy between nibbles. 'Did you want to slap her round the face? Or slap me round the face?'

Robbie laughed weakly. 'I've never resorted to physical violence. Not outside the battlefield. But yes, maybe I did want to slap you.'

'You wouldn't be the first. Though usually I deserve it.'

Robbie looked at him. I ought to be relieved, he thought. The terrible thing he believed had happened hadn't happened. But the bubble of anguish in his stomach didn't dissipate. It was the shock, he told himself. In time, the shock would wear off; his nerves would catch up with reality.

Jimmy put his hands on Robbie's shoulders and began kissing him. Robbie let himself be kissed, then he let himself be pushed back onto the bed. He opened his eyes and said: 'So, there's no one else?'

Jimmy smiled, whispered, 'No, no one,' and pinned Robbie's wrists above his head.

11

Like a House on Fire

Saul sat up in bed and looked at the luminous hands on the alarm clock. He wasn't sleeping through the night these days, not since his conversation with Jimmy in the pub. Nothing conclusive had been said, it was true. But neither had Jimmy allayed his fears. Quite the contrary.

He thought back to nearly a month ago, when he'd implored Honor to be honest, to explain her real connection to the young man who'd arrived at the house. Unlike the other residents, Saul knew full well that Jimmy's mother hadn't been in service with Honor's grandmother. He'd seen where she grew up. Neither of her grandmothers, he'd warrant, had ever risen to the status of a housekeeper, let alone employed one. If Jimmy was in fact Honor's brother pretending to be someone else, and she was covering for him – well, he wasn't sure if he could ever forgive her. He desperately hoped he was wrong, that his imagination was running away with him. For why would Honor lie about it? When her brother was sent to prison, she had cut off all contact with him – that, at any rate, was her official story, related to him after Naomi had explained his dreadful connection to Elizabeth, as she knew her. According to Honor, her new name represented a permanent break from the past. Not only had Saul accepted this, he'd felt flattered – special – that he alone knew the whole truth about her curious trajectory.

If only the prison service had provided the simplest of answers. After his letter went unanswered, he had telephoned several times, and eventually he spoke to a polite but quite intransigent lady. The sole parties privy to such information, she said, were the victims and the victims' families. But I am the victim's family, he pleaded. No, she said, I don't have your name on record. I'm Naomi Cohen's first cousin! Sorry, sir, but anyone could claim that. Would Mrs Cohen like to contact us herself?

At about four in the morning, Saul decided he was being ridiculous. He sat up in bed and lit a cigarette. The British government didn't let murderers back on the streets before they'd even served half their sentence. You were lucky to get thirty years instead of hanging. Jimmy must be a childhood friend from the East End, someone to whom Honor felt some sort of misguided loyalty. You could never truly slough off your past, after all. He of all people knew that. And yet: why had Honor wept? Why had she stayed the night and clung to him so fiercely, as though they were lovers about to be torn apart for ever?

It was no good. He gave up on sleep and made himself a cup of coffee, which he drank slowly while waiting for dawn to break. He considered his choices. Confront Honor, tell her his suspicion and risk their friendship if he was wrong. It was a serious accusation, that she would force Saul to live under the same roof as the man who'd taken everything from him. And – worse – that she would deceive him whilst doing so.

*

'Mina dear, I have a confession to make,' said Saul. 'I had an ulterior motive for inviting you out this evening.' They were at a chop house near the cinema, drinking Hungarian red wine (Saul with gusto, Mina more gingerly). 'Not that your company isn't always a pleasure in its own right, of course.'

'Ooh, an ulterior motive. How exciting. I was going to say let me guess, but I'm afraid I haven't the foggiest.' Usually when men asked her out, she grasped their motives only too bloody well. But Saul wasn't like that. If anything, women were always trying to catch his eye, while he didn't seem to notice. Anyway, he was old enough to be her father. Although she had once got a proposal from one of her schoolfriend's fathers. Mr Pickering, from number 36. She came home from the chocolate factory one summer evening and he was sitting in the front parlour, talking to her parents. Love, her mum said, Mr Pickering wants to take you for a walk. Isn't that nice? Mina was baffled, but she went with him. In the park, they sat on a bench. He pressed his leg against hers and started this speech about how ardently he loved and admired her. Gobsmacked wasn't the word. She'd never heard anything like it in her life. She barely even knew him to say hello to. Then he got a ring out. It was a nice ring, gold with little rubies and diamonds. She remembered his late wife wearing it. After a few moments of stunned silence, she said something like, thanks ever so, but I'm spoken for. It seemed the politest excuse.

At home, her parents said, all excited, did he ask you, then? When Mina said she was too young to get married, and even if she weren't, she didn't want to marry someone's dad, her mother said tartly: 'But you'll be sixteen next year. You could do a lot worse. Norman Pickering's got his own pest control business. It brings in a pretty penny. You know Hildie Burke, at number 9? Got rid of her woodworm a treat.' Mina was outraged, and not only on aesthetic grounds (his age aside, Mr Pickering was no

Dirk Bogarde). It was the notion of living for ever in the same Billericay terrace of two-up two-downs, when there was a whole exciting world out there, that struck her as offensive beyond belief. Upstairs in her room, she did some sums and decided that, with some extra shifts at the factory, she could move to London in six months.

Saul drank some wine and continued: 'Even for one as clever as you, I believe what I'm about to say would be impossible to guess. It's about our conversation on Sunday, when you told me Jimmy was lying about his past. Strictly between us – and I know I can trust you – I'm worried that young man is not who he says he is.'

The waitress brought their food. Mina popped a chip in her mouth before remembering her manners and picking up her fork (*tines pointing down, index finger on the handle*). 'Exactly what I said! There's something shifty about him, isn't there?'

'I have my suspicions about who he really is. I may be very wrong. I hope I am.' He tucked his napkin into his collar and stirred his stew. 'As you know, before the war I lived in Eastern Europe, with my wife and daughter. We wanted to leave. The Romanian government were confiscating Jewish assets, their possessions. They revoked our citizenship, placed quotas on schools and jobs. But we had one possession of considerable value. It was a portrait of my wife, Gila, by the great artist Marc Chagall. Gila's mother was a cousin of Chagall's wife, Bella, and when Gila was sixteen they went to Paris. Gila sat for Chagall, and he presented her with the painting afterwards. He was not yet as famous as he would become, and neither Gila nor her parents knew the artwork would one day be valuable.

'By the late thirties, Chagall was famous enough to be targeted by the Nazis, who classified his work as degenerate. I offered Gila's portrait to an art dealer in the Bukovina, but the sum he offered was paltry. Insulting. So many dealers were taking advantage of Jews' desperation. I knew that if we sold the painting in London, we'd receive ten times as much. So I sent it, via a travelling friend, to my cousin Naomi. She lived near the Whitechapel Gallery, and people at the gallery helped her find a buyer.' It hadn't been a great sum, the profit from selling this most precious item. Around a thousand pounds. 'The money would have been just enough to fund our escape to London, mine and my wife and daughter's.'

'Your daughter was only little, wasn't she?'

'When the war began, Marya was not yet three. She'd be around your age now.'

'Who stole your money? Someone stole it, didn't they?'

Saul dabbed his lips with the edge of his napkin. 'Naomi and her husband, Larry – a very nice fellow, he repaired wristwatches and clocks for a living – had a neighbour, Mrs Shaughnessy. Respectable woman. A widow. Her son and daughter lived with her, along with the daughter's husband. This younger couple, Elizabeth and Thomas Armstrong, they were friends with Naomi and Larry. Elizabeth and Naomi were particularly close, I believe. They worked together at one time, as waitresses at a Lyons' Corner House.' Saul remembered a photograph, possibly still in existence somewhere, of Honor and Naomi in their uniforms, with those funny black and white hats.

'Elizabeth stole the money!'

'No, not Elizabeth. It wasn't her fault, not really.'

He refilled their glasses. Then he began telling Mina what had happened, reciting almost verbatim the letter Naomi had written him from her hospital bed. He spoke as if Elizabeth were a complete stranger to them both. And wasn't she?

*

'Larry, wake up!' Naomi's voice was an urgent whisper as she poked her snoring husband in the ribs. 'There's someone downstairs.'

Larry's eyes remained closed, but his face creased into a woebegone expression. 'Don't talk nonsense, Nay. You're dreaming, just dreaming.'

From below came an unmistakable shuffle and thud. Now Larry's eyes flew open. Naomi shoved him. 'See?'

He threw off the bedclothes and pushed his feet into slippers. 'Stay there,' he told his wife. But she was already knotting the belt on her dressing gown.

Downstairs, two men in balaclavas stood in the front room. The taller one held a torch, which cut a faint greenish glow through the darkness. All the dresser drawers had been removed, their contents tipped onto the floor. Books had been pulled from the shelves, and a china samovar lay in broken pieces.

Larry advanced towards them with his hands up in a submissive gesture. 'We're not wealthy people,' he said. 'If you want the radiogram, take it. Be my guest. There's nothing else of value here.'

The shorter, rounder man nodded at his partner, who pulled a piece of paper out of his pocket and handed it to Larry. The note, written in crude block capitals, said: *GIVE US THE CASH.*

'Cash, what cash?' said Larry. 'The takings from my business go straight into the bank. Please, you've made a mistake.'

The short man nodded again, and the tall one swung the end of his torch into the side of Larry's head, making a sickening thud. Larry reeled back, but he remained upright. Naomi leapt forward and shouted: 'Are you deaf? My husband told you, you've made a mistake. There's no money here.'

Another sickening thud and a gasp from Larry. He brought his hand to his head. Blood dripped from his temple onto his fingers. A pause, and then the man hit him a third time. Larry, crouching down, his arms over his head, said bitterly: 'Tell them, Nay, for God's sake, tell them.'

Even then, Naomi hesitated before walking over to the window, lifting up the corner of the rug and jimmying loose a piece of floorboard. The tall man was right behind her, shining his torch on her hands as she extracted a Tide washing powder box from the dusty depths. As he reached out to take the box, Naomi took leave of her senses. She brought her knee up to his crotch, hard, and pulled the balaclava off his head. Yelling in pain and rage, he seized her by the throat and banged her head on the floor. As his hands squeezed, Naomi managed to poke him in the eyes. It worked, in as much as he released her neck and grabbed her wrists. She was still struggling to free herself, but she could breathe.

The other man had picked up the money box and was going towards the front door. Over his shoulder he said, speaking for the first time: 'Finish her, Jack.'

Mina blinked back tears. 'Did Naomi die?'

Saul shook his head. 'No. But she suffered a stroke and was in a coma for five days. She never walked again. She died ten years later, of an illness she might have survived otherwise.'

'What about Larry?'

'Poor Larry died the day after the attack. He had a traumatic brain injury.'

'And so Jack was Elizabeth's brother? Who was the other man?'

'Her husband. Thomas Armstrong. They were both found guilty of murder. Armstrong was sentenced to death, but it was later commuted to life in prison. Jack Shaughnessy was given thirty years.'

'But Elizabeth didn't mean for them to do it. Or did she?'

'No, of course not. Naomi told her about the money, and Elizabeth was indiscreet in telling her husband. She had no idea what he was capable of.'

'But the upshot was, you didn't leave your country,' said Mina sadly. 'Not in time, I mean.'

If only he'd tried harder to get them out, before they were trapped in the Czernowitz ghetto and the deportations started. He told Gila they ought to run away. He had a journalist friend on the outside, part of a group dedicated to helping Jews escape. She'd get them the money to bribe a guard and they'd go to a hiding place, a disused cosmetics factory. It sounded too risky, thought Gila. Too dangerous with a small child. They'd be shot if they were seen. And thousands of Jews had already been sent to Transnistria, on the eastern edge of Moldova. Maybe it would be better to join them, she said. Anywhere, surely, would be an improvement on the filthy ghetto.

Hoping to bring Gila round to his plan, Saul did a dummy run one night. With help from a friend giving him a leg-up, he climbed over the nine-foot wooden fence and barbed wire. Then, taking only back streets, he reached the factory without being seen. The next day, he walked back into the ghetto amidst a group of workers returning from the night shift at a metalworks. But when he reached home, he found his entire street empty of residents, the front doors sealed. He begged the authorities to put him on the next cattle car to Transnistria. Instead, he was sent to a forced labour camp run by the Romanian army.

Mina drank some wine – the taste of it was growing on her – and said: 'I still don't understand. Are you saying Jack is Jimmy? But how does he know Honor?'

Saul looked at her innocent, enquiring face, rosy-cheeked from the wine. A profound weariness entered his bones. He realised he had little choice but to betray Honor, discarding his steadfast loyalty of all these years. Not that being her secret-keeper was ever difficult. Not really. The young people in the house . . . well, Honor's grubby history wasn't their business. Until Jimmy came along, that is. Saul felt little responsibility towards Robbie – a grown man, albeit a rather ineffectual one – nor towards George. That flighty creature could look after herself. But Mina was a child. Wholly trusting, she would be shocked to learn he'd acted with deceit, told lies by omission. More than that: she was like a daughter to him. He realised this with a disturbing rush of sentiment. And what kind of a father withholds dangerous information from his daughter, all for the sake of protecting a lover's dignity – a lover whose judgement might be fatally flawed?

But no, this wouldn't do. The truth was that his knowledge, his agitated conjectures, simply couldn't be borne alone. He had to share the emotional burden, and there wasn't anyone else. No need to dress it up as the dictates of a moral conscience.

'The thing is, Mina dear . . .' He paused, lowered his voice. 'Elizabeth is Honor. Or rather, Honor was Elizabeth. She changed her name, you see, during the war. Then she remarried and put all that unpleasantness behind her. Understandable, don't you think?'

It took a moment for Mina to absorb the meaning of his words. Then she let out a small squeal of astonishment. She couldn't think of what to say. Or rather, too many utterances competed on her tongue. On the one hand, if anyone could understand the desire for reinvention, for having ideas above your station and putting those ideas into practice, it was Mina. And yet: what a turn-up for the books. Honor, commoner than her. From a family of yobbos. And her brother, a violent murderer, had been sleeping above Mina's head! Just across the landing from poor Robbie, who wasn't exactly what you'd call a hard nut.

Then again, she might have said the same about Jimmy. Just goes to show, she thought. 'Who else knows?' she said finally. 'Does George know?'

'No one else knows. Do you think you'll be able to carry on as normal? Treat Honor the same as always, I mean?'

'Don't you worry. I'm an excellent actress.' I can try my best, she thought, but the next time Honor comes over all la-di-da, I'll really have to bite my tongue. 'So,' she went on. 'Jimmy might be Jack. What's the evidence in favour?'

Saul smiled at her rolling-up-her-sleeves tone. 'Evidence for: he is lying about why he wasn't conscripted. We assume, anyhow. And then Honor was very upset the day he arrived. I saw that when we were alone. They offered that nonsense about Jimmy's mother working at Honor's grandmother's house. Why lie?' Even to innocent ears, he thought, nothing about that story would have rung true.

'Exactly, why lie? Did you never see a photograph of Jack Shaughnessy?'

'No. I might have, if the newspapers were allowed to publish one. It's the law in your country, apparently. The press aren't allowed to identify underage criminals.'

'That's bloody marvellous, isn't it?' She shook her head. 'But wait: can't you ask someone if he's been released? Someone official, I mean?'

'I've tried! No one will tell me anything.'

'Here,' said Mina, her eyes widening, 'you don't reckon he's escaped, do you? Tunnelled his way out or some such?'

The idea hadn't occurred to Saul. Suddenly, it seemed the likeliest explanation. Except surely an escaped convict would want to stay far away from any relations or old associations? 'There must be a way, mustn't there, that we can find out the truth?' he said. 'Given that we're living under the same roof as him.'

'Course! I'll put my thinking cap on.' She frowned. 'Would Honor do such a thing, though? Let him back into her life? I know they say blood's thicker than water. But if one of my brothers was evil like that, I'd never talk to him again as long as I lived. Wouldn't sweat over it, neither.'

And that, thought Saul, was the baffling crux of it.

For the next few days, Mina did her best to stay out of Honor's way. She feared she'd get the giggles, or otherwise act unnaturally around her, and Honor would twig the big secret was out. Mina couldn't decide how she felt about it. A bit conned, if she was honest. Her parents had only let her move into Tregunter Road because Honor, according to Mina's description, was properly posh.

'I don't know about this, love,' her father had said. 'You say there are men living in the house? It doesn't seem right.'

'No, Dad, you don't understand. It's highly respectable. One of the men is married, and the other is a widower. And I'll be sharing a whole floor with another girl, a student at the Slade School of Fine Art. I had tea with her. Her name's Sadie, she's terribly nice.'

'This girl,' said Mr Taylor, 'what does her father do?'

Mina didn't miss a beat. 'He's very high up at Peek Frean's.' He supervised the Twiglets and Cheeselets production lines at the Bermondsey factory, apparently, which wasn't *not* high up. 'Mrs Wilson is particular about her house guests – that's what she calls them. She'd never give the time of day to any riff-raff. When she interviewed me, she was wearing a gold necklace from Boucheron. I've seen it in their window in New Bond Street. Dad, it's a real chance for me.'

For a long time, Mina was intimidated by Honor's hoity-toity manner, whilst also hoping to effortlessly acquire it. Now, thinking of the way she looked down her nose – well, she had no bloody right. And if she'd shoved a murderer in amongst them without so much as a by your leave, she had even less bloody right. For all their sakes, but especially Saul's, Mina resolved to find out the truth about Jimmy. Like Deanna Durbin in *Lady on a Train*, she would carry the day with bravery and good cheer, outwitting her opponents and vanquishing villains.

Mina knocked on the office door and stuck her head in. 'Hullo, Robbie. Isn't Honor here?'

'She's out for the evening, I think. Wining and dining someone who's going to advertise. Come in, what's up?'

'Nothing,' said Mina, who'd heard Honor leave the house. 'I just wanted to offer these round.' She held a plate of fairy cakes. 'I made them to celebrate eggs coming off the ration, but it'll be murder on my figure if I scoff them all. I tried to give some to Greta, but you'd think I'd offered her a cup of poison. I'm meant to have read her mind and known about her two new root canals. I said spare me the details, please; if you don't want any, I'm sure Robbie will.' She placed the plate on his desk, then pulled over a chair and sat down. 'You can take a break, can't you?' She had prepared these lines, having decided that Robbie was the obvious entry-point to her investigation.

Robbie helped himself to a cake. 'I've been flat out,' he said. 'It's just non-stop, you know. And does anyone appreciate all my hard work? Do they hell.'

'Poor you.' She smiled sympathetically. 'How are things otherwise? It sounds like you've been getting on like a house on fire with our new resident. Must be nice to have a friend in the house. Another bloke near your age, I mean.'

He chewed a mouthful and swallowed. 'How do you mean, like a house on fire? I wouldn't say we were—'

'My bedroom's right underneath his, that's all. So I've heard you talking at night and stuff. I don't mean I've been earwigging! I think it's nice. Me and George are friendly enough, but I wouldn't call us bosom pals.'

Robbie stared at her uneasily. 'Yes, well. We're very different people, he and I, and I suppose it means we can have some interesting conversations.'

'Look,' said Mina, 'can I be honest? There something about him I don't trust. Can't even put my finger on it. I've just got the feeling he isn't who he says he is. I mean, do you know if his name's really Jimmy Sullivan?'

Robbie thought about this. 'I've no reason to suspect otherwise. After all, Honor's known him nearly his whole life, hasn't she? So that must be his name.'

'Has he told you much about Honor? Stories from before we knew her, I mean?'

'No, she's barely come up. We mainly—'

'Have you ever seen anything with his name on? A driving licence, say, or ID card?'

She was making him feel increasingly nervous, though he was loath to show it. 'Now why would I? I'm not his employer.'

'Sorry I spoke,' she said huffily. She had thought of Robbie as a highly intelligent man, with his Cambridge degree and everything. Now she wasn't so sure. Maybe all the learning in the world couldn't teach you how people tick. 'Here,' she said, to leave things on a conciliatory note, 'take another cake for later.'

Carefully shutting the office door behind her, Mina wondered if she dared poke around in Honor's bedroom. Aside from wanting to gather intelligence, she was deeply curious to see her private sanctum, which by unspoken rule was off-limits. Glancing over her shoulder, she tiptoed down the hallway.

The room was in virtual darkness, but switching on the electric light revealed an unmade bed and clothes not put away. How very slovenly. But what did you expect, with her upbringing? Mina's own room was organised with obsessive precision, each coat-hanger the same width apart on the wardrobe rail, her underclothes folded and arranged by colour in lavender-scented, wallpaper-lined drawers.

Floor-length greenish-blue curtains, either shot silk or a decent imitation, were tightly drawn. A wooden drying rack was draped with stockings and unmentionables, some that wanted mending or, frankly, throwing away. (There were no brassieres. Being all but breastless, thought Mina, must save Honor a fair few bob. Mina was saving up for an individually designed corselette from Rigby & Peller, making do in the meantime with Marks & Spencer's small cup size.) The crumpled eiderdown matched the curtains, and the padded headboard was a vivid tropical print satin. Mina saw the effect being aimed at, but the colours were too garish a mix. In her opinion a muted stripe or a check would look more modern against the wallpaper, which was mauve with a silverish repeating abstract pattern. *The cardinal virtue of all beauty is restraint*, advised Elsie de Wolfe. Mina had studied the life and works of this American interior designer, who cleverly married a lord solely to become a lady. She never lived with her husband, instead building her own fortune and sharing her homes (plural, naturally) with her female companion. If only there were classes on how to follow this exact path, thought Mina.

She considered the rather gimcrack dressing table, painted white and silver and cluttered with cosmetics: spilt boxes of powder, well-used bullets of lipstick, grimy palettes of eyeshadows with only crumbs left, jars of face cream, four or five bottles of scent. A black lacquered bedside table held nothing but a green glass dish, shaped like a lily pad and streaked with cigarette ash. Mina sat on the edge of the bed and slid open the single drawer. It contained pill bottles, handkerchiefs, and a hardback novel: *The Quiet Gentleman* by Georgette Heyer. On the cover, a man in tight breeches and horse-riding boots, a black leather crop in his hand, leant unsmilingly against a tree. Perhaps Honor wasn't such a cold fish in secret. Although Mina wasn't sure she believed the stories about her and Saul. Apart from the distastefulness of the idea, Honor's poor husband had barely met his maker when Sadie reckoned Saul was her fancy man.

Realising she'd been in the room for some minutes, Mina walked over to the door and listened out for footsteps. Hearing none, she opened the mirrored wardrobe. She longed to rifle through the dresses and coats, but there was no time. Behind some hatboxes on an upper shelf she spied a cracked brown leather portfolio, the kind carried by art students. Glad of her platform shoes, she reached in to grab it and tugged at the brass zip pull, expecting it to be stiff. But the teeth parted without the slightest resistance, revealing a mess of papers: marriage certificates, letters from the LCC about rules for multiple dwellings, demands from the Inland Revenue Department, a war widow's pension book, old National Insurance cards. The only item Mina paused on was a birth certificate for someone called John Joseph, born on 21 March 1924 to Aisling Morag Shaughnessy and Conor Andrew Shaughnessy. The headings – name, surname and dwelling place of father, and so on – were printed in English and another language too. Mina was baffled until she realised it was an Irish birth certificate: the unfamiliar words with accents over the vowels were Irish Gaelic. Had Honor's brother been born in Ireland? Not that it confirmed or ruled out that John – Jack, as he presumably became – was Jimmy. And this, reflected Mina, was the only goal.

At half past eight the next morning, Mina found the kitchen in an atmosphere of high drama. Honor was reading aloud from a newspaper to gasps and shudders from her audience of Saul, Jimmy, and Robbie. 'Oh, Mina,' she said, putting down the *Daily Express*. 'They've found *four* dead women at that house in Rillington Place.'

'What does the *Mirror* say?' asked Jimmy as Mina sat down.

'A nationwide hunt,' read Honor, 'is on for clues to the identity of the Bluebeard of Notting Hill – the killer who strangled four brunettes and hid their bodies in a shabby flatlet in west London.' At the word 'brunettes', Mina emitted a yelp and patted her hair, as though the killer might suddenly appear and drag her away.

Honor scanned the rest of the article. 'It says three of the women were aged between seventeen and twenty-five. They were found half dressed or only in underclothes. None of them has been identified, but there's a possibility that the fourth body, an older woman, is the wife of John Christie. He's the man who lived at the house for fifteen years, but recently moved out.'

Robbie put down his spoon, no longer hungry for his porridge. 'So that poor young fellow who hanged for the murder of his daughter, on Christie's evidence, and was accused of murdering his wife in that same house – are they now saying he was innocent? He could hardly keep murdering from beyond the grave, could he?'

'What was his name, that fellow?' asked Mina. 'He was an Irishman, wasn't he?'

'Timothy Evans,' said Robbie.

‘Yeah, I thought he was a Taff,’ said Jimmy.

‘That’s right,’ said Mina. ‘The Irish aren’t generally the murdering sort, are they?’

Honor looked up from her newspaper. ‘I don’t know that the poor man’s birthplace is relevant, if he was the victim of a miscarriage of justice.’ She squinted at the page. ‘Wait, no, it says the police have ruled out a connection between those murders and these ones.’

‘Well, they would say that, wouldn’t they?’ said Robbie. ‘Otherwise it means admitting an innocent man was sent to his death.’ He turned to Jimmy. ‘See, this is what I mean about capital punishment. Justice is too fallible.’

‘Maybe they were accomplices,’ said Jimmy. ‘That’s why the killings continued.’ Or maybe, he thought, Timothy Evans had been dragged into a situation he didn’t understand, had been taken over by a stronger personality. He had the mind of a child, or so it was said.

Seeing Mina’s stricken face, Saul said: ‘Let us leave the speculation to the police. A terrible business all round, in any case.’

‘It’s not far from here either, Rillington Place.’ Jimmy caught Honor’s eye, which sharply conveyed: you’re meant to be new to London, remember? ‘From what I gather,’ he added.

‘Oh, it’s miles and miles away,’ said Honor. ‘It’s a very downmarket area. A different world, really. You mustn’t worry, Mina. Anyway, they’ll catch the man soon, you’ll see.’

Mina stared at Honor. Those poor girls, she thought. Strangled and discarded like rubbish, their final moments unspeakably terrifying.

Jimmy smiled kindly at her, as if to endorse Honor’s reassuring remark, but Mina couldn’t bring herself to smile back.

Tuesday 12 May 1953

'But my dear Honor,' said Saul, his silver-flecked brows knitted with concern, 'the authorities – this Scotland Yard fellow – supposing they uncover your, how should I put it, your alias, and it occasions scrutiny? Scrutiny of a kind that—'

'Well, first of all, Britain is a free country.' Honor lit a cigarette and exhaled defiantly, as if in celebration of this fact. 'I can call myself whatever I please, and it's nobody's beeswax but my own. Second of all, as you may have noticed, when a woman marries, her identity is entirely subsumed into her husband's. I am Mrs Wilson, wife of Gerald Wilson, late of this parish.' She grinned and patted his hand. 'If you imagine middle-aged widows arouse the merest interest, let alone suspicion, then you possess a rather more colourful imagination than I've ever given you credit for.'

12

Amongst the Pigeons

'The police, they've identified two of the women in the House of Murder,' Mina told Greta, who was curious enough to pause her dusting of the landing skirting board. 'Yesterday they didn't know who any of them were. But in today's evening paper they've given two names. And listen to this: one lived in Warwick Road. That's just over there.' She pointed at the window. 'She was twenty-five, they reckon.'

'And they all died same way?' asked Greta.

'Yup. Strangulation with a ligature.'

Greta looked quizzical.

'Some type of cord, or rope,' clarified Mina.

'They were prostitutes? Runaways?'

'Well, that's the thing, we don't know! One of them was six months pregnant.'

Sighing deeply, Greta twisted her duster into a narrow strip, as though forming a ligature to hang the culprit. 'You and George, you must be very careful. No going out at night.'

'You as well, of course.' Mina wasn't sure if Greta ever went out at night. No one knew how she passed the time when she wasn't at Tregunter Road. No one had ever dared ask. But it was only polite, felt Mina, to include her in the group vulnerable to an on-the-loose sex-murderer.

Greta made a 'pfft' sound and resumed her vigorous dusting. When she reached the attic floor, she cast a quick eye over Robbie's room – all spick and span – then went into Jimmy's. She had promised not to clean in there. But whether he liked it or not, it was her job to make sure no stray coffee cups were forgotten, or damp towels left on the floor. And lo, there was a dirty ashtray at the bedside. Honor didn't allow smoking in the bedrooms – she worried about the house going up in flames – so she'd be hearing about that. Greta walked around the narrow bed to retrieve it. Something unusual caught on her peripheral vision. She crouched down and had a closer look, revulsion drawing her lips inward. Between finger and thumb she lifted a towel from under the bed. It was stiff with rusty stains, seemingly left by large amounts of blood.

She stood up, folded the filthy item into as small a parcel as possible and put it in the front pocket of her capacious apron. Perhaps it would be needed as evidence. Even better, she thought with relish, she might be called as a witness in court. Back in 1942, she had acted as a witness in Gerald's divorce, but to her great disappointment she wasn't required to attend the trial in person. She merely had to provide a sworn statement. At the solicitor's office, further disappointments had greeted her. Furry grey dust gathered in little wells where filing cabinets met the carpet. The receptionist girl wore a costume more suited to a male impersonator at a vaudeville hall. And when Greta was given a cup of tea, the saucer had a chip. Magnanimously ignoring these lapses in standards, she confirmed that yes, one afternoon she had surprised the respondent, Mr Gerald Wilson, in bed with the co-respondent, Miss Honor Petrova. The petitioner, Mrs Barbara Wilson, was out of the house doing work for the WVS. All lies, of course. The very idea of Barbara lifting a finger for anyone else's benefit! But Gerald, may his soul rest in peace, said it was the kindest way to do things, and bought Greta a crate of Mercer's Meat Stout, her favourite.

Greta shut Jimmy's bedroom door behind her and descended the stairs, cradling her apron as if it were a baby bump. On the second-floor landing, she passed him coming in the other direction. He wished her a good afternoon. She stopped and gave him a look you might give to a hairball the cat had thrown up. Then she quickened her step.

Rude old cow, he thought. What had he ever done to her?

Mina went into George's room to tell her the latest on the murders, but George interrupted her. 'Please, I'd rather not know. It's too vile.'

'But my dear, the murderer is at large. In all likelihood he's scoping out new victims. Fresh meat.' Mina said the phrase in dramatically hushed tones. 'You know, my dad thinks I ought to go home for a while, thinks London's not safe. I wrote back and told him he was being silly. Besides, I'll be eighteen in a couple of weeks. I can't go running back to Mum and Dad whenever a crime's committed within a ten-mile radius.' On the little settee, she moved a pile of clean washing to make a space and sat down. 'But he's not totally wrong, I suppose. We really must keep our wits about us.'

'A lady must always keep her wits about her,' said George haughtily. From the top of the laundry pile, she took some French knickers and put them in her chest of drawers. 'It's my understanding that these women probably lived with the prime suspect. He didn't need to grab victims from off the street. Unless Honor starts offering rooms to murderers, we can probably rest easy in our beds.'

Mina thought about this as she folded some slips. 'They – those poor girls – didn't know, though, didn't they? That they were living with a murderer, I mean. They'd never have lived there otherwise.'

Examining one of the garter straps on a longline girdle, George said: 'Mina, you've got good little sewing fingers, haven't you?'

Nodding absently, Mina took the garment. 'But don't you see? For all we know—'

George laughed. 'Saul has managed to resist murdering us so far. So has Robbie. As for Mr Sullivan – I don't believe he'd hurt a fly, do you? In fact, I know he wouldn't.'

In her own room, Mina heard Jimmy's footsteps above, the closing of his door, and his progress down the stairs. As though by chance, she came up behind him and said: 'Off out? Nice evening for it. I do love it when the days get longer, don't you? It's nearly April, at last.'

'I'm off to the pub,' confirmed Jimmy. 'Why don't you join me?'

'Oh, I'd love to, but I've got to go into work. One of the other girls is ill and I'm taking her shift.'

'Another time, then.' Jimmy doffed his hat in farewell. Mina pretended to go into the kitchen and listened for the slam of the front door. She waited another few minutes, then went back upstairs and into Jimmy's room.

Where to look, she wondered. Beneath the sloping ceiling was a neatly made single bed with an iron bedstead. Between the bed and the wall, a folding leather stool held a foil ashtray and an alarm clock. In the opposite corner, at the ceiling's highest point, was a narrow wardrobe made of mottled wood. A black cardboard suitcase with brass clasps sat on top.

Mina knelt on the floor and, craning her neck, peered under the bed. Next to some magazines – dirty ones if she was any judge; she averted her eyes – there was a Lilley & Skinner shoebox. She grabbed it and looked inside: used envelopes, letters, receipts, and goodness knew what else formed a disorderly stack. On top was a piece of thick cream notepaper, folded in half, which she opened and smoothed out. It took her a moment to make sense of it. The embossed black letterhead was an address in Westmoreland Terrace, SW1. Then, in swirly feminine handwriting, it said:

7th March, 1953

Dearest George,

The chap you want is Dr R. Jenkins, telephone BATT 3946, 23 York Mansions, Prince of Wales Drive, SW11.

Do let me know how you get on, won't you? Good luck, darling. And don't worry, it'll all come out in the wash!

All my love,
Fiona xxx

Perhaps, thought Mina, the letter was about George getting rid of her baby. But why did Jimmy have it? She rifled through the rest of the box's contents and pulled out a photograph. She didn't hear the feet on the stairs. She only heard the scrape of the door handle. Her stomach falling, she shoved the photograph into a stocking top, slid the box back under the bed and stood up. Jimmy, shoeless for some reason and holding his hat, smiled at her and raised his eyebrows enquiringly.

'Back already?' she said. 'You'll think me awfully careless, but I've lost an earring and I've searched and searched! I thought maybe it had got stuck to the sole of someone's shoe or something, so I'm having a quick look on all the floors. It's my favourite pair, too.'

'You've got dust on your nice skirt,' he said, pointing to her knee. 'My fault. I said I didn't want that old bag, the cleaner, coming in here, poking around. You can't trust foreigners, can you?'

Mina stepped forward to leave, but Jimmy closed the door quietly behind him. 'So did you find it, then? Can I help you look?'

'Find what? Oh, my earring. No, don't worry. I think it might have fallen out at work, when I was changing into my uniform.'

He gazed at her. 'You're quite the little storyteller, aren't you? Why don't you tell me what you're really looking for?'

'I just did, silly!' Nonchalantly she brushed some dust off her skirt and said: 'Well, I won't keep you.' He said nothing, just kept looking at her. His expression was calm. But she saw an odd glint in his eye, as if in spite of her breeziness he knew she was frightened. She quickly opened the door and walked down the first flight of stairs, then ran until she'd reached Saul's rooms.

Jimmy dropped his hat on the bed. He glanced towards the door, then took the pistol holster from the inside pocket of his overcoat, placing it carefully on the bedside table. I'll put it back tomorrow, he thought. Hopefully Robbie wouldn't even notice it had gone. Anyway, he'd probably have lent it to Jimmy if he'd asked. But it wasn't like borrowing a scarf or a book. He'd need to offer a reason, and what could he say? That he was supposed to take the motor car back, but ever since Saul gave him the third degree in the pub, he'd been gripped by a dreadful paranoia? Obviously Jimmy couldn't tell Robbie why he felt nervous going to east London, not without coming clean about everything. And it wasn't the right time for that. Not yet.

When the right time came, though, Robbie would understand. Jimmy was sure of it. So long as he explained everything. Put across his side of the story. For once, he thought with satisfaction, someone would listen to his side of the story.

He sat down and his racing heart began to slow. What was Mina hoping to find? Did she suspect his and Robbie's affair? Or – he wasn't sure which was worse – was Saul properly on to him?

Paul was expecting his motor car back tonight. Jimmy had promised. But going anywhere near his old area, even with Robbie's gun as protection, now felt laden with doom.

'Mina, what's happened?' said Saul when he saw her flushed excited face. 'Sit down. I'll get you a drink.'

'I went in Jimmy's room. You know, to snoop.'

She carried on talking, and he didn't interrupt until she began explaining that Jimmy had caught her almost red-handed. 'Oh no, Mina, he—'

'Nothing happened!' she reassured him. 'He was definitely suspicious, but I made up an excuse.'

Saul exhaled. 'You say nothing happened, but think of what could have happened! I can't have you putting yourself in danger like this. I simply can't. It's not worth it.'

'No, but it was worth it, because look.' She produced the photo and they both stared at it. A freckle-faced young lad in shirtsleeves and braces was posing with a bicycle, smiling, a tuft of hair escaping a neatly combed side-parting to fall on his forehead. On the brick wall behind him was an advertisement for Turf cigarettes, next to half a shop sign.

'Lavner's Domestic Store,' said Saul. 'It was in Stepney. Still is.'

The boy was unmistakably Jimmy, aged fourteen or fifteen.

'But he looks sweet, doesn't he?' said Mina sadly. 'I wonder what happened.'

Saul reached for the bottle to refresh her drink and pour one for himself. 'You girls don't have locks on your doors, do you?'

'No. I can't say I've ever given it a second thought. Do you think I ought to warn George?'

'Let's wait,' he said. 'We need to be absolutely certain, before we throw the cat . . . where do we throw the cat?'

'Amongst the pigeons,' supplied Mina. 'But then, once we're sure, what will you do? Will you make Honor kick him out?'

But that wouldn't be enough, thought Saul. He'd leave here, and then what? Unless he was stopped altogether, he'd go and do harm elsewhere. It wasn't simply a matter of vengeance, although Saul felt almost overpowered by that impetus. By the thought of how different his life might have been. But what's done is done, he thought. What mattered now was the present, the future. If he saw the threat Jack posed – and he did, there was no escaping it – wouldn't failing to act be the immoral choice?

13

More Than a Frisson

That night, no one at 42 Tregunter Road slept well.

Before getting into bed, Mina pushed her chest of drawers in front of the door and tucked a small sharp knife under her pillow. Saul had told her to keep it with her at all times, 'just in case'. She didn't need telling twice. Still, she drifted in and out of light sleep, avoiding bad dreams.

Saul, the photograph of young Jimmy in his coat pocket, walked to Gloucester Road Underground station and got on an eastbound District Line train. He didn't return until after two o'clock in the morning.

Honor hadn't slept properly in weeks, and she'd just been turned down for a new mortgage on the house. The bank manager had been quite intransigent. Wasn't there a male relative, he'd enquired, who might serve as co-applicant? He had the decency to look embarrassed, but what good did that do her? She had hoped to pay Jimmy off once and for all. Not only that: yesterday a letter had arrived from Rebecca Levene, the woman who owned Saul's Chagall painting. Mrs Levene, who had inherited the painting from her father, had always refused to sell it. Now she was emigrating to Israel with her family and apparently needed money. So she was putting *Gila with Delphiniums* on the market and giving Honor first refusal, at the precise moment she was newly penniless. How God loved a joke.

When midnight came and went, Robbie got up and knocked for Jimmy in his usual way. He saw the line of light along the bottom of the door and heard Jimmy saying, 'Shh!' then laughing. A female voice said something anxious, imploring – the tone was clear, even if the words were unintelligible. Robbie returned to his own bed and curled up in a ball. He stayed like that all night, rigid and wakeful. At six o'clock he got dressed and, in some sort of fugue state, went into Jimmy's room. In the narrow bed, George was asleep on her side, mouth slightly open and blonde hair fanned on the pillow like a halo. Her plump shoulders were bare, and a fraying black strap slipped down one arm. Where her neck met her chest, the skin was deeply flushed. Next to her Jimmy lay on his back, eyelashes casting jagged shadows on his cheeks, one arm slung above his head. His broad tuft of reddish underarm hair gleamed damply. Suddenly, Robbie got the feeling Jimmy wasn't really asleep, that he was enjoying the sensation of Robbie standing there, staring at them both. The faintest of smirks played on his lips. George, though, definitely wasn't pretending. She made rhythmic little snuffles as she breathed, and a sparkle of drool slid from the corner of her mouth.

Robbie was about to walk away when he noticed, from the corner of his eye, his leather gun holster on Jimmy's bedside table. He hadn't noticed it missing. But he couldn't reach across and take it, not without waking George. I'll retrieve it later, he thought, leaving the room with a light tread and closing the door silently behind him.

He had no idea what to do with himself. But he couldn't just sit still. So he put his coat on and went out into the bright frosty morning. He walked for maybe half an hour, his stomach aching and his thoughts slow and repetitive. Nothing made the least bit of sense – except, he realised, his own foolishness. He'd ignored what his gut was telling him, believed Jimmy's lies, and now reality had smacked him in the face.

On his return, he found Honor in the kitchen, sitting with a cup of tea and a cigarette. She didn't usually smoke at breakfast. 'You're up early,' he said.

'I might say the same to you. Where have you been at this hour?'

'I couldn't sleep.' He sat down and indicated her cigarettes. 'Could I pinch one?'

For a few minutes they sat and smoked in silence. Then Robbie said: 'Oh, you were right, by the way. About George and Jimmy having a frisson. It's a bit more than a frisson, if the fact she spent the night in his room is anything to go by.' He wondered if Honor heard the spite in his voice.

'Oh Robbie, tell me you're joking!'

'Never been more serious in my life.' He ground out his cigarette. 'She was pregnant five minutes ago, too. She had an abortion. You'd think she might, you know, curb her sociableness for a brief time. But no.'

'Pregnant how? From whom?'

'Not Jimmy, it pre-dated him. One of her many other conquests. Who can keep up?'

Honor wanted to get a drink of water, but her legs felt weak. 'I'm afraid words fail me,' she said. 'Is she all right? Was the abortion done in a hospital?'

Robbie shrugged. 'No idea.' He stood up. 'Might as well get on with some work, I suppose.'

Honor knew Robbie didn't much like George, but she was

surprised by his indifference. As for Jimmy, she thought, is he trying to hurt me through George? Not that he understood, of course, what he'd done. Neither of them did.

All day Robbie worked with a strange focus and efficiency, while Honor drifted in and out of the office. If his rejection notes were a little more barbed, a little terser than usual, that couldn't be helped.

He changed his mind hour to hour, minute to minute, about how to act when he saw Jimmy. He liked the idea of cutting him dead, remaining blank and stoical. At the same time, he longed to hear him explain himself. Apologise, even. He was owed that much, surely?

When he finished work that evening, Robbie's legs carried him to the King's Arms practically of their own volition. Jimmy was sitting at the bar, reading the *Daily Express* and eating an apple, a full pint at his elbow. He turned and smiled as Robbie slid onto the stool beside him.

'I just wanted to know,' said Robbie, 'why you couldn't be honest with me about you and George. Why was that so hard?'

Jimmy closed and folded his newspaper. 'Honest about what? What are you talking about?'

'I know you and George are sleeping together. I saw her in your bed last night.'

Jimmy took a sip of his pint and carefully set it down again, as if composing himself. 'Look, it's not what you think. We're just pals, me and George. She needs a friend, after all that horrible business with . . . you know. That's all.'

Robbie swallowed. 'I thought you liked me. At least, I thought you respected me enough to be honest. Really, it's fine. I'm not going to crumble into a thousand pieces. So you're having an affair with George. Fine. Let's have it all out in the open. What I can't stand is being laughed at behind my back.'

'Okay, listen. Last night, George came up to my room because—'

But Robbie couldn't bear to hear it. Heat suffused his face and a buzzing sound filled his head. 'You know what, forget it. I don't need an explanation. Just stay out of my way in the future. Do me that kindness, please.' He got to his feet and swiped at an itch on his cheek. He realised it was a tear. Embarrassment was too inadequate a word to describe the shrinking of his soul as he left the pub – convinced, whether it was true or not, that every pair of eyes in the place was fixed upon him.

14

Back in the Saddle

'What on earth are you talking about?' said George when Honor enquired how long she'd been involved with Jimmy. Honor had ambushed the girl as she came home, smelling of drink even though it was barely 5 p.m.

'If you must know,' said Honor, 'Robbie told me. Living on top of each other the way we are, surely you didn't think you could keep it a secret?'

'Robbie's got it wrong,' said George irritably. What did he mean, she wondered, by telling tales to Honor?

'You promised. You promised you'd keep away from him.'

'I suppose I did. I'd almost forgotten, it was weeks ago.' She was so tired. 'But does it really matter so much if Jimmy and I are chums? He's not interested in me in *that* way, so you needn't worry.'

Honor looked at George. She was pale and thinner than usual; her skin had lost that velvety plumpness and her lips had cracks at the corners. But nothing could hide her beauty. Jimmy not interested in her in *that* way – Honor had never heard anything so ridiculous in all her born days.

George had heard of girls who were themselves again in no time, who got straight back in the saddle. But for days and days after the abortion it took real effort just to drag herself about. She felt gloomy every time she looked in the mirror: her cheeks had deflated and her under-eyes were bluish-grey, as though swiped by charcoal. Even her hair, usually shiny and bouncy, looked like old string. After she brushed it, many long strands were left in the bristles. She felt exhausted, yet she slept poorly, waking with a vertiginous lurch from dreams where some version of Dr Jenkins was looming over her with his instruments. In those moments the smell of him, of that horrible flat, would seem to linger in her nose. Every morning she layered on powder and rouge until she was halfway presentable – so long as you didn't get too close. And every afternoon, whether or not she'd been to work or to see friends, she lay on her bed (the mattress now flipped), her limbs like dead weights. In these moments, time seemed to slow down. Her mind emptied out as she listened to the blood moving sluggishly through her veins, the very workings of her circulatory system an exertion too far.

Ten days after her visit to Battersea, she began to feel slightly more energetic and remembered that she ought to buy Jimmy some new towels. She went to Peter Jones, and on her return she took the shopping bag up to the attic, planning to leave it on the landing for him. But as soon as she set the bag down, he opened his door.

'New towels,' she said. 'Sorry I didn't replace them sooner.'

'You didn't have to do that. Are you busy? Come in for a minute.'

She peered past him into the tiny room. 'Oh, I . . .'

'I've been hoping to bump into you. I didn't want to intrude by knocking on your door, but I wondered how you were doing. After . . . you know.' He held the door open for her. 'Don't tell anyone, but it's my birthday today.'

'Happy birthday!' She sat on the edge of the bed.

He smiled embarrassedly. 'You won't mention it to anyone else, will you? I don't want any fuss. Anyway, how are you feeling? You still look a bit fragile.'

'Definitely still a bit fragile. But on the mend.'

'Do you know if things will be okay? When you decide to have babies, I mean.'

After a surprised pause, George said: 'I suppose only time will tell.' Her theoretical future fecundity was the last thing on her mind. 'But no, I'm sure I'll be fine. I'm just really tired at the moment, that's all. It's probably a touch of anaemia.'

'You want to drink Guinness. It's full of iron. And eat spinach, like Popeye.'

She made a face. 'Ugh, no thanks to both. I'd far sooner eat a few steaks.'

'By the way, we're breaking the rules, aren't we? Socialising together, I mean.'

She opened her mouth, hesitated. 'Wait, what *do* you mean?'

'Mrs Wilson doesn't want me anywhere near you, by the sounds of it.'

'Right,' said George slowly. 'That was my impression. But what exactly did she say to you?'

'She said nothing. She sent Mr Reznikov to have a word. Man to man, like.'

'Really? How very Jane Austen. Did he say why he'd been entrusted with this mission?'

'He didn't, no. I ought to have asked. I just think . . . I think

Mrs Wilson doesn't want me here. And doesn't want me getting my feet under the table, as it were.'

'Oh, I'm sure that she—'

'It's all right. I don't care.' He looked at her, pensive. Then he grinned. 'So those two. Mrs Wilson and Mr Reznikov. Are they . . . you know?'

George raised her eyebrows. 'Are they what?' She smiled. 'I'm only teasing. I really mustn't say.'

'Oh, come on!' Jimmy's voice was mock-outraged. He pressed George's knee imploringly. 'You have to tell me now.'

'I don't believe it, personally. But according to gossip, they were once an item. Before my time. I just can't see it. Can you?' Before he could answer, she exhaled and said: 'Do you know, I feel a bit dizzy. I think my little outing to Peter Jones has tired me out. How ridiculous.'

'You are an odd colour, you know. Here, lie down. That's the best thing if you think you're going to faint.'

George kicked her shoes off and did as he suggested. She closed her eyes. If she kept her head perfectly still, the woozy sensation lessened. She must have drifted off, because she didn't remember Jimmy lying down next to her and gently embracing her from behind. It felt so relaxing and safe that she drifted off again. When she opened her eyes, the room was in semi-darkness. She gazed at the skylight, deep sapphire with a murky smudge of moon, and remembered where she was. She must have been asleep for some time.

'Gosh,' she said, yawning. 'I do apologise. I must have fallen into a properly deep sleep. I've not been sleeping at all well lately. But that was glorious. I can hardly open my eyes; I feel like a newborn kitten.' She still had her back to Jimmy and turned round to face him. Their noses were a couple of inches apart; she looked at his thick eyebrows and a tiny round scar on his left cheekbone, then into his eyes. She closed hers again and waited for him to kiss her – which he did, but on the forehead, in a brotherly sort of way, which wasn't the idea at all. Stretching and yawning, she positioned herself so that her thighs were pressed against his. 'Everything's all right now, you know,' she whispered. 'All shipshape. In case you were—'

'Shh,' he said, wrapping his arms around her and bringing her head to lie on his chest. 'You don't have to be like that with me.'

George burrowed her nose into his shirt. She tried to remember the last time she'd been alone with a man, let alone in a bed situation, and he hadn't tried to get her clothes off. Certainly, it was before she grew breasts. A discomfiting feeling expanded in her ribs, not quite shame but something akin to it. She disentangled herself. 'I'd better go,' she said lightly.

Jimmy, sitting up, nodded wistfully and didn't try to detain her.

A few nights later, George was lying in bed ruminating on Jimmy's surprising gallantry, or restraint, or whatever it was. She kept tossing and turning; every time she edged near drowsiness, some irrepressible inner agitation made her eyes fly open. Would no man ever want her again? Was she shop-soiled, sterile, her body's subliminal signals no longer guaranteeing the usual enthusiastic advances? True, at times it had been onerous, dealing with male attention. That was putting it mildly. They simply had no compunction or scruples – this was the astonishing thing one learnt, all too early in one's romantic career. George had been twelve, still a child in every sense, when she began noticing a predatory gleam in men's eyes. And not only hormonal youths, but older men whom she'd considered ancient, paternal.

Surely those days weren't over already?

She got out of bed, removed her sleepwear of moth-eaten pullover and knee-length drawers, and slipped on a black negligee. It was an old garment, frayed and not quite clean. But she had nothing else suitable.

Her head clear and determined, she padded up the stairs and tapped on Jimmy's door. He opened it immediately, almost as though he'd been expecting her. He wore only cotton undershorts, his chest bare. Yet he looked startled. 'George, whatever's the matter? Are you ill?'

'I've never felt better. I just can't sleep. And I had such a lovely nap with you the other day. You don't mind, do you, if . . .'

'Oh . . . well, I suppose . . . yes, of course.' He drew her in and closed the door. 'Though we ought to—'

'I'll disappear first thing, don't fret.' She flung herself down on the bed and lay on her side, propping up her head with a fist.

There was another tap at the door.

'Who could that—' George began.

Jimmy, shrugging and smiling, told her in urgent tones to shush.

'But supposing something's happened?'

'Nothing's happened,' whispered Jimmy. 'Come on, let's get some sleep.'

'I know you don't allow unmarried carryings-on under your roof,' said George to Honor now. 'I certainly shouldn't want to break the rules!'

Honor lifted Lulu the dog into her lap and caressed her little head. 'George, I never, ever wanted you to hear this. You must believe me. I'm desperately sorry.'

George lit a cigarette and looked at her, confused. 'Sorry about . . .'

'I'm afraid there's no other way to say it. Jimmy is your brother.'

Friday 15 May 1953

'You mentioned on my last visit,' said DI Hilary Comyns, 'that Mr Sullivan talked about having acquired a lady friend.'

'That's correct,' said Miss Patricia Lapham, Probation Officer for Inner London. A plainish, youngish woman with a crispy permanent wave and an industrious air, she addressed Hilary politely but without particular deference. We are both busy law-enforcement professionals, her manner said. 'I encouraged it. He's the type of lad who'd greatly benefit from the influence of a sensible girl. Settling down and getting married can work wonders, you know. I was also helping him apply to take a City and Guilds qualification. He was interested in fashion design.' She said this with a note of indignation, as though she took Mr Sullivan's betrayal – if betrayal it was – more personally than the abscondment of an ex-con with less refined aspirations.

'Do you recall anything else he shared about his girlfriend?'

'Well, as I said before, I don't remember his mentioning her by name. Only that she was very beautiful and worked as some type of model. Now that I'm repeating this to you, I realise it sounds fanciful. But I didn't get the impression he was making it up. And in my line of work, one's intuition for lies becomes acute. In yours too, of course, Detective Inspector.'

15

I'll Swing For You

'My *brother*?' George stared at Honor, waiting for her to laugh, to say she was joking.

'He is also a criminal, in prison until very recently. So as you see, it's rather vital that you—'

The doorbell rang and they both started. George began speaking, but Honor shushed her. Greta's heavy footsteps were heard as she went to answer the door, then muffled voices as she spoke to the visitor.

'It sounds like a woman, doesn't it?' said Honor. 'George, go and have a peep out the window and see who it is.'

Who cares! thought George, desperate to resume their conversation. But she did as Honor asked, then came and sat back down. 'It's just a girl. A chum of Mina's maybe. She's standing there waiting. Rather rude of Greta not to ask her in.'

'Oh, you know Greta. Marvellously unencumbered by decorum. Really, she's wasted on us. She'd be a great asset to the prison service, I've always thought.'

'Anyway, you were saying. Jimmy—'

Greta stuck her head round the door. 'A young lady wanted to know if Jack lives here. I said, you mean Jimmy? Is Jack another name for Jimmy? I thought Jimmy was nickname for James.'

Honor concealed her consternation with an expression that said: why are you bothering us with this?

'I look for Jimmy but cannot find him,' Greta went on. 'She say she will come back later.'

'Well, we'll mention it to him when we see him,' said George briskly. 'Surely it's your home time, Greta? We mustn't keep you.'

'She was pretty,' pursued Greta. 'Not pretty like you, George. But attractive, clean. Good clothes. Maybe she's Jimmy's girlfriend?'

'But you said she asked for Jack?' said Honor. 'Sounds like she had the wrong house.'

'George, what's the matter?' said Greta. 'Are you not feeling well?' The girl looked like she'd seen an *apparition*, she thought.

Honor stood up. 'Greta, when did you last see Jimmy?'

'It's opening time,' said George. 'He'll be at the King's Arms. But Honor, I really—'

As Greta left the room, Honor murmured: 'I'm sorry, George. I'm so sorry. We'll talk about this later, I promise. You won't tell anyone, will you? No, of course you won't. I'm sorry,' she repeated. 'I must go.'

Honor speed-walked over to the Fulham Road. From a hundred or so yards away, she saw Robbie leaving the pub, looking extraordinarily glum. She was about to raise a hand in greeting when he crossed the road, seemingly to avoid her. How peculiar.

Inside, Jimmy was sitting at the bar with a half-drunk pint of beer, talking to the barmaid. 'Elsie!' he said. 'What are you drinking?'

'Don't call me that. I'll swing for you, so help me God I will. Get me a whisky. I'll be over there.'

She sat in a booth and lit a cigarette. For the first time since Jack's return, anger was surpassing anxiety.

'So,' he said, bringing their drinks over. 'To what do I owe the—'

'You said no one knew where to find you.' She took a large sip. 'That was the whole point. No one is even meant to know you've been released. So why did someone just come to the house asking for Jack?'

He looked disbelieving. 'Who did? What did he look like?'

'She. Greta answered the door. Said she was young and pretty.'

'Oh.' He half preened, half shrugged. 'What are you worried about, then?'

'If she knows, whoever she is, then who else knows? I can't have this. I just can't. Imagine if Saul found out. He's already curious about you.'

'He won't find out, though, will he? Not unless you tell him, and you're not going to do that.' Jimmy leant back and raised his eyebrows, challenging her to say otherwise. 'Anyway, if it weren't for your rotten husband, none of it would have happened.' And if Thomas hadn't been the first adult to give him any attention, to act like he mattered a measly jot, Jimmy might not have been so willing to do his bidding. 'You knew what he was like,' he went on, warming to his theme, 'but you still told him about the cash next door.' Saul losing his wife and child was Elsie's fault, thought Jimmy. And he himself lost the best years of his life. What did she lose? Nothing. 'Then you sodded off and left me to rot in prison. For fourteen years. Can you even imagine how that feels?'

It was meant to be thirty years, thought Honor. She remembered the night Jack turned up at Tregunter Road. The gut-punch shock of it. No one had informed her of his release. Then again, she wasn't easy to trace. So how had Jack managed it?

'They let you out, then?' she'd asked, sitting down next to him in the drawing room. She didn't know what else to say. He looked the same, she thought with amazement. Taller, and broader, but the same.

'No,' he said. 'Someone sent me a cake with a file baked in. Course they let me out.'

'But . . .'

'But why?' He smiled. 'Wouldn't you like to know.'

'Actually, Jack, I don't care.' She rubbed her right temple. 'You're out for good, though? That's it; you've served your sentence?'

He nodded. At HMP Brixton, he said, he'd befriended a man of around his own age, Ronald Macneice. Ronald worked for his father-in-law, Albert Cooper, a prolific racketeer whose enterprises snaked like a vascular system through the West End underworld. (Honor had heard of this man – everyone had – but she remained blank-faced.) Scotland Yard were building a case against Cooper, apparently, and had tried to make Ronald turn Queen's Evidence. 'When he wouldn't, the bastards trumped up a charge against him,' said Jack. 'Claimed he'd burnt down an amusement arcade for the insurance.'

'Heaven forfend,' said Honor.

The evidence Scotland Yard possessed of Ronald's primary activities, namely running illegal baccarat clubs, was insufficient to use as convincing leverage. But as he told Jack, not only were these establishments unlicenced for gambling, they also existed solely to disunite wealthy men from their fortunes. 'And there was me,' said Honor, 'thinking that only decent, honest people ran gambling dens.' Even Jack, cloistered from society since 1939, had heard of some of the toffs and tycoons who'd lost tens of thousands of pounds in a single night at Ronald's tables but were too embarrassed – or too frightened they'd be prosecuted for gambling – to go to the police. The main trick that duped them: playing cards whose marks signalling high, low, or zero were invisible unless you knew exactly what to look for. Honor had to concede it sounded clever.

She wondered what Jack had done to invite these confidences, whether his friendship with this Ronald had been genuine. As a child, he was never popular with other boys. Or maybe it was more that he'd chosen to keep himself aloof. There was one boy who was his special friend, she remembered – a chubby little lad who was incessantly picked on. But not by Jack, who got into scraps on his behalf. Paul Linton, that was his name. Goodness knew what became of him.

'People have this idea,' said Jack, 'that men in prison don't talk about their crimes. What rubbish. They barely talk about anything else. Anyway, I knew what the information was worth, didn't I?'

'Loyal to a fault,' said Honor.

'Oh, you want to talk about loyalty?'

'Not really, no. Go on.'

Previously, he said, Ronald had been willing to go to prison for eighteen months rather than turn on his overlord and father-in-law. But were he faced with a much longer sentence, it would likely be a different story. Jack had a suspicion that Scotland Yard would deem collaring Albert Cooper, who had eluded prosecution for decades, worth the price of his own halved sentence. 'I was right, wasn't I? Not just a pretty face, you see. Naturally, my release is hush-hush. I'm going by a new name. Just in case. And who would ever come looking for me here? It was hard enough for me to find you.'

'How did you?'

He ignored the question. 'Nice of you, by the way, to keep in touch.'

She started to speak, but he cut her off. 'Do you know, in fourteen years I didn't have a single visitor? And the only person who ever wrote to me was Mum. Then she died, and there was no one. Got anything to drink?'

She got up to pour them drinks. He continued: 'I heard Mrs Cohen died, too. Pneumonia, was it? Shame.'

'Exactly, you've served your time,' said Honor now. 'So why don't you move on with your life? You could go abroad. America, anywhere.'

'I could. That sounds like a good plan, actually. I'd need proper money, of course. To pay for my passage, set myself up once I'm there. Maybe I'll buy a business. A little going concern.'

Honor blew a thin stream of smoke from the corner of her mouth. 'The bank said no to the loan,' she said. 'So that's it for money. You've cleaned me out. There's no point in you hanging around any longer. And whatever's going on with George, it stops now.'

'Look, I can't help it if I'm irresistible, can I?'

She looked at him curiously. Did he think she'd be jealous, or fearful that he'd take George away from her? Or did he imagine that she'd want to protect the girl, and therefore be extra motivated, financially speaking, to be rid of him?

'I'm being serious,' she said. 'It's time you moved on. I want you gone by midnight. Tell the world my secrets if you want. I don't care any more.'

‘That’s not fair. At least give me time to fix up somewhere else to stay. Be reasonable, Elsie.’

‘I’ve been more than reasonable.’

He got a look on his face she’d seen before, but not in decades: petulant, defiant, and pitiable all at once. ‘You know, I did loads of reading in prison.’ He tipped an ice cube into his mouth and crunched it, frowning. ‘Especially about the law. Did you know the average sentence for bigamy is nine months?’

‘I’m sorry, I don’t follow.’ He may be bluffing, she thought. Don’t make it easy for him.

He made a clucking sound of disapproval. ‘Poor old Thomas. Do you think it gives him comfort, as he lives out his days eating prison slop and sleeping in an eight-by-six cage, that he’s still got a wife on the outside?’

She opened her mouth to speak. He held up a warning finger. ‘Trouble is, any widow’s inheritance would be invalidated. That’s the house and Mr Wilson’s war pension. No more house, no more lodgers. The income from your little magazine isn’t much, is it? I suppose you might apply for a waitress position at a Lyons, like in the old days. Then again, they prefer younger girls in those places. You might have to go out skivvying. I suppose it was good enough for Mum.’

There was a terrible pause. Then Honor said: ‘You don’t know what you’re talking about.’ She’d meant to sound dismissive. But panic was seeping out. Her fingertips tingled. She fought the urge to stub out her cigarette on the back of his hand. Straightening her spine, she shifted back in her seat. ‘You know nothing about my life. Nothing. So don’t you dare think you can threaten me. If you ever—’

‘Or you’ll do what?’ said Jimmy with a mocking grimace. A part of him recognised this fight as senseless, understood that he’d be better off simply disappearing. But another part remained a terrified boy sitting alone in a cell, knowing his sister was swanning round London and never giving him a second thought. In the opinion of that terrified boy, the score wasn't yet even.

It was a good question, thought Honor. She'd do what? 'Why don't you go and pack your things?' Her tone hovered between furious and mollifying. 'Pack your things, get out of my house, and forget you ever had a sister.'

For some time Robbie had been lying on his bed, his face jammed into a pillow, thinking that he ought to start packing his things. He could find a cheap hotel, he supposed, just for a couple of nights, whilst he decided what to do. If he took a suitcase tonight, he could ask Honor to put his remaining worldly goods, such as they were, into store. Perhaps he'd go abroad. A bonus inducement to fleeing the country: it was Easter next Sunday. He'd be expected in Dorking. Gathering the family to celebrate Christ's resurrection was one of his mother's stalwart expectations, which one defied at one's peril. The prospect of sitting down to lunch with his sisters and their husbands – tedious, unappetising specimens all – and their innumerable snotty-nosed offspring made Robbie feel murderous.

But the real point of escaping to France, Italy, Spain – it hardly mattered where – was knowing he could walk down any street and never bump into Jimmy or George.

He looked at his wristwatch: nearly seven o'clock. Jimmy would be in the pub for a while yet, but at some point he might come home for supper. I'd better go down to the office now, thought Robbie. Get my address book and other odds and sods whilst the coast is clear.

To his horror, as he placed his hand on the banister, he heard

Jimmy coming up the stairs. Robbie turned back, and as he did so, Jimmy stopped on the second-floor landing and rapped on a door. 'Come in!' trilled George, obviously expecting him.

An alarming heat suffused Robbie's temples, his forehead. He had to sit down, right there on the carpeted stair, to steady himself. Am I ill? he wondered. Has all this torment caused an aneurysm? But no, he realised after a moment or two. This wasn't an aneurysm. It was rage. Unclouded, ungovernable rage.

George heard a soft knock on her door. 'Come in!' she called, assuming it was Mina or Honor. 'Oh!' She jumped to her feet from her sitting position on the settee. 'Jimmy. Hullo. Is everything all right?'

'Sorry to disturb you. I was just at the pub with Honor, and—'

'She told you too?' George blurted the words out.

'May I?' He indicated the straight-backed chair by the dressing table. She nodded and he pulled it closer. 'Yeah. Says I've got to leave tonight.' He sat down. 'She discussed it with you, then?'

'I beg your pardon? I mean – sorry, Honor's kicking you out? Why?'

He sighed. 'Oh, I dunno. She's sick of me, I expect. Everyone always gets sick of me. It's just . . . I like it here. I like all of you.' He crossed his legs and glanced towards the window. What he didn't say – couldn't say – was that he wasn't lonely any more, and it felt miraculous. 'I was wondering – d'you think you could talk to her, ask her to let me stay, even just for another week? She'd listen to you. She admires you, thinks the world of you, everyone says so.'

George sat back down heavily. She looked at her stockinged feet, then at Jimmy. She remembered trying to seduce him, sleeping pressed up against him, and felt ill. 'I'm awfully sorry,' she said. 'But I couldn't possibly get involved. Honor makes her own decisions when it comes to the household. It's not my place to interfere. I'm sure you understand.'

He came and sat next to her. 'I do understand, of course. It wouldn't hurt to try, though, would it? I'd be no end grateful.' Even by tomorrow, he thought, Robbie might have calmed down. Then Jimmy would make him see the truth, clear up this farcical misunderstanding.

George said nothing, just tilted her head and considered him with a sort of chilly contempt. As though he were a bothersome stranger. He felt his face flush with humiliation. 'How about this,' he said lightly. 'We could do each other a favour. Obviously I'd never think of telling anyone about your little . . . your little mishap. Because there'd be trouble if I did, wouldn't there? Your friend, what's her name, Fiona? The one who wrote to you. She might get two years. Life is the maximum, but in this day and age that's not likely. The doctor will be in the most trouble. Dr Jenkins, isn't it? You'll be seen as more of a victim than anything else. I reckon you'd get six months. Possibly the sentence will even be suspended. Except it'll be in all the papers, won't it? I can see the headlines now: Society Beauties in the Dock for Procurement of Abortion.'

George got to her feet and stared down at him. The ceiling light accentuated the rings around his eyes and cast a yellowish glow on his cheeks. He stared back at her, no longer vulnerable but closed off, remote. She was frightened and also incensed, on the brink of tearful hysterics or physical violence. 'How dare you,' she almost whispered. 'Get out. Get out of my sight.'

Jimmy lifted his hand to knock on Robbie's door, then hesitated. Maybe first he'd talk to Honor. If she dug her heels in, he'd ask

Robbie to leave with him tonight. After setting him straight, of course, about George. Maybe Robbie could get the truth from the horse's mouth. She'd certainly want to quash the rumour! Except, of course, he'd probably rather die than raise the subject with her. But if Jimmy suggested – pleaded – that he do so, wouldn't that be evidence enough? The thought was cheering, and he went downstairs with a lightened heart.

Part 2

16

No Proof We're Lying

Jimmy lay on his front on the drawing room rug. His face was in profile and a thick scarlet cloud expanded over his upper back. His visible eyelid flickered and his body gently convulsed.

'Oughtn't we try to stop the bleeding?' said Mina. 'Aren't you meant to apply pressure or something?'

'Is he – is he still alive?' said Robbie. Muscles can keep twitching like that after death, he thought. But Mina was right: they should stanch the wound. So why was he rooted to the spot like a useless bystander?

'I know,' said George, 'we'll check his breathing.' She produced a compact from her handbag and held it to Jimmy's slackened mouth. 'I can't tell! Honor, can you?'

Honor peered dubiously at the mirror. 'I think Robbie's right. I think he's dead.'

Saul rolled up his shirtsleeve and lifted Jimmy's hand, pressing two fingers inside his wrist. 'Maybe a faint pulse?' he said. 'Difficult to judge.'

The blood continued to bloom across the rug, a flower growing in fast motion. Jimmy's upper body suddenly lurched. His eye rolled back in his head. Then he was still.

They looked at each other, sensing shared guilt – but also, perhaps, relief.

At length, Honor said: 'I don't know about anyone else. But I can't help wondering if we should deal with this privately.'

Saul said: 'You mean . . .'

Robbie swallowed and took a step back, away from the body.

'We could telephone the police, of course,' said George. 'There'd be a huge kerfuffle. And what good would it do? The police can't bring him back, can they? And they might completely misinterpret the situation.'

'But the body,' said Mina. 'What will we do with his body?'

Saul looked at his wristwatch. 'It's after ten. Soon, everyone in the neighbourhood will be in bed. No one will see if we put him in the Anderson shelter. Just while we decide what to do.'

'Honor, your poor rug!' said Mina.

'I know,' said Honor. 'I think even Greta will have met her match with this stain.'

'Do you suppose anyone will come looking for him?' Mina looked anxiously at Honor.

She drew on her cigarette. 'It's a good question. I'll think about how best to handle it.'

George blurted: 'You told me he was a criminal, Honor. Does that mean—'

'A *criminal*?' said Robbie. 'What sort of—'

'The worst sort,' said Saul, with an air of conclusiveness. 'He was in prison, and not for long enough.'

Robbie opened his mouth, but Honor spoke first: 'Maybe we'll get rid of his things and say he moved out. Or simply claim he never came home tonight.'

'You were at the pub with him this evening, weren't you?' said George. 'Does that mean you'll be considered the last person to see him alive?'

She was surprisingly calm in a crisis, thought Honor. 'Well, possibly, yes. But the important thing is that we agree on a version of events, and all back each other up should we ever be required to. That way, there'll be no proof we're lying.'

George put her arm around Mina, who rested her head on the taller girl's shoulder.

'Honor's right,' she said. 'So long as we stick together, everything will be fine.'

Robbie looked at George, then at Jimmy's feet, which remained neatly shod. One trouser leg had ridden up, exposing a worn-through sliver of sock where the shoe rubbed against his heel. 'Sorry,' muttered Robbie. 'Sorry, I . . .' As he bolted from the room, George came out after him, asking if he was all right. Halfway up the staircase, Robbie turned round and started saying yes, he was fine, but then he said: 'George, what did he do? What was the crime, I mean?'

They stood there, each with a steadying hand on the banister. 'I've no idea,' she said. 'I take it he didn't mention anything to you?'

Robbie shook his head and sat down awkwardly. 'Nor you? Even though you two were . . .'

'Were what?' Her voice was sharp.

'Well, I mean, you were . . .' His brain ached inside his skull, and the right words eluded him. 'Having a sort of affair.'

Now George sat down too, a few steps below him. Frowning, she pulled her knees to her chest and stuck her chin out. 'Is that what he claimed?'

'No, I . . . It doesn't matter.'

'But it does matter! We were having nothing of the sort. He

was kind to me when I was in a tricky spot, and once I spent the night in his bed because . . . oh, I don't know, I was feeling insecure and wanted company. But we just slept, like children.' She wasn't sure why it seemed so important to convince him. After all, he didn't know Jimmy was her brother.

Robbie had the oddest expression on his face, and George went on: 'It sounds silly, I know. It's perfectly true, though.'

He stood up. 'Tell the others I'll be back downstairs in a moment. I just need to . . .' But he hurried upstairs without finishing his sentence.

17

Physique Pictorial

On Saturday morning, the entire household overslept. Unsurprisingly so: last night's group effort had taken more time and energy than anyone had anticipated.

Once Jimmy was deposited in the Anderson shelter, they mopped and scrubbed the drawing room's parquet floor, refilling buckets of hot water and bleach until squeezing the mop left the water barely pink. In the end, the wood looked perfectly clean. But whether an application of luminol might reveal vestiges of blood, no one was sure. (Mina provided a lesson in this key tool in the detective's arsenal, courtesy of film thriller plots.) A replacement rug would be acquired, Honor promised. Everyone insisted they'd chip in for the cost. It was bizarrely reassuring, thought Robbie, the feeling of cooperation that had enveloped them. As in wartime, strife and fear made for unlikely collaborators.

A siege-like mood spilled into the weekend. For the moment, it was agreed, no visitors would be admitted. Since nobody felt much like going out, nor being alone, they ate their meals together and passed the time playing cards and charades. Mina even called in sick to the cinema. (She, who'd never been ill in her life. Like most healthy people she regarded the very idea of illness with scepticism.)

It was Robbie who, after lunch on Saturday, brought up the question of what to do with Jimmy. His poor body, abandoned like rubbish in the freezing cold! It was all Robbie could see, all he could think about. 'I know it's still chilly out and everything,' he began, trying to sound reasonable, prudent, as though he was merely weighing the practicalities. 'But we can't leave him in there indefinitely.'

'You're right,' said Honor. 'Of course you're right. There are some spades in the Anderson shelter, aren't there?'

'You mean we . . .' said Saul in a scandalised whisper.

'Unless you've got any better ideas?' she said. 'If we all pitch in, it oughtn't take too long.'

'Fine,' said Saul. 'But let's wait until at least midnight.'

'I suppose,' said Robbie slowly, 'it'll be easier to move him after rigor mortis has begun to dissipate.'

'Mina, I'll lend you some old rags to wear,' said George.

'I'm sure,' said Saul, 'that we can manage without Mina's help.' He gave her a reassuring smile. 'In fact, I'm sure Robbie and I can manage it between us.'

Robbie looked startled, evidently not so sure.

'Greta will be here in the morning,' said Honor, smoothing out the *Sunday Times* women's page in her lap. 'We must decide whether to get rid of Jimmy's things.'

Robbie put down the *Observer* section he was pretending to read. The newsprint had been shimmering past his eyeline like ants on sugar. He wondered when he'd be able to sleep again. This morning, he'd finally drifted into a fitful drowse as the sun came up. Then the sound of church bells had jerked him back into painful consciousness, his pyjamas drenched in sweat.

He heard himself speak and was disturbed by the evenness of his tone. 'Let's look at it from both sides. We could be proactive. Wait a few days then report him missing, purport to be worried, as all his clothes et cetera are still here. That's what an innocent person should do, isn't it? Or might it look suspicious?' He bit his thumbnail and frowned. 'God, I don't know.'

George, curled up at one end of the sofa, had appeared to be snoozing, but she opened her eyes. 'No, I think you're right. It would give the appearance of innocence, and the police won't care anyway. I knew a chap who vanished for three months, and his family were told a grown man can go missing any time he likes, that it was none of their affair.'

'Where was he?' asked Mina. She looked up from the game of patience she'd been playing, seemingly for hours, whilst tensely cross-legged on the rug.

'Oh, he'd taken up with some sort of loony religious order. Turned up like a bad penny.'

'But,' said Saul, 'your friend probably wasn't known to the police before, was he?'

Honor tapped the ash from her now perpetual cigarette. 'Saul's right. The police might be interested if we tell them Jimmy has disappeared. And having them sniffing round – well, I don't know if my nerves can take it.'

'What, then?' said Robbie. 'We dispose of his stuff, and afterwards? If anybody ever asks, we say he moved out?'

'Who's going to ask?' said Mina. The poor girl wasn't looking well, thought Saul. Her eyes were puffy, her skin pale. 'Because if someone decides to start wondering why . . .'

'No one's going to ask,' said Honor. 'But yes, let's get rid of his things, then to all intents and purposes he's moved out. I did tell him, at the pub on Friday, that he had to leave.'

'Seems simpler that way, certainly,' said George. 'Tidier.'

Mina gathered all her playing cards in a heap and sighed shakily. 'Doesn't anyone else feel that maybe we've made a huge mistake? We could still go to the police. Tell them it was an accident. Why would they not believe us? After all—'

'Mina darling, come and sit next to me,' said George. 'Come on.' Mina clambered up from the floor and George grasped her hand. 'No one is going to the police. Not now, not ever. Is that perfectly clear? Everything's going to be fine. Anyway, it's too late. We've buried him. What do you suggest, that we dig him back up again?'

'But . . .' Mina's lower lip trembled.

Saul shot Honor an aghast look and said: 'George is right, Mina dear. We must be sensible. Getting the police involved at this stage would be . . . would be . . .'

'Suicidal,' muttered Robbie, examining his chewed-to-the-quick thumbnail. 'Utterly suicidal.'

'All right then,' said Honor decisively. 'I'll sort out Jimmy's room now. Saul, would you give me a hand?'

'We can't go on like this,' said Honor, closing the bedroom door behind them. 'Not talking about it. Even if you tell me you hate me, we must somehow clear the air.'

'I don't hate you,' said Saul. 'But I am awfully confused.' He sat on the end of the bed and looked up at her, dark-eyed and baleful. 'Why didn't you come to me? When Jack arrived, why didn't you tell me what was going on? I take it he was threatening you with exposure, with telling people who you really are – but I knew all that anyway. If you'd confided in me, I might have helped. Instead, you let that monster live here whilst lying to me about it.'

Honor waited to see if he'd finished. She wanted him to get it all off his chest. Then she sat down too. How she wished that was Jack's only bargaining chip! 'You must think me pretty feeble,' she said, 'if you imagine such a silly threat was all it took.'

'What, then? Tell me! What possible reason can there be to withhold anything now? He's dead! Thank God, he's dead! I'm sorry, I know he was your flesh and blood. But you can't blame me for rejoicing.'

'No need to apologise,' she said. 'And I can assure you, I'd have gone back to being Elsie Armstrong from Stepney if it meant seeing the back of Jack. I'd have done it like a shot.'

'Well, now you don't have to.' Saul sighed with awful weariness. 'Were you *ever* going to tell me about him?'

Honor smoothed the edge of the counterpane. 'I thought I could pay him to go away. And then things would return to normal. I didn't want to upset you needlessly. But he took nearly everything I had, and it wasn't enough. I even asked the bank for a loan.'

Maybe I ought to tell Saul the truth, she reflected. But she could hardly bear to think of it, let alone confess it. Some truths slashed a rent in one's existence when spoken out loud, a rent that could never be repaired. Once, she'd thought that love could enact some sort of exoneration. No, not exoneration, that was the wrong word. She wasn't only thinking of her conscience (and certainly not her eternal soul). By sleeping with Saul, by trying to make him fall in love with her, she'd hoped for an exorcism. A reprieve from being haunted by the past. She hadn't realised that her lies, her guilt, would keep them disconnected, estranged, even when physically entwined.

And yet . . . She let herself think back to the first night they spent together, now more than five years ago. She had sensed some mutual well of affection, a lovely unfamiliar brightness and security, a happiness both physical and emotional that remained, tantalisingly, just outside her grasp. Like something in a dream.

'Since we're bringing everything out into the open,' said Saul, 'I ought to tell you – Mina knows everything. I confided in her when I began to have my suspicions about Jimmy. A couple of weeks ago.'

Honor sat up straight. 'Everything? You mean . . .'

'I mean she knows you were Elsie Armstrong, that Jimmy was really your younger brother, Jack, that he and your husband went to prison for what they did. I'm sorry, Honor. I had to talk to someone. Don't worry, though, she knows I told her in confidence.'

'Well.' She was more lost for words than angry. 'I suppose it hardly matters now.' After a long pause she said: 'How did she react?'

'She doesn't think badly of you. Not after I explained what happened to Naomi and her husband. Who wouldn't want to put all that behind them?'

This seemed to bring them to a tentative accord. They began gathering Jack's possessions and putting them in his cardboard suitcase. There wasn't much: a few items of clothing, a shaving kit, some paperback novels.

'Surprisingly educated taste in reading,' remarked Saul, holding up *The Power and the Glory* by Graham Greene and *The City and the Pillar* by Gore Vidal. 'Perhaps I shouldn't be surprised. He was your brother, after all.'

'That's the tragedy of it,' said Honor. 'He was very bright. Began reading at three.'

She knelt to check under the bed. There was a shoebox, a

few magazines and a much smaller cardboard box. It was heavy, thought Honor, and she saw why: it contained bullets.

'I'll dispose of those, shall I?' said Saul, taking them. 'What the devil are those magazines?'

The covers of *Physique Pictorial* showed lifelike, artistically rendered drawings of extremely muscular naked men, their dignity protected, just barely, by wisps of fabric or, in one case, the breeze-blown mane of a horse being energetically straddled. Inside were actual photographs of a similar nature: weight-lifters demonstrating their prowess, cowboys enjoying the sun on their bodies, and other wholesome examples of male health and fitness.

'Published by the Athletic Model Guild of Los Angeles,' observed a stunned Honor.

'Did you know Jack was interested in – um – body-building?' said Saul.

'I did not know that. In fact, you might say I hadn't the faintest clue.'

Poor Robbie, thought Honor, sitting back down in the drawing room. Of everyone, he knows the least about the man whose death we're conspiring to hide.

Strange to contemplate, thought Robbie, how no one knew Jimmy quite like I did.

How unutterably bizarre, thought George, that Jimmy was somehow my brother. The second Honor had said it, she had known it was true. It was the way she had uttered the words, as though she'd rather be saying literally anything else. Then Greta had come in and started talking about Jimmy's pretty visitor, whereupon fate picked them all up and spun them round. Last night, George had buttonholed Honor and begged for a private conversation, only for her to plead a bad headache. Then this morning she offered to accompany her to the newsagent's for chocolate, but Mina had declared herself 'positively gasping' for fresh air and tagged along. Honor would have to explain herself, in the fullness of time. George had her own theories. But that was all they were, theories.

'Did Jimmy have any other friends, do you know,' she asked, 'or people who might miss him?'

Honor was about to say no, she didn't think so, when Robbie piped up: 'Oh hell, I just remembered. What about that friend who lent him the motor car?'

Nobody seemed to know about the motor car, so Robbie explained how Jimmy had driven him to the printer's a few weeks ago. 'He may have given it back. But if not, it's probably parked somewhere nearby. Christ! How could this have slipped my mind? Of all the stupid . . .'

'What was the name of the friend?' asked Honor. She hadn't thought Jimmy had any friends, not any more. No one had ever visited him in prison, as he'd lamented.

'No idea,' said Robbie. 'I ought to have asked him. I don't know why I didn't. Although for all we know, of course, the friend doesn't even exist. The motor car might be stolen or something.'

'Exactly, it probably was.' For God's sake, thought Honor. If Robbie went on like this, getting his knickers in a twist over every little hitch, they were done for. 'Still, why not go and see if you can find it.'

Obediently Robbie rose. He grabbed his overcoat from the hallway and left the house. It was just gone 5 p.m., still sunny after a bright spring day. A moist, leafy smell drifted through the deserted street.

He walked west, towards Brompton Cemetery. There was an

odd lightness in his head, in his legs, but at the same time a crushing sensation gripped his torso, as though he'd been run over by a tank and was slowly expiring from internal injuries. Idiotic metaphors kept coming to mind. *My heart's been ripped out. I'm all smashed to pieces. I'm dying inside.* And yet he wasn't about to curl up and die. If he were, why worry about anyone finding out what they'd done? A selfish survival instinct, he knew, was feeding the thrum of panic, of adrenaline, that dulled all the pain and propelled his movement down the street.

He saw the motor car, the rust-rimmed Ford in whose passenger seat he had sat the day his life changed for ever. It was innocently parked outside number 50. Was it bad news, he pondered, that Jimmy hadn't returned it to his supposed friend? They might come looking for it. This was precisely the type of loose end that caught people out, as Mina would no doubt remark.

'The motor car's there,' Robbie announced. 'Parked just down the road.'

'Thank you, Robbie,' said Honor. 'We've been talking it over, and we've decided what to do. If you agree, that is. This might actually be rather useful.'

He sat down and looked at her.

'You know how to drive, don't you? None of the rest of us does, you see, and—'

'Yes, I do, but—'

'Supposing you drive the car to London Bridge and leave it there. Take the Underground back. We'll have left something in the car identifying Jimmy. His wallet, say. If and when the car is discovered, it will appear that . . . well, you know.'

'That he took a long walk off a short pier,' supplied Mina

helpfully. This was no time to be squeamish, she thought. 'Delivered himself to a watery grave. Became fish food.'

Good grief, thought George. Where did she learn these phrases? 'It's a good idea, Robbie,' she said. 'If it looks like he took his own life, then there's no mystery for anyone to solve.'

The idea of driving the vehicle across London terrified Robbie. Supposing he was stopped by the police? It seemed a dreadful risk to put on his shoulders alone. 'All right,' he said. 'I suppose I'll do it in the morning.'

Honor and Saul exchanged a look. 'Now might be better,' said Saul. 'If you don't mind, of course.'

Robbie frowned, his misgivings plain. 'Do I have a choice? I mean—'

'I tell you what,' said Honor. 'I'll come with you. We'll get the Inner Circle back and I'll buy you a drink at the Sloane Square platform bar.'

They left the room, and Mina stood up and shouted after them: 'You will wear gloves, won't you?' She sat back down. 'Fingerprints,' she said with a do-I-have-to-think-of-everything glance at Saul and George.

'I suppose you've considered that you can never sell the house,' said Robbie, carefully changing gears as he sped up on the Fulham Road.

Honor looked at him. 'You mean . . .'

He grimaced. 'Exactly.'

A double-decker bus, all lit up and billowing exhaust fumes, pulled out in front of them. Honor gazed out at the darkening evening. 'Listen,' she said, 'I know we've been through a lot. But for all our sakes, you need to stop worrying about getting caught. I'm not going to sell the house. No one's coming looking for Jimmy. But you need to believe it, and act accordingly. A lie can become the truth, you know, so long as you're willing to convince yourself, first and foremost. So the truth is that a young man called Jimmy stayed with us for a while, and then he left. A brief and wholly unimportant episode in our lives. Now please, let's change the subject and talk about something more cheerful.'

Except it wasn't that easy. Neither of them spoke for several minutes. Then Honor said: 'I'm assuming you've guessed by now that Jimmy wasn't the son of my grandmother's housekeeper.'

'If I can be frank, I had my doubts about that from the outset.' They slowed to a stop at a red light and Robbie lit a cigarette. 'You were related, weren't you?'

She smiled, but she was taken aback. 'What makes you say that?'

'It might sound strange, but you have the same eyes. I know they're different colours, but they're the same unusual shape. Slanted, as though there's foreign blood. It's rather beautiful,' he added.

'Aren't you observant? And yes. He is . . . he was my younger brother.'

She began, haltingly, to describe the events that led to Jack's imprisonment. By the time she'd finished, they were at Hyde Park Corner and Robbie seemed not only shocked but shaken.

'Thomas is still in there,' she said. 'We never divorced. Jimmy said he could expose me for bigamy.'

Robbie gripped the steering wheel and kept his eyes on the road. He didn't trust himself to speak. So Honor had allowed – invited! – this chaos into their lives. And hadn't seen fit to alert them to the loose-pinned human grenade living amongst them.

'He arrived out of the blue!' said Honor, reading his face. 'I had no time to think, or decide what to do for the best. He put me in an invidious position, an impossible position, don't you see?'

Robbie drew deeply on his cigarette. His thin, elegant fingers were stained with nicotine and he had three days of dark stubble, making him look almost rakish.

'I suppose I do see,' he finally said. Looking at Honor, he felt a kind of excitement build up in his chest. 'Seeing as we're spilling our guts,' he said, 'did you know Jimmy and I were having an affair?'

'Oh Robbie. I'm so sorry, I—'

'It's all right,' he cut in, embarrassed. 'None of it matters now, does it? I thought it was . . . I thought he and I were, oh, I don't know, real. But I didn't know him at all. Let alone that he was a convicted murderer.' His tone was ironical. In a small, helpless gesture, he shrugged. Then he said: 'I asked George if there was something between them. She insists not. Do you believe her?'

She'd hardly admit to a fling with her own brother, thought Honor. 'I don't know what to believe. You saw them in bed together, didn't you?' She paused. 'Still, he was a homosexual. I'm convinced of that.'

Horribly close to tears, Robbie bit the corner of his lip until he tasted blood. 'Some chaps are ambisexual, aren't they? Horatian, they used to call it.'

'Is that what you are, then?'

'Gosh. Now you're asking.' Keeping his eyes on the road, he said: 'No, I wouldn't say so. I think I'm oriented in the one direction. I just didn't realise until recently.'

What a nuisance sex was, thought Honor. Life would be so straightforward, so *civilised*, without it.

Monday 18 May 1953

Cradling the receiver between ear and shoulder, his back to the road, Robbie held a tuppence over the slot. He looked at the advertisement on the telephone box wall: *Weetabix makes an ideal summer snack*. Then he looked at himself in the small, square mirror. Under the harsh yellow light he appeared gaunt. Spectral. Finally he pushed in the coin and asked the operator for Bishopsgate police station.

'Hello,' he said, 'I'm telephoning to report an abandoned vehicle. Yes, I'll hold the line . . . That's right, it's a rusty Ford Anglia, blue and cream. It's parked at the bottom of Fish Street Hill, at Upper Thames Street. Suspicious, I thought. Not to mention an eyesore. I work in the area, you see. No, thank you, I'd rather not leave my name.'

18

An Inspector Calls

It was astonishing, thought George as she strolled home on a sunny May afternoon, how one could simply move on from ghastly experiences. Not quite six weeks had passed since they'd buried Jimmy. And yet, it occurred to her now, for the past few days she'd scarcely thought about him. She'd even given up brooding over how, exactly, she and Jimmy had been siblings. Honor still insisted it was the truth but that for George's sake – for her sake alone! – she couldn't explain any further. Downright baffling.

George had always wondered, when reading about criminals and murderers, how they coped with the constant fear of being found out. True, she'd had a few sleepless nights early on. But given the efficient way everything had been dealt with, there seemed little to worry about. No one had come looking for Jimmy. Not yet, at least. In any case, the house's residents were beginning to palpably relax, to resume normal routines, admittedly by gradual, varying increments. Herself included. She was even seeing someone: Rory, a producer of BBC documentaries, of all things. Judging by what he'd told her, his subjects were terribly worthy and boring. Still, he was relatively good fun. When he'd chatted her up at the cheese counter in Selfridges Food Hall, she'd taken in his wholesome pinkish face and expensive-looking steel watch on a thick wrist. It was less love at first sight than 'you'll do' at first sight. Over a glass of champagne, he told her about his jazz gramophone records. As contemporary versions of 'come up and see my etchings' went, this was a cut above a stamp collection or a battalion of model aeroplanes (both had been offered to George as enticements from fully grown men). Following a suitable amount of persuasion, she'd accompanied him to his flat in Hallam Street. As soon as they'd taken their clothes off, she realised she'd done the right thing.

She turned into Tregunter Road, enjoying the sight of her shadow stretching over the chalky pavement. As she approached the house, she saw a man going up to the door and ringing the bell. A shiver of fear went through her. Understandable jumpiness, she reflected. But it was all right: he was a non-descript chap in early middle-age, wearing a dark suit and homburg hat. He appeared dully harmless. Not a likely associate of Jimmy's, at any rate.

Greta opened the door and looked at the man without saying anything.

'Good afternoon, madam,' he said. 'Am I speaking to the lady of the house?'

She frowned darkly. In her hands she held a red checked tea towel, which she slowly folded in two and threw over her shoulder, like a chef. '*Who* are you wanting?'

'I'm Detective Inspector Hilary Comyns, Metropolitan Police. I was hoping to speak to a Mrs Wilson.'

Greta's nostrils flared, as though detecting a bad smell. 'Police? Where is your uniform?'

George hurried up the porch steps. 'Hello, Detective Inspector,' she said. 'Hello, Greta, don't worry, I'll look after our guest.'

Greta gave one of her *please yourself* shrugs and retreated into the house. George held the door open for DI Comyns. 'Do come in. And please don't mind Greta. She's a refugee, you know. Her country was invaded by Jerry. We make allowances. If you'd like to go in and take a seat, I'll see if Mrs Wilson is at home.'

'Thank you, Miss . . . ?'

'Georgina Mountford-Owen. Back in a jiffy.'

'A policeman?' said Honor. From her tone, she might have been saying, 'A circus clown?' She was in her usual position behind her desk, cigarette holder between her fingers and drink at her elbow. Her tomato-coloured lipstick had worn away at the centre, as though a child hadn't finished colouring her in. 'Robbie, do you know what this is about?'

'Other than the obvious, you mean?' Robbie, who stood with his back to the door, spoke in a frantic whisper. 'Of course I don't. Why would I? George, what did he say exactly?'

George removed a pile of books from a chair and sat down. She felt light-headed. 'He wants to see Honor. He asked Greta if she was *the lady of the house*.' She affected DI Comyns's deep voice and south-of-the-river accent.

'What a cheek!' said Honor, forgetting to whisper. 'Greta's pushing sixty, and—'

George gestured at her to keep her voice down. 'Hadn't we better focus on the matter at hand? This might have nothing to do with Jimmy. Let's hope not. But it'll seem a bit suspicious if we leave the detective twiddling his thumbs for half an hour.'

Honor stubbed out her cigarette and sprayed herself with perfume, rubbing her wrists together and saying: 'You're right. I'll go down now. You two stay here. Is anyone else at home, by the way?'

'I think Mina's out,' said Robbie. 'Don't know about Saul.'

'Honor Wilson, a pleasure. Have you been offered any refreshment? Tea, coffee, gin?'

DI Comyns shook her outstretched hand and they both sat down. 'Nothing for me, thank you, Mrs Wilson, thank you very much. I'll come straight to the point. It's about a Mr James Sullivan. I'm given to understand that he is, or was, your lodger, is that correct?'

'Oh no! Has something happened to him?'

'I was hoping you could tell me that.'

'Gosh, really? I do hope he's all right. But I'm afraid he doesn't keep in touch. Since he moved out, I mean.'

DI Comyns produced a small notebook and said, pencil poised: 'And when was that, exactly?'

She pressed her lips into a thoughtful moue. 'Um. March, I think. Yes, it was late March. I remember, because Easter was just around the corner. He's not in any sort of trouble, is he?'

'We'll have to see about that. Were you aware of his criminal record?'

'Oh yes.' She didn't elaborate, and he smiled. What the smile meant, Honor wouldn't have liked to say.

'And he asked to stay here because his late mother had once been a servant in your family's employ, is that correct?'

Honor nodded.

'The thing is, Mrs Wilson, Mr Sullivan was helping us with certain other … certain other investigations. He'll be called to appear as a witness at court. But no one's seen nor heard from him in weeks. So anything you might be able to tell us would be extremely helpful. For instance, did he leave a forwarding address?'

'No, he didn't.' She said this in a reproving tone, then leant forward and lowered her voice conspiratorially. 'What sort of crime has he witnessed? Oh, but you don't suppose he's been – what's the word – nobbled?'

His mouth pursed with apparent amusement. Then he frowned and swallowed. 'At this stage, I'm following all potential lines of enquiry. If you wouldn't mind explaining: why did Mr Sullivan move out?'

'I think I'd better be honest, Inspector. I asked him to leave. Things weren't very cordial. He went off in a huff, as it were.'

He scribbled in his notebook, and Honor wondered if he was quoting her verbatim.

'He has failed to register a new address with his probation officer,' he said, 'which he is legally obliged to do.'

She gave a small shrug. 'My dear, I do so wish I could help.'

'What was the nature of your falling-out?'

'Our falling-out?'

'You said you asked him to leave.'

'Well, it was only meant to be temporary, his stay here. There wasn't really room. So it wasn't fair on my other house guests. But he took it rather personally.'

DI Comyns nodded and licked a fingertip to stroke back a few pages in his notebook. 'Can you confirm, Mrs Wilson, who else lives here presently?'

'Of course. There's Robbie, Mr Robert Trafford. But I can assure you, he won't know any more than I do. And there are the girls. You met the Honourable Miss Georgina Mountford-Owen, and then there's Miss Wilhelmina Taylor. She's only eighteen, so . . .' She didn't mention Saul, since he lived in the separate basement flatlet. Aware this was a technicality, she nevertheless hoped to get away with it.

'I see. Might I have a word with Mr Trafford, then?'

Unlike George, Robbie hadn't stopped fearing this day would come. As he walked slowly down the stairs, his mind went to the most catastrophic of places – even though Honor, when fetching him from the office, had hurriedly told him that the man knew nothing, only that Jimmy had vanished.

'Robbie Trafford,' he said as he entered the drawing room. 'How do you do. And how can I help?'

'Good afternoon. I'm sorry for the intrusion. This won't take long.'

Robbie sat down. Thank God the man hadn't shaken his hand. He had a desperate urge to run his palms over his trouser legs. Instead he pressed them onto the edge of the armchair seat, hoping he wouldn't leave damp marks.

'As I was saying to Mrs Wilson, I'm trying to track down James Sullivan. I understand he was a friend of yours?'

Robbie opened his mouth to respond, trying to produce the right expression: incredulous, but not too incredulous. More surprised. A mixture of surprise and concern. 'Well, not really, but we lodged across the landing from one another. Passed the time of day sometimes, you know.'

The man nodded and said nothing. An excruciating silence hung in the air. It's a technique, thought Robbie. He means me to start yabbering. Well, I wasn't born yesterday.

DI Comyns looked around the room and said: 'This is a nice house, isn't it? How long have you lived here?'

'Must be four years now, give or take. Mrs Wilson and I work together. We run a literary magazine.'

'And what did you do before that? Workwise, I mean?'

'I was at Cambridge. And before that the army.'

'Where did you serve?'

'Egypt. Eighth Army.'

'Oh really? I was in Palestine.' He took a cigarette case from his pocket. 'Smoke?' He lit Robbie's and his own cigarette, and said: 'I'm sorry to have to ask this, but is Mr Sullivan a homosexual, as far as you're aware?'

Robbie drew deeply on his cigarette. 'Gosh. I really wouldn't know. It's hardly the sort of thing he'd talk about, is it?' He congratulated himself on using the conditional present tense, even as nausea curdled the contents of his stomach.

The inspector dipped his chin and said lightly: 'What about you, Mr Trafford?'

Robbie looked at him, confused. 'What about me?'

'Look, I wish I didn't have to be so personal. And I ought to make one thing clear: I have no interest in bringing any charges for . . . for . . .' DI Comyns glanced towards the door, which was half an inch ajar. Robbie went and clicked it firmly closed. 'I need to examine all lines of enquiry,' the inspector went on, his eyes following Robbie's movement. 'I'm sure you understand.'

Robbie sat down. 'I'm not sure I do. What on earth does this have to do with me?'

'You and Mr Sullivan were overheard arguing one evening. At the King's Arms pub on Fulham Road. Several witnesses said you were very upset.'

He felt his face turn ashen. Before he could respond, DI Comyns said in an alarmingly sympathetic way: 'Do you need a glass of water?'

Robbie shook his head, swallowed some gluey saliva and said: 'I am a bit parched. I'll just make myself a drink. I don't suppose you . . .' The man held up a demurring hand. Robbie went over to the sideboard and filled a glass with one third whisky and two thirds soda water. He took several large gulps before sitting back down.

'Perhaps you could tell me about it,' said DI Comyns. 'The argument. Perhaps the onlookers got entirely the wrong end of the stick. Wouldn't be the first time.'

Focus, thought Robbie. Don't panic. You're finished if you panic. He took another large sip of his drink. Then he said: 'There was nothing to it really. We bumped into each other, and Mr Sullivan made some rather offensive remarks to me. Casting aspersions.' He stubbed out his cigarette. 'I'm married. My wife and I are separated just at present. But we both hope that's a temporary state of affairs.'

'Right. I see. I'll reiterate, if I may, that you needn't worry about incriminating yourself. By which I mean, don't lie to me to conceal a crime in which I have no professional interest. That will only cause trouble for you.'

'I'm not lying. And if *I* may, I resent the insinuation. As I say, my wife and I—'

'Unfortunately, the barmaid at the King's Arms recalls quite a different conversation between you.'

'A barmaid? You can't seriously be taking the word of a . . .' Robbie stopped, uncertain how to finish the sentence.

DI Comyns consulted his notebook. 'Millicent Turnbull, thirty-five. Widowed, lives with her mother. Keen church choralist. Former Wren. Nice lady. It's unclear why she should make up stories.'

'People misremember things, don't they? Or, as you put it, they get the wrong end of the stick.'

'Hmm. Mrs Turnbull was confident she'd overheard some type of jealous spat. You were aggrieved, she said, over Mr Sullivan's relationship with another man.' He glanced at his notebook. 'George. Who is George?'

I might help myself, thought Robbie. Say who George is. Claim she was having an affair with Jimmy. Deflect these dangerous accusations. But he knew he mustn't drop her in it. Not if he ever wanted to look at himself in the mirror. They had to stick together: that was the pact. 'As I say, Detective Inspector, whatever this woman thinks she heard, she's mistaken. The only George I know, aside from our late King, of course, is my great-uncle, George Higginbotham. He keeps bees in Somerset. I don't suppose he socialises in the same circles as Mr Sullivan.'

DI Comyns remained poker-faced at this facetiousness. He jotted down some notes, which Robbie took as another attempt to unnerve him. He hadn't said anything useful, surely?

'I appreciate your time,' said the inspector, replacing his notebook in his blazer pocket. 'Before I go, I'd like to speak to Miss Mountford-Owen. Perhaps you could ask her to—'

'Certainly,' said Robbie with excessive alacrity, jumping to his feet. 'Best of luck with your investigation.'

'Robbie, for goodness' sake, calm down,' said Honor in a cross murmur. 'You said he didn't seem to care about your affair with Jimmy. So I don't see there's any reason to panic. And you denied it, in any case. He can't prove otherwise, can he?'

'That damn barmaid.' He sat down and rested his forehead in his hand. 'How dare she eavesdrop and repeat private conversations. Jobs like that ought to have a code of conduct attached to them.'

'He didn't guess, then, that George was George?'

'Didn't seem to. But you know these detectives. They play everything close to the chest. I got the feeling the whole time that he was testing me. Did you get that feeling? He was trying to trip me up.'

'Be that as it may,' said Honor, 'oughtn't we to tell George about this? If the detective inspector thinks George was having an affair with Jimmy, he'll wonder why she concealed it. Won't he?'

Robbie shook his head. 'Please don't tell her. I don't want her to know about me and him. I honestly couldn't—'

'But Robbie, she ought to be told that she may fall under suspicion. It's not fair to keep it from her.'

He looked at her with pure anguish.

'All right,' she relented. 'We won't tell her. But we'll have to revisit this decision, depending on what happens.'

'Right, right. What did you make of him, Comyns?'

She thought about it. 'I'm afraid he's one of those quietly clever types. Presents a diffident face to the world, but underneath, his brain is working nineteen to the dozen. That said, he didn't seem to think Jimmy had been killed, just that he'd absconded. If they've got cases resting on his testimony, I don't wonder they want to track him down.'

'Did you know he'd be expected as a witness in court?' His tone held a hint of rebuke.

'No! I didn't realise the police still needed him. Stupidly, I thought he'd simply told them what he knew in exchange for his release, and that was that. It was to do with a prisoner friend of his. A fellow who'd entrusted him with all sorts of confidences. Boasts, I suppose.'

'What sort of a friend?'

Honor raised an eyebrow. 'Well, quite.'

'This is all very exciting,' exclaimed George. She kicked off her sandals and tucked her feet underneath her. 'I've never met a policeman before. What do you suppose has happened to poor

Mr Sullivan? You don't think he's come to a sticky end, do you?' She widened her eyes.

'I . . .' DI Comyns glanced down at the cork heel of George's shoe, resting sideways on the rug.

'He always struck me as very much the sort of fellow who knew how to look after himself. Wait, that came out wrong. I don't mean he seemed capable of violence. But you can never really tell with people, can you? I had a school friend who—'

'Miss Mountford-Owen, if I could stop you there. All I'm doing presently is talking to people who know him. He has absconded from his parole, you see. You're not in touch with him, I take it?'

George caressed the beaded brooch on the neckline of her dress, as though absently pondering. But the man's eyes didn't stray from her face. 'I'm trying to remember if I've seen him,' she said. 'In the street or anything, since he moved out. But I don't think so.'

'You don't consider him a friend?'

'I like to think I'm nice to everyone I meet. Naturally, when he took a room here, I tried to be kind, because I gathered he'd had a tough time. One should always be charitable, or so my parents taught me. Second chances and all that.'

'Did he have any girlfriends, do you know?'

'I never saw him in the company of any girls, as far as I recall. But that doesn't necessarily mean anything, does it?'

DI Comyns looked at her without speaking. He was not an unattractive man, she thought. Perhaps forty or forty-two, he had wide grey eyes that tilted down at the outer corners, giving him a sympathetic, mournful mien. Neatly oiled black hair. Bookish specs. The bluish tint of a five o'clock shadow emphasised the thinness of his lower face. He seemed thoroughly decent. The only countervailing feature was his nose, which was prominent and crooked. At a certain angle, it made him look almost disreputable.

'What about the other young lady who rooms here?' he said at last. 'Were they . . .'

'Mina?' George laughed. 'Gosh, no. Mina wouldn't give him the time of day.'

'A beauty, is she?'

'Um . . . let's just say she has her sights set on a more advantageous match. I hope that doesn't sound sneering. I don't mean it to. I can quite see why climbing the social ladder is an appealing prospect. For a particular type of girl, that is. I'm afraid I've rather slid down in the other direction. As an hon.'

He didn't react to this attempt at rank-pulling. Either he didn't know what she meant, or he wished to convey indifference. 'I'd like to speak to her – is she at home?'

'No, she rarely is. I can ask her to contact you, perhaps?'

DI Comyns rose to his feet and picked up his hat. 'No need. I might drop by again. Would you please thank Mrs Wilson for me? I must be going.'

George saw him to the door. Her head was aching. What had she even said? It was all a blur. Had she struck the right note? And why, of all the filthy luck, was he so undistracted by her feminine charms?

Hilary Comyns wished Miss Mountford-Owen a pleasant evening. Nice girl, he thought. But troubled. He saw it quite clearly. All that forced vivacity, the flirtatious mannerisms. No doubt this was a long-time successful strategy. She probably couldn't stop doing it if she tried. And why was an honourable living in a Chelsea rooming house in the first place? What had gone wrong to lead her there?

He walked back the way he'd come, north-east towards Hyde Park, and replayed the conversations in his mind. Shame about Mr Trafford: he was patently terrified. Well, who wouldn't be? But Hilary had meant what he said. He wasn't interested in making trouble for the fellow – he just needed to find Jack Shaughnessy, aka James Sullivan. Mr Sullivan had told his probation officer he had a new lady friend, so why hadn't anyone admitted to meeting her? Unless the lady friend didn't exist and was simply a cover story for romantic leanings in another direction entirely.

If it came to it, of course, he could force Mr Trafford to be more forthcoming. There'd be evidence somewhere to be used against him – there always was. But Hilary lacked the stomach for such machinations. People couldn't help who they were, could they?

As for Mrs Wilson: what an odd duck. Certainly not your average landlady. The court record admitting the late Mr Wilson's will to probate had his widow's age as twenty-nine, which would make her, what, thirty-four now? Yet she acted like a dowager aunt. Another queer thing: when he'd looked for records of her from before her marriage, he couldn't find anything. She seemed to materialise into existence during the war. Her maiden name, supposedly, was Petrova. A Russki, perhaps. There was no trace of an accent, but if she were foreign – had been a penniless refugee, say – it might also account for the couple's frankly vast age difference.

Later that evening, Mina knocked on Saul's door and stuck her head round. 'Did you hear? A copper came calling!'

'Come in, Mina! Have you just got home?' Her cheeks were flushed and an errant curl had escaped its hairpin.

'A little while ago,' she said, sitting down and spreading out her full skirt to avoid creasing. 'George filled me in. She seems very sanguine about the whole thing, I must say. She found the policeman charming, apparently. That's as maybe, I told her, but that's part of his job, isn't it, to weasel information out of people, and in that way collar wrongdoers. He didn't speak to you, then?'

'I was out, as it happens.'

'Thank heavens I was out too! Can you imagine? At least now, if he comes back, we won't be caught unawares.'

'We must remain on our guard, certainly. But it ought not to come as a huge surprise that Jimmy's disappearance has been noticed. It was bound to be. There's no reason to think any of us will fall under suspicion, is there?'

Mina considered this. 'So long as they don't have a body, they can't charge anyone with murder. They can suspect all they like, I suppose, but that's the bottom line.'

Saul wasn't sure this was true. 'There you are, then. No need to worry unduly.'

Easy for him to say, thought Mina. 'Could I have a cigarette, please?' she asked.

'Of course.' He proffered his case and lit it for her. 'I didn't think you smoked.'

Mina held her cigarette aloft in straight fingers and gazed moodily into the middle distance. 'I'm trying to learn.' She took a tentative puff and exhaled poutily. 'I've been studying Lauren Bacall. She's a marvellous smoker, don't you think? The trouble is, it makes me feel like puking. Sorry. But it does.'

He smiled. The poor child did look green. 'You'll soon get the hang of it, I'm sure.'

With a determined frown, she took another drag. 'Is Honor worried, then? About the policeman? I mean, in her situation . . . It's a bit dicey, isn't it? If I was pretending to be someone else, the last thing I'd want is the attention of the law.'

She was right, thought Saul. If the police learnt that Jimmy was Honor's brother, what then? She'd always seemed so confident her secret was safe. *I've covered my tracks,* she once said. *Nothing can connect me to the past. Elsie Armstrong might as well be dead.*

'Well,' he said, 'Honor seemed rather sanguine too. Her former self, as it were, is so far in the past, it's as though she can't conceive of anyone – even a police detective – raising her ghost.'

19

As English As You or Me

'Good afternoon,' said Hilary to the ticket seller at the Classic Cinema. 'I wonder if you can help me. I'm looking for a young lady called Mina Taylor. Is she working today?' The girl was slouching in her chair and sucking on a sweet. She blinked at Hilary, as though this departure from the usual demands of her job were a challenge too far. Impatient, he flashed his badge.

That did it. She dropped her insolent expression and stood up. 'I'll fetch 'er,' she muttered, and went off, glancing over her shoulder before quickening her step.

When she returned with another girl duly in tow, they were whispering and giggling. The ticket seller nudged her friend and nodded pointedly at Hilary.

'Miss Taylor?' he said. 'I'm sorry to interrupt your work. I'm Detective Inspector Hilary Comyns. Might we have a quick chat? Nothing to worry about.'

She stared at him, an appraising glint in her eye. In her uniform of belted jacket, white blouse and black collar-ribbon, this slight young girl seemed oddly authoritative. Like a boarding-school headmistress, or a female SS guard.

'I'm afraid you've caught me in the middle of a shift,' she said in confident, slightly theatrical tones. 'I can't abandon my post, you see.'

'I'm sure the manager—' Hilary began.

'Tell you what,' she said soothingly, 'I finish at five. If you'd like to come back then, perhaps?'

He glanced at his wristwatch. 'Very well. Five o'clock.'

Hilary almost didn't recognise Miss Taylor in civilian clothes, which had transformed her from spinsterish headmistress to Hollywood vamp. Her peach-coloured dress matched her coat, which had bracelet-length sleeves showing two rows of pearls on her left wrist. She wore imitation lizard-skin shoes, a white cap with a small spray of purple feathers, and freshly applied orange lip paint. A sharp eye tooth bore a tiny orange smudge.

'So sorry to keep you waiting,' she trilled. 'I hope you haven't been too inconvenienced.' He detected elocution lessons in her clipped consonants, and remembered what Miss Mountford-Owen had said: that Miss Taylor was a social climber. He didn't doubt it. Pure resolve radiated from her like heat.

'Not at all,' he said. 'Can I buy you a cup of tea?'

'I expect you've been told about my visit to your residence,' said Hilary once the waitress had taken their order. 'And that I'm trying to trace Mr James Sullivan.'

'You expect right,' she said. Cheekily, he wondered, or merely plain-spokenly? 'I heard all about it, don't you worry about that.

It was *the* most exciting thing ever to happen at Tregunter Road. I was quite sorry to have missed it, I don't mind telling you.'

'May I ask: how did you come to live there? Where did you meet Mrs Wilson?'

'Oh, she answered my advertisement. In *The Lady* magazine. I didn't want to live just anywhere. I wanted something suitable. You know, with nice people.'

'And Mrs Wilson is nice, is she?'

The girl looked at him steadily. 'Of course.'

'Is she Russian, do you know?'

'Russian?'

'Born in Russia. The Soviet Union.'

She tilted her chin down. 'I'm afraid I've no idea what you're implying.' She seemed affronted. 'Honor Wilson is as English as you or me. I mean, really. You've only got to speak to her to see that.'

The waitress arrived with the tea things and Miss Taylor smiled at her with great warmth – the solidarity of one working girl to another, thought Hilary.

'Right,' he said. 'My mistake.' He stirred some sugar into his tea and offered her a cigarette. 'So, I daresay you know what my next question will be.'

She nodded and leant forward so he could light her cigarette. She turned her head and in a slow, sultry way let a thin jet of smoke stream from the corner of her mouth. Hilary imagined her practising the gesture in front of a mirror. 'The whereabouts of Mr Sullivan,' she said, 'are unknown to me.'

This phrasing also seemed practised, he thought. 'Were you two friendly?'

'I prefer,' she said grandly, 'to keep myself to myself. I'm terribly busy. I certainly wouldn't have time to befriend strange men, even if they are living under the same roof. Not to say . . . I mean,

I get on well with everyone. And Saul, well, you might say he's like an uncle to me. But that's different, he—'

'I'm sorry,' interrupted Hilary. 'What was the name you mentioned?'

'Saul Reznikov,' said Mina slowly, as if realising she'd made an error. 'He lives at Tregunter Road with us, in the basement.'

'For some reason,' he said, 'I know that name.'

'Oh yes, Saul is a published poet.'

But Hilary, whose literary tastes began and ended with the Hardy Boys books of his childhood, felt the name was familiar for quite a different reason. At that moment, though, it eluded him.

'So, this Mr Reznikov, he's a chum of yours? A good chap, is he?'

'The very best of chaps. Now, he *is* foreign. He's from somewhere . . .' She made a vague swirly shape with her cigarette. 'One of those places where the Germans did terrible things. He lost his wife and daughter. Can you imagine?' Her little nostrils flared. 'So yes, you might say I'm proud to know him. George and I are fairly pally, too. But I barely exchanged two sentences with Mr Sullivan, I—'

'George?' he said. 'Who do you—'

'Sorry, Miss Mountford-Owen. She's been . . .'

Momentarily Hilary stopped listening. How stupid of him. George. Georgina. Of course.

'Forgive my interrupting,' he said, 'but I don't want to take up your entire evening. If I could ask one more question. Were you aware that Miss Mountford-Owen and Mr Sullivan were romantically involved?'

Miss Taylor replaced her teacup in its saucer and looked at him with an expression he could only describe as nonplussed. She drew on her cigarette, wincing as though she'd inhaled too hard.

Then she opened her mouth to speak. Finally she fixed him with her shrewd green eyes and said: 'I know it's your job, Detective Inspector, to ask questions, even if those questions might be impolite. I don't know who's been saying such things. I don't want to know, I'm sure. But I'll thank you to tell them they're mistaken. George is the daughter of a baron. Her portrait's been painted by famous artists. The very idea that—'

Hilary held up a placating hand. 'It isn't my intention to besmirch anyone's reputation. But I'm afraid this isn't idle gossip. I have the information on good authority. Naturally, it's none of my business. Except Miss Mountford-Owen lied to me about it. Why do you imagine she might have done that?'

Miss Taylor widened her eyes and pressed her lips together. For a horrible moment he thought she might burst into tears. But she just sat up straighter, ground out her cigarette, and said: 'If you don't mind, I must be going now.'

He hadn't the heart to detain her. Still, he insisted on seeing her home. It was a lovely evening, light and mild, the sky's pink-white tint reflecting the blossom petals scattered like confetti over the pavement. As they walked, Miss Taylor resumed her forceful, jaunty demeanour. In an offhand sort of way he was able to bring up Mr Trafford, whom she seemed to like. 'He's married, you know,' she said. 'Some people are surprised about that. They think he's not the marrying kind. He's just bookish, though. There's nothing wrong with that, is there?'

'No,' said Hilary, smiling to himself. 'Nothing.'

Christ on a cracker, thought Mina as she let herself in with her latchkey. George and Jimmy. Who else knew, she wondered, and who on earth had told the policeman? It was a bit much for George to have kept it a secret. In the circumstances, as it were.

Mina had properly been put on the spot. Unless it wasn't true? Maybe the detective was fishing for information. That was what detectives did, after all. Was he looking for a murder motive? *Cherchez la femme?*

Mina knocked on George's bedroom door and said: 'It's only me.'

'Perfect timing,' said George when Mina entered. 'Zip me up, could you, darling?' She was half in a sleeveless rose-print dress. 'I'll breathe in.'

The straps of her shell-pink brassiere were grey with dirt, Mina noticed with a grimace, and her underarms wanted shaving. After some manipulation and frantic tugging, Mina managed to force the dress's zip up, and they both sighed with relief.

George stood in front of the dressing table mirror and, leaning forward, stuck a hand down her front to arrange her breasts. 'Did you need something, Mina?' she said, straightening up and considering her reflection. 'Rory's picking me up in twenty minutes.'

Mina sat down on the little settee. 'Continue with your primping, don't mind me. I just had an encounter with DI Comyns, that's all. He came to find me at the cinema. George, I'm worried.'

'You mustn't worry!' She picked up a can of hairspray and spritzed her new short fringe. 'There's nothing he can pin on us. I think he's rather a pet, don't you? Now, which earrings, the paste or the enamel?'

'The paste. George, why didn't you tell me you and Jimmy were having an affair? He knows, you know. Comyns.'

In the mirror, Mina saw George's face fall. It's true then, she thought.

George sat down next to her. 'Tell me *exactly* what he said.'

'He asked did I know that Miss Mountford-Owen and Mr Sullivan were romantically involved. Because he had it on good authority that you were.'

'And what did you say?'

'I said it was completely out of the question, that he'd got his wires crossed.'

'Well, precisely so. Thank you, darling.' She stood up. 'Have you told Honor?'

'No, I've only just—'

'I must have a word with her about it.' She reached down and touched Mina's shoulder. 'Really, don't worry. Everything's going to be fine.'

'You *knew*?' said George as Honor paced around the office, alternately smoking and biting a thumbnail. 'Why the hell didn't you tell me? For Pete's sake, of all the—'

'We didn't know he'd worked out it was you!' said Honor. 'He thought George was a man.'

George looked at her with a mixture of bemusement and exasperation. 'We? Are you going to explain, or—'

'I don't want you to upset yourself. Let's go downstairs and have a drink, at least.'

She followed Honor out of the room. 'You know what this means,' she said. 'All my lovers . . .' She paused. 'I mean, the few men within a certain time frame . . . they're going to end up murder suspects, aren't they? A jealous lover is textbook motivation. I won't be perceived as having a motive. Not unless . . . Oh God, Comyns doesn't know about me being Jimmy's sister, does he?'

'No, no, of course not, I—'

'Why of course not? How am I meant to understand anything, when you won't even tell me who he was, or how the hell we were related?'

In the drawing room, Honor made them both a stiff drink.

Then she told George about Robbie and Jimmy having an affair, about the barmaid at the King's Arms overhearing them arguing about someone called George, about Robbie swearing Honor to secrecy. 'I did say, though, I did warn him we might have to tell you. I'm sorry, George. But you can see my position.'

'I think I'm going to be sick. I wasn't even aware Robbie was . . . I mean, I had my suspicions. We all did, didn't we? But . . . well, I don't know what to think any more.'

'It's all been very hard on him. On top of everything else, he has to worry about being arrested for this other thing.'

George remembered her conversation with Robbie on the stairs, after he'd fled the scene of Jimmy's death. 'Have you any idea why he formed this misapprehension in the first place? About Jimmy and me, I mean?'

As Honor began explaining that Robbie had seen George in Jimmy's bed, there was the sound of a key in the front door, then someone wiping their feet.

'It's Robbie,' said George. 'That's his step.' She raised her voice. 'Robbie, can you come in here, please?'

'George,' said Honor in a warning tone.

He entered the room in his shirtsleeves. He looked younger than his years, thought Honor. Younger and extra vulnerable. He'd shaved that day, and the sun had brought out some freckles on his forehead.

'So apparently,' said George, a nasty edge to her voice, 'our chum Detective Inspector Comyns is apprised of this supposed . . . well, I'm not going to say love triangle. I daresay he might, though. How could you keep this from me, Robbie? Do you have any idea what it must look like?'

As George spoke, Robbie stood there and stared miserably at the floor.

'I didn't have time to tell you,' he said. 'When you went down to speak to him, I'd only just learnt that he knew.'

'And you've not had ample opportunity to tell me since?' She pushed back a lock of hair irritably. 'So you were jealous? How extraordinary. You know, I had a feeling, back then, that you were giving me the cold shoulder. But you've never liked me, so I didn't think much of it.'

Robbie sat down next to her. 'I'm sorry. I'm truly sorry. I never ought to have kept it from you. Any of it. All I can say is that I've not been in my right mind. All of this, it's scrambled my brain. I feel ill all the time. I can't sleep. I can't think straight.'

The doorbell rang. 'Oh blast,' said George. 'That'll be Rory.' She stood up. 'This conversation isn't over.'

'Robbie, you've got to pull yourself together,' said Honor. 'I agree, it's not ideal that Comyns seems to have got his teeth into this idea – the love triangle, as George put it – but remember, he's got it wrong. And if you think about it logically, if either of you had killed Jimmy in a jealous rage, why would you be covering up for each other?'

He shakily lit a cigarette and nodded. 'Yes. Yes, if you put it like that, I suppose . . .' He frowned. 'But you know what I'd hypothesise if I were him? That in the scenario you describe, we'd both be compelled to cover it up due to the risk of scandal. I mean, if either of us were charged with Jimmy's murder, the whole sorry imbroglio would be publicised!'

'You're thinking too hard about it,' she said. 'Remember, not only are you in possession of the real facts, but you're also far more intelligent than Comyns.'

'I wouldn't be too sure. He's clever. You said so yourself. He's not some bumbling bobby.'

Honor was trying to stay positive for Robbie's sake. But she couldn't argue with that, not convincingly. 'Look,' she said, 'what has he actually got? A barmaid's claim to have overheard things. Snatches of conversation in a busy, noisy public house. That wouldn't stand up in court, would it? It's hearsay. Inadmissible evidence.'

He smiled ruefully. 'You sound like Mina. But even if that's true, don't you think we ought to try and – I don't know – help Comyns focus on a different theory?'

'And how do you propose we do that, exactly?'

He thought about it, smoke billowing dragon-like from his nostrils. 'A suicide note! You could say you've realised a letter from Jimmy arrived some weeks ago, but it got hidden or lost until now. I can forge his handwriting. The letter could say goodbye, don't blame yourself, et cetera.'

'What about the postmark on the envelope? That can't be forged, can it?'

'We could reuse an old envelope somehow. Or say it was hand-delivered. Wait – even better, that he pushed it under your bedroom door and it went beneath the carpet. Then when they find the motor car at London Bridge, it will all make sense.'

Honor shook her head and sighed. 'I don't know. I think you're panicking. Let's not rush into unwise decisions. I say we wait for the time being. Let's see if the whole thing doesn't blow over.'

As soon as she said the words, she realised how silly they sounded. Trouble like this didn't just blow over. Not without enormous luck. And Honor knew better than to rely on luck.

20

Concocting Connections

It had come to Hilary suddenly whilst he was bathing, his mind partially elsewhere, the reason Saul Reznikov's name was familiar. He featured, of course, in the original case file for the murder of Laurence Cohen and the attempted murder of Naomi Cohen, for which Jack Shaughnessy, aka James Sullivan, served fourteen years. Mr Reznikov was Mrs Cohen's cousin. Wasn't that curious, that Mr Reznikov and Mr Sullivan ended up living under the same roof all those years later? More than curious, in fact. Certainly beyond the bounds of coincidence.

Sitting at his desk at Scotland Yard, the contents of the file spread out in front of him, Hilary smoked contemplatively. As witness statements testified, the money stolen by Shaughnessy and his brother-in-law – stolen and never recovered – was meant to have given the Reznikov family safe passage out of Nazi-infested Eastern Europe. In the event, it seemed only Saul himself made it. Indeed, hadn't Miss Taylor said he lost his wife and daughter?

Hilary tried to put himself in Mr Reznikov's shoes. So many murders were petty, impulsive acts by damaged people. Pitiful people. But if this was the act of long-overdue vengeance Hilary suspected it to be – well, it had a sort of tragic grandeur. He couldn't honestly claim he wouldn't have done the same, given such provocation.

It was Shaughnessy who remained a puzzle. Assuming he'd been able to track down Mr Reznikov – a big assumption – why would he have wanted to? It didn't make any sense. Unless it was the other way round, and Mr Reznikov had somehow lured him to the house in Tregunter Road.

The telephone rang.

'It was found where? Hold on.' He reached for a pencil. 'Got it. No, I'll be right there.'

In less than half an hour, Hilary was sitting in a small back room in the police station on Bishopsgate, examining the contents of James Sullivan's wallet. It had been found in the glove compartment of an abandoned motor car by London Bridge, quite five miles from Tregunter Road.

'You mentioned,' he asked the young constable, 'that the person who called it in wouldn't leave a name?'

'That's right, sir. He just wanted us to know about the motor car. It was an eyesore, he said. Ought to be taken away and used for scrap metal.'

'What sort of a person was he, would you say?'

'Sort of a person, sir?'

'Young, old, well-mannered, gruff, anything that struck you?'

'Um. I'd say neither young nor old, sir. Sounded educated, if I'm any judge.'

'And you haven't contacted the registered owner?'

'Not yet, sir. My guv'nor said that Scotland Yard had circulated the wanted man's details, so protocol was that—'

'Good, good. You can leave all that to me. A cup of tea would be nice, Constable . . .'

'Abbott, sir. Constable Abbott. Coming right up, sir.'

The wallet contained no money save for a few pence. Otherwise, there was a National Insurance card, a couple of dog-track betting slips, a library card. Nothing revealing or useful. Well, he'd see what the vehicle owner had to say for himself.

Paul Linton was a tall young man with receding brownish hair and a strong brow. He'd be rather handsome, thought Hilary, were it not for his cowed expression, that vague air of persecution. Though it probably brought forth a certain instinct in women.

They sat in the tiny front room, Mrs Linton relegated to the kitchen, the children in bed and Hilary doing his level best to lull Mr Linton into a trusting state.

'You're under no suspicion,' he reiterated. 'I just need your help in clearing a few things up. So, you were saying that your Ford Anglia is lost, but not stolen?'

Mr Linton looked even more disheartened. 'Anything that's going on, can my name be kept out of it? The children . . .' He trailed off. 'I haven't been in trouble with the law since I was a kid.'

'Did you lend your motor car to somebody?'

Mr Linton glanced towards the door. 'An old friend.'

'All right. Good. Your friend's name?'

'Jack Shaughnessy. He's not even really a friend any more. We sort of grew up together, and then lost touch. Will I get the car back?'

It took a certain amount of gentle interrogation to get at the whole story, but eventually it all unspooled. The two boys were friends from before they could walk. Reading between the lines, Jack was the steelier, more confident child, who defended chubby, sensitive Paul from local toughs. But when fifteen-year-old Jack was arrested for murder, Paul's parents insisted he cut off contact with his friend. Soon after, the Lintons moved to Walthamstow, and when Paul was eighteen, he was sent to the front. He hadn't heard from Jack again until recently.

'He needed the motor car to get started with his new job,' he said. 'I said he could have it for a few weeks. Margaret hated it anyway. I used to spend my Sundays fixing it. She said I was more interested in engines than in her and the little 'uns.'

'What was Mr Shaughnessy's job?'

'Delivering things? I'm not sure. But look, he said it was all a mistake, what happened back then. No one was meant to get hurt. That's why they let him out early. Because the parole board believed it wasn't his fault. Jack never got none of the money, neither. His sister took it.'

'This is Elizabeth Armstrong?'

'She stole the money and ran away with it, Jack said. That's why it was never found. Elsie disappeared with it.'

Hilary jotted down some notes. 'Did Mr Shaughnessy mention anything to you about the victim's family? Or about Mrs Cohen's cousin, to whom the stolen money belonged?'

Mr Linton shook his head. 'He only talked about his sister owing him the money.'

'Has he made contact with her?'

'I think so. I mean, he knew where she lived. He was planning to go sniffing round, talk to the neighbours and that. Find out what she was calling herself these days.'

'But you said she'd disappeared – how did he learn her current whereabouts?'

Mr Linton pursed his lips guiltily. 'I went to the house. You know, where it happened. In our old street. I was meant to ask Mrs Cohen if she ever heard from Elsie. But Mrs Cohen was dead. Another lady was living in the house. She said she used to look after Mrs Cohen. We got to talking, and she said she had an address for Elsie. She wasn't sure if it was up to date, though. Elsie was wonderful to poor Naomi, she said. Visited her, paid for things.'

'Do you have the address?'

'I gave it to Jack. I don't remember the name of the street. South-west, somewhere.'

'Could you try a bit harder to remember? Really think.'

'I'm sorry, I . . .'

'Don't worry. What was Jack's state of mind when you last saw him? Was he unhappy, or worried about anything?'

'He was the same old Jack. Nothing ever really got him down. If I'd spent half my life behind bars, I'd be bitter, I reckon. Or depressed. But he wasn't.'

The door opened and a small boy toddled in, carrying a shredded blanket and sucking his thumb. He removed it to say: 'Dada, dada, story.'

'Sorry,' said Mr Linton to Hilary. 'Horace, I thought you were asleep. Dada's talking to his friend just now.'

Horace considered Hilary. 'We're having a treat party, with cakes,' he informed him. 'You can come,' he added with a benevolent dip of his chin.

'He means a street party,' said Mr Linton. 'For the Queen's coronation. It's all a bit of a silly fuss if you ask me. But the children will enjoy it. When I was a boy, we had a street party for King George's silver jubilee. A photographer from the local paper was there, and me and Jack were on the front page. My mum was tickled pink. It went straight in the scrapbook. D'you want to see it?'

'Certainly,' said Hilary politely.

'Maggie,' he called. 'Mum's old scrapbook. Where is it?'

'Just a moment,' Mrs Linton shouted back. After a few minutes, she brought in a large wallpaper-covered book, handed it to her husband and scooped up Horace, who began wailing at the injustice of being taken back to bed.

'Here we are,' said Mr Linton. 'Look at Jack. You'd think butter wouldn't melt. And that's me. Right little fatso, wasn't I?'

The boys, aged around eleven, were sitting at the end of a long table decorated with twisted crêpe-paper garlands. All the children, and some of the adults who stood behind them, wore party hats and were smiling at the camera.

'Who's that?' asked Hilary, pointing to a young woman in a nip-waisted jacket, her hair sculpted into regimented waves. Surely it couldn't be . . . except it was, he'd almost swear to it.

Mr Linton smiled. 'Would you look at that. It's only Elsie, isn't it? I forgot she was in the photograph.'

'How old is Elsie in that photo?'

'Let's think – twenty-five, twenty-six? She was quite a few years older than Jack. He was one of those unfortunate surprises. His mother used to say she'd shut up shop, and let her guard down just the once, after taking a drink to celebrate the British leaving Ireland. She was from Cork, you see.'

'So you don't know anyone who keeps in touch with Elsie?'

'No one. We lived down the road from her for years. But when all that unpleasant business happened, she vanished. Never even visited her mother. It was a shame for Mrs Shaughnessy. She was a widow. Then her son went to prison, and her daughter buggered off. Excuse me, ran away. Mrs Shaughnessy died not that long after. She couldn't have been much more than fifty.'

Hilary took all this in, then said: 'Do you believe Elsie stole the money?'

Mr Linton shrugged. 'I dunno why Jack would make something like that up. What would be the point?'

Mina got off the bus and spotted George coming out of the newsagent's. 'Hullo, George,' she said. 'I haven't seen you for days. Is everything all right?'

They walked along side by side. 'I've been at Rory's all weekend,' said George. 'But I simply must change my clothes. Nothing's happened, has it, at Tregunter Road?'

'No, nothing. Not since my encounter with the detective.' Mina paused. 'George, why did he know before I did about you and—'

George cut her off. 'There is no me and Jimmy. Was, I mean. So I take it Honor hasn't told you about the barmaid? At the King's Arms?'

'No, what about her?'

George looked at her wristwatch. 'It's past opening time. Come and have a drink at the Six Bells. My shout. I don't know about you, but I'm fed up with secrets.'

Mina gaped at George. 'Lovers?' She said the word as though for the first time, with not only scepticism but also bewilderment. 'But Robbie isn't like that, is he?'

'I'm afraid some men are, darling.' George took a large sip of her gin and mint. 'They can't help it, you know.'

'And . . .' Mina looked quizzical, then hesitated. 'What about women? Are they ever . . .'

'Of course.' George was about to launch into some boarding-school stories, but the poor girl looked so discombobulated that she thought it best to change the subject. 'But Mina, listen, I was wondering if you could explain – what is the history between Jimmy and Saul? Honor won't tell me. What did Jimmy do to him that was so terrible?'

'Oh George, it's too awful. They never should have let Jimmy out of prison. And Honor shouldn't have let him live with us. The lies that woman has told, I—' She stopped herself and sighed. 'But none of it is my story to tell, I'm afraid. Not unless Saul says he doesn't mind.'

The barman came over to them at the back of the snug. 'Excuse me, ladies,' he murmured apologetically. 'The two gentlemen over there wish to buy you a drink.'

They looked in the direction of his nod. The men were maybe thirty-five, officey-looking, with three-piece suits and ties. Harmless enough, thought George.

'One more for the road?' she said. 'I think we deserve it, don't you?'

When Mina and George came in from the pub at around 7.30, they were met by a frantic Honor. 'They've taken him!' she said. 'They've taken Saul!'

'Who has?' said Mina.

'Comyns. He came with two other policemen. They searched the house – turned it upside down, from top to bottom – and then they arrested him. Oh girls.' She grabbed George's arm. 'What have we done?'

Tuesday 9 June 1953

'We'll have to see what Robbie says,' said Honor. 'I mean, we must assume his fingerprints are on the gun.'

'And if we wipe it,' said George thoughtfully, 'we'll also remove—'

'Precisely. But darling, I mean it: you only have to say the word and I'll drop the idea. Apart from anything else, to kill a man in order to fend off suspicion for a different man's death . . . well, in Agatha Christie stories, the so-called auxiliary murder is usually the key to the villain's downfall.'

George laughed. 'This is real life, not a story written to a formula. And what's the alternative? We sit back and let Saul be tried for murder – even hanged? No. I couldn't live with myself. And neither could you.'

21

A Well-Turned-Out Little Thing

1939–40

If it weren't for Thomas needing ready cash to pay for his solicitor and counsel, Elsie knew he'd have kept his lip buttoned about where he'd hidden the money, the thousand pounds he and Jack had stolen from Naomi and Larry. As it was, he had little choice. He trusted her more than any of his friends, or his rotten family. More fool him. And fair's fair: she gave the solicitor enough to get the ball rolling. There was no possibility of them getting bail, in any case. Nor of being found not guilty. Though she supposed a clever KC could make a difference when it came to sentencing. But they didn't deserve the help that money could buy, did they?

And you deserve it, do you? enquired the reproving angel on her shoulder. Yes, she thought, as it happens, I do. With something like relief, she gave herself over to amorality, to ruthless self-preservation. Her treachery to Naomi was somehow consigned to an inaccessible chamber of her mind. She deserved to escape, to uproot herself from the poverty and sordidness into which she'd been thrust by accident of birth. And here, unexpectedly, was her chance. She'd be an utter fool not to take it. Jack and Thomas gone, likely for good; nearly one thousand pounds at her disposal. And war all but certain, impending chaos she could disappear into.

The weather was volatile that August, one might even say ominous: stormy, with thunder and lightning and hailstones. On the evening of Sunday the 27th, after her mother had gone to bed, Elsie went to her own room and slid open the sash window. The warm damp air rushed at her face, smelling salty and riverish and filling her with a restless excitement. She felt in the grip of possibility, a novel and glorious sensation. She wouldn't take much with her, she decided. Just a small suitcase. After all, the first order of business should be buying a new wardrobe. The thought made her blush with happiness. French silk underwear. Silver kid evening shoes from Jacobus. A velvet dinner dress from Enos Ltd. Dressmaker suits from Molyneux. Blouses from Liberty's.

She thought about leaving a letter for her mother. But really, what was the point? What could she feasibly say? There were no words to justify her actions. More to the point, she didn't care to justify herself. From the moment she was born, not a single human had prioritised her well-being, including – no, especially – her parents. She hadn't been sorry when her father died, and she'd shed few tears over not seeing her mother again. Thank God she and Thomas had no children. He was mystified that she'd never conceived during their six years of marriage. But she'd always known it was unlikely, if not impossible. Occasionally guilt, even regret, had pricked her. Yet how glad she was now! A child would be a good deal harder to discard and forget.

She left home soon after dawn and waited for the first Tube. She travelled a few stops, then sat in a café in Marchmont Street, WC, for a couple of hours before presenting herself at a ladies' hostel off Russell Square. It was a dreary and anonymous sort of place, which was for the best. Until she'd effected her transformation, she didn't wish to draw any sort of attention to herself. And there was plenty of time – all the time in the world, in fact.

The following days and weeks passed in a pleasant haze as she did little but stroll around the West End, shopping and sitting in tea rooms. The haze was heightened by blurry sporadic lightheadedness thanks to her commitment to a strict diet outlined in *Vogue* (she studied the magazine like it was divine scripture). Coffee, tea, wine, eggs and beef were allowed; verboten were starches, milk and cheese, fruit and vegetables. Her cheekbones began to emerge, her eyes looked larger, and her collarbones were gratifyingly prominent. Her waist, however, still measured twenty inches. When it measured eighteen, she would have attained her ideal shape.

For her appointment at the Harley Street plastic surgeon, she dressed carefully in a puff-sleeved alligator-green rayon crêpe dress, tightly belted and hitting just below the knee, and a grey fox stole. Mr Nigel Lacey, an elderly silver-haired man smelling of cigars and carbolic soap, regarded her with an urbane twinkle.

'Young lady,' he said, 'my job is to repair disfigurements caused by injury, or by some defect of nature. Unless you are concealing a hideous deformity with that delightful costume, I fear you have wandered into my office by mistake. I'm a surgeon, not a god – I cannot improve upon perfection.'

Elsie – or Bianca Skelton, as she was temporarily calling herself – laughed. 'A surgeon and an expert flatterer. What I'm hoping you might do, Mr Lacey, is remove the bump on my nose.' She turned her head to display her profile.

Mr Lacey emerged from behind his large desk and brought his face close to Elsie-Bianca's. He ran a finger down the bridge of her nose, then grasped her chin between thumb and forefinger and moved her face from side to side. 'Are you perchance an actress, Mrs Skelton?'

She grasped at the idea gratefully. 'I'm on the stage, yes. My management thinks I have a chance to be in films, but I've been told I don't photograph well.'

'And what does your husband think?'

'He's very supportive of my career. He's in the arts himself.'

'Hmm.' He sat back down. 'It should be a simple operation, very simple indeed. We break the bone, then reset it. If I might make a recommendation – it's not necessary, and yet . . .'

'Oh, but please.'

'A small chin enhancement, to go with the new nose. Again, it's very simple. We pop in a little crescent of cartilage, just to give a firmer prominence. A more elegant facial silhouette, as it were. We'll put you to sleep, of course. You won't feel a thing.'

She brought a hand to her chin. 'Will there be a scar?'

'A tiny one. No one will notice.'

She smiled. 'How soon can you fit me in?'

Once the bruises had faded, it was nearly Christmas. The newspapers were full of Mr Chamberlain's visit to France, where he was inspecting the units on patrol. These consisted of mostly rural men from the north of England, many of whom would never see their homes again. In a way, reflected Elsie, Jack and Thomas were better off where they were.

She had found a flatlet in Bird Street, near Selfridges, and she entrusted the next stage of her transformation to the Selfridges hair salon. A slight young Frenchman, his braces holding his trousers high on his waist, attended on her. He struck Elsie as frail, defenceless. She hoped he'd be allowed to spend the war there, in that pink-painted room smelling of coconut shampoo and peroxide, far away from the battlefield. But when he unfolded her mousy-brown chignon and raked his fingers through it, staring at her critically in the mirror, she realised she was in confident hands. Emboldened, she told him: 'I want something dramatic. Something sophisticated. I'm not frightened of a big change.'

He brightened at this. 'I think,' he said, 'your style is *à la garçonne*. We cut to here' – he sliced his hand across the back of her head – 'and dye it black. Yes?'

Having offered him carte blanche, she could only agree, despite her mild terror. But ninety minutes later, when he removed the dryer and began arranging her new hair, she saw she'd been right to trust him. Not only did she look years younger, you'd never have taken her for an English-Irish jailbird's wife from Stepney. She appeared glamorously, indefinably continental. With her new straight nose and firmer chin, she might even pass for an aristocrat, she thought. A debutante.

'Tell me honestly,' she said to the clever Frenchman, 'looking at me now, what age would you guess me to be?'

He finished smoothing a side-curl with his fingertip, considered her, and said with apparent sincerity: 'Twenty, perhaps twenty-one.'

And so, three months after her thirty-first birthday, she knocked ten years off her age.

After around six months of freedom, the money, which had seemed inexhaustible, began to run low. Elsie – now Honor

Petrova, a name she chose after buying a set of Louis Vuitton luggage monogrammed HP at a Christie's auction – turned her mind to finding work. Since she'd have sooner died than go back to waitressing, she embarked upon a correspondence course in typing and shorthand. She also invented an education: boarding school in Geneva, finishing school in Fontainebleau. Guided by the announcers on the BBC, she began to alter her voice, lowering its pitch and sharpening her consonants, mimicking certain words as practice: bot-tull; iss-yu; evacu-ay-shun of civil-yins. Her neighbours, listening through the thin walls, must have thought her quite potty. She didn't care.

Despite all this, it took a fair amount of courage to present herself at the secretarial agency. She feared they'd take one glance and see her for what she truly was. The first challenge was the girl on reception. She was on the telephone when Honor entered the rather modest rooms, situated unpropitiously above an ironmonger's in Goodge Street. Lawton and Grey, the firm was called. Honor had chosen it from the telephone directory, the sole criterion being that the name sounded smart, but not too smart.

'Mm-hmm,' the girl was saying to her interlocutor. 'All right, then.' She rolled her eyes at Honor to indicate that whoever it was, they were tiresome. When she rang off, she sighed cheerfully and handed Honor a clipboard and a ballpoint pen. 'You're new, aren't you? Fill this in – don't worry if there're bits you can't answer, just leave them blank – and then I'll send you in to do your typing test.'

For some reason the possibility of a test hadn't crossed Honor's mind. Oh well, she thought, the worst that can happen is they'll turn you out. She filled in the form carefully. Her handwriting had always been decent, at least. Then she was taken into the main office and placed behind a monstrous Imperial contraption with large round keys.

She'd never actually touched a typewriting machine before; her correspondence course had only required her to move her fingers across a diagram printed on cardboard. It took surprising strength to press down the keys. She managed only twenty words per minute, with fifty per cent accuracy.

'I'm awfully sorry,' she told Mrs Grey, an older lady with stiff white hair and a yellow jersey. 'I haven't had much practice. I'm sure I'll improve.' She had seven pounds and six shillings to her name.

But Mrs Grey seemed unconcerned. 'We'll find you something where typing isn't the main task,' she said, running an evaluative eye over Honor's outfit. 'You're a well-turned-out little thing. Decorative. And' – she put on her spectacles and looked at the filled-in form – 'you must speak French.'

Oh God, thought Honor. Please don't ask me to demonstrate.

'Marjorie,' said Mrs Grey, turning her head. 'Is the file for that publisher, the one in Vigo Street, on your desk?'

Marjorie (presumably Mrs Lawton) was a younger, plumper woman with a well-powdered face and an Hermès scarf knotted around her neck. She strolled across the room holding a buff-coloured folder. As she returned to her desk, she trailed a faint delicious cloud of Femme de Rochas.

'Ah yes,' said Mrs Grey, glancing through the file's contents. 'You might do very well for this. Do you like reading?'

'Adore it,' said Honor.

'I'll give the chap a ring. But I'm sure he'll consider you more than suitable. His firm isn't exempt from conscription, so he's lost several young men. We'll be in touch.'

'Hilda Grey tells me you speak French,' said Gerald Wilson. 'I was stationed in Nîmes, you know, during the Great War. *Votre internat était-il francophone?*'

Honor smiled and nodded, panic in her eyes. Ah, thought Gerald. Either she or Mrs Grey had exaggerated. He wondered what else she'd lied about. 'Not married, then?' he asked. 'Any boyfriends?'

Back on safer ground, Honor told him no. 'I've not been in London long, you see. My parents are still on the continent.' *Con-ta-nint*. 'So I'm trying to make a go of things by myself. People have been so kind. Like Mrs Grey. And I'm awfully keen to get to work. I'm sure I can turn my hand to anything you need me to.'

Gerald was a man of the world. He'd striven far from less-than-ideal beginnings and knew rank desperation when he saw it. Poor wretch. He hadn't the heart to disappoint her. She'd find other work, of course, there was no question of that. But the idea of this fragile girl in a bustling typing pool or, worse, on a factory line where she'd be sitting prey for men less cultured, less scrupulous than himself – well, it was somehow not to be borne. She wore a tiny ruby around her neck: it rested on the dip of her clavicle and emphasised the whiteness of her skin. He'd never seen skin quite like it. Not a mark or a freckle, no suggestion of a flush nor the tint of a vein. Her hair was cut severely above her ears, not a style that generally met with his approval. Barbara had long blonde hair that he enjoyed unpinning, winding round his hands. Yet looking at this child, with her elongated neck and sharp jawline, he suddenly understood the appeal of the gamine.

'Why don't I start by organising things a bit in here?' said Honor, looking around at the mess of books and papers in Gerald's office. He realised he hadn't spoken for several moments, and that she thought he was mulling over whether to employ her.

'Goodness me, no,' he said. 'No need for that. Can you start on Monday? Mary, my secretary, will be here then. She'll show you the ropes.'

I'm a soft old git, he thought. But the expression of pure relief on the girl's face was all the reward he needed.

Or so he'd have sworn. A sense of paternal responsibility, nothing more, guided his thoughts during Honor's first weeks of employment. Protecting her innocence seemed a duty commensurate with his worthiness as a man. Only upon war – upon history itself – was that worthiness wrecked. When David and Michael went MIA, only a month apart, Honor was a fount of sympathy and selfless tender ministrations. His wife, Barbara, white-faced and mute with grief, turned in on herself. She was unable to process the enormity of it. Her beautiful sons, aged twenty-three and twenty-one, wiped out senselessly. As she raged silently against the universe, Gerald sought solace in the only way he knew how.

But if that was how Gerald and Honor's relationship began, it soon became a true love affair, at least for Gerald. And the depth of his passion for Honor, he discovered, all but eclipsed any guilt. I'm only human, he told himself. What man of nearly sixty could resist this exquisite raven-haired creature, who at twenty-two had the body of a fourteen-year-old girl and yet somehow possessed a bedroom repertoire as heady as the coquettes in the blue-lamp brothels on the Western Front? Such gifts, he had supposed, were uniquely French. He was very happy to be proven wrong.

It was perhaps to Gerald's greater astonishment that Honor's editorial knack, and her eye for sellable work, emerged as quite superior to the Oxbridge fellows who used to work for him. She absorbed his teaching with almost masculine facility, soon becoming indispensable. When it was announced that young unmarried women were to be called up, she pointed out an obvious solution. She could be strangely forthright in that way.

But Gerald didn't have to think about it. That very lunchtime, he went out and bought a two-carat diamond ring from Hancock's, conveniently two doors down from their offices.

With scarcely a hint of guile, Honor declared herself the happiest girl in the world.

22

A Legitimate Provocation

Hilary had come to his decision reluctantly. Yet in the end, he saw no other path forward. He only wished he could make the arrest quietly and unaccompanied. There was no question, after all, of Mr Reznikov causing any trouble. But it was out of his hands: he was obliged to attend Tregunter Road with Chief Inspector Lish of the Chelsea Constabulary and Lish's junior colleague, Detective Inspector Hodge.

Lish hammered forcefully on the front door, no doubt meaning to frighten the residents out of their wits. They heard hurried footsteps approaching. When Mrs Wilson opened the door, her expression of outrage turned to masked terror at the sight of them, three rigidly poised men in mackintoshes. Hilary knew then, knew without question, that she was hiding something serious. Her skin was a bloodless grey; the black stuff on her eyelashes had smudged like soot. She suddenly looked every second of her real age – which, he now knew, was forty-four.

'Detective Inspector, you've brought some friends,' she parried. 'But how nice. Please, come in.'

'Good evening, Mrs Wilson,' said Hilary pleasantly. 'I apologise for the intrusion. It's Mr Reznikov we're here for. Can you please fetch him?' But Lish had already peeled off from the group and found the back stairs. 'Down here, is he?' he called, leaving the rest of them no choice but to follow him.

'Please,' she said, pursuing Lish down the stairs. 'You must knock. You can't just go barging—'

Lish shouldered the basement door open and went in. Mr Reznikov, obviously hearing the commotion, was on his feet and doing up the top button of his shirt. Before the ambushed man could speak, Lish said: 'We are policemen from the Chelsea Constabulary and New Scotland Yard. We have come to arrest you on charges relating to the disappearance of Jack Shaughnessy, also known as James Sullivan. I must inform you that we're going to search these premises.'

You might make your enjoyment a bit less plain, thought Hilary. Lish was a large lubricious Scot with thick sideburns and huge fingers – the type of man blessedly unacquainted with self-doubt. His colleague, Hodge, though not exactly shy and retiring, was made of finer, more austere stuff. He had dark eyes – Italians or Spaniards lurked in his family tree, suspected Hilary – and a watchful air. Hilary saw him extend a consoling hand to Mrs Wilson, who was quietly weeping and shooting reproachful glances at all of them.

Mr Reznikov, who had said nothing, began shaking with a dreadful violence. Hilary could hardly bear it and announced his intention to begin searching at the top of the house. 'Who's upstairs?' he asked. But Mrs Wilson seemed not to hear him.

*

As he stepped onto the landing, Robbie Trafford emerged from one of the attic bedrooms. He blinked at Hilary, like an animal who'd been woken, and said: 'Are we all to be arrested?'

'Why should you think that?' replied Hilary. 'It's Mr Reznikov who has been arrested. But I'm afraid I must search your room.'

Mr Trafford stood aside without objection, then sat on the edge of his neatly made bed. Methodically, conscious of the man's eyes upon him, Hilary went through the desk drawers. He fanned a pile of typescripts, scanned some letters and glanced through notebooks.

'You've written a lot, haven't you?' he said. 'Are those novels?'

'Partial novels, yes. A load of old rubbish most likely.'

'I'm sure that's not true.' He realised he was rushing his task, eager to finish searching the room before Lish and Hodge appeared, as though he knew what he was about to find. Mr Trafford, he felt, knew too. There emanated from him an air of surrender to his fate.

Hilary could easily have missed the notes and very nearly did: they comprised four scrappy pieces of paper, folded in two and tucked into the elastic of an out-of-date desk diary. He looked at them, then at Mr Trafford, who'd turned his head towards the window, jaw set and fists clenched. The contents of the notes – brief, cod-poetic, vulgar yet not without a certain inventive eroticism – surprised Hilary less than the handwriting. It was delicate and ornate, tiny and precise, lending the crudest words a sort of spiritual intensity. Who among us, he thought, could fail to be seduced by the composer of such a hand?

'Why didn't you burn these? Why not get rid of them after I first came here, if not before?'

Mr Trafford turned to meet his gaze. With an almost imperceptible shake of the head, he conveyed that he knew he ought to have done, he knew it very well, yet had found himself unable.

'So it was you and the girl Georgina.' Hilary spoke quickly and very quietly. 'He was playing you off against each other, was that it?'

Shrugging helplessly, Mr Trafford said: 'But why are you blaming Saul?' He spoke in almost a whisper, matching Hilary's vocal pitch. 'He wouldn't harm a fly. Nor would I, but—'

'His motive is plain. Yours is . . . well, yours is murky. Mr Sullivan couldn't have blackmailed you without implicating himself.'

'I thought sexual jealousy was an accepted motive.'

'Mr Trafford.' Hilary pulled out the desk chair, hitched up his trousers, and sat down. 'Do you want to make a confession?' He was half-joking. This man plainly wasn't capable of murder. Still, he was curious to see what he'd say.

'No, no, don't be absurd. If Mr Sullivan has died, I'm very sorry about that.'

Hilary still held the love notes in his hand. 'Not heartbroken, though?'

Mr Trafford said nothing.

'Anyway,' said Hilary, 'in films, it's often the case.'

'That the motive is jealousy, you mean?'

'In real life, it's usually money. Money, or revenge.'

From beneath them came a sound like glass smashing. 'That's George's room. In her case, going through the billets-doux of her lovers may take some time.' Mr Trafford smiled, and in his smile was bitterness and contrition and actual grief. It was shocking. Looking back much later, Hilary wondered if that was the moment he made his decision – or if, in fact, he'd made it the moment he laid eyes on the notes. Either way, he slid the incendiary evidence into his pocket and stood up. 'I'm not going to show these to anyone,' he said. 'Not unless I have to, at any rate.'

'But—'

'I'm not being kind, if that's what you think. If the counsel for Mr Reznikov – or for whoever ends up in the dock for this – if they got hold of them, just imagine the tale they could spin. The jury would have reasonable doubt coming out of their ears.'

Mr Trafford took a sharp intake of breath and said: 'What makes you think he's actually dead, and hasn't just run away from his troubles? I wouldn't blame him.'

Hilary gave him a look of playful warning that said: I won't be drawn any further. For a shade longer than necessary, Mr Trafford held eye contact, his pupils expanding a tiny, unmistakable fraction. How the body gives us away! Hilary felt the hint of a smile play across his lips. Then he lowered his chin, brought his fist to his mouth, and cleared his throat. 'Stand up, please. I shall have to check under your mattress. Will I find anything else?'

'Let's start at the beginning, Mr Reznikov. Why don't you tell me when you first heard the name Jack Shaughnessy.'

Saul lit the first of many cigarettes and looked directly at Comyns, who was sitting across from him. He sensed no malevolence, only the focused intention of a man keen to do his job effectively. 'It was in 1939, before the war,' he said. 'Naturally you're familiar with Mr Shaughnessy's criminal record. So, yes, it was after my cousin and her husband were attacked in their home.'

'Hmm,' said Comyns. 'Horrible business. Please forgive my confusion, but how was it that you then became the lodger of Mr Shaughnessy's sister? You do know Mrs Wilson is his sister?'

'How did you . . .' Saul blurted. So Honor's cover was blown at last. His head ached as he tried to think through the ramifications.

'It's true, then? Honor Wilson is Elsie Armstrong?'

He swept a hand across his hair. 'It's quite simple. Not long after I moved to London, in 1947, I met Mrs Wilson at a party. A literary sort of affair. Her husband was in publishing, you know. Then I met her again, or rather I met Elsie. It was at my cousin's house. At Naomi's. Mrs Wilson used to visit her. They were old friends, and Naomi didn't blame Elsie for what her husband and brother had done. Why would she? It wasn't her fault. And Elsie was very good to Naomi, financially and otherwise.'

'Does that mean you were one of the few people who knew who Mrs Wilson really was?'

'I was the only person. I mean, aside from Jimmy. Mr Shaughnessy.'

'Right. So then, in the present day, Mrs Wilson lets her wayward sibling come and live with her. Why?'

Why indeed, thought Saul. 'I suppose he threatened her with exposure. With telling the world she was a fraud. She had put superhuman effort into changing her . . . changing her identity. Making a good life for herself. I cannot blame her for not wanting to . . . to throw it all away.'

'I must say,' said Comyns slowly, 'I find that generous of you.' He reached for his cigarette case and lit one. 'It was thanks to Shaughnessy, was it not, that you didn't manage to bring your family to Britain before it was too late?'

'I didn't say I was happy about it. About his living there in the house with us.'

'That's putting it mildly, surely? If I were you, I'd have wanted to kill him. I cannot imagine a more legitimate provocation. I'm sure a jury would agree. It's a classic crime of passion.'

Saul laughed, a short and bitter guffaw. 'Detective Inspector. My wife and daughter died ten years ago. I haven't been walking around ever since in a perpetual state of violent anger. As for committing murder, I've never even been in a physical altercation. If Mr Shaughnessy has turned up dead somewhere, that's very unfortunate. But it's nothing to do with me. And I know for a fact that you have no evidence otherwise – except for, perhaps, what's the phrase?' He'd heard it from Mina. 'Circumstance evidence.'

Comyns smoked and narrowed his eyes at Saul. 'The thing is, Mr Reznikov. You're the only person at Tregunter Road with a clear motive. I must tell you, that means I can charge you with the capital crime of murder. But perhaps I'm barking up the wrong tree. I'm not infallible – I'd be the first person to tell you that. Perhaps new evidence will emerge that exonerates you. But if not . . .' He stubbed out his cigarette, lifted his right shoulder, exposed his right palm. A fey gesture, thought Saul. 'You don't seem like an evil man, Mr Reznikov. You understand, however, that a life has been taken. Someone, therefore, must pay.'

'Shouldn't my solicitor have arrived by now?'

'I'll go and check in a moment. Of course, even without his presence, you don't have to tell me anything. I can't force you to speak. There are some things you ought to know, though. When I said you were the only person with a clear motive, I wasn't being entirely truthful.'

'Forgive me, Detective Inspector, but you're making very little sense. First you accuse me of murder, then you say there's another suspect. Whoever this man is, he is presumably roaming the streets, at liberty to kill again. Meanwhile, you're wasting time cross-questioning me about trivialities, such as my personal relationship with Mrs Wilson.'

Comyns half smiled. 'You said Mrs Wilson let her brother live at her house because she feared her real identity being exposed. I wonder if you realise his blackmail material was far more serious?'

Saul felt a coldness in his bowels.

'That money, stolen from your cousin's house and never recovered.' Comyns paused for effect. 'She took it.'

'What a ridiculous thing to say. I—'

'Think about it. How else was she able to achieve such an astonishing self-reinvention? As you said, a whole new life.'

'Her husband was older, successful. He had—'

'Ah yes. Mr Wilson. Unfortunately, a bigamous union. The former Elsie Armstrong is still married to Thomas Armstrong, residing at Her Majesty's pleasure. I visited him the other day. He had some choice words for her, I can tell you. Mr Reznikov, are you feeling all right?'

Saul opened his mouth to reply. His tongue stuck to the roof of his mouth. 'What are you saying?'

'I'm saying that perhaps it wasn't you who killed Mr Shaughnessy. I can't make up my mind, is the thing. Mrs Wilson's motive, whilst a different kettle of fish to yours, is fairly persuasive. She wasn't only to be exposed as a female Walter Mitty, you see, but as a ruthless criminal.'

Could it all be lies, wondered Saul, an interrogatory technique designed to elicit useful information?

'Before Elsie Armstrong became Honor Wilson, before she began working at the firm where she and her husband met – well, her would-be husband – she was already dressing in expensive clothes, furs, jewellery. And according to Thomas Armstrong, nearly a thousand pounds in stolen cash – yours – was hidden in a lock-up. It disappeared along with his wife when he was still on remand.'

Saul blinked. Then he covered his face with his hands.

Comyns reached over the scarred and pitted wooden table and touched Saul's wrist. His fingertips were cool and soft. 'Mr Reznikov. Why don't we prepare a witness statement, you and I? You can explain how Mrs Wilson killed her brother. Then you can go home. Or I can arrange for a hotel, if you don't wish to go back to Tregunter Road. She destroyed your life once, didn't she? Don't let her destroy it all over again.'

23

A Cuckoo in the Nest

'I thought it would be nicer to go for a walk,' said Hilary, 'and talk informally, rather than at Scotland Yard.'

He and George entered Brompton Cemetery. From the brightness of an early-June afternoon, they were plunged into cool shade. Tall ancient beeches overhung the wide path bordered by ivy-clad stone crosses, carved angels and flat marble memorials. The dead were the only witnesses to the conversation about to take place.

'Is that usually a consideration of yours, then?' said George. 'Being nice?' Her tone was teasing, but she looked straight ahead with a sober expression.

'Ah, I mainly meant nicer for me. There are some days I can't bear being stuck in an office.'

'Oh? I've never worked in an office. I've always thought it sounded rather convivial. Do you have a tea lady who comes round with a trolley?'

'Certainly. She has biscuits, too.'

'You seem to get out and about a lot, though. I suppose one must, as a detective.'

Comyns took his cue. 'Obviously you're aware that your house underwent an official search. I trust it didn't take you too long to rearrange everything.'

George gave him a sidelong glance. Underwent! As though the house had volunteered itself for the experience. And that sterile phrase, *official search*, connoting nothing of the reality of it. They'd left a complete mess. A vase had been smashed, her personal items pawed through, dresses and coats pulled out of the wardrobe and left on the floor. 'It ought not to be allowed,' she said. 'How would you like it if you came home to find the place ransacked?'

'I apologise. My colleagues from the constabulary – they are . . .' He made a vague gesture, apparently unwilling or unable to describe their shortcomings. 'In any case, they couldn't fail to notice a very large stain on the underside of your mattress. Blood, by the looks of it.'

'Are you married, Detective Inspector?' asked George.

'No, I'm—'

'Yet you understand the workings of the female body?' She was being sarcastic. Still, she had her doubts. There was something ascetic about Comyns, this elegant man who spent his days wading through moral filth whilst remaining miraculously, conspicuously spotless.

'I saw it myself. It was—'

'Not menstrual blood? Would you be prepared to swear to that in court?'

'Miss Mountford-Owen, you seem to be putting words into my mouth. If you say there is an innocent explanation, then please, there's no need for us to go into detail.'

George's cheeks burned. The indignity of it. Irritably she said: 'Well then. If you think I can help you to frame Mr Reznikov for something he didn't do, I'm afraid you've got another think coming. What that poor man must be going through. Have you no conscience? He was persecuted by the Nazis, you know.'

'I do know. But do *you* know his history with Mr Sullivan?'

She extracted a hanky from her cardigan sleeve and blew her nose. 'Excuse me. A touch of hay fever.' She had gathered, of course, that Jimmy had committed some horrific wrong against Saul in the distant past. Mina had confirmed as much, whilst refusing to divulge the gory details. Honor, too, refused to explain the two men's erstwhile connection – which made George suspect it had to do, somehow, with Jimmy and herself being siblings. She felt like she was going insane, being kept in the dark about the fabric of her own life.

'Why does it matter,' she said, 'what I know and don't know?'

He indicated a bench. 'Shall we sit?'

The bench's horizontal iron slats pressed coldly through her cotton skirt. She longed for this encounter to be over, to be in her room with a cup of tea, listening to the Light Programme. As he started monologuing about how Saul wouldn't have been arrested were it not for certain evidence, but that pieces were missing, George's mind split into two. One half paid attention to Comyns while the other half deliberated over how Jimmy could have been her brother. Was she adopted? Though she could scarcely imagine her parents, of all people, assuming responsibility for an unwanted baby. Then again, perhaps she didn't know them at all. Perhaps everyone harboured unfathomable secrets. All this time, she realised, she'd lived among strangers at Tregunter Road. It had never occurred to her to be wary or mistrustful. Yet, except for Mina, they had all misled her as to their true selves, had concealed cataclysmic facts.

George was circling ever faster around this ruminative helter-skelter when Comyns said, 'Mrs Wilson's brother,' pulling the whole of her attention back to him.

'I beg your pardon,' she said. 'Could you repeat that?'

'Mr Sullivan. He was Mrs Wilson's brother. Her real name is Elizabeth Armstrong, and she comes from an impoverished background.'

She smiled, almost involuntarily. So she, Honor, and Jimmy were siblings. Amidst all her anger and befuddlement, the thought of Honor as her sister made George feel warm inside.

'Forgive me,' said Comyns, 'but you don't seem surprised. Mr Reznikov gave me to understand that nobody knew of Mrs Wilson's prior identity.'

'No, I am surprised. I'm a little confused, though, as to what I'm even doing here. How do you think I can help with your investigation? Seeing as you're evidently much more in the picture than I am.'

'I suppose I wanted to give you the chance to tell the truth. Your relationship with Mr Sullivan—'

'There was no relationship. I don't know how much clearer I can be.'

'Were you jealous that he was carrying on with Mr Trafford? Is that why things ended between you?'

She laughed. 'Don't be ridiculous. I didn't even know about that. Nor would I have cared less if I had.'

'And you wish to maintain your position that Mr Sullivan's whereabouts, his fate, is unknown to you?'

'Of course I do. It's not a position, as you put it. It's the truth.'

As George was pondering hers and Honor's blood relationship, Honor was trying to calm herself by making up her face. Now that Saul understood the depth of her wickedness, she mused, spitting on a tiny brush and rubbing it on a mascara cake, now that the past had finally caught up with them, it was almost a relief. When he strode into the kitchen the morning after his night in a police cell, she saw straight away that he knew, that he hated her and always would. How Comyns had found out about the theft, Honor couldn't begin to fathom. It was a credit to him, really. And now he meant to pit them against each other. 'He doesn't have enough evidence to take me to trial,' Saul had said. 'That's obvious. But he thinks I'll turn on you. Believe me, I'd do it. My only fear is that he won't believe you acted alone. Not the burial and everything. And I don't want any of the young people implicated. Especially not Mina.'

Honor tilted her dressing table mirror to get a better light. She'd lost too much weight, she knew, and it wasn't doing her any favours. Not at her age. As a younger woman, the extreme slenderness she'd maintained had been chic. Girlish. Now, as she scrutinised her face, she saw the edges of her eye sockets pressing against the skin. Her front teeth – which at some stage had acquired perfectly symmetrical tobacco stains – seemed to protrude as the flesh around her mouth waned. It reminded her of how Gerald had looked during his last days. She smeared on more panstick and added coral-coloured rouge. That was better. I must go to the office, she thought, and help Robbie. Despite an encroaching sense of futility, they were planning to publish *Vista*'s summer issue in August. Yet she continued to sit at her dressing table, wondering why she couldn't move.

For the hundredth time, she went over her own conversation with Comyns. When he had ambushed her yesterday, in Peter Jones's glass and china department, she'd been rather rude to him. 'Are you following me, Detective Inspector?' she said. 'Hoping to catch me in a criminal act?' This won't do, she thought, and immediately softened her tone. 'Actually, I'm looking for a new vase for George, to replace the one those officers of yours smashed. You can help me choose it. Lulu' – and here she indicated her dog, whose little ears pricked up at the sound of her name – 'is not an ideal shopping companion. Her taste in home decor runs to gaudy.'

And so she and Comyns browsed together. To the store's other clientele, the gaily dressed housewives on a quest for a wedding gift or a new teapot, they doubtless looked for all the world like a normal couple.

'How is Mr Reznikov?' asked Comyns.

'He's bearing up, I suppose.' Honor stopped to consider a small Murano vase in swirling shades of green. 'He'll be better once you drop all charges against him.'

'I must say, I find it creditable, the loyalty you two share. There comes a time, however, when you must think of yourself.' He spoke softly. If an innocent person had been eavesdropping, they'd have heard nothing but compassion in his tone. 'That you didn't obtain a divorce from your first husband – well, obviously I only investigate crimes of a more serious nature.'

She turned to him with a radiant smile. 'Do I hear a "but" coming, by any chance?'

'Mrs Wilson, you're an intelligent woman. Whether or not you choose to cooperate, Mr Reznikov will in all likelihood be tried for murder.'

She tried to interrupt, but he kept talking: 'But as I understand it, for you to be branded a bigamist has wider consequences than mere loss of reputation.'

'And you have it within your power, do you—'

'Of course.'

'To shield me from prosecution, you mean. That's one thing. But I don't see how you could legalise my marriage, if concrete evidence emerged that invalidated it. And therefore jeopardised my pension, my house. Speaking purely hypothetically, of course.'

'Of course. And I can assure you, Mrs Wilson, far deeper wrinkles have been smoothed in the cause of a greater good.'

Well, reflected Honor, he would say that, wouldn't he. Though she supposed it was the sort of arrangement one could get in writing, under lawyerly advisement. Not that she was actually considering it, mind you. It hadn't come to that. Not yet.

She placed a hand on his arm. 'Now, I haven't seen anything nicer than that little green vase, I don't think. Have the Metropolitan Police got an account here?'

For the rest of the day, George kept wondering: who *am* I? She even considered asking Venetia. When George was born, Venetia was fourteen, so she'd have known about a cuckoo in the nest. Yet supposing it wasn't the Mountford-Owens who'd always lied to her? Supposing Honor was lying now, for heaven knew what reason? She certainly had form, if Comyns was to be believed. And what had Mina said? 'The lies that woman has told . . .'

George imagined the impatient disdain on Venetia's face, were she to relate the pickle she was in. And where would she even begin? *The silly cow's really lost her mind this time*, her sister would think. *Succumbing to crackpot delusions*. It was an anxiety of hers, being written off as mad. She remembered a cousin, Lettice, who went slightly cracked after having her fifth baby. She was found roaming the carpet and fabrics department of Marshall & Snelgrove wearing nothing but her dressing gown. In the middle of January, too. Apparently it was a nice dressing gown, pale yellow brocaded satin with soutache embroidery, the sort of thing that could almost pass for evening wear. Nonetheless, Lettice was carted off to a loony bin in Shropshire and given weekly electroshock treatment until she seemed herself again. Except she never quite did.

George would have to talk to her putative mother, then.

When she rang her, Lady Susan sounded surprised but not displeased. 'There's nothing wrong, is there, darling? Or it is good news?'

'No news,' said George, 'either good or bad. I just need to talk to you about something. Daddy won't be there, will he?'

'Oh no,' her mother said offhandedly. 'Your father is in Ireland. Something to do with horses. You know me, I don't ask questions.'

On the train to Winchester the following afternoon, George mentally rehearsed ways of broaching the subject. There was definitely no need to bring up the police business. Yet she could hardly claim to have pulled from thin air the notion that she was some sort of foundling.

It was even more difficult than she had imagined. Mother and daughter walked around the garden and looked at the roses. They drank two cups of tea and smoked several cigarettes. Still she couldn't find the right words. Susan was midway through an impenetrable anecdote involving a dismissed churchwarden, corruption in the May Queen election, and a visiting troupe of Italian rope-dancers when George could contain herself no longer.

'Mummy, are you actually my mother?'

Susan didn't look appalled, or shocked – merely uncomprehending. 'I'm sorry, darling?'

'It's just that . . .' George picked up the heavy onyx cigarette lighter and started playing with its chrome mechanism. 'It's difficult to explain. But I learnt recently that I've got a brother and a sister other than Arabella and Venetia. And there's such an age gap between me and them – I thought perhaps I had different parents. I don't want to cause a flap, or upset anyone. But I'd dearly like to know the facts of the matter.'

Susan removed the lighter from her daughter's hands and set it back down on the coffee table. On the sofa next to her was Sheba, a fifteen-year-old golden retriever, whose neck she slowly stroked. Sheba rested her head in Susan's lap and blinked at George accusingly.

'Look, Georgie,' began Susan, 'I was going to tell you eventually. It just never seemed to matter particularly. It's a common enough thing in families, after all. But you're right; you may as well know. Charles isn't your real father.'

Oh, thought George. Oh. Why hadn't she thought of that?

Susan twisted one of her rings around her middle finger, centring the sapphires. 'You remember my friend Sir Alec St John Gardner?'

With difficulty George summoned the image of a ruddy man with large teeth and hawkish brows. 'You mean to say . . .' She must have looked squeamish, because Susan shook her head and smiled. 'He was terribly handsome as a young man. I wouldn't expect you to see that, not now. But age comes to us all. Who'd believe I was once considered a beauty?'

But the ghost of that beauty remained, thought George, despite the wrinkles and ravages. And Susan still made the effort, still reddened her lips and wore pearls at her ears, tucked a pale silk scarf into the neck of her cardigan.

'He knows about you,' Susan went on. 'There wasn't much room for doubt. Charles and I . . . Well, I'm sure Alec will be delighted if you acknowledge him. Not publicly, of course. But he's always said you're a smashing girl, a chip off the old block. You ought to write to him. Tell him I said to.'

'Wait – so does Daddy know too?'

'Naturally. Why do you think he dislikes you, darling?'

'My personality?'

They both laughed. 'Well, that too,' said Susan. 'No, he was irritated at my carelessness. He didn't mind who I had affairs with. But he didn't want to bring up another man's child. He found it unseemly, or humiliating or something. Infuriating man. It wasn't my fault. I was forty-five when I realised I was having you. I assumed it was my change of life. The penny only dropped when you started kicking. Charles said I was so ancient, you'd be a mongol. He said he'd put you in an institution. But you were a lovely little baby. Much nicer than Arabella or Venetia. Wailing red-faced wretches. I couldn't wait to hand them over to Nanny. Perhaps you took after Alec. You didn't cry or fuss, just gazed at everything with those huge gas-blue eyes. I really don't know what I'm doing here, you seemed to be thinking, this simply isn't what I signed up for, but I suppose I'll give things a fair shot.'

She looked at her daughter intently. It was almost, thought George, as though she was seeing her for the first time since she was a baby. 'You were at school with Daphne Gardner, do you remember? And you came out together.'

'Gosh, good old Daffy, yes. I've not seen her in ages. She was a scream. She winked at the King, you know, when we were presented. She said he winked back, but no one else saw it. She was probably pulling my leg.'

'She married an Eyetie, didn't she?'

'That's right. Count Alfonso of Caserta. Actually a rather dear little man.'

'Ah, yes. I suppose the title makes a difference.' Susan sighed. 'You must have met all the Gardner children at one time or another. I always feared you'd take up with one of the boys – though I don't believe the youngest are Alec's.' She smiled. 'I can't tell you how glad I am this is all out in the open!'

Whereas I'm more confused than ever, thought George. 'Did

Alec . . . does Alec have other offspring out of wedlock, do you know? Perhaps with a woman of not quite the same class?'

'Knowing him,' said Susan with a wryly raised eyebrow, 'I wouldn't rule it out.'

Monday 15 June 1953

'Goodness me,' said Mrs Orla Rosenfeld, bringing red-lacquered fingertips to her chest. 'When you asked to speak to me about someone I used to know, I had quite a few candidates in mind, if you catch my drift.' She winked at Hilary, who very much caught her drift, and pushed a plate of iced lemon creams towards him. 'Have another, Inspector.' The biscuits had been chosen, suspected Hilary, to coordinate with the yellow lampshades and arrangements of daisies in Mrs Rosenfeld's immaculately modern Mayfair drawing room.

She closed her large teeth over a biscuit, chewed rapturously, then continued: 'But little Elsie Shaughnessy! I've not thought about her in donkey's years. And yes, that's right, we were waitresses together in . . . when was it? Gosh, I'll be showing my age here, but it must have been 1922, 1923? Then she had a baby. She wasn't married, poor girl.'

'Actually,' said Hilary, 'that's what I wanted to ask you about. May I smoke?'

24

A Chip Off the Old Block

George arranged her legs across the blanket they'd spread on the lawn and wiggled her bare toes, throwing her head back to soak up the warm sunshine. Honor, who held an old paper parasol, told her she'd get freckles if she wasn't careful.

'I don't care,' said George, eyes closed. 'I don't care if I turn as brown as an Indian.'

'Look at the garden,' said Honor guiltily, reclining on her elbows. 'I must get a man to come and tidy things up. Though I must say, you'd never know where we dug. Do you remember, Robbie planted some poppies there, because he said they'd spread and grow quickly. Now there are only a few poppies and an absolute riot of wild bugleweed. Mother Nature colluding in our scheme.'

George turned her head lazily in the direction of Jimmy's grave. 'Is that what those purple flowers are called, bugleweed? Pretty. A little bunch will look nice in my new vase.'

'I feel there's an apt literary phrase for that. Since Comyns paid for the vase, I mean. Poetic justice? No, that's not right.

Ironic juxtaposition, maybe.' Honor swatted away a bumblebee. 'Robbie would know.'

'So,' said George, 'I went to see my mother yesterday.'

'And how is Lady Susan?'

'Full of revelations, as it happens. Well, one revelation mainly. It turns out my real father isn't Charles, but some old swain of Susan's. Sir Alec St John Gardner. Does that name mean anything to you?'

Honor put down her parasol and sat upright. She opened her mouth to speak. Then she leant forward and touched George's shoulder. 'Is she . . . is she completely sure about that?'

'Evidently so. Reading between the lines, Susan and Charles were no longer sharing a bed by the time of my conception. But what I don't understand – what I'm hoping you'll tell me – is how Sir Alec got together with your mother. Yours and Jimmy's mother, I mean. He was your brother too, wasn't he?'

'Oh, but George.' Honor smiled, and her face seemed to shed all the anguish of the past months. For a moment she looked like the old Honor. 'This is wonderful news.'

'I suppose so. He sounds like a nice fellow, Alec. Nicer than Charles, at any rate. Which doesn't set the bar very high, of course.'

'Indeed not,' said Honor with feeling. 'But what I mean is, if Charles isn't your father, then you and Jimmy were no relation. Charles was *his* father, you see.'

George opened her mouth, but found herself dumbstruck.

'I haven't talked about it in nearly thirty years,' said Honor. 'I was fourteen, and my father had taken me into the West End to apply for a job at a hotel.'

*

Elsie, ascending from the depths of the hotel, found her way back to the service door. She stepped into the brightness of the August afternoon and was momentarily disorientated, unsure in which direction to walk for the Strand. Her father, Conor, would be waiting with great impatience.

But to her surprise, he was talking animatedly to a man she'd never seen before. He was a few years older than Conor, she assessed, and a toff. She could tell from his gold watch-chain, but also from the way he stood, as if his head, though large, weighed less than other people's. He caught Elsie staring and gave her a look she couldn't decipher.

'Ah, here she is at last,' said Conor. 'Elsie, Field Marshal Lord Mountford-Owen saved my life at Ypres. Carried me away from the gas when my leg was shattered.'

'How is the old leg?' asked Lord Mountford-Owen. 'You kept it, didn't you?'

'Oh yes, they pinned it back together all right.'

'So, young lady,' he said to Elsie, 'did you get the position?'

'They'll write, they said. Which probably means no.'

'It had better not,' said Conor. 'She left school weeks ago. Was turned down for a post as a machine operator at the pencil factory. She didn't look strong enough, they said. Not strong enough, my foot. Look at her, healthy great girl.'

Lord Mountford-Owen eyed her unblinkingly, like a lizard. 'No more school, eh?' he said. 'All grown up?'

'My fourteenth birthday was in May,' said Elsie with a note of defensiveness. She didn't understand why he was bothering to talk to her. Grown-ups, especially gentlemen, usually acted like she was invisible. Either that or they looked down their noses, like she had no right to breathe the same air as them.

'Well, they know me here,' he said, gesturing up at the Savoy Hotel & Restaurant sign. 'So don't you worry, I'll put in a good word.'

Do what you like, she thought. Who wants to skivvy in a kitchen anyway? Not her.

'Elsie Shaughnessy?' the man shouted from across the room. He advanced towards her, tall and thin, wearing white like the kitchen staff, except his trousers and jacket were snowy and unblemished. 'You're wanted upstairs, ducks. Well, don't just stand there, look lively.'

She'd been on her feet for nine hours, scrubbing pans, scouring grease off the stoves and peeling and chopping endless piles of vegetables. She put down her potato knife and looked at the man. 'Have I got the sack?' she said hopefully. It was her fifth day, and she wasn't sure how much longer she could stick it. After a day of slaving, she was expected to sleep in a poky little room with two other girls. Ivy snored like a Zeppelin raid and Myrtle droned on endlessly about her fella in the navy, who had promised to marry her when she was sixteen. Rather him than me, thought Elsie, having seen Myrtle without her foundation garments.

The tall man looked her up and down. 'No time for chit-chat, and take that filthy apron off, for Gawd's sake. No, leave it there. We'll find you something to put on.'

She followed him out of the warren of kitchens, through the din of different languages making themselves heard above oven doors slamming, plates clashing, heavy footsteps ferrying everything from half a cow to a barrel of live trout. They went up a narrow metal staircase and emerged into the cave, or so it was known: a sort of staff hub with noticeboards and lockers like at railway stations. 'Minnie,' he yelled, 'be a treasure and get this girl a waitress's uniform, will you? Then send her to me.'

Oh, thought Elsie, I'm being promoted. Already. Fancy that.

A motherly coloured lady appeared through a door, one of

several flanking the cave. After she'd rootled around and found a uniform for Elsie, she sent her into a little side office to get changed. The black dress with a frilled white pinafore was much too big. She turned up the dress's cuffs and pulled the pinafore's belt twice around her waist, knotting it at the back.

'Sorry, darlin',' said Minnie in her singsong West Indian voice, 'we got no other girls your size. Now, take yourself along the corridor and through the double doors to Mr Edwardson.'

'Who is Mr Edwardson?' she managed to ask. 'I mean, what is his position?' He was someone, she presumed, with the authority to promote her.

'The head floors-waiter, of course. Go on with you, and watch you don't trip on that hem.'

'Thank goodness,' said Mr Edwardson when he saw her. 'About blooming time.' He handed her a silver tray holding a bottle of champagne in a brass bucket and two glasses – flutes, Elsie thought they might be called. 'Steady as you go. Get the lift up. Suite 325. Don't look so frightened, he won't bite.'

'But . . .' she began as Mr Edwardson turned his back on her and began berating a carbuncled youth in a gold waistcoat about smudges on a cocktail glass. 'I ought to smash this over your head,' he hissed, 'and I just might.'

Elsie quickly retreated, gripping the edges of the heavy tray as though it were the most precious thing in the world.

With difficulty, she balanced the tray on one arm and knocked on the door of Suite 325. Perhaps she'd get a tip! She'd buy herself a Flake, her favourite. Elsie had a sweet tooth. The smell from the cakery had been making her mouth water all day.

Of all people, the man who answered the door, in his shirt-sleeves and bare-headed, was Lord Whatshisface from the other day. 'Ah, Miss Shaughnessy,' he said warmly, as if he was expecting her. 'Please, come in.' He held the door open. The room she entered was high-ceilinged and softly lit. She had a general impression of pinks and reds, of fringed lampshades and gold-framed looking glasses. Her footsteps were silent on the thick carpet.

'Shall I put your champagne down here?' she asked, indicating a low marble-topped table. She looked around for Lady Whatsherface. After all, there were two glasses.

'By all means. And please, sit down for a moment and tell me if they're treating you well here.'

'Oh, but I think Mr Edwardson will expect me back downstairs.'

'Nonsense.' He sat down on the gleaming pale settee and patted the area next to him. 'Elsie, have you ever tried champagne? May I call you Elsie? And you must call me Charles. Champagne isn't to everyone's taste, but you strike me as a girl with a sophisticated palate.'

He poured two glasses and handed one to her. She sipped. It was sharply chilly and bitter on her tongue. Altogether unpleasant. 'Mm,' she said. 'Very nice.'

'Cheers.' He clinked his glass against hers. She took several more sips. With each one, she found herself disliking the taste less. 'Do you know,' he said, 'I have a daughter, Arabella, who's just about your age. But she's not nearly as pretty as you.'

Unused to compliments, indeed never having heard she was pretty – quite the contrary – Elsie had no words, no formula to respond. After several moments she said: 'Has Arabella got any brothers or sisters?'

'My younger daughter, Venetia, is eight or nine. I haven't got any sons yet. But I'm not concerned. Some men set great store by perpetuating the family name, don't they? But why should I care? I'll be dead and gone.' He laughed, and Elsie laughed too. She liked the way he talked to her, as if they were on equal terms and she understood the world as he did. He refilled her glass and she drank. It gave her a queer sensation of blurriness, of recklessness. I haven't a care in the world, she thought. Why am I always griping and complaining?

'I've no brothers or sisters,' she said. 'My mother said having me put her off the whole enterprise.'

'Did she really? What a cheek. Still, you wouldn't like having brothers, I'm sure. Little boys are ghastly creatures. I ought to know, I used to be one.'

She smiled. 'Mammy asked God not to send her any more babbies. Why don't more people do that, I wonder? Then there wouldn't be so many unwanted children in the world.'

'Well, my dear Elsie, I'm afraid it's not quite as simple as all that. God cannot always control husbandly zeal, unfortunately.'

She must have looked confused, because he said: 'Girls like you are taught, I take it, how babies are made?'

'Kissing?' she said uncertainly. She'd gathered there was also nakedness involved but was far too shy to say so.

'Well done, yes, that's certainly a part of it.'

He refilled her glass again and she sipped. She felt relaxed and very tired. 'I've been at work since eight o'clock this morning,' she announced. 'And I only had a sausage and a tomato for lunch.'

'You poor child. You must be exhausted. Go and have a rest. There's a bedroom in there.' He pointed at some gilt-patterned doors. 'Have a nice lie-down before you clock off for the evening. Don't worry, I'll clear things with your superiors downstairs.'

Elsie stood up and hiccupped. 'You're ever so kind,' she murmured, moving towards the bedroom.

The bed was huge, covered in a pink satin quilt with a mauve pleated skirt to the floor. She took off her shoes and lay down.

As soon as her eyes were closed, she drifted off to sleep. She wasn't sure how much time had passed before she became aware that Charles had removed her pinafore and was unbuttoning the front of her dress. When she resisted, sleepily, he said she mustn't get her uniform creased, that was all. Except then he lifted her arms above her head and pulled off her vest, followed by her bloomers and stockings. She shut her eyes, hideously embarrassed, as he ran his cold hands all over her body. To her astonishment, he put his face between her legs and started biting and sucking. She quivered with terror and shame. But she only cried out and began to struggle when he shifted himself upwards, so that his face loomed over hers, and moved in a manner that caused her unbearable pain.

'Shh,' he said, rocking back and forth with a violent rhythm, leaning on one elbow and holding her down with the other hand. 'Keep still, there's a good child.'

He was covered in spongy amber hair, like an orangutan. She'd had no notion men's bodies were like this. As the wooden bedhead drummed against the wall, the pain increased in ferocity. Elsie sobbed, wondering what she'd done to deserve it.

Charles kissed her face. 'You're a dear little virgin, aren't you?'

His breath came in ever more rapid gasps.

Sweat dripped onto her face and stung her eyes.

She thought she might be sick.

All of a sudden he yelped as if in agony and slumped onto a pillow, still as a corpse.

She wondered if he had died. But then she felt the disappointing thump-thump of his heart.

She pulled herself out from under him and stood up to gather her clothes.

*

Elsie never went back to the hotel after that night. To placate her father, she got a new job the very next day. It was easy: she saw the Help Wanted notice in the window of Maud's Tea Rooms and Confectioners, marched in like she owned the place and told Maud she'd been a waitress at the Savoy and that Mr Edwardson, the head floors-waiter, would provide a reference.

He had seen her after, face tear-stained and puffy, hair a mess, a bruise beginning to show on the side of her neck. Despite his entreaties, she wouldn't – couldn't – say what had happened. Only that she was resigning. He must have felt pretty guilty, because in a letter to Maud he called her an exemplary employee he was sorry to lose.

Maud and her sister, Phoebe, were already in charge of two waitresses, Nellie and Orla. Elsie made three. Everyone was nice, but Orla was her particular friend. She was twenty-five, with shingled hair, and had worked in all sorts of places, including on a Cunard cruise ship. Some evenings she took Elsie home to her room in a big house near Victoria Park, and showed her how to pluck her eyebrows and draw kohl pencil around her eyes to look like an Egyptian. Orla, who'd been engaged three times, said that what she didn't know about men would fit on a postage stamp. Elsie accepted the spirit of this claim whilst wondering at the metaphorical logic.

On Christmas Eve, Elsie and Orla were left to close up early. After the last stragglers had gone and Orla bolted the door, she sat down with a sigh and rubbed her ankles. 'My veins are starting to bulge,' she said mournfully. 'Just my damn luck, eh? My legs are my best feature, too. Everyone says so.'

Elsie, who was dragging a wet cloth across the tables, said: 'You want to wear compression bandages. My mum swears by 'em.'

'What, and look like an old granny? No ta.' Orla reached in her pocket for her cigarettes. 'Sit down, Els. Have a gasper.'

'Don't mind if I do,' said Elsie, accepting a Woodbine.

Orla lit it for her with a grave look on her face. 'Els, we're good pals, aren't we? You'd tell me, wouldn't you, if you needed my help with anything?'

'Like what?' Elsie puffed on her cigarette, enjoying the whirling-head sensation.

'Look, don't take this the wrong way. But have you noticed you've put on a bit of weight?'

Elsie laughed. 'Is that it? I'm not offended. I'm growing into a woman, that's all. Mum even told me it was time I got some brassieres. I must say, they do give you a nice secure feeling. But d'you reckon I ought to stop eating sweets? I don't want to turn into a big elephant.'

'What about your monthlies? You haven't missed any, have you?'

Elsie frowned. 'How do you mean?'

'Girls, when they get to a certain age, start bleeding regularly, don't they?'

'Bleeding? Where?'

Orla looked even more worried, and started talking about wombs and the body getting ready for babies, and the womb lining falling out when a baby didn't start growing. It sounded absurd to Elsie. But Orla was the most knowledgeable person she'd ever met, so it had to be true.

'Does it happen to all girls, though?' The only time she'd seen blood in her underclothes was after the unspeakable night at the Savoy.

'Well, yes, eventually.'

Elsie considered this. 'And then once it starts, it happens every single month?'

'Unless you're going to have a baby. And that would be because you've been to bed with a man. Elsie, is it possible you're going to have a baby?'

Elsie stubbed out her cigarette, put her hand over her mouth, and ran to the WC.

'Please, please don't tell Dad,' begged Elsie, tears running down her face.

'It's not something we can keep secret,' said Mrs Shaughnessy, who was sitting on the edge of Elsie's bed. 'Orla's right, you're showing. I don't know how I didn't notice, except you're still just a little girl to me. Oh Elizabeth, how could you? How could you let this happen?'

'But Mammy,' sobbed Elsie, 'why did you never tell me? Why didn't you tell me the things men do? I didn't understand. I didn't know how to stop it happening.'

Mrs Shaughnessy tutted sadly. 'You ought to know better than to let a boy get you alone. I hope I've taught you that if nothing else.' She frowned. 'What's his name? I'll go and talk to his mother. We might be able to get Father Donaghy to marry you if we do it quickly. You'll have to wear a loose dress, but goodness knows you'd not be the first girl who—'

'But I don't want to get married. I can make it go away. There are things you can—'

The slap came so fast, Elsie didn't see her mother lift her hand. 'If I ever, ever hear you say anything so evil in this house, Elizabeth Theresa Shaughnessy, you'll get more than a slap, is that understood?'

Her cheek tingled and she tasted blood; a back tooth had loosened. 'I'm sorry, Mammy. Please don't hate me.'

Mrs Shaughnessy stroked her daughter's hair. 'My poor wain. It's all going to be all right. We'll manage, just you wait and see.'

*

Elsie began having nightmares. She dreamt of a monster growing inside her, a half-human, half-animal creature whose tentacles spread through her limbs and wrapped themselves around her insides. Every night she woke up as she was about to choke to death. She became terrified of sleep, so she stayed up reading library books. She read *Jane Eyre* and *Great Expectations* twice through, marvelling at the depth of emotion and drawing strength from the triumphing of Jane and Pip. The days ran together dully as she grew fatter and sleepier, dragging herself around and mindlessly eating leftovers off customers' plates, until one evening in late January Maud told her not to come back. 'We can have another look at the situation,' she said, not unkindly, 'when you're through this difficult patch.'

Elsie nodded numbly. If left alone with her thoughts all day, without work as a distraction, she knew she'd go mad.

After she left the café, she walked slowly up Roman Road, picturing herself falling under the wheels of a bus. She'd wake up in hospital, bruised and bumpy but alive and, crucially, no longer pregnant.

'Els, hold on.'

She turned round to see Orla trotting along in her rabbit-fur hat and long wool coat. Snowflakes clung to her fringe and eyelashes. 'You look like a Russian princess,' said Elsie.

'Why didn't you wait for me?' Orla hooked her arm through Elsie's. 'Brass monkeys out tonight.'

'Maud gave me the boot, didn't she? Mean old cow.'

'Come on, it's not her fault. It's not good for business, is it? She's trying to run a respectable establishment. Everyone can see you've got no ring on your finger.'

'It's so unfair,' said Elsie. 'I just want to be normal.'

'Quick, let's run across the road before this motor car.' They held onto their hats and scooted to the other side. 'Did you think about, you know, what we discussed?'

'I can't, Orla. I wish I could, but my mum would kill me. And my dad. He barely says two words to me any more as it is. Just looks at me like I'm the Whore of Babylon.'

'You know, sometimes it happens without the girl even doing anything. You could pretend it was an act of God. Like he decided you were too young to be a mother.'

'Or I could say I was run over by a bus!' The idea made her feel more cheerful than she had in weeks.

'Come home with me now. No time like the present. We'll stop and get a quarter-bottle of whisky on the way. Just . . . just don't ever tell anyone I helped you, will you?'

'What on earth did you do?' asked George. 'You were, what, five months gone?'

Honor nodded. 'Nearly. Orla said she'd done it herself lots of times, and that the baby would still have to come out but it would be tiny and dead. I didn't care, so long as I didn't have to go on with it. Anyway, she gave me some quinine in whisky – a far too large dose for someone my size, I realised after. It made me sick and unbelievably dizzy. Then she showed me how to use a douching apparatus. Hot water, with a poison in it, I assume. Poor Orla. She was so sorry for me and wanted to help. It wasn't her fault. But I got so ill I ended up in hospital for nearly a week. I'd contracted some kind of infection. All I remember is a tremendous amount of pain, and the nurses saying I'd die if the infection went into my bloodstream. The subtext being it would serve me right. They told me that if I lived, and my baby lived, it'd be damaged. A cripple or a moron or both.'

She was still weak and feverish when her mother picked her up from the hospital and told her they weren't going home. They were going to Ireland, and never you mind about the war there.

Honor tried to never think back on those weeks, which existed as a sealed-off nightmare, not compatible with a life she could bear living. She and her mother stayed in a two-room cottage, a shack really, made of whitish stone, with a thatched roof that stank of mulchy decay. More than anything, she remembered being cold all the time. There was never enough firewood, nor food. They ate a lot of kippers. (To this day, smoked fish turned Honor's stomach.) The privy was twenty yards from the house, and it had no flush, just a pit. Sometimes, when her mother was asleep, she'd think about killing her and then herself. Or she fantasised about running away. But where could she go? After half an hour of trudging in the snow, she'd have died of exposure.

When she went into labour, a month early, her mother fetched a local woman to help. Mrs Doyle, indescribably offensive with her spiderwebby sideburns and shiny red hands, her multiple layers of unwashed skirts, trudged into the bedroom and said: 'God almighty, what's with all this bleating and yelling? You'll raise the dead from their graves with that infernal racket, and that'd be all your poor mother needs, now, won't it?' Then finally – who knew how many hours later – 'Ah, would you look at that, it's a boy; it's a lovely wee boy.' The baby looked more like a pupa, so small and slimy and compact. So colourless.

'But he lived.' George said this quietly.

'He was tiny, but seemed physically all right. It was my mother who insisted on keeping him, taking him home. I wanted to wrap him up and leave him on some church steps. Either to die or to become someone else's problem. She said if I did that, I'd no longer have a home under her roof. That she'd leave me there in that Irish hovel. I think she soon regretted her decision, though.' Honor paused to light a cigarette and lean into the shade. 'I know all babies cry, but Jack never stopped. He screamed all day and all night. Even I, who'd never looked after a baby, could see there was something not right about him. As a toddler, he began to get this look in his eyes. It's hard to explain. It was like you couldn't see a real person there. When he'd do something naughty and we'd slap him, he didn't flinch or react. He seemed amused. Scornful, even. I know it sounds ridiculous.'

'You thought the nurses' predictions were being borne out.'

'Well, wouldn't you? I'd tried to kill him, and this was the consequence. I can't even pretend I felt guilty, though. Or guilt is too simple, too facile a description of what I felt.' Honor brushed away a tear with a violent swipe. 'The real guilt came later, when he murdered that man.'

George stared at her. 'Go on.'

And so Honor told her, at last, about Saul's cousin Naomi, and Naomi's husband, about the painting and the money, about abandoning Thomas without divorcing him, even about taking the stolen money herself. 'I can't defend it. I suppose I was already so damned. Because of my actions, a man was dead and a woman paralysed, so what more was a bit of theft? Of course I'd no idea what was actually happening to the Jews in Europe, or what was to come. But I was so focused on myself, I'm not even sure it would have made any difference. I'd been trapped in a nightmare since before reaching adulthood. And I saw a way out.'

'But I don't see that you can blame yourself for Jack's badness. How do you know he wouldn't have turned out like that anyway? I mean, look at who his father was. What made Charles such a rotter? I guarantee you his mother didn't try to abort him. If Cressida Mountford-Owen couldn't direct a servant to do something, it didn't get done.'

Honor laughed. 'But that's precisely it. That's why I wanted to get to know you. I orchestrated it, you see, you moving in here. If you were a horrible person, I reasoned, even an odd person, then Charles's bequeathed heredity could be blamed for everything.

My conscience should be a bit lighter. You can imagine my disappointment when you were an utter joy.'

George made a face. 'I don't know about that. God, it is funny, isn't it? In a farcical way. And now that Charles isn't my father, you can revert to your original theory. If it helps, my sister Venetia is a soulless bitch. And my other sister, Arabella, was never the full ticket.' Honor laughed again as George protested she was serious. 'And supposedly my real father thinks I'm a chip off the old block. Score one more for nature over nurture.'

The low sun cast a patchy radiance across the oblong of garden where Jack lay, turning the poppy petals a translucent orange. Honor lit another cigarette and gazed into the distance. 'Comyns wants me to help him convict Saul. And in return, he'll give me immunity against prosecution for bigamy. Even retroactively legalise my marriage somehow. I'm not going to do it, of course. But if I lose this house . . .' She gestured to the bottom of the garden.

'You've got to tell him, you know. Saul. You've got to tell him everything you've told me.'

'It won't matter. He won't forgive me, and I don't think he ought to.'

'Maybe, maybe not. But I'm not sure forgiveness is the point. These big secrets are poison, don't you see?'

They were both quiet for a moment, then George grinned and patted Honor's shoulder. 'Anyway, we've got two tasks: make Comyns drop the charges against Saul, and somehow make you innocent of bigamy.'

'When you put it like that, it sounds most straightforward.' Honor smiled ruefully. 'George – you were all right, weren't you, when you had to get yourself fixed?'

'Oh, yes – but how did you . . . ?'

'Robbie told me.'

'Ah. It was pretty ghastly. Painful. Annoyingly expensive. But it worked, which is the main thing.' She gave a slight shudder. 'Those policemen saw my bloodstained mattress, unfortunately. Comyns tried to frighten me with it. Don't worry, I gave him short shrift.'

'Thank God they didn't pull the drawing room rug up,' said Honor. 'Useless, really. I could tell Comyns despised those other policemen. They weren't intelligent like him. Especially that big Scot with a drinker's face.'

George bit her thumbnail thoughtfully. 'You can't have been the only one, can you? Charles, I mean. He might still be doing it now.' Picturing Honor as an innocent fourteen-year-old, she reached out to touch her cheek. Honor covered George's hand with her own. In the wordless look they exchanged – vindictive, pained, extraordinarily resolute – a decision was made.

25

Daddy's Dead

'I've been meaning to ask,' said Robbie to Honor, who was spooning tea leaves into the pot. 'When you and Saul went through Jimmy's stuff, did you find my pistol? It was in a leather holster. Jimmy had taken a shine to it and pinched it from my room.' Only when the house was searched did Robbie wonder about the gun's whereabouts.

'Your war pistol? It wasn't in Jimmy's room. At least I don't think so.' She thought back. 'No, it definitely wasn't.'

'That's odd. I wonder where it's got to. If it was anywhere in the house, the police would have found it. And wouldn't they have loved to?' Although, he thought, if Comyns had found it in his room, he might have withheld it from evidence, as he did with Jimmy's notes. His reasons for doing so were pragmatic, Comyns had said. Not for the first time, Robbie wondered if this was true. A guilty thrill fluttering in his throat, he turned away to reach for teacups.

'You'd think they'd have come across it,' said Honor. 'But I wouldn't be so sure. The whole exercise seemed pretty slapdash to me. Let me ask Greta. She's probably tidied it away somewhere.'

She found Greta in the second-floor bathroom, scrubbing the tidemark from the bath. 'So sorry to interrupt,' said Honor, offering obeisance as one always had to, 'but you haven't seen a gun lying around anywhere, have you? It's Robbie's. From his time serving. He thought Jimmy had borrowed it at one point.'

Greta removed her orange rubber gloves, hung them over the edge of the bath and straightened up, one hand supporting her lower back. She seemed uncharacteristically abashed. Even sheepish, thought Honor.

'The one in leather case?' she asked.

'Yes, I think so. Why, have you seen it?'

Greta bit the corner of her lip. 'I . . . I believed . . .'

'You believed what? My dear, no one's accusing you of anything. Perish the thought. I assumed you'd put it in a safe place, that's all.'

'I put in safe place. Under my bed. I saw it in Jimmy's room and it frightened me. He is not good person. I plan to tell you, but then when I come on Monday, he has gone, so I . . .' She trailed off.

'You thought there was no need to mention it. Understandably. So it was on that Friday, was it, before he moved out?'

'He didn't want me cleaning in his room. Why? Because he had things to hide.'

I'll say he did, thought Honor, remembering the bodybuilding magazines.

'But then,' went on Greta, 'the pretty girl came asking for him, asking if he lives here. So I come upstairs to look for him and see the gun. Maybe he wants to kill us all, I think. Hide us in the walls, same as House of Murder. So I take it and go home.'

'Gosh. Thank goodness he's no longer living here. You may have saved our lives!'

Greta nodded, happy to acknowledge this accomplishment.

'Perhaps you could bring the gun back tomorrow? I rather think it has sentimental value for Robbie.'

A couple of days later, shortly after 11 a.m., the telephone rang. George, who was about to leave for work, picked up the line in the entrance hall.

'Georgie? Oh good, it's you.' The voice was breathless.

'Venetia? Is everything all right? You sound—'

'Daddy's dead. They found him this morning. Sorry to tell you like this. Muggins here has been given the task of phoning round to break the news. Awful, isn't it?'

'What do you mean, dead?' George had heard this phrase in radio plays, usually followed by *I just saw him yesterday; he can't be dead.*

'I know, darling. It's hard to take in. He was found by a chambermaid at the Savoy. Shot, apparently. A gun by his side. The police are saying it looks like a suicide. There was no theft, no break-in. He was in bed. But I can't see Daddy topping himself, can you? Why would he?'

'Well, I—'

'I must warn you, Georgie, it's going to be in the papers. We can't stop it. The hotel staff have already talked to the press. But look, I'm afraid I must dash, I've got dozens of people to telephone. Can you catch a train home today? I'll be there tomorrow. Diana's got a tea dance this afternoon. She can't miss it. Why couldn't this have happened in a couple of weeks, when the season was over?' With that, Venetia rang off.

*

'George told me the news,' said Honor to Comyns, 'before she left for Hampshire to be with her mother. Then I read about it in the late edition of the evening paper. I realised I had to come clean. About everything. I'm willing to make an official statement.' Through the windows of Scotland Yard, the morning sun burnished the Thames a fuzzy orange-gold. She felt a sense of unreality, of observing herself from outside. 'I think of you as an eminently reasonable man, Detective Inspector, and I believe you'll understand why I felt unable to be . . . to be completely candid before. But now everything has changed.'

Comyns's expression was some combination of neutral and sceptical. 'Mrs Wilson, I'm eager to hear whatever you wish to tell me. As for making an official statement, let's take one thing at a time. You learnt of the death of Lord Charles Mountford-Owen, the father of your friend and lodger Georgina, and you believe it has to do with Jack Shaughnessy?'

Honor explained, in concise, even tones, that Jack was Charles's natural son. 'It was the oddest coincidence when George came to live with us. It felt like fate, in a way. Naturally I didn't tell her – it's too unpleasant a fact to hear about one's parent, isn't it? And Jack lived most of his life believing I was his sister. It was only when the two of them began . . . Well, when I found out, I didn't know what to do. The only thing I *could* do was explain to Jack how he came to be born. He was very disturbed by it. Well, of course he was. Flew into a rage. At Charles for his brutality and abandonment, and at me for lying to him all those years. That's the real reason we had a falling-out. You'll recall you asked why he left in a huff, and I offered some silly excuse.'

'Mrs Wilson. Are you suggesting Mr Shaughnessy is responsible for the murder of Lord Mountford-Owen?'

'I'm not suggesting anything. I'm merely apprising you of various pertinent facts. I don't exaggerate when I say Jack flew into a rage. Such was his state of mind, I wasn't surprised when he seemed to fall off the face of the earth. Any ideas of fulfilling his responsibilities, of getting his life on the right path were probably eclipsed by the madness that took hold of him.'

Comyns nodded inscrutably.

'One other thing. George thinks it's impossible her father would have committed suicide, as is being theorised. "I've never known a person with a stronger sense of self-preservation," she said.'

He nodded again, more slowly. 'You said I'd understand why you weren't more candid before. I'm not sure I do understand. I mean, given all that's at stake. For Mr Reznikov, especially.'

Honor found a hanky in her handbag and pressed it to the back of her neck. The room was very warm. 'Allow me, then, to enumerate my reasons. When Lord Mountford-Owen was living, to bring such an accusation against him, with no material proof, would have created a scandal. I've never wanted people to know I used to be a common little girl called Elsie. I couldn't let my first marriage be exposed, nor be sued for slander. After all, a man in Lord Mountford-Owen's position would be highly motivated to brand me a liar. Also, I was trying to protect poor George, both from the knowledge she'd committed incest and from her father's immorality.' She replaced the hanky in her bag. 'But here's the twist in the tale. George was sired by another man entirely, as her mother divulged not two weeks ago. So that puts quite a different complexion on things.'

'Doesn't it just?'

Was that sarcasm? Honor wasn't sure.

'Why do you suppose,' he said, 'that Georgina's mother chose now, of all times, to reveal this family secret?'

'You'd have to ask Lady Susan. Though I gather George's real father is keen to know his daughter. Before it's too late, as it were.'

'When you were a girl, and you became pregnant from this . . . this unwanted encounter, did you confide in anyone about the father's identity?'

'Only one person, and I swore her to secrecy. I'm sure she'll remember. Orla Rosenfeld. She used to be Orla Quinn. We worked together at a tea shop. We've lost touch, but I occasionally see mentions of her and her husband in the papers. They run several West End nightclubs and Orla owns a racing-car team.'

Comyns noted down these details without comment. 'All right. Let's imagine you're correct, and Mr Shaughnessy has murdered the man he believed to be his errant father. Why have several months elapsed since he found out? If he was in a rage, as you say, would he not have acted on that rage immediately?'

'I don't pretend to understand the workings of my son's mind,' said Honor tartly. 'I never have. But just because he had a motive, it doesn't follow he had the means and opportunity. Those might have taken some time to acquire. George says her father – the man who wasn't, in fact, her father – had kept the same suite at the Savoy for decades. He stayed there during the week. For sittings at the House of Lords. But Jack couldn't have known that, could he? I certainly didn't, and at any rate I didn't tell him to which room I was lured in 1923.'

'Mrs Wilson, I'm afraid I must ask: where were you between the hours of eight and ten on Wednesday evening?'

She thought about it. 'I was at home. We were all at home that evening, I believe. Is that the time of death, then? It's quite specific. I thought the body was only found in the morning.'

'It's my understanding that hotel guests reported a sound like a gunshot at around nine p.m. The management, no doubt wishing to prevent panic, claimed somebody had let off a firework. But the condition of the body, when it was found, suggested that death had occurred at least twelve hours earlier.'

'I take it the gun has been dusted for fingerprints? Needless to say, I'd be happy to let you have mine.'

After a frantic few days of following every lead, Hilary saw no choice but to drop the charges against Mr Reznikov. Not that he was convinced of the man's innocence. Frankly, he could barely make head nor tail of the whole blasted affair, which wasn't exactly a sterling endorsement of his investigative skills. He needed a holiday, he mused as he walked through St James's Park in the softening evening light. That was what people did in the summer, they went to the seaside. But the prospect of taking a single room in a Bognor Regis or Bournemouth guest house, of making polite small talk at breakfast and trying to fill the long, empty days – well, it filled him with something approaching terror.

In any case, he couldn't leave London. Not until this mess with Jack Shaughnessy had reached some form of conclusion. It didn't seem credible that he was still alive and yet had managed to fly completely under the radar. But fingerprints didn't lie, and the pistol on Lord Mountford-Owen's bed yielded, quite clearly, several of Shaughnessy's. Another person's, too. But not Mrs Wilson's, nor the dead man's. It was a British service revolver, a .38 Webley. Not exactly rare. Privates weren't meant to keep them as war souvenirs, but many had. Why would you leave the gun behind, though? To make it look like a suicide, he supposed – and yet if that was your plan, why not make sure the prints of the putative self-murderer were on the handle?

For whatever it was worth, Mrs Wilson's lunatic cleaning lady, Mrs Kovačević, claimed to have seen a gun – or at least the leather holder – in Mr Sullivan's possession. Then there was the testimony of the hotel manager, a Mr Walter Edwardson. A likeable fellow, affable and silver-haired, someone for whom exposure to the full ghastly gamut of human behaviour had, Hilary inferred, bred compassion rather than misanthropy. Yes indeed, Mr Edwardson confirmed, he had noticed someone fitting Shaughnessy's description 'loitering around' the lobby on the night in question. 'To tell you the truth, I nearly had him removed. I guessed from his shoes – those crêpe-soled jobs worn by reprobates – that he was up to some skulduggery. I ought to have gone with my instinct and turfed him out. Although . . . but no, one mustn't speak ill of the dead.'

'You didn't care for Lord Mountford-Owen?'

'He was very rude to the staff. The girls, especially, were frightened of him. When I was head floors-manager, I instigated a policy of sending only male waiters with room service. I might be speaking out of turn, but I wonder if he seriously upset a young waitress or chambermaid, and her young man decided to take matters into his own hands.'

On Honor's return from Scotland Yard, a letter was waiting for her. She opened it immediately and stood reading in the hallway. An odd expression formed on her face, both amused and incredulous.

Ben Yehuda 8
Hadar Ha'Carmel
Haifa
Israel

Thursday, May 28th, 1953

Dear Honor (if I may),

I thought you might be interested to know that I was recently contacted by the Jewish Museum in London, who hoped to borrow Gila with Delphiniums *for an exhibit. The chap I sold it to gave me permission to pass on his contact information, so I expect the painting will be on show there at some stage.*

It's not the same, of course, and I know how disappointed you were when I had to sell Gila *to someone else. But perhaps you and Mr Reznikov should like to see it in person, as it were?*

All my best wishes as ever,
Rebecca (and family)

26

My Enemy's Enemy Is My Friend

'Don't be sad, dear girl,' said Saul.

Mina watched dolefully as he folded up shirts and placed them in a suitcase.

'Just because I'm moving out,' he said, 'it doesn't mean we won't still be friends. I'll be coming to the cinema every week as usual. You won't even notice I've gone.'

'It won't be the same, though, will it? And won't you be lonely, living in rooms by yourself?'

'A little, perhaps. But I'll manage. Before long, you'll be moving out yourself, I'm sure. You'll be getting married, or travelling abroad, or doing any number of exciting things.'

'We were meant to all stick together. That was the plan. Supposing Detective Inspector Comyns comes back? Or those other policemen?'

Saul put down the shirt he was holding and sat next to Mina on the sofa. 'If any of them come back, or if you're even a little worried, you'll tell me immediately. I'll never let anything happen to you. It's just . . . it's Honor I can't live with.' She had told him, in what seemed to be a desperate plea for mitigation, that Jack was really her son and how he came to be born. Tragedy begets tragedy, thought Saul, now even more determined to get away from her.

Mina pursed her lips in an unhappy moue. 'Do you hate her that much?'

He half nodded, half shook his head. 'I can't see her. I can't be around her. Now that I'm not legally confined to this address, I . . . I must go.' Poor Mina. He didn't want to desert her. After all, he had embroiled them in this present disaster.

'Mina,' he said, 'you don't ever think about it, do you? The night Jimmy died? You mustn't.'

'I do try not to. Sometimes pictures come into my mind for no reason. It's strange. But whenever that happens, I quickly think of nicer things. Why, do you think about it often?'

'No,' he said truthfully. 'Not often. Occasionally I'll be reminded. And then I tell myself it wasn't our fault. That's all that matters.' He squeezed her hand. 'We'll soon forget it altogether, won't we?'

It was the night before Jimmy died, when the first dominoes were toppled, that played on a loop in Saul's head. Over time, the evening had taken on an ever more artificial and hallucinatory quality, like a half-remembered Hitchcock film. Only the beginning remained sharp, lifelike. He could see himself on the District Line, Mina's filched photograph of adolescent Jimmy in his overcoat pocket. Then he had exited Whitechapel station, walking purposefully, any fatigue or trepidation blotted out by his ferocious resolve.

There were two public houses within spitting distance of Honor's childhood home: the White Hart and the Blind Beggar. Neither was Saul's sort of place. But for his purposes, the more disreputable the better. He looked at his wristwatch: just after 8.30. Hopefully a busy drinking time.

Moving from the freezing dark street into the Blind Beggar was like being embraced by a warm, fusty cloud. In the public bar, the vegetal smell of rain-damp wool mingled with acrid shag tobacco and the occasional enlivening waft of women's scent or hair lacquer. Saul's eyes stung and he wanted to sneeze. Pretending to clear his throat, he pressed a finger to his nose and edged his way through the throng to the bar.

The barmaid, he saw as he ordered a drink, would be too young to remember residents from the 1930s. A dark zaftig girl in a low-cut red frock with a starched white collar, she barely looked old enough to be serving. Yet she carried herself with remarkable poise, casually fielding quips while pulling the tap handle, no drop spilt nor hint of fluster aroused. 'Oi, Agnes,' said one young man with a badly scarred cheek and too much hair oil, 'you tryna give me a heart attack, leaning forward in that get-up? You know I got a murmur. Too much excitement and I'll fall off me perch.' Agnes, placing a pint on the bar, enquired: 'Isn't Reenie carrying again, Raymond? How'd she manage that, then, immaculate conception?'

As Raymond clarified that 'a bit of the other' when you were married was as thrilling as having a tooth stopped, Saul turned away and spotted a very old man sitting slightly on the outside of a group, seemingly deep in his own thoughts. 'Excuse me,' he ventured, 'I wonder if I can ask: have you lived in this area a long time?'

The man looked up at him and breathed in wheezily, as though to gather the strength to speak. 'I was born round the corner in Sidney Street. And I'll be ninety next year. Is that a long time?' A mischievous twinkle entered his eye. 'I'd say so, wouldn't you?'

Saul smiled and agreed he would. 'Do you recognise this boy?' He handed him the photograph. 'He's older now, but he used to live nearby, in Redmans Road.'

The man held the photo at arm's length and squinted. 'I'm not good with faces,' he said apologetically. 'Is he your boy?'

'Oh no, nothing like that. Thank you anyway, I—'

'Hold up. Davy! Have a look at this fella's picture. He's looking for this lad.' He turned back to Saul. 'Davy's my boy.'

Davy was indeed a younger, more vigorous version of his father, smartly dressed in a three-piece brown suit and red tie, a half-drunk pint of frothy bitter in his hand. 'Let's have a butcher's, then,' he said.

'He lived in Redmans Road, the fella says,' supplied Davy's father.

'Do you know,' said Davy, 'he don't half look familiar. But . . . no, sorry, mate. I can't place him.'

'The photo is old,' said Saul. 'It must have been taken sixteen, maybe seventeen years ago.'

'D'you have a name for him?' asked Davy.

'I'm not sure,' said Saul. 'But it might be Jack Shaughnessy.'

Recognition spread across Davy's face. 'But isn't that . . .' He turned towards the bar. 'Mick, come here a minute.'

Mick bounded over. Around Davy's age, sixtyish, he was skinny and gangling with a jutting Adam's apple.

'What was the name of that kid, only a nipper, who got a lifer for murdering that bloke? It was him and someone from the same family. Fifteen or twenty years ago.'

'It were Conor Shaughnessy's son, weren't it?' said Mick, Adam's apple bobbing like a red buoy at sea. 'Good thing he weren't alive to see it.'

'Mick,' said Davy, 'look at the picture. Is that Jack as a kid?'

Mick peered at it and frowned. 'Yeah, I reckon so. Don't you?'

Saul tipped back the rest of his whisky. He'd known Jimmy was Jack. Of course he'd known. But so long as there was reasonable room for doubt, he'd held his emotions at bay. Now, only a sliver of doubt remained. Hot sweat prickled under his shirt collar. He gripped his glass tumbler. 'I am indebted to you both,' he said calmly. 'If I can trouble you with one more question. As Davy says, Mr Shaughnessy was sentenced to life imprisonment. And yet he's been released. Can you offer any speculation as to why that might be?'

Davy and Mick exchanged a glance. 'I can think of one reason,' said Davy. 'He's a squealer.' Seeing Saul's face, he went on: 'He's told things to the police. In a bargaining arrangement, like.'

'If you really want to know,' said Mick, 'there are certain people who . . . who might've heard about it. Or who'll be able to find out for you, at least.'

'If you ask them nicely,' added Davy. '*They're* not very nice people, though.'

'Where might I find them, these people?' said Saul.

He was given directions to a billiards hall not half a mile away. 'Talk to Bill White,' said Davy, 'or his cousin Terry White. If it's all the same to you, don't say we sent you.'

The billiards hall stretched across the basement of a red-brick building. Evidently once grand, it had columns flanking the raised main entrance and Grecian-style stone reliefs on the curved window pediments. But the stucco was filthy and at least two windows were taped up with cardboard. Saul lit a cigarette. Then he stepped down from pavement level and pushed open the double doors beneath a red enamel sign proclaiming, in jaunty white script: *BILLIARDS Club and Café Bar.*

He blinked and looked around the cavernous space. Eight or ten billiards tables, ornately carved from mahogany, were each lit by a low-suspended roof-shaped lamp. Drinks were served at a rectangular hatch in the wall. Around forty men were spread out, either playing a game or sitting at small round tables. An atmosphere of vague menace seemed to hang in the air. Perhaps it was his imagination, his expectations having been primed by Davy and Mick. A few glances came in his direction, but no one appeared to take his presence amiss.

He asked the elderly barman for a whisky and, handing over the extortionate sum of two shillings, asked if Bill or Terry White were in attendance that evening. Before the barman had a chance to respond, a thick-necked man in his early middle years spun round and said: 'Who wants to know?'

Saul introduced himself. 'I'm told either Bill or Terry might help me with . . .' He wasn't sure how to continue. 'Some information I'm seeking.'

'You're not a copper, are you?'

'Course he's not a copper; he's a Yid, int he?' This was from a younger, carroty-haired fellow who was only slightly taller than his billiards cue.

'Yids can be coppers, don't be so prejudiced!'

'Gentlemen,' said Saul hastily, 'I can assure you, I'm not a policeman. If you could assist me by pointing out either of the Mr Whites, I'd be most grateful.'

The younger man, chastened, said he'd fetch Bill. From where was unclear; he left the building and was gone for some ten minutes. When he returned, he was accompanied by a slender, dark-suited man, no older than thirty-five, with tortoiseshell spectacles and a soft, almost gentle voice. 'Pleased to meet you,' he said. 'Billy White. Mr Reznikov, is it? What are you drinking?'

Fresh drink in hand, Saul followed Mr White to the back of the room. Like Moses's parting of the Red Sea, his approach caused a cluster of tables and chairs to empty of their occupants.

'Please,' said Mr White, 'take a pew. Tell me how I can be of assistance.'

'This is very obliging,' said Saul. 'I hope that young man didn't drag you away from anything important.'

'You mean do I come running for any stranger who asks for me?' Mr White grinned.

Saul was startled: that was precisely what he'd wondered.

'I do not is the answer. Little Barnaby told me that a well-mannered chap of the Hebrew persuasion wanted to see me or Terry. Well, those may not have been his exact words, but that was the gist. I thought you might work for Chaim Levy.'

Saul was intrigued, but he knew he mustn't be sidetracked. 'No, I'm actually not from around here. I'm trying to identify this boy, who is now a man of around thirty years of age.'

Mr White took the photograph, holding it carefully by its edges. He had beautifully manicured fingernails and a gold wedding ring. 'It's Jack Shaughnessy. He was in my brother's year at secondary school.' He handed back the photograph. 'What do you want with him, then?'

'As you may know, he was in prison for a long time.'

'Yeah, I heard he'd got out.'

'Do you know *why* he got out?'

'I might do.' Mr White's sanguine demeanour altered a fraction: he was clamming up. Not that it mattered. Saul had what he'd come for. Yet his curiosity wouldn't let him leave.

'You're familiar, I'm sure, Mr White, with the saying: my enemy's enemy is my friend?'

'Jack's your enemy, is he?'

'More than I can put into words.'

'You want to track him down? You're not the only one, from what I've heard.'

'No, no,' said Saul. 'I know exactly where he is. But I had to ascertain he is indeed who I suspected. So thank you, thank you kindly.'

Mr White gave an *it's nothing* salute and said: 'D'you need to be somewhere? Why don't you come for another at a place round the corner?' He finished his drink and stood up. 'I got a feeling your enemy's enemy will be pleased to make your acquaintance.'

Saul's third venue of the evening was a private drinking club occupying the top two floors of a Georgian terraced house. A warren of interconnected spaces with crystal chandeliers, Persian rugs, and red flock wallpaper, it brought to mind an Arab souk. A gramophone record was playing one of those affecting black American singers, her voice equal parts brash and mournful.

Unlike at the billiards hall, a male sanctum, here there were as many women as men. Saul had the impression, however, that the female patrons were of the companionate rather than wifely type. Indeed, a matriarchal older lady, apparently the establishment's hostess, was heard briskly admonishing a teenage girl in a spangly gold costume for some moral infraction. 'You think this is a knocking shop, do you? Learn how to behave, Shirley, or you can sling yer hook.'

Mr White conducted Saul into a small upper room with an uncurtained window overlooking a street lamp. Its peach glimmer, sickly and artificial, supplemented the scattered pools of yellow light inside.

With the door shut behind them, it was quiet, the music from downstairs but a faint hum.

Around a square card table sat four or five men, smoking and talking. A game had recently been completed, it seemed, and a pile of cash still sat in the centre of the green baize. Saul wondered that the winner hadn't pocketed his gains. But it was a show of might, he realised, to assume no one would dare steal what wasn't theirs.

'All right, Billy,' said one of the men. 'You missed me get taken to the bloody cleaner's. Does your pal want a game?' Gravel-voiced and suntanned, perhaps fifty-five, he wore a diamond tie clip and a crocodile wristwatch. This wasn't mere prosperity, thought Saul, but a headier, more assertive quality. He was flashy, that was it. Saul had heard the word used, but he'd never seen it so conspicuously embodied.

With three shillings and ninepence in his pocket, he was relieved when Mr White said they weren't playing poker but that he ought to talk to Mr Reznikov, as they had something in common. He then bent down and whispered to the flashy man, who glanced at Saul while listening and nodding.

He beckoned Saul to sit. 'And get our new friend a drink,' he said, to no one in particular.

The rest of the group melted away.

'Albert Cooper, a pleasure.' Saul's right hand was grasped and imprisoned within Mr Cooper's large, hot, and profusely hairy pair. 'So,' he said tenderly, '*talk* to me.'

'Well, I . . .' Saul longed to extract his hand; he was about to do so when Mr Cooper released him to pick up a half-smoked cigar. 'As Mr White perhaps mentioned,' Saul continued, 'I've recently seen Jack Shaughnessy. It came as a shock, you understand. I'm a relation of the couple who suffered at his hands. And I'd believed he would remain in prison for a good deal longer.'

'I do understand.' Mr Cooper tapped his ash. 'And you know where he is, do you? At this moment, for instance?'

'I know where he lives.'

This elicited a broad smile. 'Smashing. You write down that address for me, and—'

'Can I ask: what is your dispute with Mr Shaughnessy?'

'Is your accent Russian or something? It's charming. Isn't it charming, Patsy?'

A heavyset blonde girl had appeared and was placing two crystal tumblers on the table. She looked at Saul from beneath painted lashes and murmured agreement as she removed the dirty glasses and put them on a tray.

Mr Cooper patted her bottom by way of a dismissal and said: 'It's my son-in-law. He was inside with Shaughnessy but was meant to be getting out soon. Now . . . now he's looking at another ten-stretch, with Shaughnessy's testimony. It's not fair, is it? It's not right. My daughter Kathy's at home with two kiddies who need their father.'

Saul sipped his drink, a delicious single malt Scotch. 'What will you do?'

Mr Cooper released a dense plume of cigar smoke. 'I'll have to see, won't I?'

'If I give you the address,' said Saul, 'can I have your assurance that no other resident of the house will be harmed? Women live there. So does an entirely blameless young man of about Mr Shaughnessy's age. I'd hate there to be any—'

'Cock-ups. Course. You have my word.' Mr Cooper picked up his glass. 'Cheers.'

Saul got into bed some time after two o'clock in the morning. There was no possibility of sleep. Each cell in his body squirmed with tension, his thoughts swimming from one alcohol-blurred rumination to the next. When dawn broke, soon after five, he washed and dressed. Then he waited.

He heard people coming and going as usual. Each time the doorbell rang, he stood at the front left of the room, under the porch, where he could hear the caller's voice. At around 5.30 in the evening, a woman asked for Jack. Do you mean Jimmy, enquired Greta, and went to look for him before telling the woman he was out. Saul peered out from behind the curtain to glimpse her as she walked away. She was young and beautiful, with a sharp profile and a noble bearing. Her dark hair was tucked under a fur hat and she carried a toffee-coloured handbag shaped like an envelope, its gold clasp glinting in the gas-lit street.

Surely, thought Saul, her manifestation was not a consequence – or rather *the* consequence – of the previous evening?

For the next several hours, the house remained quiet. At some point, despite sitting upright on the sofa, Saul sank into a deep sleep.

Jimmy came downstairs, regretting his barney with George. Stupid of him to threaten her like that, not to mention pointless. Posh girls weren't scared of getting nicked. They thought it only happened to proles. But it was true, what he'd said about Honor. She'd do anything George asked. Jimmy didn't understand it, personally. Then again, there never was any understanding his sister. Nor women in general, frankly. Last night, George was all over him like a rash. Now she was treating him like something on the sole of her shoe. What changed?

He hadn't even wanted to get her involved. Honor's bigamy was meant to be his trump card. But she threw it back in his face. Maybe she didn't believe he'd make good on his threat. And he wouldn't, so long as she didn't kick him out on the street tonight. Something prideful in him was unwilling to let that happen, as though it might prove the final, fatal blow to his dignity.

Jimmy was all right for money: of the four hundred pounds Honor had deigned to part with, most was left. Renting some nice rooms, or even his own flat, shouldn't be a problem. Except he didn't want to live alone. He kept picturing it. Eating out of tins and staring at the walls. Coming home to an empty house, no one asking how his day had been. He'd go round the twist, he knew he would. Other people were loved and cared for – couldn't it be his turn?

If he told Robbie they ought to get a place of their own, would he laugh in his face? Or be appalled at the recklessness of the proposal? Jimmy wasn't sure he could work up the nerve to come out with it. Ought he first to insist that Robbie talk to George? But if he agreed to – admittedly a big if – would George bad-mouth Jimmy? Almost certainly she would, and something rotten too.

I just need time to think, he thought desperately. He couldn't banish the fear that if he left Tregunter Road before making things up with Robbie, they'd never see each other again.

No one was in the drawing room, so Jimmy went into the kitchen. Honor was sitting at the table, a half-eaten cheese sandwich set aside in favour of a cigarette – several, going by the butts in the ashtray. She said nothing, just glared at him and gripped her tumbler of whisky. Her scarlet lipstick marked the rim like a blood smear.

Honor was exhausted. She couldn't face another confrontation. 'I think I've made myself quite clear,' she began. 'Nevertheless, I shall make myself clearer—'

'You don't get it, do you?' Jimmy sat down across from her, pulled the plate towards him and bit into the sandwich. 'Your problem is . . .' He paused to chew and swallow, waggling his finger at her as he did so. 'You've had a lifetime of stepping over other people to get what you want. Never any consequences for you, isn't that right? Well, sorry, Elsie, but now there are. You think I won't grass you up for having two husbands?' He ate the rest of the sandwich. 'Just watch me.'

'But I've done what you said you wanted. I've given you back the money – the money that by rights belongs to Saul!'

'Well, you've given me a bit of it. And maybe it does belong to him, but it won't bring his family back, will it? To me, it's less than I'd have earned over fourteen years, if I weren't stuck inside. So I don't think it even makes up for—'

Honor got stiffly to her feet. 'Jack, please. I've got a splitting headache. I've had enough.' She left the room, glass of whisky in hand. He followed.

'You won't be the only one getting arrested,' he shouted at her back. 'George'll be getting her collar felt an' all.'

She swung round. 'What are you on about?'

'It's funny, actually. Abortion and bigamy have similar penalties under the Offences Against the Person Act. Maybe you two can share a cell at Holloway.'

Taking a step back, Honor placed a hand on the drawing room door jamb. She brought her glass to her lips and tipped back what was left.

They stood there without saying anything, eyeing each other, their stubborn wills in deadlocked combat. Then he gave her a strange placatory smile. For a brief moment, she saw his father's face in his.

An angry man was shouting at Saul in a language he didn't understand. He tried to shout back, but no sound came out. He was at the camp in Tăbărăşti, shovelling rocks, and the camp was also the cinema where Mina worked. It wasn't safe for her there, he suddenly realised. Why had he never told her that before? He must find the girl and help her escape. If only he wasn't so cold! Then maybe he'd be able to unstick his bare feet from the icy gravel. The only way to unstick them, it seemed, was to keep shovelling.

The clattering of the rocks grew so loud that Saul was jolted awake. Above his head, several thumps shook the ceiling. The light fixture vibrated, glass against metal. He had a foul taste in his mouth and a dull throb in his left temple. What time was it?

Mina, her feet aching after a long day, had arrived home and let herself in with her latchkey. An unfamiliar and irate feminine voice issued from the drawing room. Intrigued, she pushed open the door to see a strange young woman in a fur hat. She was yelling at Jimmy, who was backing away from her towards the fireplace.

'I won't let my babies grow up without their father. My children are innocent. They're not going through what I did because of a toerag like you.'

Mina was so admiring the young woman's coat, a shawl-collared pink and grey tweed with deep mink cuffs, that it took a moment to notice she had a gun. That was stylish too, gold and mother-of-pearl. She pointed it at Jimmy, who lunged and managed to knock it out of her hand. Then with incomprehensible speed he was on top of her. He slammed her head against the floor once, then twice, then three times. Mina started screaming.

The girl's face turned a terrible shade of purple.

She whimpered pathetically.

There was nothing else to do. Mina grabbed the knife from her handbag and plunged it into Jimmy, somewhere near the top of his spine. It made a queer scraping noise. Or maybe Mina just felt it. A roar of pain was muffled by a gurgle. He was face-down, slumped and sort of threshing on the girl's upper body. She pulled herself free, got on her hands and knees to crawl to her gun, and stood up. Somehow her fur hat had remained on her head. Her breath was coming in hoarse staccato bursts.

'Are you all right?' said Mina. 'Are you hurt?'

Saul appeared, almost immediately followed by Honor, Robbie and George. They all started talking at once and the girl pushed past them out of the room. The front door slammed.

'Mina,' said Honor, placing a hand on her shoulder.

Mina looked down. She hadn't realised she was still holding the knife. Dropping it, she burst into tears.

A fine spray of darkening blood had patterned her lavender coat. Like a Japanese painting, thought Honor.

Epilogue

On a dull afternoon in early December, the clouds thickening and the air tawny with smog, Honor stepped out of a taxi at the Jewish Museum in Tavistock Square. Their new exhibition, *Jewish Artists in the École de Paris, 1905–1939*, featured several Chagalls, including *Gila*. Naturally, Honor was curious to see this likeness of Saul's wife as a girl. More importantly, she sought the identity of its current owner. Having sold the lease of the basement flat at Tregunter Road, she could now potentially, finally, afford to buy Saul's long-lost painting.

She entered the exhibition space, just two small interconnected rooms, and affected the demeanour of a normal visitor who was interested in all the artworks, not just one. She paused in front of a Modigliani sketch of a nude woman, forcing herself to contemplate its merits (the harsh lines produced a certain mesmeric quality, she conceded). A landscape by Soutine was, to her mind, excessively kitschy and childlike, liable to give one nightmares. Several portraits by an artist of whom she'd never heard – Moïse Kisling – were actually rather lovely and surprisingly modern, all variations of an archetypal woman (Kisling's sexual ideal, no doubt) with huge elongated eyes and a reed-like neck.

And here was *Gila*: painted circa 1927, the typed plaque

advised, when the artist was around thirty and in his 'flower period'. Gila would have been in her mid teens. Deep pinks and greens dominated the small square picture, with the girl's pallid face, capped with inky swirls of hair, marked out firmly in profile. Her shapeless dress flowed down, stopping just short of tiny bare feet. In the foreground were magenta flowers with eye-like pistils; in the background, a navy sky and crescent moon. Honor wasn't capable of assessing it objectively. It resounded with dreadful significance and could hardly do otherwise.

The present owner didn't want to sell, or so she'd been told. And neither Rebecca Levene nor the exhibition curator was at liberty to divulge his identity. If only I could get a few minutes in his company, thought Honor with frustration. I'd talk him round. It wasn't that presenting the picture to Saul would mean all was forgiven, or even that he'd start speaking to her again. It would be a tiny gesture, she knew. But it would be *something*.

A girl with a long black plait and spectacles, wearing a name tag identifying her as museum staff, was talking to a group of visitors a few feet away. Honor waited for their conversation to end, then caught her eye.

'Isn't that one beautiful?' said the girl, whose tag said *Rachel S*. 'It's a favourite of mine.'

'I just love it,' said Honor. 'I've actually got a personal connection to the model. She went on to marry one of my friends.'

Rachel gasped appreciatively. 'Gosh! How fascinating, I—'

Honor interrupted her: 'I forget, just at this moment, the name of the current owner. Mr . . . ?'

'I'm afraid we only disclose the names of our lenders with their express permission,' said Rachel apologetically.

'Of course. Rebecca Levene, whose father bought it during the war at a rather good price, is also a friend. I remember she sold it earlier this year. The chap's name is on the tip of my tongue.' But she could see Rachel's professionalism was not to be breached.

'It's a funny thing,' said Rachel. 'You knowing the original Gila. Just yesterday we had a school party in, and one of the girls said her mother's name had been Gila. She'd never come across the name before. Well, it's hardly commonplace in England, is it?'

'It certainly isn't,' said Honor. 'Was the girl herself English? How old was she?'

'Well, they were Advanced Level students – you know, those are the examinations they're doing now instead of Highers – so about seventeen, I imagine. But yes, she was English.'

'Forgive me,' said Honor after a too-long pause, 'but I don't suppose she was called Marya, was she?'

Rachel frowned thoughtfully. 'I believe so. Why? She wouldn't be the daughter of Chagall's Gila, surely?'

'Probably not,' said Honor. She swallowed; her throat was dry. 'Which school was she from, if I may ask?'

'Queen's College, in Harley Street.'

Saul looked at the girl sitting composedly in Honor's drawing room, and marvelled at her Englishness. She wore a checked blue and white woollen suit, exquisitely well-fitting yet to his mind far too grown-up. Pearls were at her ears and throat. Her hair was cut to the nape, with stiff question-mark curls framing her face. When she spoke, she sounded like an announcer on the wireless.

It had been Mina, appointed as Honor's ambassador, who came to convey all the facts that Honor had painstakingly verified. Marya and Gila had been at Transnistria for a month, said Mina, crammed into a filthy barn with hundreds of other terrified souls. When Gila died from dysentery, a girl called

Natalia Yivlinsky, barely in her teens and newly orphaned, took charge of Marya. They didn't leave each other's side, even after they were placed in a ghetto orphanage and, in 1944, sent back to Romania. In December 1944, the girls, now aged seven and fifteen, boarded a ship bound for Britain, where Natalia had distant relations willing to take them in. So it was that Marya grew up in some splendour in a house in Marylebone, the doted-upon youngest daughter of a banking family. All she knew of her beginnings: she was born in the Bukovina and her mother's name was Gila. Her adoptive parents, the Barnetts, had tried to trace any surviving family. They concluded there was none.

Saul had wondered if he'd recognise his daughter in some primal sense, responding to the call of blood, or if she'd be a total stranger. Neither and both, he realised. She was a stranger, of that there was no doubt. Honor, after welcoming Marya and bringing them tea, had tactfully left them alone. In fact, she ought to have stayed. A middle-aged man and a young girl could only be uncomfortable in each other's strange company. He felt sorry for Marya. Worse, he saw she was sorry for him.

And yet: she was the very image of her mother. The curve of her nose, the sharp tilt of the eyes, even the shape of her fingernails. It was all Gila. A feeling of constriction arose in his throat and he had to look away. 'I'd very much like to meet Natalia,' he said, helping himself to a biscuit. 'It sounds as though you owe her your life.'

Marya nodded gravely and took a small sip of tea. 'She's got two children of her own now. They call me Auntie Riri. They live in Wimbledon. Her husband's a nice fellow. He works at Peat Marwick Mitchell & Co.'

Saul couldn't think of anything to say to this. He smiled at her, feeble, helpless.

'Isn't it strange,' she said, taking the social reins, 'that we both came to live in London? By sheer chance.'

'Or perhaps it's not chance,' offered Saul. 'Perhaps it's *bashert* – ordained.'

Scepticism crinkled her sensible little brow. 'Do you believe in that sort of thing? I'm not sure I do.'

He thought of Jack Shaughnessy, of the violence of his conception and death. Had the one ensured the other? By extension, was Jack's disastrous imprint on his own life inescapable, his and Honor's paths always bound to cross? 'If I'm perfectly honest,' he said, 'I'm not sure I do either. Still, it's a nice idea, isn't it?'

After seeing Marya out, Saul went upstairs. Honor's bedroom door was open, and he found her sitting at the end of the bed, small black-stockinged feet on the floor. She looked at him, her ruined-doll face betraying in an instant all her yearning and dread. A loosening feeling, like ribs unlatching, grazed the inside of his chest.

He sat down next to her. 'That didn't go too badly, I don't think. Poor girl. What a surprise to land on someone. Yet she behaves with such equanimity. I suppose it's her upbringing. The English stiff upper lip!'

'No,' said Honor, turning to face him. 'No, it's not that. She gets it from you. Tell me, when in your life have you ever caused a scene? Even after . . . after everything came out, you didn't so much as raise your voice.' She smiled. 'You'd be calm in an earthquake.'

He smiled back at her. 'And you – how are you keeping?'

She glanced down at her lap. 'Oh, you know.' What could she say? She felt dangerously on the verge of tears, of begging for forgiveness, of making irretrievable declarations of love – of causing, in short, exactly the sort of scene Saul himself would never cause.

He frowned and opened his mouth to say something, then seemed to think better of it.

Honor, bravely, said: 'How about a drink?'

Saul stood up and held out his hand. 'A drink would be lovely.'

In the spring of 1954, a thirty-one-year-old man called Ronald Macneice – the son-in-law of elusive gangster Albert Cooper – went on trial at the Old Bailey for several counts of fraud and larceny, all relating to his running of illicit baccarat clubs. The key testimony of Mr James Sullivan, who was Mr Macneice's confidant and erstwhile cell neighbour at HMP Brixton, was to be offered in written form. But this constituted inadmissible hearsay, submitted the defence. Justice Peregrine Shackleton, presiding, heartily agreed. The jury found they had no choice but to acquit Mr Macneice on lack of evidence. Two weeks later, he was declared a free man and went home to his wife, Kathy, and their two small children.

Shortly thereafter, in a turn of events no one (well, almost no one) connected to the fate and fortune of a notorious crime family, Mina became the proprietress of a fashion emporium. The aptly named Mina's, next to Asprey and opposite Finnigans in New Bond Street, carried only the most chic and exclusive labels from Paris and Milan. For Mina, this meant frequent buying trips, stays at the George V and the Palazzo Parigi, and – for promotional purposes – never being photographed in the same outfit twice. Her financial backer, a Mr A. Cooper, left all business decisions to her. Indeed, he was the very definition of a sleeping partner, his identity known only to Mina herself.

After six months, the shop's turnover was so high that another Mina's opened in Knightsbridge. She found a flat in nearby Belgrave Square: three thousand square feet, on the first floor, and laterally converted across two wedding-cake houses. Her parents and brothers, back in Billericay, were impressed but not entirely surprised by the levels of swank to which their little Wilhelmina had ascended. By 1965, every major city in Britain had a Mina's, as did Palm Beach, Beverly Hills, and Madison Avenue.

Mina never married. Instead, she maintained several beautiful homes, cherished a series of purebred poodles, and entertains lavishly to this day. Her long-time dresser, a retired flamenco dancer called Antonia, is devoted to her mistress and takes care of her every need. All the national newspapers have a Mina Taylor obit ready to go, but at eighty-nine, she shows little sign of slowing down. She tirelessly keeps the world apprised of her latest style diktats (on TikTok) and dog photos (on Instagram).

At Christmas 1953, George got engaged to Rory Goodwin, and their July nuptials – the society wedding of the year, trumpeted *The Sketch* – were held at the bride's ancestral home in Wickham, near Winchester. A family friend, Sir Alec St John Gardner, walked her down the aisle. The six bridesmaids included banking heiress Miss Marya Barnett, the bride's niece Miss Diana Rutland (she fainted during the ceremony, poor thing, doubtless on account of the hot weather rather than the celery-only diet prescribed by her mother in preparation for the big day), and Miss Wilhelmina Taylor, owner of the madly popular new Mayfair boutique, Mina's. In the days that followed, Miss Taylor kindly took the time to inform anyone with an interest – well-wishers, Fleet Street diarists, fashion-page style arbiters – which guests had bought their wedding attire at her shop.

The newlyweds were quickly blessed with little Daisy Rowena then little Alasdair Archibald, nice babies who nevertheless proved what George had always suspected: motherhood was a crashing bore. Thank goodness for nannies and bottle-feeding.

George and Rory remained happily and, by enthusiastic mutual agreement, un-monogamously married, until that rainy June night when Margaret Thatcher secured a third term as prime minister and George – perhaps unrelatedly – died in her sleep of a heart attack. She was only sixty, but everyone agreed it was nice she went doing what she loved best. Her daughter, Daisy, organised a group show in her honour at the Saatchi Gallery. Entitled *Modern Muse*, it gathered portraits of George from over three decades by artists from the avant-garde to the old guard. The *Evening Standard*'s waspish art critic declared that only one painting, a 1953 gouache nude by the Royal Academician Auden Quennel, 'manages to convert with mystery and melancholy, without glossy pretension or puerile literalism, the raw material of its bovine, slack-thighed subject to attain an elevated and abstracted ideal, a feat of keenly discerned delicate spirit transcending concupiscent flesh'.

'Concupiscent?' thought Robbie, reading the paper on the Tube. 'He doesn't know the half of it.'

After publishing one final issue, Winter 1953, Honor folded *Vista* in favour of a more profitable venture: resurrecting her late husband's book publishing firm in partnership with Saul. Reznikov & Wilson put out twelve titles in their first year: a mix of fiction, memoir, and biography. For the sake of the bottom line, they tended towards the middlebrow, but never the trite. Honor also vetoed 'Angry Young Man' novels, anything with a whiff of Beat Generation, stories about girls having careers, and racy content unless French or homosexual (ideally both).

Saul moved back to Tregunter Road, first into George's old room, and then into Honor's. It was an odd union, they both privately reflected, yet their delight in each other only grew with the rapidly passing years. To Honor, being accepted for all she was – all he knew her to be – was something in the order of a miracle. Saul, for his part, relaxed into loving coexistence with the purest gratitude, entrusting his heart to Honor's spindly and – of this he was happily assured – unyielding clutches.

The question of marriage never arose, even though Honor's widow status was now legal. George's real father, Sir Alec, had obtained advice on her behalf from a relation of his, Sir Theo Rainey KBE, who happened to be the Director of Public Prosecutions. This excellent fellow explained that according to the law, a second marriage was not illegal if the previous spouse was thought to be dead. Well, as Honor confirmed in an affidavit, her sincere belief had been precisely that. In 1939, Thomas was condemned to hang for his crimes. How could she have known his sentence was later commuted to life in prison? She'd left her old world behind, even changing her name (no law against that). Certainly, she no longer kept in contact with any members of either the Shaughnessy or the Armstrong family. At the time of her wedding to Mr Wilson, in 1941, she was to all intents and purposes a widow.

Marya came to tea every Sunday. All she ever knew was that her father and Honor had met through literary circles after the war. She found Honor strange and mannered, yet not unlikeable.

With only Honor and Saul left at Tregunter Road, which was now reduced in size as well as population, they hardly needed a daily woman. But they couldn't bring themselves to let Greta go, even after she was no longer physically capable of the household chores. Instead, Honor secretly hired an energetic young couple to come on Saturdays, allowing Greta to potter around fruitlessly all week. Finally, at the age of seventy-five, she was persuaded into a very ritzy old folk's home on the pretext of 'having a rest'. She soon got used to being waited on hand and foot, and was unaware that the home's staff called her, not quite affectionately, 'a right old character'.

In the winter of 1985, in the space of four weeks, Saul had a major stroke, putting him in a wheelchair; Honor was diagnosed with end-stage lung cancer; and Reznikov & Wilson was acquired by a publishing conglomerate for a very substantial sum. When Honor died, Saul went to live out his days at Mina's chateau in Vence, near Nice, where he was looked after by two very pretty and very strict French nurses. Mina was often there, the doting Antonia in tow, as was Marya, who was now a brittle divorcée, soignée as ever, with three children and a red Mercedes convertible she drove much too fast.

Robbie was senior commissioning editor at Reznikov & Wilson, and eventually managing director. He never stopped despairing of the excrement that passed itself off as literature. He could do so much better! Except that would involve finishing a manuscript and showing it to someone, hurdles he could never quite surmount.

The buyout seemed an appropriate time to retire. He was nearly sixty-five, and he fancied doing some travelling before he was too decrepit. Hilary, with whom he'd lived quietly for more than three decades, had taken his police pension twelve years earlier. Some people struggled with retirement, but Hilary had no trouble filling his days with lovingly executed domestic tasks, long walks along the river and – above all – thinking. He liked to tend to the front garden of their small house in Cheyne Walk,

Chelsea, and replay old events in his mind. Often, his thoughts returned to the investigation of 1953, and its missing puzzle pieces. He knew Robbie had withheld much of the truth. Obviously he had his reasons, and it made no difference to Hilary's feelings. Yet it continued to preoccupy him.

The missing persons investigation of James Sullivan, aka Jack Shaughnessy, was closed in 1960, and he was declared presumed dead.

No other suspects were ever questioned for the 1953 murder of Lord Charles Mountford-Owen. It remains an open cold case.

Acknowledgements

My deepest thanks to Cara Lee Simpson, Caitlin Landuyt, Katya Ellis, Jade Hui, Josefine Kals, Abbott Kahler, Maud Newton, Rob Williams, Carla Josephson, Nithya Rae, Anna Skrabacz, Erin Osman, Olivia Barber, Thérèse Coen, and Iris and Stephen Garman.